A SUMMER KISS

Jack cupped his hand at the back of Lissa's head and wound his fingers through the silken luxury of her hair. "We are alone for now. For as long as we want."

Rain tapped on the porch roof overhead, dripped off the leaves, drummed against the earth, fell like a curtain of silver black around them. They were truly alone. Jack caught hold of her collar, released the top button hidden beneath a fluff of lace.

Her kisses burned through his blood, thundered through every part of his body. She was home and heaven, need and want, wife and lover.

Her fingers plucked at his shirt buttons, smoothed away fabric until there was only air between them. He felt her need, not just for sex, but for a man to depend on, a man to trust.

Yet even in her urgent kisses, in her tantalizing fingers curling through his chest hair, there was a holding back— of her heart, of her deepest self.

He wanted that part of her. Wanted her to know he was a man she could trust. Now and until the end of time.

Books by Jill Henry

HANNAH'S HEART
LISSA'S GROOM

Published by Zebra Books

LISSA'S GROOM

Jill Henry

Zebra Books
Kensington Publishing Corp.

http://www.zebrabooks.com

ZEBRA BOOKS are published by

Kensington Publishing Corp.
850 Third Avenue
New York, NY 10022

First Printing: July, 1999
10   9   8   7   6   5   4   3   2   1

Printed in the United States of America

To treasured friends old and new:

Leslie Barstow, the loveliest person I know.
Jolene Haskins, speed demon and fellow writer.
Vicki Lemonds, your friendship lights up my days.
Henry Strickler, my very best friend of all.
And to Jack Redmond, in memory. I owe you one.
I'm thinking of you wherever you are.

Chapter One

"When's my new pa comin'?"

"I thought he'd surely be here by now, Chad." Lissa Banks stepped out onto the log cabin's front porch and squinted through the towering pines. The sun was quickly slipping from its zenith, grazing fluffy white clouds on a determined descent toward the mountainous horizon.

It was well past noon. He ought to be here by now. There was no denying it, even considering every possible delay.

Her hopes felt like a rock rolling downhill, growing steadier by the minute.

She smoothed the escaped wisps from her braid and took a deep breath. Her future husband had sent a wire promising to arrive two full days ago, and the drive up from Billings to her home in Sweetwater County took less than half a week.

He was coming, wasn't he?

She felt a tug on her skirt and looked down at her son, not yet five, uncertainty wrinkling his brow.

Her child sighed. "Maybe he died, too."

"Oh, Chad." Lissa knelt and ran a hand across the worry lines wrinkling her son's face. He was too young for such concerns. "I'm sure he didn't die. Delays happen all the time. Why, you remember the letter he sent us. He said he's coming, and he will. Maybe he's lost. Mr. Murray is from St. Louis. He's used to a big city and buildings, not mountains and pines."

"Maybe the trees are scarin' him," Chad confided. "They're awful tall."

Lissa's heart thumped. "Yes, they are. Remember how Mr. Murray said in his letter he'd build you a tree house to play in? Won't that be something to look forward to?"

Worry eased from the dear little boy's face. "I guess. Mama, how's he gonna get a house up in a tree?"

She smoothed the errant curls back from his eyes. "You'll see. Come, help me put away the food. We can always make a sandwich for Mr. Murray when he arrives."

"I guess."

Lissa stood and watched her little boy march, head bowed, across the cabin. How could the man break his word? How could he disappoint a child?

"Oh, Winston." Chad thudded to a stop at the table, shaking his head. "Mama, she's doin' it again."

A gray, striped tabby uncurled herself from one of the chairs seated around the carefully set table and peered up at the boy.

"Just as long as she stays off the table." Lissa skirted the stove and reached up into the polished pine cupboards for her biggest crock.

"She's washin' me again, Mama," Chad announced.

Sure enough, the old mother tabby had hold of Chad's ears with both paws and was industriously licking the top of his head, blond curls and all.

"It tickles, Mama." He giggled, but he didn't pull away.

"She must have noticed what a dirty little boy you've

become," Lissa teased as she carried the empty crock to the table.

"I shouldn't have played in the barn!" Another giggle came as the cat affectionately started licking his face.

Warmth settled back into Lissa's chest. She'd missed her son's laughter, the lightness of family banter, the deep comforting rumble of a man's voice in her kitchen. How she missed Michael.

She made quick work of putting away the prepared food. Had Mr. Murray been here on time, he would have been able to enjoy her pot roast and the fresh bread she'd made this morning to keep her mind off his arrival.

That she would marry a man she didn't know troubled her greatly, but she wanted to keep her ranch and this home Michael had built for her with his own hands. She could not hold onto her land alone. She needed a husband and his gunpower to keep the rustlers troubling the countryside from running her out of business.

"Mama, can I have a cookie?"

"Just one." Lissa covered the bread.

"Winston and me'll share." On his sturdy legs, Chad stretched to lift the lid from the jar on the table.

What would she do if Mr. Murray didn't come? What if—oh, it hurt too much to think about. She had no relatives, no one to help.

What about the wedding scheduled for tomorrow? Lissa felt her throat go dry. She pictured the kindly Reverend Burrow waiting patiently behind his pine pulpit to seal a marriage short one waylaid groom.

Please be on your way, Mr. Murray. Please be a man of your word.

Lissa knew hopes were only that. She'd waited far too long now. It was best to take action: Go to town. Check with the postmistress to see if her groom-to-be had written. Speak with the minister and cancel her wedding plans.

It was for the best.

Disappointment kicked her as she wet a clean cloth and wiped down the table. A giggle from the floor before the hearth, where Chad and his kitty sat together, captured her attention—and reminded her of what was truly important.

Chad broke off a small bit of molasses cookie and held it out to the tabby, who took the treat with a dainty nibble. Then he broke off a piece for himself.

Such a sweet boy, he deserved this home, to grow up on the land his father wanted him to have one day. Somehow, she would find a way to keep Michael's long ago promise.

"Go find your hat, Chad." She laid the damp cloth down to dry. "We're going to town."

"Yippee!" He jumped to his feet, chewing down the last bite of his cookie. "Do I getta drive Charlie?"

"We'll see. Now hurry along."

Lissa reached around to untie her apron. The cabin looked tidy and cozy. It was nothing fancy, snug and small. Michael had splurged with their meager savings, framing in glass windows so she could enjoy the sunshine during the long Montana winters.

Crisp white curtains framed the glass now, sparkling from a thorough cleaning. The floors, the sills, the furniture, even the black stove, all shone, polished to impress the man who would be her husband—the man who might not keep his word.

"Mama. I got my hat."

"And I have mine." She lifted her best starched-crisp sunbonnet from the peg by the back door. She fished her reticule from behind the dishtowels stacked neatly in the drawer. "Are you going to hitch up Charlie for me?"

"Mama, you know I'm not that big." Chad laughed as he dashed out through the leanto into the cheerful sunshine.

Lissa found a smile stretching her face. She shut the

door tightly, locked it, and stepped past the gray tabby sunning herself in the dry grass near the garden.

"Mama, Charlie's eatin' me." Chad's happy voice echoed like sunshine through the hay-scented barn.

With the sun heating her back, Lissa stopped to watch. Life on this ranch was often hard, but it was more often wonderful. The sight of the small boy standing before the gigantic Clydesdale, the horse affectionately nibbling Chad's hat brim, made a bubble of happiness expand inside her.

Everything would work out—with or without Mr. Murray. She would think of something. Lissa fetched the heavy leather harness from its peg in the tack room and led the big bay workhorse out into the yard. Keeping one eye on Chad, who stroked his sticky hands down Charlie's fetlock, she hitched the gelding to the small wagon.

"Come here, cowboy." Lissa held out her hand.

Her little boy gave Charlie a final pat and dashed straight toward her, the felt brim of his hat flopping in the wind.

The mountain lion's growl shattered the peaceful Montana forest. Marshal Jack Emerson drew his horse around, heart pounding. That cat sounded mad, and too damn close for comfort. The mustang sidestepped, nervous, nostrils flaring wide to scent the air.

Jack patted the mare's neck, calming her, but his senses were on alert. Hair prickled along the back of his neck at another low, threatening growl. No doubt about it, that cat was too damn close for comfort. Mountain lions were territorial. Maybe she was only letting loose a warning, so Jack and his prisoner would simply move on.

Squinting against the harsh afternoon sun, he circled the skittish mustang back around, caught hold of the lead rope tied to his saddle, and made sure the second horse packing the bandit Dillon Plummer didn't bolt. The last thing Jack needed was to hunt down Plummer a second time.

"That cat's trouble, Emerson." Dillon's gravelly voice grated like chalk on a blackboard, and was as unwelcome.

"So, now you're an expert on mountain lions?"

"No, but any fool can hear the signs."

He heard the silence, all right. The larks had quieted. Now even the wind breezed to a halt. He heard no chirp of grasshoppers, no snap of insects, not the buzz of even one fly circling the horses.

Jack slid the rifle out of the holster. He might be tired of his job here in Montana—he'd seen nearly every inch of the territory—but moving on to Wyoming was a better way to leave his job than being eyeballed as cat food. If that mountain lion meant business, then so did he.

He hadn't been named the best marshal in his department for cowardice. When it came to a fight, Jack Emerson knew how to win, whether his enemy was man or beast. He thumbed back the hammer.

The rustle of leaves turned him around. He aimed, but already the great golden cat was airborne, front paws extended. Jack got off one shot before the mountain lion slammed into his shoulders. Sharp claws tore across his chest. Jack hit the ground on his back. He heard his mount's terrified whinny, heard Plummer's shout, saw the cat's sharp-teethed jaws. Jack wrapped his fingers around the walnut stock of the rifle and swung.

The blow dazed the animal, and a second knocked the predator from his chest. With a furious snarl, the cat turned, sprang. Jack's thumb grazed the trigger and the bullet fired.

The hundred pound cat slammed him to the ground again, razor sharp claws skidding across his left arm and chest. Jack looked up into lifeless eyes, felt the cat's body shudder. It was dead.

Rolling the animal off him, he tried to stand. Wheezing,

blood dripping from beneath his shirt, he felt damn shaky. Pain lanced down his breastbone, tore across the bend of his arm. *Great. Just great.*

Looking around, he saw nothing but trees, rocky earth, and wild animals. No rangeland, no civilization in sight. And where was his horse? Plummer was probably galloping away as fast as his mount would take him toward the state border.

Well, Jack had been in worse straits. At least he had his rifle. There was a town just a ways back. He remembered seeing the fork in the weed-grown trail he'd been following. Maybe he could get word to his boss, pick up a horse, and find a soft bed for the night. He took a step, winced at the pain in his ankle. Probably he'd cracked the bone again. It hadn't healed fully from his last run-in with an outlaw.

"Hold it right there, Marshal," came that gravelly voice, irritating and triumphant.

"Plummer?" Jack spun, cocked the rifle, but the gun flew from his hands. It hit the lee side of a boulder, a bullet hole through the stock. "That was my best rifle."

"It's my rifle now." A slow, dangerous sneer twisted across Plummer's scarred face. "I'm going to enjoy putting down the one lawman sly enough to bring me in. Say good-bye, Emerson."

Jack was a dead man and he knew it, looking into the barrel of his own Colt, aimed directly at his forehead. "Why? I didn't hear you hiding behind that boulder. You could have shot me in the back. But you didn't."

"I want to see the look in your eyes, Marshal. I want to see you beg for mercy."

"Men like you don't have mercy."

"Or a conscience, either." Plummer smirked, taking pleasure in his situation, obviously enjoying the power to give life or take it away.

"Give it up, Plummer. You won't get far."

"Sure, I will." The outlaw laughed. "And you won't rest in peace knowing I'm going to steal your badge, take your gunbelt and ride your horse to my freedom."

"What freedom are you going to have when you've killed a United States Marshal?"

Plummer laughed. "Everyone between here and Wyoming will take a good look at me and say, there goes a United States Marshal protecting the good citizens of this territory. The poor saps won't recognize me, Dillon Plummer, until after I've already taken what I want from them."

Black rage tore through Jack's heart. He hated men who used their firepower to harm others, their strength to hurt those weaker.

Sheer emotion drove him forward. With a shout, he sprang and wrapped his fingers around the nose of the revolver, trying to wrestle it out of Plummer's grip. He felt the weapon fire, saw the flash of light, heard the whiz of a bullet. A streak of fire slammed into his skull.

Jack's head flew back. He lost his balance and fell. All went black as he hit the ground.

Chapter Two

"Mama, Charlie's not behavin'."

"Yes, I see that." Lissa tightened her hands on the thick reins behind her son's tiny grip. The workhorse had stopped stock still in the middle of the road, lifted his nose to scent the wind, and given an earsplitting bellow.

"Get up, Charlie." Lissa snapped the reins. "I'm not in the mood for this."

She wasn't. She had too many worries, too many uncertainties, and the humiliation of canceling a wedding many had advised her against. She remembered Maude Hubbard's prune-faced prediction that Mr. Murray would never show.

"Charlie ain't behavin'. He's in big trouble." Chad shook his head in great disapproval.

"He is." Lissa smacked the gelding's backside with the length of the reins, not hard enough to hurt him, just to remind him who was supposed to be the boss.

Charlie nickered, lifting his nose. He probably scented something on the brisk wind kicking through the low slung pines. Dust skidded along the road in little waves, motes shimmering in the lemony rays of sunshine. Lissa breathed deeply and tasted the smell of rain, but nothing else.

Then she heard it—an answering nay, high and anxious. A bay gelding wheeled around the corner into sight, lather streaking his reddish barrel and flanks, his dark eyes white-rimmed.

Lissa took one look at the worn saddle, and her heart stopped. An empty saddle meant a fallen rider. There weren't many travelers on this road, especially not this time of year. Hope flamed in her chest. Could this be John Murray's horse?

She snapped the reins hard. "Get going, Charlie."

The gelding took a powerful jump forward. Lissa set Chad on the seat beside her, quieted his worried questions, and stood up, searching the ground for signs of a fallen man. Charlie shied, rocking the wagon to a stop as he kicked out with his front hooves. Lissa nearly toppled, but caught herself on the hard wagon's lip. There, in the dust alongside the road, were the bloody pawprints of a mountain lion. They looked very fresh.

"Get up, Charlie." The wagon bounced around the rocky curve in the road.

A man lay sprawled on his back, blocking their path. Lissa jerked the reins. Charlie whinnied, tossing up his head, sidestepping to avoid the man as the wagon stopped. Heart pounding, she set the brake, scooped her son into her arms, and hopped to the ground.

Was it John? Setting Chad down, she snatched up her skirts and ran. She didn't know for certain—she'd never met the man face-to-face. He was so still. Could he be dead? Blood stained the earth and, she saw as she dropped to her knees at his side, his hair and face.

Fear washed over her. She studied him, as much from curiosity as from need to assess his injuries. Such a big man, from ruffled blond hair to scuffed boots. Lissa laid her ear against the broad span of male chest.

Relief washed over her at the sound of the steady thump-*thump* of his heartbeat. He was alive, and that was good, but how seriously was he injured? Blood oozed from beneath the thick waves of his hair, staining it, the ground, and his tan cotton shirt.

This was Mr. Murray. He matched the description he'd given in his letters—sun-browned and weathered, brawny and strong, long, dark blond hair, square jaw, as tough looking as an outlaw.

Not even her neighbors used this road.

"Is he dead?" Chad asked, his voice small and afraid.

Her heart twisted. She brushed the curls from Chad's sad eyes. "No, cowboy. But Mr. Murray is injured. Can you run and get the blanket from beneath the wagon seat?"

The child dashed off, feet kicking up dust on the road. Clouds overhead obscured the sky. A storm was brewing. Whatever lay ahead, it couldn't be good for this man unconscious before her, this man so hurt.

Charlie pranced, agitated, and that's when she saw the mountain lion. First, panic seared her to the spot. Then she bolted upright, determined to protect her son and this injured man. Then she saw that the cat was dead, shot straight through its heart.

Not many men could shoot and kill a mountain lion at close range. Admiration for this stranger flowed into her chest. Maybe she'd been right in bringing this man into their lives. If he could face down a wildcat, maybe he could scare off a band of pesky rustlers.

"Here, Ma." Chad ran up with both little arms clutching the bulky, wool blanket to his chest, eyes worried. "Is he dead yet?"

"Not in the last few minutes. He'll be fine." She somehow knew deep down inside that he would be. "I have to wrap his injuries first. Will you help me?"

A solemn nod. Chad's eyes were pinched with uncertainty. He'd lost one pa. He looked scared that he might lose another.

Mr. Murray looked seriously injured, no doubt about that. Lissa untied her petticoat and slipped out of the simple muslin garment. Kneeling beside Mr. Murray, she began tearing the fabric in long, fat strips. "Hold these high, out of the dirt," she instructed Chad.

Mr. Murray didn't move. Lissa couldn't help noticing the handsome, square cut of his face or the golden lashes curved against his cheek as she laid a hand gently beneath his head and began wrapping the vigorously bleeding wound. His blond hair felt thick and soft. He'd journeyed so far, only to be injured two miles from her ranch—all this way, just as he promised.

Hope burned in her heart. Accepting his offer of marriage had been the right thing to do. Caring for him now, well, it already made her feel like his wife—as if they *could* build some kind of a life together.

First, she had to get him to the doctor—but how? This fine specimen of hard male muscle looked far too heavy for her to carry.

"Chad, help me slide this blanket beneath your new pa. We'll have to drag him. There's no other way."

"How are we gonna get him into the wagon?"

"I'll think of something." Lissa gently lifted John's bandaged head in both hands, vowing to do her very best by him.

The doctor stepped into the sedate, dark, wood-accented parlor and adjusted the top button of his collar. "Mrs. Banks? Your groom is going to be just fine."

"Thank you, Doc." Lissa rose from the sateen-upholstered divan, smoothing her skirts to hide the way her hands were shaking. As the hours passed, she'd regretted her promise to Chad. She'd been afraid John Murray would not live. "Can I see him?"

"Of course." The stout, balding man gave her a serious nod before leading the way down the hall. "Mr. Murray woke up a few minutes ago, but he's sleeping now. I'm going to keep him here overnight. A skull fracture is nothing to take lightly."

"A skull fracture?" Dear God. Her knees shook. Her heart rocketed against the confines of her chest. The injury was much worse than she'd guessed.

Holding tightly to Chad's hand, Lissa managed to make it down the hall and into the dark, quiet room without stumbling. She'd known several men who'd died of the same injury. Surely, it was a good sign John had woken up.

If only she could talk to him now, ask what might make him more comfortable.

"He's still sleepin', Mama." Chad's face twisted as he stood at John's bedside, one hand wrapped tightly in hers.

"The doctor says he's going to wake up tomorrow and go home with us." Lissa brushed her son's frowning brow, wishing she could soothe away his grief as easily. Michael's death had been hard on her, too, but she was an adult, not a child who couldn't understand the cycle of life with the same experience.

"Your new father is going to be fine, I reckon." The doctor stepped into the room and managed a meager but worried smile. "Come with me, Chad. Let's ask my wife if she can find you a glass of apple cider. If it's all right with your mother."

Lissa nodded. She waited until she was alone with John before she pulled over the plain wooden chair and sat beside the sleeping man, just as a wife might.

"You gave us a real scare." She gripped the string handle of her reticule tightly, staring hard at her white knuckles.

"I'll forgive you this once, but you're never allowed to hurt yourself like this again. Ever."

"Who are you?" His words came like a low, deep rasp, grating across the stillness of the room, startling her.

"You're awake." The room was dim. She could hardly see his face.

"I guess so." He tried to sit up and groaned.

She laid one hand against his chest to stop him. "Lie still. Doctor's orders."

"I don't care much for doctors." His voice was warm and low, but not harsh, pleasant as twilight, deep as night.

Her hand still lay on his chest. She felt the solid heat of his bare male skin, and the hard strength of the layers of muscle beneath her fingers. Her pulse skipped. This magnificent man of steel and strength was hers?

John rubbed his forehead with one hand, encountering bandages. "Tell me, how did I get here?"

"You were thrown from your horse."

"I was?" He moaned and leaned back into the fluffy pillows.

"A mountain lion must have jumped you. You took a bad blow to your head, too, but you'll be fine." Lissa waited. "You don't know who I am?"

"Should I?"

Her heart skipped a beat. Perhaps he was more injured than the doctor had first thought. Perhaps—well, she shouldn't borrow trouble with worry. She had more than she could deal with already. "I suppose we don't need to settle things between us right now. You need to rest."

"But I—"

Footsteps knelled on the floor behind her. "Your bride is right, Mr. Murray. What you need most is to heal. Everything will look clearer in the morning."

Lissa watched John's face, shadowed and drawn. Pain etched lines around his eyes and mouth, drew a hard frown to his intelligent forehead. Was it normal he couldn't remember how he'd been hurt? That he didn't know who she was?

Fear sluiced over her like cold water. Whatever was wrong, she would stand by him. She would take care of him until he was well.

"Let's step out into the hall, Mrs. Banks." Doc's voice dipped low as he gestured toward the lighted corridor.

Lissa followed him and closed the door so John could sleep.

"Confusion isn't uncommon after such a trauma," Doc said now, tugging at his high-collared shirt. "How long it will last is anyone's guess. If that bullet had been any lower, it would have killed him."

"Bullet?" That made no sense. She'd seen the mountain lion—

The doctor continued. "As it was, it cracked his skull without entering his brain. I can't really tell you more. If his memory is impaired, then the damage may be more than I first feared."

"I see." Lissa's stomach gripped. Suddenly the problems with her ranch seemed small compared to John Murray's prognosis. "Would you mind if I stayed at his side tonight? Perhaps just having someone with him would help."

"That would be fine. It seems to me he's one lucky man to be getting a wife like you."

Lissa blushed, unsure of what to say. She only knew the doctor was wrong. She was the lucky one. She owed John Murray—who'd come to protect her ranch and help raise her son—more than she could ever repay.

"First let me find someone to watch Chad for the night and check on my stock," she said. "Then I'll be back."

Dizziness nauseated him as he stepped away from the closed door. His head hurt more than if six oxen had stampeded right over the top of his scalp. Every breath he took stabbed pain through his skull.

His mind—his memory—was one unending, gray fog. No images could penetrate it. He'd learned two things about himself. He had a serious injury. And the pretty, softspoken woman who'd sat beside him was his bride.

Did that mean he was already married?

Just trying to remember shot a throbbing spear of pain across his skull.

He inched to the bed and lay down, more afraid than he'd ever been. He couldn't think. He couldn't remember.

Darkness nudged his vision. He leaned back into the pillows and fought to stay awake. His eyes closed.

"But what about the wedding tomorrow?" Blanche took down china cups and saucers from her sideboard.

Good question. Lissa stared down at her hands, then at the crocheted lace cloth covering the carved round table. "I don't want to rush him. He's had a bad injury. We'll probably postpone the wedding."

"I'll let the reverend know." Blanche sounded sad. "You must be disappointed. You've been counting on your Mr. Murray to help you. You need him very much."

Lissa blushed. "Well, I—"

"I know you haven't said one word of complaint, but it can't be easy trying to keep up with the work on your ranch." A kettle rumbled on the polished black stove.

"It isn't so bad." Lissa set her chin. Her troubles and her burdens were nothing she intended to lay on anyone's shoulders, no matter how close they were or how good a friend. "Besides, John Murray is Michael's cousin. It's not as if he's a perfect stranger. Michael knew him well growing up."

Michael had always been fond of John, and they'd corresponded over the years. When she'd written Michael's family telling of his death, John had offered whatever help she needed. He'd lost his wife and son the previous year and felt as if he needed a change, a place to escape his memories and grief.

"I didn't say one word of criticism." Blanche set the steeping tea on the pretty table, her face kind, her eyes shadowed. "A woman in these parts needs help just to survive."

"I know what others are saying." Why did it hurt so much? Why did it matter what people thought? "That I'm desperate enough to marry any man sight unseen."

"I'm not judging you, Lissa." Blanche sat down beside her, the scrape of the chair against the wood floor, the scent of an apple crisp cooling, the comfort of friendship making it easier to accept what had to be done.

"I can't defend the ranch myself." Lissa heard the ripple of Chad's laughter just outside the window as he played with Blanche's son in the grass yard. "It won't be the first time I married without love. Michael was good to me. We had a fine marriage. I got a close look at John Murray while he was unconscious. He has an honest face and laugh lines around his eyes, so I know he isn't harsh. I have hopes he'll make a kind husband."

"You don't have to convince me."

No, but I need to convince myself. Lissa's throat hurt. Sure, she had other options, but she wanted to keep her home. She'd promised Michael.

"It's the right thing to do." There could be no room for doubts. She would believe it with all her heart, and make this marriage work. "That apple crisp sure smells good."

"Go ahead and change the subject," Blanche teased, the same gentle light present in her voice that surrounded their friendship. "But it won't change my mind. I don't know what I would do if I lost my Jeremiah, but I tell you this—I'd keep right on living. You and I are mothers. We have no other choice."

Lissa's heart twisted. "True. I'm doing this for my son." *For Michael's son.*

"Besides, I heard from young Betsy—you know, she's Doc's nurse—that your John is a very handsome man." Blanche wriggled her eyebrows. "Heard tell he was one fine specimen, with shoulders to make a full-blooded woman swoon."

"Stop that," Lissa blushed. "You're talking about my husband-to-be."

"Lucky you." Blanche chuckled. "Now, how about a nice cup of tea before you head back over to the doctor's?"

Even in the dark, he was an impressive man. Just enough light from the lamp turned down low brushed across his pillow, washing his face. And what a strong face it was: Straight nose, not too large, but not small; thick, curly, blond lashes in half-moons against his cheeks; high cheekbones; a strong, square jaw; a dimple in the center of his chin.

Most of all, she liked the lines drawn into the skin beside his eyes and cut around his mouth, as if he were a man who knew how to smile and laugh.

Please, let him be a good husband.

She'd not confided her fears to anyone, not even Blanche. What was he like inside, past the handsomeness of his face? Was he fair, or judgmental? Did he have a quick temper, or a slow, steady patience?

At least she'd made the decision to come to town when she did, and found him. Her heart clenched, remembering how vulnerable this big man had looked, sprawled unconscious on the road. She tried to quiet her uncertainty about how he'd come to have a bullet wound at all.

He'd come. He kept his promise. Surely that was a good sign.

John moaned low in his throat, then rolled his head on the pillow, his face contorting with pain.

"Easy, now." She laid a hand on his cheek. The heat of him, the rough feel of the day's stubble whiskering his jaw, made her pulse jump.

His hand closed around her wrist. Such well-shaped fingers, tanned by the sun, callused as if he knew how to work, and work hard. He twisted on the pillow to look up at her. Shadowed eyes met hers, glazed with pain. "Thirsty."

"Let me pour you some water." She lifted her hand, and his grip fell away. Lissa stood, nervousness flowing through her veins.

If only she weren't so shy, perhaps it would be easier. She feared he would find her less than he hoped—less pretty, less desirable, less everything. Lissa knew he was a man tough enough for the job ahead of him. She so wanted him to be pleased with her, too.

Her hand trembled as she filled the tin cup. She clinked the pitcher against the basin accidentally. When the intensity of his gaze latched onto hers, though, she felt surer. His steady presence felt like strength. John Murray was a substantial man. Hope warmed her like sunshine.

"Here. Don't sit up." Lissa lowered the cup to his lips, but his hand caught the cup, as if he weren't used to being waited on.

He sipped, the relief audible in his sigh after he swallowed. "Thank you."

At least he was polite. *That's a very good sign, right?* "Would you like more?"

"Later, perhaps." He sank back into the fluffy pillows. "Has the doctor been in to check on me?"

"Less than twenty minutes ago." Lissa found the edge of the chair and eased into it.

"What did he say? Am I going to be all right?"

"Yes. He said you must have a harder head than most men. In this instance, that's a good thing."

A smile stretched across his generously cut mouth. An attractive smile, simple and easy, brought out twin dimples in his cheeks.

Warmth bubbled in Lissa's chest. "You're looking better than you did when I found you."

"You brought me here?" His interest was quick and sharp.

"Yes. You must have fallen off your horse."

"Must have?" Frown lines puckered between his eyes. "Were you there?"

"No, I found you lying on the road leading to my ranch."

"And you brought me here all by yourself?" His blue gaze fastened on hers, curious, measuring.

She felt the impact like a touch to her face. "Yes. I laid you on the blanket I keep beneath the seat and dragged you to the tailgate. Then I hoisted you up into the bed of the wagon."

"You're strong for such a little thing." He had a gentle voice, gentle eyes.

"I'm a country girl." She shrugged, uncomfortable with his compliment. She wasn't used to them. "Lucky for you I am fairly strong, or I never would have managed to pull and push you into the wagon. My son is too small to help."

"Your son?"

"I suppose you don't remember anything about him, either." Sadness crept into her voice, and she couldn't stop it.

"No. I'm sorry."

Somehow that made the situation worse, more hopeless. Chad was one of the reasons she had even considered John Murray's offer of help, why she'd written him about the towheaded little boy so different from Michael, a child who needed a father, a home, someone to help protect and provide for him.

John had answered with a promise to bring his guns and his might. He'd worked as a deputy for years. He knew how to fight for what was right. He also vowed to love Michael's son as he had once loved his own.

"How old is he?" A quiet question.

"He'll be five this July." She dipped her chin and stared hard at her hands, folded tightly in her lap.

"You love him. You're a good mother." He rubbed his forehead, encountered the bandage. "It's in your voice."

"Oh." She blushed, a pretty wash of pink across her delicate nose and cheeks.

"It's a nice thing to see, a woman who loves her child. Not all families are that way." His voice rumbled pain through his head, and just saying the words made him hurt.

How did he know about families? Maybe the doctor was right—he would be fit as a fiddle come morning. All he needed was sleep. How could he rest, though, when so much troubled him? The gray, painful fog of his mind beat through him. The questions he wanted to ask speared like lances through his rib cage.

The doctor had called this woman his bride. So, were they married? Did her son call him father?

Pain jammed through his skull. He gritted his teeth. He watched her rise from the hard-backed chair, her gray-checked skirts rustling around her ankles as she carried the tin cup back to the pitcher and filled it.

For him. She did this for him.

What was their relationship? How much did he care for her? He tried to remember any detail at all as she strolled toward him. This bride of his was a fragile-boned woman, lean and petite, and graceful. Kind, too—he could read it in her face, see it in her movements. He knew nothing else about her, other than that she loved her son.

Did she love him?

"Would you like more water?" Her voice was soft as a creek singing over stones.

"Yes." He was damn thirsty, even if the water upset his stomach.

She leaned toward him again, and he breathed in the scent of her—faint cinnamon and sunshine. His heart kicked in his chest.

He wished he could remember her, remember anything. All he felt was loneliness, and a painful blackness he couldn't think past.

The water tasted cool, and it wetted his throat and all the way to his twisting stomach. Pain rocketed through his head. He leaned back into the pillows.

She touched his cheek, her fingers gentle. How many times had she touched him like that? His eyes fluttered shut. He could not keep them open. He wanted to. He needed answers. He had to know who the hell he was.

There was only darkness.

Chapter Three

Morning light edged between the curtains, casting a gentle grayness across his face. Lissa stretched the kinks from her spine. Sitting in that chair all night, watching over John, hadn't been comfortable.

She'd gotten little sleep, especially since the doctor came every hour to wake him, but staying by her groom's side had been the right thing to do. She felt that all the way to her soul. This man had kept his promise to her. She would do anything she could for him.

Doc startled her. "I'll keep an eye on him if you want to attend the service."

Lissa gasped, surprised, when she saw him standing in the threshold, looking as haggard as she felt. Was it already that late? "I don't feel right about leaving."

"Trust me. That man of yours is going to be bedridden for some time. There will be plenty of time for you to watch over him. Go ahead and take a break. You need to go stretch your legs and check on your son."

Lissa hesitated. She did want to go to church, yet was it

right, leaving John here alone? She did need to see the minister and thank him for his trouble, even if Blanche had already told him there would be no wedding.

"I'll just be gone a short while."

"Fine. If all is well, you can take your man home this afternoon." He stopped, glanced down the hall. "You have someone waiting for you out front."

Chad—and probably Blanche and her sons. Lissa reached for her reticule, her gaze sweeping across John's still form. His bandaged, broad chest was bare beneath that sheet, rising with each steady breath. He still looked so pale, despite his suntan. She hoped that when he opened his eyes he would remember everything—including his promises.

"Thank you, Doc."

"It's what you pay me for. Take your time." Seriousness lit his intelligent eyes. "I know you have arrangements to make."

"Or unmake." She waited while the doctor stepped aside and let her through the threshold.

"Ma!" Chad's voice echoed in the hall as his footsteps pounded across the wooden floor.

"Walk, please," she said automatically, but already she was kneeling down and her son was against her, his arms clenched tightly around her neck. "I missed you."

"We had pancakes for breakfast. With huckleberry jam." Chad released her, his eyes wide with the excitement of having spent the night with his best friend, Blanche's son, and with what could only be the same tightly lined worry that settled on his face the day Michael died.

"Sounds like you had a great time." She brushed back a mop of fine, blond curls from his eyes.

"Yep." Chad bit his lip. "Is my new pa gonna wake up?"

"He's been awake several times during the night." Lissa took his hand and wished she could wash away his fears as easily. "Mr. Murray is going to be fine, but he's not well enough to take me to church today. Maybe you could be my escort?''

"Oh, Ma." Chad shook his head. "Do I have to sit next to any girls?"

"Does Mitsy Buchman still have a crush on you?"

Chad sighed, his burdens great.

Footsteps caught her attention. She looked up. Blanche Buchman looked perfect, as always, all dressed up for church, yet her gaze held sorrow and worry, for she knew how very much Lissa needed a man to take care of the rustlers.

Lissa stood, chest tight. "I can't thank you enough for helping me out."

"And I can't do enough for you." The smile of friendship reached all the way to Blanche's eyes. "Your son is so well-behaved that he makes my three look like wild coyotes."

Lissa let a chuckle warm her. She knew Blanche was just trying to ease her worries.

"Does he remember?"

Lissa shook her head. "The doctor hasn't examined him this morning. He's still sleeping."

"Then the wedding is off?" The question held such great sadness that Lissa's throat closed.

"I can't impose any expectations on John. It isn't fair. He's an injured man." Lissa took Chad by the hand. "Son, why don't you go outside and play with Ira?"

"But what about my new pa?"

"The doctor will watch over him. Don't worry."

The towheaded boy dipped his head and trudged down the hallway, feet dragging.

My new pa, the boy had said.

His chest ached, emotion lingering as the child disappeared from his sight. Pain cracked through his head, and he leaned heavily against the threshold.

It was Lissa's voice that drew him, soft as morning sunshine and twice as warm. "Yes, I think it's safe to assume the wedding is off. At least, until Mr. Murray is feeling better."

He thought about that. He was Mr. Murray. It didn't sound right.

"Lissa, what about the danger? Those cattle rustlers are getting violent." About the same age with dark hair and eyes, the second woman had real concern in her voice. "What will happen if your Mr. Murray doesn't marry you?"

"Then I can't hold onto my cattle. I'll go bankrupt." Her voice came again, gentle and sensible. He only saw her from behind, the set of her thin shoulders and her steely, straight spine. "It can't be helped. I'll not pressure an injured man into a marriage he can't remember agreeing to, no matter how much I may need him."

Pain speared through his skull. Whoever this woman was, he'd made a commitment to her, promises that should not be broken.

"Perhaps the doctor will have better news." The second woman sounded hopeful.

"Even so, it would not be right." Lissa formed a small and delicate fist at her side. "I hope he remembers, of course, but I can't count on it. I can't *wish* him healed. I'll just have to wait and see what happens. Perhaps he'll be well in a couple of days, and then he and I can talk. Maybe he'll remember his promises to me."

"What will you do if he doesn't?"

"I'll face that situation if it happens."

He edged away from the door. Gray fog blocked every memory, every thought, but he did know several new pieces of information. He'd made a vow to Lissa Banks to marry her. Dangerous men were bothering her. She could go bankrupt. Her son was expecting a new father.

His knees wobbled just from his thinking of the enormity of such a commitment, such a staggering responsibility. This didn't seem right, this agreement of his to marry, and yet he must have a link with this woman, a bond. She'd sat at his bedside all the night through with her gentle touches, cups of water, and her steady, comforting presence.

He was a man of honor. What should he do?

"Mr. Murray?" A light rap on the door woke him.

He squinted at the tall man, thin and bookish, standing uncertainly in the threshold. "Do I know you?"

"Not formally." He tipped his hat. "I'm Jeremiah Buchman, the town's schoolteacher. I'm a friend of Lissa Banks and her former husband."

He rubbed his brow. "You know Lissa?"

The quiet man gestured toward the empty wooden chair. "May I come in?"

"Of course." The conversation he'd witnessed between Lissa and her friend troubled him. Perhaps the teacher could bring some answers. "I'm afraid I can't remember if we've met."

"I know of your condition. I've taken the liberty of speaking with the doctor." The chair scraped as Jeremiah Buchman positioned it, then sat. "He says your memory hasn't improved."

"That's true."

"Then I should tell you how pleased I am to finally meet you in person, since we have corresponded." The teacher pulled a white envelope from his coat's breast pocket. "This is the letter you wrote me last month, after you proposed to Lissa."

He didn't understand. This was a small town. Why wouldn't he know the schoolteacher? Why would he write a letter? Didn't he live here? Pain slammed through his skull. He couldn't remember.

"This will answer all your questions, I think." Jeremiah handed him the envelope. This teacher might be a quiet man, but his gaze was sharp. He'd come as Lissa's friend, a protector to a woman alone and in danger.

Head hammering with pain, he lifted the flap and withdrew the letter. Parchment crinkled as he unfolded it. A bold hand written with care stared back at him. His handwriting? There, at the bottom, was his name. John Murray. That didn't seem right. Perhaps he went by a nickname.

Dear Mr. Buchman,
    I know you were close to my cousin Michael and to his widow Lissa.

His throat tightened. His cousin died. He couldn't remember Michael. Sadness crept through his chest.

    That is why I am writing you. Surely by now you know of my proposal to Lissa and of her acceptance. Since I am a stranger to you and to my future wife, I wanted to write you to ease any worries you may have.

The city named in the address beneath his name was St. Louis. He'd come from St. Louis to marry a woman he'd never met? This Lissa, with her soft voice and small son and the ranch she was near to losing?

He skimmed the rest of the words which listed promises, good intentions, and the vow to protect her from gun-toting outlaws. That pricked his interest. He thought that sounded right, that he was capable of handling men who lived on the wrong side of the law.

Then his gaze caught the last line of the letter. "I am a man of my word," he read. "Michael would want me to

look after his family, especially since I have lost my own
wife and small son. I come with the best of intentions. I
will protect Lissa."

He'd lost a family. Was that why he couldn't remember?
He didn't want to? Did grief explain the darkness wedged
in his heart like an ax?

"This has filled in some of the gaps in my memory."
He refolded the letter. He slipped it into the envelope.

"I'm glad I could help." Jeremiah's eyes were friendly
but questioning, too. "Lissa's future is in jeopardy, yet she
has canceled the ceremony for your sake."

"When was I to marry her?"

"Today." Jeremiah rose. "Sunday service begins in less
than an hour. I'd best get home and gather up my family."

As he watched the teacher leave, jumbled emotions
twisted inside his chest. He tried to remember. Only dark
gray fog and pain answered. Buchman was hardly a confidence man, out to fool him. He had no doubt the schoolteacher spoke the truth, that Lissa expected and needed
him to marry her.

He sat up, fighting the dizziness. He knew what he had
to do.

Hanging up the dishtowel to dry in the sunny corner of
Blanche's kitchen, Lissa leaned forward just enough to
glance through the window to the street outside. She could
see Doc's clinic with the sign swinging on the awning in
the brisk morning breeze.

"You didn't need to help with the dishes, Lissa."
Blanche's hand brushed hers with a connection of friendship, of caring—a connection that tugged at her heart.

"It's the least I could do, Blanche. You fixed me breakfast, and I know it's made you late this morning."

"Not at all. We just have to round up the boys and find

Jeremiah." Blanche set the empty basin on the table. "I'm glad you and Chad are joining us today."

Lissa tried not to think of her situation during the walk through the burning bright sunshine. Dust kicked up from the heels of the boys' shoes as they tried hard to keep from running and playing, with a few quiet reprimands.

Chad walked steadily in the same subdued way he had since his father died, with chin down, hands shoved deep in his pockets.

Would John Murray regain his memory? If he did, would he still want to help her? Or had his injury changed things between them?

"Lissa?" A man's voice broke through her thoughts.

She spun around to face Ike Palmer, town sheriff, so smart looking in his black vest, trousers, and polished boots. The badge on his chest glinted in the new day's light, and the puckered frown on his brow as he looked her over made her feel drab in comparison. She still wore yesterday's dress, for she hadn't bothered to change. The gray gingham garment was serviceable, but not her Sunday best.

"Ike. I'm surprised to see you headed to church." Normally the lawman avoided the weekly service.

"Today is different. I was looking for you. I hoped we could speak privately." He cast his gaze behind her shoulder and tossed Blanche a withering glare.

"I'll catch up," Lissa told her friend. Then she waited, squinting against the rising Montana sun. Chad took one glance back at her, then trudged along with the Buchman family.

"I've heard of your groom's unfortunate accident," Ike began, removing his crisp black hat. "Perhaps it was the hand of providence. Perhaps I'm the man you should be marrying."

"I've already heard your offer, Ike. You know it would never work." Lissa set her chin. "You're the sheriff. You have a responsibility to live in town. And I would never be happy in the cramped little apartment above the jail."

"I would buy the finest house here in town."

"I love the ranch. And you hate it. I can't change my preferences any more than you can change yours."

"But I would protect you."

One look at the jut of his chin and the sparkle of want in his narrow eyes shot regret straight through her heart. "It would be a sure path to unhappiness, and you know it, Ike."

"You could live in town, and *still* have a garden."

The man was thickheaded. Lissa gritted her teeth. It wasn't just the gardening. It was the scent of fresh mountain air every morning, the cycle of seasons from the new life of spring to the barrenness of winter. It was all she'd ever known and loved. That, and the freedom it gave her. When a person had their own land, they truly had independence.

Besides, her husband was buried on the hillside just yonder from the cabin, facing the rugged peaks of the Rockies and the setting sun. Her babies were buried beside him. She could never leave.

"Always remember I want the best for you, Lissa." Ike smiled. He truly was a dashing man, handsome in a pampered sort of way. "Will you ask me if you need help?"

She'd asked him to chase off the rustlers, but he hadn't made good on his promise—not like John Murray.

"Lissa!" Susan Russell called above the sounds of the street and the gathering crowd outside the white peaked church.

"Good-bye, Ike." She walked away with some sadness. Once, before she'd met Michael, she'd had a brief crush on Ike Palmer. Of course, she was a schoolgirl then who had no idea what she wanted in a husband, in a man.

"Lissa." Jeremiah's hand felt cool in hers as he met her on the top step. "Blanche is in the front row watching over Chad. She thought you would want to sit next to her today."

"I will." Lissa swallowed hard, uncertain how to walk through that door. Her decision to marry a man from so far away, a man she'd never met, had sent tongues wagging all through Sweetwater Gulch. Now she would have to meet their judging gazes again.

One step inside the church, and cold sweat dampened her palms. She looked up at the families crowding the rows and rows of handcarved pews, and saw more than one pitying gaze. Murmurs rose like a tidal wave, crashing over her.

Embarrassed, Lissa lowered her eyes and somehow made it to the front of the church, next to her son and best friend.

"You look nervous," Blanche said in her gentle voice. She reached over to pull one of her boys off the back of the neighboring pew. "Whatever happens, it's meant to be. You remember that. Everything will work out just fine. I can feel it in my heart."

"I hope so." Pesky tears hurt in her throat and burned in her eyes. She hated being so vulnerable, that for all the struggling she did to make it, she couldn't do it alone— Not unless she learned how to outshoot cattle rustlers.

Then, like a cold wind through a meadow, the congregation's chatter silenced. Lissa felt a prickle along the back of her neck. She turned.

John Murray stood in the threshold, strong-shouldered and handsome in a white cotton shirt and dark trousers. A white bandage hugged his forehead, and a wave of dark blond hair swept over it.

The air was squeezed in her chest. He shouldn't be out of bed. He shouldn't be standing. He looked ready to fall over in a dead faint.

"It's him," Chad breathed at her elbow. "My new pa came."

"He sure did." Lissa watched as John strode down the aisle enduring dozens of curious gazes, his chin up, his step sure, his dark blue eyes focused on her.

Only on her.

"I've come to marry you, Lissa," he said when he settled on the bench beside her. Up close she saw how pain lined his face and paled the tanned skin around his eyes.

Marry her? "But you're too injured. You must recover first."

"I've recovered enough. Let me show you I'm a man of my word. Will you be my wife?"

Chapter Four

"My real concern is for you."

Lissa's words made him look at her, *truly* look at her. Selflessness flickered in her blue eyes like sunlight on water, like the honesty of dawn and raindrops and a warm southern wind. John felt his throat fill. He could not swallow past the way she made him feel—valuable, worthy.

"You must be in terrible pain." She laid her hand on his forearm, her touch gentle. "I don't see how you managed to get yourself out of bed."

"I guess I'm a pretty tough man." He shrugged.

Her gaze narrowed. "You forget I'm the one who found you unconscious on my road, bleeding and helpless. You're lucky to be alive, and you ought to be resting, John. I want to marry a well man, not one who can't remember the agreement he made with me."

"I know why I'm here, and that's enough." It had to be. He had nothing but a mind full of darkness, and nowhere else to go.

"It's not enough for me." Her voice low, she leaned toward him. "I don't want to take advantage of you."

"You won't be."

A little frown crinkled across her forehead. "You may not realize what I've asked of you—"

"To be your husband," he interrupted. "To defend your ranch. To be a father to your son."

That frown deepened. "The cattle rustlers are dangerous, John. I can't ask you to take risks unless you know what they are."

He pressed the heel of his hand against his bandage and tried to will away the blinding pain. "I'm not afraid of risks or a few ruffians."

"It's a good deal worse than that." Hesitation tensed her face. "The rustlers have already killed one man, a rancher with land near mine. And my neighbor was seriously wounded last month. I wrote you. You probably don't remember."

"No, I don't." He winced as pain cracked his skull in two. He laid his hand against the side of his head. "But I'm not afraid. I made a vow to you, Lissa, a vow I will keep. Even if I can't remember. Even if men have died fighting those criminals."

"Why aren't you afraid?" Her words, whispered now, were almost lost on the rustle and clatter of last minute worshipers clamoring for seats, but he sat so close to her—head tilted, almost touching hers—that he couldn't miss a single word, a single breath, a single look.

Her soft, bow-shaped mouth quirked at the corners with her concern for him, a stranger. A shivering, hot glow began deep in his chest. He could not seem to force his gaze from the shape of her mouth or stop breathing in her sweet, cinnamon scent.

"Do you know what I'm more afraid of?" he confessed as a single note whined from the pipe organ and a cacophony of notes formed the introduction to a hymn.

Her eyes widened in silent question.

"Having nothing."

"Why, you don't have nothing. You have us."

"Exactly. Right now that's all I do have. That's every-thing. You and your boy. I have no other future, no other life." His voice caught, and he was thankful the congrega-tion rose with the spirit of the hymn, leaving him some privacy. "Don't take that away from me. Marry me today. Get it over with."

"It's a wedding, not a hanging."

"That's a matter of opinion." He winked, so she knew he was joking, and he was rewarded with the sight of humor sparkling in her eyes, crisp and clear. "Is that a yes?"

"It's a yes," she breathed. "As long as you're certain."

"I'm certain."

"And as long as your condition doesn't worsen. I'll not have you fainting at the altar, John Murray."

"I'll be sure to wait until after we seal our vows with a kiss." He liked the thought of brushing her soft lips with his. He liked it very much.

Blushing, she bowed her chin, hiding her face and eyes beneath a veil of curls which escaped from her braids.

Chad leaned against his knee. John looked down. The small boy looked up, his neatly combed hair rippling back from wide, happy eyes. Although he didn't appear to know the words, that small detail did not keep Chad from singing along—loudly and off key. John rumpled the boy's hair, and was rewarded with a broad grin.

He felt her gaze on him, and he bit his lip to keep from laughing. Lissa covered her mouth with one slim hand. Merriment sparkled in her eyes.

"Do you know the words to this?" he whispered.

"Try looking in the hymnal."

He fumbled with the book. He wasn't sure what he was supposed to be looking for on those red-trimmed pages.

Apparently, in the life he couldn't remember, he wasn't a churchgoer.

Lissa reached for the hymnal and belatedly searched through the pages. She glanced over another woman's shoulder for the correct number.

"Sorry," she whispered, half giggling.

She must not be a regular churchgoer, either.

Even though he had the lyrics in front of him, he didn't sing. His head pounded with a fury that made him weak, that sickened his stomach. He was content to listen to Lissa's soft, sweet soprano, and Chad's singing the wrong words half a beat late.

When the hymn was finished the congregation fell silent, and so did Chad, pleased with his vocal performance.

The minister's voice rose in prayer. John stood silent, aware of the boy gazing up at him, aware of Lissa at his side. Every time their gazes met, her eyes lit with silent amusement.

Just looking at her made him hope. She was a better woman than most. He didn't know how, but he knew. Her face was delicately formed by a small, straight nose and high cheekbones. The tiny lines at the corners of her eyes and mouth had to have been etched there by a million smiles.

She was his future now. He took solace in that.

"Looks like there will be a wedding, after all." Blanche wrapped her up in a hug while a crowd gathered on the church lawn. "See, I told you everything would work out. And I was right. He's a *handsome* one."

"Yes, he is." Lissa's gaze fell on her husband-to-be. Her heart clenched at the sight of his strong shoulders braced against what had to be enormous pain, pain he endured in silence while he spoke with Blanche's husband. "Chad likes him, too. That's the most important thing."

Blanche's smile was pure happiness. "I'm so glad. Look, there's so much to do if we're going to get you married this afternoon."

Lissa's pulse skipped. A wedding. That's what she wanted and needed, yet it felt so final. By tonight she would be John Murray's wife.

Again, she turned to study him, the length of the crowded churchyard between them, and met John's smile. His gaze warmed her and gave her courage. He didn't look panicked, the way she felt. He looked calm, confident, without doubts.

If only she could feel the same.

He strode toward her, his face pale and drawn but determined. "Doc said I had to see him before I left town."

"Are you sure you're feeling up to a wedding?" Lissa held back her hand, uncertain whether she should act on the urge to touch him. He wasn't her husband yet. "You're looking ashen."

"I feel fine, considering."

He wasn't fooling her—he was seriously injured. Yet he was determined to keep his word, to marry her.

She realized that he might be doing this as much for himself as for her. What would it be like to wake up with no memory, with only emptiness? Did he feel lost and alone? Perhaps marrying her gave him somewhere to belong, someplace to be needed.

He leaned close, smelling of clean man and sweet pine forest. "I'll get your horse and wagon ready."

"You don't have to—"

"Yes, I do. I'm your husband now, remember?" His eyes seemed to smile, flickering midnight blue like the deepest part of dreams.

"I'm not likely to forget." And how could she? He towered above her, all solid man and determination. Beneath his warm demeanor, she sensed John Murray was a man who got what he wanted.

"Neither am I. You saved my life, Lissa." He squinted down at her, the sun in his face.

Her heart twisted, and she heard what he did not say. "I was just protecting my best interests," she answered instead, meaning to tease when she felt otherwise.

He smiled, and she knew he understood.

Footsteps pounded on the earth behind them. The tightness in Lissa's throat eased when she saw her son dashing toward her, his hat brim flapping in the wind, his smile wide as the sky.

"Mama!" He launched himself against her skirts and held her tight. "We were playin' tag."

"It looks like you were having fun." She tugged on his hat brim and earned his chuckle.

"Yep." Then Chad tilted his head and gazed up at John. "You got a big owie. Does it hurt lots?"

"Not too bad." The big man gazed down at the boy with kindness in his voice, in his eyes, on his face.

"You fought a big, mean mountain lion." Pride held up the boy. "Everyone said you were brave."

"I guess I was probably pretty afraid, too." He had no memory of battling the wild cat. Only the deep claw marks on his chest testified to the struggle.

"I get afraid sometimes, too." Chad shrugged and looked down at the ground. "My pa died."

Sadness twisted through her, leaving her weak. But then John knelt down, one knee in the dirt, to look at her son on his level.

"A pa is mighty important to a boy."

"He sure is." Chad rubbed his eyes. "Mama said you're my pa now. You're gonna make the nights better."

John glanced up at her, a question written plainly on his honest face.

"Nightmares," she mouthed.

He placed one capable hand on the boy's little shoulder. "I'm going to make the nights better, partner."

And in that moment, when trust shone through Chad's grief like morning sunshine through fog, Lissa knew she would always be in debt to this man who could make such promises. She believed he would keep them.

John halted his horse after he circled the last bend in the road. Aspen and cottonwood leaves rustled in the wind, and the boughs of pine and fir swayed, scattering moving patches of shadow on seed-tipped grass. The scents of pollen and pine blended on the prairie fresh air.

A yellow-throated lark zipped past, wings spread. John watched as the bird darted amid meadows thick with purple and gold wildflowers. Lissa's ranch—the land he'd traveled so far to protect, to claim.

His breath stilled at the sight of neat rows of split rail fences marching across flat expanses of field and then climbing rolling hills into the far distance. Well-groomed horses stood drowsy in the hot afternoon shade. All this was framed by dense green forest and pastures where, in the distance, dark spots of cattle napped in the afternoon sun.

He looked to his left and saw a neatly built, whitewashed barn. A tidy log home was at the center of the scene, facing west and the setting sun to take in the distant view of the blue tinted, snowcapped mountains.

Speechless, he sat atop the bay and stared at the land— his land, his and Lissa's. Ever since he'd opened his eyes in Doc James's clinic, nothing had felt right, not his name, not this convenient marriage. But this—this rugged and beautiful land—did.

Somewhere down deep where dreams lived, past the bleak fog of his memory, something sparked to life in his chest. A recognition, a piece of emotion, one that twisted hard in his throat and left him weak. He remembered a

yearning for endless meadows and fresh air and a ranch
of his own.

Whatever had happened to him, he remembered that.
It only proved how right his decision was, his determination
to marry Lissa.

Slowly sounds tore him away from admiring the view,
the land that would be his. John headed the bay up the
drive and took it all in—the parked buggies, wagons, and
buckboards. Trestle tables were set up in the clipped grass
yard. He heard the ring of childrens' voices laughing, playing a game, somewhere out of his sight.

While he'd seen the doctor and bought necessities at
the store, Lissa and her friends had been busy.

That was all right with him. His gaze missed nothing,
not the neat, solid build of the cabin or the glass panes
so clean that they reflected the sun's rays like glints of fire.
Not the neat yard and the organized beds of well-tended
flowers, or the garden patch stretching out behind the
clothesline, small plants reaching toward the Montana blue
sky.

"Are you Mr. Murray?" A lean, bearded young man
strode close. "I'm Will Callahan, Lissa's ranch hand. It's
a pleasure to know you."

John dismounted and shook the man's hand. "Good to
meet you, Will. Need any help?"

"Nope. Got the horses tended to, and the chickens roast-
ing. I will take your gelding, though."

John handed over the reins, then swung the stiff new
saddlebags from behind the worn saddle. He thanked the
hand and headed toward the house.

A woman nearly crashed into him and almost lost her
plate of fragrant cornbread. "My goodness, excuse me!"

He let her pass through the doorway before he dared
step foot inside the house.

Neat and cozy—he'd expected that much. Lissa's caring
hand was everywhere. The polished furniture shone. Color-

ful, hand-braided rugs brightened the honey wood of walls and floor. Touches like a colorful quilt hung on the front room wall, the cloth over the table, and the crocheted lace at the windows all whispered the same word: *Home.* John's chest tightened. He suspected he hadn't had a place to call home for a long time.

"The bridegroom is here!" Blanche Buchman emerged from the hallway, dressed in ruffles and lace. "John, you aren't dressed. And look—" She craned her neck to see out the window. "The reverend just pulled in. Quick, step into Chad's room and get into your good clothes."

He didn't argue, didn't see how he could. He swung the saddlebags over his shoulder and stepped into the small, sun-filled bedroom.

The trill of women's laughter and the scents of competing perfumes faded when he closed the door. He took in the room. He was glad to see Lissa's touches there, too. A handmade quilt with fabric cowboy hats and horses decorated the corner bed. Matching curtains framed the small window. A cat reclining on a pillow stopped licking, studied him, found him wanting, and resumed her grooming.

John set his bags on the floor. He needed to get ready for his wedding. Lissa was counting on him. So was Chad.

He had discovered something today that troubled him. When he mounted his horse at the livery stable, the stirrups were a few inches too short. He'd dismounted and looked at the buckles. A crease worn into the leather showed the stirrups had been at the shorter length for a long time.

Odd—the livery owner had sworn it was John's horse and saddle. Not wanting to argue, he'd thanked the man and headed home, all the time wondering why he had a horse that wasn't his. The animal shied from him, didn't nicker or show signs of recognition.

Had he been robbed? Had the robber taken his horse and left him with a lower quality animal? The gelding was no expensive horse, but worthy. His billfold was still thick with money.

John unbuckled his packs. Inside were the clothes he'd purchased for his wedding—a white shirt, a black tie, trousers to match. He laid the garments on Chad's bed and considered them.

He could hear Lissa's voice, muffled by the thick wood walls, low and pleasant as she talked with her friends. The anticipation in her voice was unmistakable. He couldn't burden her with his worries. They weren't worries, really— just questions needing explanations.

There was a logical explanation. He felt certain of it. He was just nervous, that was all. Any man would be. Besides, if he wasn't John Murray, then the real one would have shown up for the wedding. As far as he could tell, he was the only John Murray in attendance.

Just nerves, he told himself. Someone had tried to rob him, failed, and shot him in the head. It wasn't the first time such a crime had happened in this frontier land.

As far as husbands went, Lissa knew she couldn't find a better candidate than John Murray. Blanche squeezed her hand. "Nervous?"

"Very." Lissa ran her hands down the rich satin overskirt of her dress, smoothing the expensive fabric. The garment had been an impulse purchase during her and Michael's last trip to Billings, and it hurt to remember.

"You look beautiful, just the way a bride should." Blanche sighed, the brush of her hand on Lissa's that of comfort. "You're doing the right thing. You know that."

"I do." *Think of the future. Think of what's at stake.* She and Chad needed John, and she had the feeling John needed her. Why else would he insist on marrying her, just as they had planned? Nerves clamped in her stomach, leaving her nauseated and unsteady. "I need to be alone for a few minutes."

"Of course." Blanche stepped back. "I'll be waiting for you. In front of the minister. With your handsome groom. I'll try to keep my hands off him."

"You're a married woman," Lissa teased. "Behave."

"I'm not making any promises." Blanche pranced from the room.

Alone, Lissa studied her reflection in the bureau's beveled mirror. A pale face stared back at her, and she winced. She was not at her best. Exhaustion bruised the skin beneath her eyes. Tension crinkled around her eyes. Goodness, it was a wonder John hadn't taken one look at her and run for Canada.

Lissa turned to study her room—the bureau with half the drawers empty and waiting for her new husband's clothes, the bed made crisp and neat, all ready for tonight, where they would sleep together. Her stomach flip-flopped.

She was ready for this. She was. In a few minutes she would become John Murray's wife. She would have a new name, a new husband, and a new future.

There was only one last thing to do.

She grabbed the bouquet she'd picked from her garden, a collection of white-petaled daisies, purple asters, and yellow-centered sunflowers. The house felt empty as she ambled down the hall. Everyone was outside, anticipating the wedding, and she wanted it that way. She needed to do this alone.

On a sigh, Lissa pushed open the kitchen door and stepped out into the late afternoon sun. Sunlight slanted through the gracefully limbed pines, and she hurried through the dappled shade, past the vegetable garden, to the rising hill beyond.

Michael's headstone faced the sun and the distant peaks of the mountains. Her feet felt heavy as she approached.

She shifted her stiff skirts and knelt before the grave. Like this marriage today, hers and Michael's had been a practical one, but love had grown from it.

She would not make that mistake a second time. Over the years of her life, she'd buried those she had loved one by one: her parents, her brothers, her babies, and her husband—everyone but Chad. After the grief and heartache, Lissa had to face the truth. She had no more pieces of her heart to spare.

"Forgive me." She knew it was time. She had to let go, move forward, but she would not forget.

She laid the flowers on Michael's grave and blew him a kiss. It was the last time she would visit this site, the last time she would let herself ache for what might have been.

Love was unnecessary to survival, but one's heart, that was very important, indeed.

Lissa rose and headed back to the house. Her skirts rustled in the seed-tipped grasses as she walked. Larks and finches and blue jays chirped in the meadow and up high in the trees. As she tried to leave her grief behind, the birdsong felt encouraging, a sign that she was doing the right thing.

She looked up, startled to find John leaning against the side of the house, hands tucked in his trouser pockets, waiting for her. How handsome he looked, how dependable. His shoulders were straight and unbowed, his chin cocked, his mouth looking ready to smile. She blushed, hoping he couldn't guess her thoughts, and lowered her gaze.

"Saying good-bye?" he said, that gentle and low voice beckoning her close.

His understanding touched her, and she could only nod.

"I'm glad to know you loved your husband so much. That's something a man wants in a wife." He held out his hand. "Come, our guests are waiting. Unless you've changed your mind?"

"No. Have you?"

"Not a chance." He knelt down and lifted a bunch of flowers from the ground, a spray of wild roses. "I picked these for you."

"You're thoughtful."

"No, I just want to please my pretty new wife." He smiled, and the world seemed brighter. He towered over her, all steely man and might. He pressed the flowers into her nervous hands.

He wanted to please her. He thought her pretty. He wanted to marry her. She feared John Murray wanted something she couldn't give him.

"Marrying me won't be so bad," he said, trying to tease a smile from her. "I don't swear. I don't snore. I don't drool in my sleep."

"Truly admirable qualities in a man."

"I think so, too." He offered his hand, palm up, his big fingers relaxed. She studied his hand, so strong, extended to her in friendship.

Friendship, she could accept. She laid her palm against his.

"Do you, Lissa Banks, take this man to be your lawfully wedded husband?" Reverend Burrow's baritone drew a hush from the gathered crowd—and from Lissa's chest. She couldn't breathe as she felt all eyes turn to her. Beneath the satin of her only good dress, her knees wobbled. Her hands clutching John's bouquet grew clammy. After these words, there was no going back.

"I do," she said clearly, and earned her groom's relieved smile.

Late afternoon sun slanted at a long angle through the windows of her garden porch where they stood, casting both shadows and slivers of golden light. The brightness haloed John, set his shoulders and the crown of his blond hair ablaze.

"You may kiss the bride," Reverend Burrows instructed with approval warm in his voice.

Lissa's heart stopped. Kiss him? The ceremony had slipped by so quickly. She wasn't ready. Now, she wet her lips and looked up. John's lopsided grin met her gaze.

"Prepare yourself," he whispered low, so that only she could hear. "I've been told I devastate women with a single kiss."

"How do you know? You still don't have any memory."

His eyes twinkled. "Fine. I was lying. I just wanted to make you laugh. You look nervous."

"That's because I *am* nervous."

"Kiss her, already!" some man shouted from the crowd, and everyone laughed.

She studied his mouth. Thin cut lips, strong to match his rough-hewn face. Would his kiss be overwhelming and powerful like the man, or tender like his smile?

"I won't bite," John promised her. "Well, not this time."

When his lips found hers, she was laughing. The first brush of his mouth to hers felt warm and soft, as if testing her response. Then he broke away ever so slightly and drew in a breath, a whisper against her sensitive mouth. His dark eyes flickered, hinting at his intent. Before she could brace herself his kiss claimed her again, hot and firm, just short of possessive, and demanding enough to make it clear:

They were man and wife.

Chapter Five

"Yes, you really found a good one," Blanche whispered. "Now you can keep your ranch. I say that for selfish reasons, you know." Warmth twinkled in her gaze. "I didn't want my best friend to move far away from me."

"Neither did I." Happiness wrapped around Lissa like a snug wool blanket.

Sounds of the celebration supper filled the air—the laughing ring of children's voices, the drone of men discussing crop prices and the beef market, and the clang of tin dishes as many finished eating at the trestle tables set out in her yard, brushed by the low rays of the setting sun.

It would be dark soon, then time for bed. She remembered John's kiss, remembered the feel of his arms enfolding her, still tasted the heat of his mouth on hers.

"Look at him," Felicity James sighed over her half-eaten slice of wedding cake. "It's so romantic. You have just met, but he sees only you, Lissa."

Sure enough, across the crowded yard John glanced over his shoulder as he walked the reverend the rest of the way to the horse barn. His gaze pinned hers like an arrow finding a target. A half-smile graced his lips. He entered the barn and disappeared from sight.

Every woman seated around Lissa's table sighed.

Flustered, she reached for the creamer. "He looks at me because he doesn't know anyone else. Maybe he's shy in crowds. Maybe he feels lonely."

"Or maybe he's falling in love with you." Susan Russell dipped her fork into the creamy white frosting of her untouched sliver of cake. "Felicity is right, Lissa. This is so romantic."

More sighs.

Lissa spilled three dollops of cream before she managed to pour any into her steaming cup of coffee. Romantic? She wasn't looking for romance. Those dreams had been buried along with Michael.

"We all saw how he kissed you," commented Maggie James, Felicity's older sister, as she measured three teaspoons of sugar into her cup of tea.

"We all saw it," the women muttered at once.

Lissa grabbed her spoon and stirred her coffee so hard it slopped over the rim of the cup and into the saucer. "It was a mandatory kiss. Everyone who gets married has to kiss like that."

"Not like that," Blanche argued. "A peck on the cheek—"

"Even on the lips—" Susan interrupted.

"Would suffice," Blanche completed, apparently knowledgeable on the subject. "When Jeremiah and I were married he gave me a polite little smooch."

"That's all John did," Lissa assured them.

"Ha!" Four women challenged her.

"That was no polite kiss," Blanche declared. "I was standing right next to you, Lissa, and I saw the way his mouth covered yours with the possessive claim of a man branding his wife. He left you breathless."

"I was nervous."

"You didn't look nervous. You looked eager," Felicity teased.

The women erupted into laughter, and Lissa resisted the urge to give her friend a small kick beneath the table.

Awareness skidded over her like rainwater. She looked up and saw John emerge from the barn, walking beside Reverend Burrows and his old white mare. The minister mounted up. John rubbed his brow, trying to hide a grimace as he turned away.

Her heart beat with concern for him. He wasn't well. He might walk with the power of a hero, with the strength of a giant, but he was ashen with pain.

When John ducked into the shadows of the barn, disappearing from her sight, Lissa stood. "Excuse me please. I need to check on my husband."

"What do you suppose they are going to do in that barn?" Maggie speculated.

"You heard her. She's going to check on her man."

Blushing, Lissa didn't know what to say. She turned, trying not to think in the same direction her friends' thoughts were already heading—to the marriage bed and her first night as John Murray's wife.

She stepped into the dim interior of the barn. The scents of warm horseflesh and sweet hay greeted her. A calf mooed from her pen, joined by a dozen other plaintive cries. A pink tongue darted out between the slots of wood and she laughed, hurrying to catch the calf before his strong teeth could clamp around the hem of her dress.

"You have a gentle touch with them." John's voice rose out of the dimness, accompanied by the sound of his uneven gait.

"They're just babies." She ran her hand over the calf's velvet warm nose. "You look a little pale."

He stopped near enough for her to see the slant of his

mouth, upturned in one corner, and the hint of a dimple etched into his cheek.

Up close, his complexion looked gray against the crisp white of the bandage at his brow and the shirt's snowy collar. He shrugged, a single lift of one dependable shoulder. "I'm still standing. I think that's a good sign."

She laughed; she couldn't help it. This sense of humor hadn't come through in John's letters. She was surprised by it, and immensely pleased. "Before you collapse in a heap, I think I ought to take you to bed."

"Already? The guests are still here. What will they think?" Then he winked.

She knew darn well why he was winking. Heat crept across her face. "They will assume you need your *rest.*"

"Ah, but a newly married man doesn't need rest." His chuckle was as rich and deep as a waterfall. He rubbed a hand over another eager little calf's head. "Are these orphans?"

"Unfortunately for them."

"Fortunately." John watched her slim hands pet the animals with tender affection. He didn't miss the gleam of love in the calves' eyes. "They think you're their mother."

"They do." She extricated the hem of her gown from between a set of determined bovine teeth. "I raise the gentlest milk cows around. And every year I pick a bull calf to raise."

"Let me guess. You have the gentlest bulls, too."

"Yep. I've made some good money that way over the years. My bulls are in great demand."

That surprised him, and didn't. He suspected few women enjoyed barn work—much less handling big dangerous animals—but when Lissa smiled he could see the size of her heart, the gentleness she held toward all living things.

"You said you always wanted your own land." She gazed up at him, a worry settling around her eyes.

"I have." He knew it, deep in his heart. It was the only thing since he had opened his eyes in the doctor's clinic that felt right, in place, as if it belonged to him.

"I thought you didn't remember anything." Her voice was so hopeful. She must want him to remember.

That's what he wanted, too. "I don't. I just know it. I can feel it."

That satisfied her. Her soft, blue gaze radiated light, and it captivated him, made him want to do anything to ease the worry around her eyes, to tease a smile from her lips.

Her lips—his gaze arrowed there. He had not forgotten the supple heat of her mouth. Their kiss had been all too brief, but it haunted him. He wanted more.

"There's something I need to tell you." He gestured toward the back of the barn, where green pasture beckoned through wide double doors.

She fell in stride beside him. "Good or bad?"

He shrugged. "Not so bad. It's just—" He sighed. "None of this feels right. Maybe because I'm lost. I don't even know who I am."

She looked stricken. "I shouldn't have let you marry me. I tried not to pressure you. Now I see I should have insisted—"

"No. I don't regret our marriage."

"You should have waited until you recovered." Worry thinned her voice. "I thought—"

"We did the right thing, Lissa." He laid a hand on hers. Her skin felt cool, and he sensed the fears she kept hidden from him—fears to which she had every right. "What else could I have done? Leave a woman unprotected from dangerous rustlers? I spoke with some of the men today. I know what's going on around here. And how close you are to losing your entire herd." *And her ranch.*

She met his gaze, all fire, her chin set for a fight. "So you married me because I was helpless?"

"No." He stepped closer. "I married you because I said

I would. Because your little boy is counting on having a new pa. Because I can see in your face how much you need me. I'm not questioning this agreement between us."

"Then what?"

"My name." He looked away, took another step toward the green grass. Wind scattered the scent, growing steadier now as evening lengthened. He smelled a storm on the way.

"What about your name?" She followed him, lifting her skirts above the ground. The fading sunlight brushed her with golden pink, the light glinting in her hair, glowing richly across her skin.

"I don't think I was called John before I was injured. I mean, maybe I had a nickname."

"Do you remember?"

"I'm trying."

A gunshot echoed in the distance. Lissa stepped away from him and faced the hills, the gentle meadows and rolling slopes of her pastureland. Adrenaline shot into his blood. He didn't need to guess. While Lissa made fists of her hands, he strode back into the barn.

"Those damn rustlers," she cursed, fury edging her voice. "This is my wedding party."

"No better time to hit." He caught the bay gelding by the neck and tested the rope lead. It would have to hold. "Nearly every man in the area is in your yard, unarmed."

"Will!" Her voice echoed in the rafters above.

John swung up on the bay's back as footsteps drummed in his direction. He saw Will Callahan bounding into the aisle at the same time, the young man all business. John headed for the hardware stored up high on a dusty shelf. The guns were shadowed, but he chose the best weapon there, an old single shot pistol, then grabbed a tiny drawstring poke. Had to have bullets in it.

Lissa's eyes widened. "John, you can't ride after those rustlers. Please, you're not—"

"I can catch them." He wheeled the gelding around and headed toward the double doors and the twilight world beyond.

At a full gallop, the bay drummed up dirt and gravel as they sped past the scattered crowd. Already men were running toward their horses as angry voices discussed the rustlers. A cheer rose from the crowd when John sent the bay hurling over the four-foot high fence.

"After him, boys!" Jeremiah's call carried on the wind.

Every gallop of the gelding shot white hot pain through John's skull, but he didn't turn from the threat. His mount chewed up ground and drew nearer to the second volley of gunplay.

The rustlers were firing rifles to drive the herd. That meant there couldn't be more than a few men.

The horse crested another rise, giving John a good view of sweeping fields and more hills. Then his pulse caught. *There:* He saw an ominous flash of darkness moving in the distance—the rustlers.

He pressed the bay harder and clamped his thighs tight to the horse's flanks, balancing his weight as the seasoned animal bounded downhill, skidding on his haunches in the lush grass.

Now that he'd found them, John's greatest concern was how to stop the thieves. He carried only a single shot Colt, older than the hills—not a good weapon to fight a band of well-armed outlaws.

Another hillside hid the rustlers from his view. At least John had surprise on his side. Those varmints probably figured everyone was too intoxicated after Lissa's wedding supper to notice the distant echo of gunfire. The outlaws wouldn't be expecting company.

The gelding's front hooves dug into the earth, propelling them up a steep hillside. Clods of dirt flew as the bay galloped all out, foam flecking his neck and withers, tangling in his windblown mane. This horse had the heart of a warrior, but no animal could run full-out for long.

There, at the base of the hill below, he spotted his prey. Knowing he could not confront the men, for he counted six of them to his single gun, he drew up the gelding hard. Four legs went rigid as mighty hooves tore into the ground, and the bay's head came up in a sudden, well-executed stop.

John slid to the ground, gripping the gun in one hand. He checked the chamber, inserted a single bullet. His gaze never strayed from the rustlers. He counted twelve, but when he closed one eye he saw a wavery, unfocused six. His hindered eyesight was going to cause him problems.

Well, it was too late to think about it now. He knelt in the grass, piecing together a strategy. He ignored the pain in his head, in his chest, in his ankle. Nothing mattered more than showing these men they couldn't push him around, or steal a helpless woman's cattle. When he aimed, his hand shook. He steadied the gun on one knee.

Take out the leader, his instincts told him. He studied the men below, all busy trying to drive the panicked herd north while the cows kept dashing in all directions.

John watched a man in a black shirt lift his hand and point, as if barking orders. His harsh voice rose with the wind, but the words came distorted and impossible to decipher.

That's the one. He thumbed back the hammer and aimed. Two images stared back at him, blurred and wobbling. He closed one eye, and the images joined into one. His hand still shook, and he waited, cursing himself and his injury. Soon, the men would be out of range. He had to fire now.

He heard hooves drumming the ground behind him, and he pulled the trigger. Fire sparked, thunder roared, and the leader of the rustlers tumbled from his saddle.

The outlaws swung wide toward the hill, jerking their rifles upward. John squeezed off another shot, and a second man fell. Gunshot volleyed across the crest of the hill and he dropped to the ground, thumbing another bullet into the chamber.

"You're a good shot." Will Callahan nodded approval as he crawled low in the tall grasses.

"I caught 'em by surprise, but now the tables are turned. There's no cover and we can't follow them like this."

"I'm no slouch when it comes to a good fight." Will readied his rifle. "What about Lissa's cattle?"

"The cows are scattering. The rustlers won't take the time to drive them, not with us on their tail. How many men were behind you?"

"Counted about twenty saddling up when I rode out of the barn."

John rubbed his brow. Damn, he hurt. "We trail them, keep to the south of this hill, in the trees. We'll try to jump them, take out a few more of their men before we engage in a gunfight."

"The odds will be even, then."

Fewer bullets peppered the hillside as the renegades raced for their freedom.

"They're running north." John risked his neck for a look. "Let's go."

"Whatever you say, boss." Young and determined, Will flashed him an approving nod. "Here, take my extra Colt."

"Much obliged." He accepted the sparkling revolver. Now, he was properly armed and ready—except for the horse. The damn gelding shied away from him, dodging his attempt to catch the single lead rope.

"Easy, fella," he crooned, and grabbed again.

Again, the horse evaded him. He snagged the rope and pulled in the reticent horse. Wincing against the pain, he hopped onto the animal's back and joined Will on the downside of the embankment, galloping hard for shelter and the line of trees.

Of the two men he'd shot, only one lingered on the

ground. John saw at a distance that the man was too injured to move, much less reach for his gun and try to shoot them in the back. His bay took the lead.

By the time they reached the clearing, the rustlers were waiting. A bullet sank into the tree trunk near his head, and John wheeled the bay back into the cover of the woods.

"I miscalculated that," he confessed. Damn, but his pounding head made it hard to think. "I need more ammunition."

"Got it." Will reached into his shirt pocket and laid a handful of bullets on John's palm.

"They're coming after us. Take cover."

Shots tore through the grove of alder and maple. John slid from his mount and ducked behind a solid tree trunk. Will, safe behind a moss-covered boulder, fired in return. John thumbed bullets into the empty chamber, spun it, and waited. The gunfire grew nearer.

"See to the other men," he shouted to Will. "They are going to ride straight into this."

With a nod, Will disappeared on foot, the brush and thick limbs obscuring him within seconds. John listened and waited before he wove through trees and bushes, and listened again.

A snap of a twig came from ahead of him, and to his right. He thumbed back the hammer, holding the revolver steady with both hands, and closed one eye. The world spun with his dizziness, but he concentrated hard.

Then he saw the slant of a cowboy hat and the flash of a rifle. His finger squeezed the trigger, then froze. He wanted to see the man before he brought him down. He didn't know if the men from the wedding party had caught up with them. He didn't want to shoot one of the good men.

A slant of shadowed twilight, dispersed by wind-tossed leaves, shivered over the man—not friend, but foe, rough, ugly, unkempt, unwashed, and dangerous. John fought to keep the gun steady, then fired.

Missed.

"Damn."

The dizziness was only getting worse, but it was no excuse. He thumbed back the hammer, and the gun jammed. He slammed it hard against his palm. Then, when the chamber didn't turn, he banged it against the side of a tree trunk.

His heartbeat tripled. Worry licked at his spine. His mind remained clear and calm, though, as he tried to spin the stubborn chamber. It turned, but already he saw the shadows in the underbrush. He dropped to the ground as fire flashed. A bullet bit into his flesh along the outer edge of his bicep, enough to make the arm hurt too much to use.

Angry now, John rose up and aimed with one hand. The rustler was already running, and John did, too. He crashed through fern and flower, tripped over rocks and rotting logs. Holding the gun steady, he squeezed off a single shot and grazed the rustler's hat. He aimed again, his last bullet, as the toe of his left boot caught in a rotten log and he tumbled forward.

The gun flew from his hand, hitting the ground and firing wild. John held out both hands, but he was already falling.

"Jeremiah!" Lissa called out as she swung down from Charlie's broad back. Twilight began to deepen, but even in the dimness she could see the devastation on the man's face.

"Lissa, you shouldn't be here. Not with those rustlers on the loose." Jeremiah strode toward her, his hand extended, as if to turn her and lead her from the meadow.

"I heard gunfire." Cold fear banded her chest. "Where is John?"

Jeremiah stared off at the horizon where night began. "I'm sorry, Lissa. Callahan and Miller are carrying him out."

"He's dead?" Her body failed her. She rocked against Charlie's flank, and the big horse held her up as shock turned her limbs and mind numb. *Dead.* "But he—"

"No." Jeremiah's hands caught hers, but she couldn't feel them. "He's been shot, Lissa. He's pretty weak—"

The doctor had warned against further injury. She tore away from her old friend's grip, hampered by the bothersome skirts of the fashionable dress. "Where is he? I have to see him."

"He's—"

Movement in the wooded grove sent Lissa racing across the wildflower dotted field. Will Callahan emerged from the shadows, striding alongside a tall, wide-shouldered man. Dark hair blowing in the wind, John faced her, a wry pinch to his mouth.

"I'm sorry, Lissa. I almost had them."

"Looks like you put a bullet in half the gang." Will swept off his hat. "Lissa, your groom is quite a shot."

John shrugged, lifting one shoulder, then wincing with pain. "It wasn't so hard. Next time I'll be well enough to bring those outlaws down, and that will be the end of their raiding."

"And harming innocent ranchers." *Or killing you.* Lissa bit back the angry words. "You're bleeding."

"Took a bullet in the arm. Nothing serious."

"Nothing serious?" *Really?* He could barely stand up. Crimson seeped through the bandage across his forehead, and spots of red stained his shirt. "You've torn your stitches."

"Good thing we invited Doc to the wedding," he said in that voice—low, not flip, strong and deep and confident.

She caught his injured arm. "That's no excuse, and you know it."

"You're in trouble now." Jeremiah winked at him across Lissa's blond head.

Big trouble—he gazed down into her fiery eyes and saw the hidden fury. So, the quiet little sparrow had passion. That intrigued him. He would have figured her for a warm sort of woman, cozy and comforting, not a steel-spined spitfire.

She kept it well hidden. He could see that. She shielded that fury behind concern for his arm. She tugged the seared cloth away from the bullet wound.

"Ow," he hissed.

"Sorry." He didn't think she was. "That bullet didn't just graze you. Doc needs to take a look at this."

"No more doctors." He meant it, even if the pain in his head threatened to bring him to his knees. "I just need to lie down for a bit."

"You need stitches." Jaw tight, Lissa wrestled a folded handkerchief from her pocket. Her full skirts swayed with her savage steps. "Stand still, John."

"Why are you so angry?" he whispered, aware of the dozen men watching him, curious about the newlyweds' first fight.

"I'm not angry." She avoided his gaze as she tied the cloth tight around his injury, then knotted it.

Sharp pain sliced through his biceps. John, sensing he shouldn't argue, clenched his teeth. She was afraid. Anyone could see it. Tears glittered in her eyes, unfallen and stubborn, as she reached up to check the bandage at his brow.

"You've torn open the wound, but these stitches might have held." She stepped back. "Can you make it back to the house?"

He caught her hand between his, felt her trembling. She'd been afraid for him. She'd been afraid for herself and her son. He could guess why. She needed him. She needed a man's protection in this rugged country.

"Don't worry, Lissa. I won't get myself killed." He offered his hand to help her up onto her broad-backed Clydesdale.

"You'd better not." She smiled thinly through her worry. "Michael doesn't have any more unmarried cousins."

She mounted with a rustle of satin and a whisper of lace, her graceful beauty striking against the raw power of the surrounding wilderness.

She was no delicate flower, easily battered by a hard north wind. She was like a willow, able to bend but not break.

Warmth expanded in the center of his chest. He liked this woman and her combination of fragility and strength.

Chapter Six

"I made you some fresh tea." Lissa stepped into the room—her bedroom—and was startled to see John shirtless before the window.

"Tea sounds great." He turned, appreciation tugging at his mouth. The sheen of lantern light caressed the sun-kissed skin of his back, illuminating delineated muscle and spine.

"I brought a slice of wedding cake, too." She set the tray on the bureau, her pulse thundering in her ears.

She saw the reflection of the bed in the mirror. The big, four-poster frame dominated the room. Her colorful garden basket quilt seemed to draw attention to the soft expanse of feather ticking and plump pillows.

"After enduring Doc James's stitches a second time, I could use some sweets." He spoke over the clatter of the flatware and tin dishes.

"You have a sweet tooth?" she found herself asking just to cover the nerves clenching around her stomach.

"I must. I'm awful partial to that cake."

"You didn't mention it in the letters."

"I guess I didn't mention a lot of things." He nodded toward the window, darkly reflecting the room. "This is really something, this place you have here."

"I'm glad you think so." She saw the lift of his chin, the gleam of satisfaction in his gaze. "You said you've always wanted a ranch of your own. Are you disappointed?"

"In this spread?"

She nodded, nerves clenching more tightly until she couldn't breathe. So much depended on this man—her happiness, her son's, their very future.

"How could any man want more?" Sincerity rumbled in his voice. "I never imagined a place like this could be mine."

"You like it, then? The barn's roof needs repairs, and—"

"I'll fix it." He let the curtain fall.

"The house is small."

"I like small." Lamplight shifted across the planes and contours of his face, masculine and striking, and kind as the night was long—so kind. "I'm happy I'm here."

"So am I." Her heart thudded. Kindness in this man, practically a stranger, came as a surprise. He'd been cool in his letters. Perhaps, she thought now, his emotionless tone in his writing had more to do with his losses and grief.

"How are you feeling?"

"You mean the stitches? They're sore, but I'm tough." His arm brushed hers. Awareness skidded across her skin. "Judging by the scars all over me, I'm used to a few scrapes."

"A few scrapes? You were shot. Twice."

"I wish I could remember the man who gave me this." He rubbed his forehead. "I'd like to haul him in to the sheriff."

"No one recognized the man you shot today." She

watched him spoon sugar into his tea—such strong hands. "He isn't from around here. At least, not that anyone knows."

"The rustlers must avoid town. Probably wise." He set down the spoon, leaving the tea swirling in the simple tin cup.

For the first time, Lissa truly wished she had nice dishes, something fine for this man to drink from. Michael's family came from money, and the scent of fineness clung to John, in the straightness of his posture, in his easy command of those around him.

She'd come from plain people herself, and later, as an orphan, she'd had even less. Now, she wished she could give her new husband all he deserved. He had risked his life today, when he could barely walk, to protect what was theirs.

"I suppose a lot of the folks around here knew when I was arriving." He sipped the hot, soothing tea, his gaze watching her over the rim of the cup—intelligent eyes.

Lissa wondered what he was thinking. "Why, yes. The wedding was planned ahead of time. We agreed."

He set the cup down. "And by the looks of things, the entire town was invited."

"Times have been hard around here. With the diphtheria passing through this last winter and the drought before that, people deserved a good party." She avoided the bed and pulled the hardwood rocker out from the corner.

She thought of offering it to him, but he reached for the plate and fork and turned toward the window. His limp was more pronounced. She remembered the doctor mentioning a cracked ankle.

She settled her weight in the rocker, and a joint in the wood creaked.

"Maybe I wasn't robbed," he said, so grim that even the ticking of the clock seemed to still.

"What do you mean?"

"I mean, maybe someone was waiting. Maybe someone wanted to kill me. Why else would I have a bullet wound in my forehead? Maybe it wasn't a robbery attempt. Maybe those rustlers figured they didn't want a man with a gun running them off. Cattle can be a valuable business, especially rustled cattle."

Lissa paled. "But there was a mountain lion. Surely that wasn't planned."

"It was common knowledge when I was supposed to arrive, and where I would be riding." He set down the plate with the cake half-finished, with a clank on the bureau's edge. "From what I hear, half the town had an opinion about you marrying a city dweller you'd never even met."

"You think the men stealing my cattle tried to kill you?"

"They've killed before."

She said nothing. He watched her stare hard at her hands, her face a hard line. "And they thought they could steal my heifers while we were getting married."

"Looks that way to me." He couldn't tell if she was angry or frightened. He didn't know her well enough to interpret the stiff line of her jaw. He knelt beside her and covered her hands, so tightly clenched, so surprisingly strong, with his. "Don't you worry, Lissa. I know one end of a gun from another. No outlaw has killed me yet. I'm not about to let that happen now."

"I want your word." Her chin lifted. Fire flashed in her eyes, that passion he'd seen a hint of before. "I don't want you to risk your life over this."

"You could lose this place. *We* could lose it." He squeezed her hands gently. They felt cool against his skin. "We're in this together now, Lissa. You and me. I don't want you to worry. I'm not a reckless man, but I am a damn good shot."

"That's what Will said." She breathed the words, soft

as music, drawing like melody. "Whatever you did out there, you impressed him."

"He's young."

"He thinks you can rid this place of those violent rustlers." Something attractive, something that looked like pride, glimmered in her eyes, strengthened her voice. "I don't want to bury another husband. I want you to remember that the next time you race off with a gun."

"I'll remember." He ached to brush away the curled tendrils of gold that brushed the sweet skin of her brow, but he held back. "I want this to be a good marriage. A real one."

Her throat worked. "So do I."

Her gaze traveled to the bed, neatly made and waiting, and guessed her anxieties. "Is Chad in bed for the night?"

"He was hoping you could come read to him, like you promised in your letters. But I told him you didn't feel well tonight."

His brows knit together. "What other promises did I make?"

"To build him a tree house. To take him riding."

"Easy enough promises to keep." Good humor tugged at his mouth, warmed his words. "What promises did I make you?"

Her gaze strayed to the bed. "You said you'd give me time."

"I see." He paused, silence falling between them. "That's one promise I don't want to keep for too long."

She blushed. So male-hot and iron hard, he squeezed her fingers gently, the way a lover might. She had hoped some memory would return to him so that they would not have to discuss this. Again, she stared at the bed.

"It's late." He stood, moving away with his limping gait, head held high despite the pain. "I'm going to go to sleep. Which side of the bed should I take?"

Her throat closed. "The left side."

Michael's side. As if he heard her thoughts, he said nothing. The knell of his boots stopped at the bureau. Light brushed across the muscular planes of his back and highlighted the crisp white bandage on the outer edge of his upper arm. At least he understood she needed time before they . . . before they were . . . intimate.

Still, that bed was small. The thought of lying beside him made her breath catch.

She heard the sound of fabric hitting the floor and leaped from her rocker. He was undressing! She caught a flash of white drawers, lean hips, and bare thighs. She headed straight for the door.

"I guess I should have warned you." His voice trailed out into the hall. "I just figured you'd seen more of me than this when I was unconscious."

"I didn't." The words tangled in her throat. She watched his hands hesitate at the waistband of his drawers, as if he were thinking twice about slipping them down. "Did you happen to buy a nightshirt when you went to the store today?"

"I don't wear one." His eyes sparkled.

Goodness. That meant . . . His hands stayed on his hips, ready to whisk those drawers off at any moment. Flustered, she fumbled for the doorknob. "I don't think I'm ready for this."

"Then you'd better leave." He winked.

Her face grew heated. She closed the door. John Murray was much more of a man than she had anticipated—maybe even more than she wanted.

He expected a real marriage. She was afraid, because he wanted what she could not give.

"Jack."

He spun away from the steel bars of the jail, the ring of keys in one fist. Sunlight slatted through the open door, offering a glimpse of the dusty street. A tall man filled the threshold, a badge on his chest. "Here's another reason why you can't leave. You'll miss locking up the criminals. Face it. You like the power."

"I would like something different." His own voice and the yearning for wide open spaces.

Jack, Jack, Jack . . . .

He sprang up in bed. Pain drummed in his head, making the dream fade. He tried to snatch back the pieces, tried to remember. He'd almost had it—the sliver of an image, of something tangible. What was it? He was in a jail. He was locking up a criminal. He was leaving his job. Yes, that was right.

Was the dream a piece of true memory? It had to be. He had read in Jeremiah's letter how he had once been a deputy, and he already knew he wanted his own ranch. This only confirmed it, and made something more important clear.

Jack, Jack, Jack . . . The name echoed in his head, cracked with the pain through his skull. He tried to remember, but there was only blackness and a void.

His breathing slowed. Moonlight peeked through the edges of the curtains, painting the room with a pale glow. The room felt silent. He turned and saw the bed beside him was empty.

Lissa filled his mind—her cinnamon scent, her musical voice, the light of her smile. He could relax now. All the pieces fit. The troubled feeling in his gut was better now. He knew what was wrong. He knew what was right. Finally.

A floorboard creaked in the hallway. He waited as the doorknob turned and Lissa's presence filled the room. The swirl of cotton, the pad of quietly placed feet, the sweet rhythm of her movements. "You're awake."

"Yep." He rubbed his brow, wishing away the pain. He needed a clear head. He had the rustlers, this new marriage, and this woman to figure out—no easy task. "I remembered my nickname."

"John is a pretty hard name to shorten." She reached for her buttonhook, and it rattled against the wooden surface of the bureau.

"I know my own name when I hear it. Call me Jack."

"Jack? That doesn't sound right." She leaned forward to unbutton her shoes. "Michael always referred to you as John, although your father is also named John. You mentioned it in one of your letters."

"That explains it, then. It's awkward having two Johns in the same family." Yes, that explained it, all right, and he was glad.

"Do you want me to call you Jack?"

"I do."

"That will take some getting used to." She stood, shoeless, and her smile was nervous. "Are you sure——"

"I'm sure. Look, I got shot in the head. Have pity on me. Call me Jack. It will make me happy."

"Jack." She tested the word on her mouth, those supple soft lips shaping the name like a kiss.

It was no struggle at all to remember the texture and heat of her lips to his, and the sweet wondrous taste of her mouth. "You need to undress?"

She dipped her chin. "I hadn't planned on sleeping in my clothes."

"I won't peek, I promise." He scooted back down beneath the covers, rolling on his side away from her. "That's going to be a hard promise to keep."

"Try." Nervous laughter filled the room, glowing like lamplight.

"A true test of my willpower." He squeezed his eyes shut. "Why is Will your only ranch hand?"

Fabric rustled as it hit the wood floor. "He was the only one who stayed after Michael died. The others feared I couldn't keep the ranch afloat, and left."

More fabric rustled. He swallowed. The thought of those garments sliding off her body left him breathless. He heard a drawer pull open. Cotton whispered. He wondered if she were naked, her skin gleaming like a pearl in the pale moonlight.

If he'd had any doubt about his attraction to his new wife, he had his answer now. It didn't matter how much pain racked his body or hammered through his skull. He was rock hard.

The mattress dipped slightly as she settled in beside him. The bed felt far too small. She was inches away, probably naked beneath her nightgown. That thought only made him harder.

"Good night, John—Jack."

"Sleep well, Lissa."

The sheets rustled as she rolled away. All fell silent save for his breathing and the clock's steady ticking.

How was he going to sleep now? He stared at the wall, his every thought of her.

The minute Lissa opened her eyes against the graying light of morning, she felt his presence, a male heat, the weight of his substantial body in bed beside her. He slept on his back, the sheet puddled around his waist. The thin muslin hugged his lean hips and the length of his thighs, hinted at his nakedness beneath.

Goodness! She shouldn't be gaping at him. Blushing, she slid out from beneath the covers and snatched her fresh clothes. Leaving Jack to sleep and heal his wounds, she stepped out into the hallway, heading toward the kitchen.

The mornings were still cool, but not nippy. The first light of dawn met her as she lit the stove. Soon fire crackled to life, and she hurried out of her nightgown. Keeping one ear toward the bedrooms, both doors closed tight, she heated enough water to wash with.

By the time the rooster quit crowing, the sun was up

and she was dressed in her favorite pink gingham and on her way to the barn.

" 'Morning, Lissa," Will Callahan called, drawing water from the well.

"Good morning to you," she sang.

This was the first morning in a long time that her burdens weren't heavy. She poured grain into Patches's trough. The milk cow lowed in greeting. "Good morning to you too, sweetie." The cow nudged her hand in thanks before rolling her tongue in the tasty oats.

"Were there any problems last night?" she asked Will when he returned with two five-gallon buckets which sloshed with each step.

"None that I heard. Or Pete, either." Will hoisted one bucket hip high, ready to fill the cow's bin. "I think your Mr. Murray gave those rustlers a much needed message. They'd better move on to easier pickings, or they'll be sorry."

"That's all I want," she said. Yet, as she thought of the dead man John—rather, Jack—had shot yesterday, she shivered.

She hadn't wanted that. She hadn't wanted her desire for justice to end in anyone's death, even a criminal's.

Will emptied the bucket and moved on to Charlie's stall with the second. The great Clydesdale lifted his velvety nose and affectionately lipped the ranch hand's shirt.

Troubled, Lissa drew her milking stool into the stall and settled down against the warm cow's flank. Patches gave a low moo of contentment as she crunched on her grain.

Lissa set the bucket between her feet and caught hold of the cow's udder. Gently, she curled her forefinger and thumb around one teat, then a second. She squeezed downward in rhythm, keeping a steady stream of milk hissing into the bucket.

The old tomcat let out a *meow* and hopped up into the

hay feeder. Patches watched in fascination as the feline waited for his pan of morning milk.

The familiar morning routine calmed Lissa, but could not put to rest her growing unease. Jack Murray's hopes for intimacy last night had been unmistakable.

Her heart stopped. She hadn't thought she would need to deal with that part of marriage—not yet, anyway. In his letters he'd said he wasn't ready to love again, but in time he would like more children. So would she, but Jack was still very much a stranger, despite all he had risked for her.

She thought of the way he'd galloped out of the barn in pursuit of the rustlers. He looked like a man who went after what he wanted—and got it.

What would he think when he realized she had lied to him before half the town, before the minister and God and her own son?

She would honor and cherish Jack Murray, but she would not love him. She would never be foolish enough to give her heart away again.

He felt watched. He opened one eye.

"Hi, Pa." Chad's grin felt as bright as the morning sunshine dusting the room.

Damn, but his head hurt. Jack rubbed his brow. "How long have you been sitting there?"

"Forever." Chad shifted against the headboard, sitting where Lissa's pillow should have been. "You must have been real sleepy."

"I guess." Jack tried to sit up. Dizziness confused his senses. "Where's your mother?"

"In the barn. She got lots of babies to feed."

Well, barn work wasn't Lissa's job anymore. He moved, and his entire body knotted into one enormous ache. *Great.*

Well, maybe he didn't need to bound out of bed, after all. He'd take it slow and easy.

"When I get an ow, Mama gives me cookies." Chad held out his hand. "Want one?"

He studied the boy who was now his stepson—a nice looking child, sweet and kind like his mother. Jack's gaze fell to the grubby cookie. "How long have you been holding onto that?"

"A while."

"Break it in half, and we'll share."

Pleased, Chad obliged. Crumbs tumbled onto his trousers and the sheets. Jack chuckled. He felt lighter, happier, with a chunk of cookie in his mouth.

"Your mother's a good cook."

"She has apple bread in the kitchen." The boy's eyes lit. "And sausages keepin' warm. I'm not supposed to touch the stove. Mama says."

A gray tabby leaped up on top of the bureau, rattling a china jewel box.

"Winston!" The boy clamored from the bed and dashed across the room. "You ain't supposed to be up there!"

The cat appeared unimpressed.

Jack watched as Chad hauled the feline from the bureau, nearly dropping the animal twice. The cat wrapped both paws around the child's neck.

"I'd better take her outside." Chad tromped across the floor, leaving cookie crumbs and bits of dirt from his shoes in his wake.

Chuckling, Jack tossed off the sheets and stood. Now, to find his clothes. He tried the top bureau drawers, neatly filled with precisely folded, fresh smelling woman's things. When he bent to investigate the bottom drawers, his body screamed in protest.

Damn, but being injured could sure take the steam out of a man.

Then he caught his reflection in the mirror, saw a bruise

purpling his forehead, creeping beneath the bandage wrapped around his head. More bandages covered the crest of his upper arm and the breadth of his chest.

There were older injuries evident, too, wounds he could not remember. Scars peppered his legs, streaked like knife cuts or run-ins with barbed wire fences. There were a few puckered ones, maybe bullet wounds—one to his thigh, another through his opposite calf—and fresh cuts from his fall in the woods yesterday.

Whatever his past life had been, the life he couldn't remember, it had been a tough one.

Where were his new clothes? John looked around, then tried a lower bureau drawer. He smelled sweet cinnamon and saw folds of petticoats. He'd better try another. There—he recognized the few shirts he'd picked up ready-made at the general store. His baggage must have been taken by the men who tried to kill him.

Chad raced into the room and skidded to a stop at Jack's elbow. "Whatcha doin'?"

"Just looking for a shirt."

"Wear a blue one," was Chad's serious advice. A frown crossed his small brow. "That way we can be the same."

"Blue it is."

The boy was easy enough to please. Jack grabbed the cotton shirt and slipped it on. He rolled up the sleeves and breathed in the faint scent of cinnamon and sunshine from being kept in Lissa's bureau—her doing, no doubt. He was grateful for it, for all day long he could catch the scent of her every time he inhaled.

Having a wife wasn't such a bad thing, he thought as he stepped outside and caught sight of her at the well, drawing water. The wind snapped her pink checked skirts and whipped the golden silk of her curls across her face. She was slender and graceful and strong.

Every inch of his body responded to her as she bent to

retrieve the full water bucket. What a nicely rounded fanny she had. Even with his striking headache, he couldn't help admiring her all the more.

Yes, a wife was a very good thing.

"What are you doing just standing there?" Lissa called, shielding her eyes with one hand. "I could use some help."

Even from so far away, her smile shone bright enough to touch him. "As you wish, milady."

She gave a laugh, sweet as the morning air. "You'll change your mind when you see what I have in store for you. After I rinse out these pails, I have to clean the calf pens."

"Clean out pens? I don't remember agreeing to shovel manure," Jack teased as he handily reached past her and lifted the heavy bucket from the well.

"Trust me. You did."

The tempting lure of her voice made him look up as he poured the fresh, cool water into her small washtub. "I'm not certain I should trust you, Lissa. I have no memory, and it seems to me now is the perfect time for you to take advantage of me."

"Take advantage?" She quirked a delicate golden brow. "Me?"

"Sure. You tell me I was supposed to marry you. Now I'm supposed to clean out pens. Seems to me you could tell me anything, and I'd have to believe you."

"It does seem that way." She knelt down and sluiced a small pail through the clean water. "I forgot to tell you something else. You agreed to muck out the entire barn for me twice a day."

Then she laughed, and he knew whatever the blackness in his memory, the void of his past, it didn't matter. Not if he had her to fill his present and his future with that light, breezy laughter.

* * *

"Are you telling me Murray shot a man through the heart at long range with a skull fracture and, according to Doc, double vision?"

"That's what I'm tellin' ya." The deputy leaned back in his squeaky chair. "According to Doc James, Murray shouldn't even be walking. An injury like that would put most men in bed for a month."

Ike Palmer pushed away from his desk and stood. The late spring sunshine blew in with the hot air from the open window. Anger punctuated his steps as he stormed to the window and gazed out at the street.

Murray was trouble, no doubt about that. Ike didn't like trouble in his town. And he especially didn't like how Murray had married *his* woman.

Lissa might have refused his proposal a few times, but he was certain she'd change her mind. In time.

Well, a man like Murray was easily dealt with. All it took was one well-placed bullet.

Chapter Seven

She couldn't stop watching him while he worked. Sunlight kissed the line of his back and shoulders as he climbed down the ladder. The boughs of the great green maple shook in protest. While she had only been teasing about Jack working in the barn, he had refused to lie in bed, even when she'd ordered him.

Lissa plucked another shirt from her basket of rinsed clothes and shook out as many wrinkles as she could. Really, she ought to be concentrating on her work, but her gaze kept finding Jack, shirtless in the afternoon heat, over and over again. The white bandages on his brow and chest and upper arm made him look rugged, rougher than any man she'd ever known.

Her heart turned over. Good thing he was tough as an outlaw. She wouldn't want anything to happen to him, to this man who was bringing laughter back into her son's life.

"Wanna go to town?" Chad ran hard, nearly knocking

over her basket of whites, puffing for air. "Pa said to ask ya."

"I have to hang the laundry." She caught a clothespin from the hanging bag.

"Let me help." Jack's voice, low and deep, cascaded over her like the wind.

She spun around, her skin strangely shivering from the caress of his words. The bandage hugging his bare chest did not diminish his appeal. A dusting of light hair sprinkled across his dark skin made her throat close.

"Come to town with Chad and me." He rescued a sheet from the heaping basket. "I need to buy lumber for the tree house."

"Gonna be a big tree house." Happiness brightened her son's face.

"How big?" She secured the shirt to the line.

"Very big."

It was good to see her son carefree again. Lissa's heart squeezed. "Jack, are you sure you know what you're doing?"

"How hard can it be?" He fumbled with the wooden pin. Once hung, the sheet tumbled to the grassy earth. "Oops. Harder than it looks, apparently."

"Make sure you shake out any bugs." Really, what did he think he was doing? "Not being able to help Will is driving you to do housework."

"A sorry state." Jack nimbly shook out the sheet, his teeth visibly clenching as he moved his injured arm and ribs. Yet there was no harshness, no cursing, nothing but an easy humor. "I'm going to try this again. Chad, grab that other end for me. It's dragging in the clover."

"A bee's on it." Chad took a quick step back. "Don't like bees."

"Why, dagnabit, it's a good thing I have my hat."

Lissa watched, slowly feeling the last of her reluctance scatter. The great big man swept off his hat and swatted

at the bothersome bee. The insect lifted into the air, buzz-
ing and diving at him. Jack beat his hat harder, earning
giggles from Chad and a growing warmth in her chest.
She so liked this man of strength and humor.

He went back to hanging sheets—rather badly—but
when his blue gaze caught hers and held, she forgot any
protest, let him hang her sheets crooked. Jack Murray had
brought laughter to their home again. As far as she was
concerned, he was worth his weight in gold.

Jack felt curious gazes studying them as they rode
through town. He ought to be holding the reins, ought to
be guiding that big, stubborn Clydesdale down the street,
but Charlie had refused to move when Jack took the reins.

"It's not a surprise," Lissa had said in that light way of
hers, soft like spring breezes. "I raised Charlie from a foal.
And he still misses Michael."

Didn't everyone? Jack bore no malice toward the cousin
he did not remember, but he didn't need to be a genius
to know how she felt. Lissa might smile, but the sadness
shadowed in her eyes was unmistakable—a sadness she
was working to put behind her.

"They are all wondering why you aren't driving." She
spoke low to him, leaning close so her words wouldn't
carry.

The tantalizing scent of her filled his head. "I'm injured.
They will just think I'm a weakling."

Her gaze slid over his shoulders. "Hardly. Not with the
way you rode off after the rustlers on our wedding day."

He shrugged. What mattered was that he hadn't stopped
those ruffians, black-hearted opportunists who would take
advantage of a newly widowed woman.

"You should stop by and let Doc check those wounds.
Whoa, Charlie." She drew back the reins so gently that
the big horse probably didn't even feel it.

Charlie stopped, meek as a kitten, in front of Russell's General Store. Lissa set the brake with ease.

"I don't need a doctor," he assured her, "but I'm glad you care."

Her eyes widened. He could see her shift back a few inches. When he helped her out of the wagon, she laid her hand on his palm with the lightest touch. Maybe he shouldn't have said that. Maybe his new wife didn't feel for him.

Not that she wasn't warmhearted. He could see it in her movements as she made sure Chad got safely to the ground and his clothes were on straight. She took a second to button Chad's top button and dust bits of leaf and twig from his hair.

"Good afternoon, Lissa," Susan Russell greeted from behind the counter. "And how nice to see your son and husband with you."

"Hello, ma'am." Jack tipped his hat to the pleasant-faced woman. "Come on, Chad. I fear those women are going to start talking. If they do, we'll never get what we need."

"Mama talks a lot." Chad's grave statement made Lissa laugh.

"No peppermint for you," she said, but her eyes were bright.

Not every woman was kind to her child, Jack knew. A stern mother who had planted herself in front of the bolts of fabric slapped her small daughter's hand when she reached to touch the pretty fabric. The resounding smack tore through Jack.

A glimmer of grayness haunted his memory, but he lost it and there was only the void.

"We need some nails," he told the boy, steering him down the farthest aisle from the door.

"We got hammers," Chad informed him as they passed a wall of carpentry tools.

Jack stopped and considered. The child was old enough to help out, to learn how to hammer, to know the satisfaction of building something with his own hands. "This here's a small one, just your size."

"Oh, boy." Chad reached up with both hands, eager to hold the small hammer, a replica of the larger ones, for grown-ups.

Jack fought the rise of feelings for this child he hardly knew. He was his pa. He was responsible for Chad and for the blond, pretty woman whose voice filtered through the store, light and sweet. It staggered him, and yet it made him glad, too.

"Are you coming next Thursday?" Susan asked after she'd cut a length of cloth for Mrs. Halverston. "We've missed you. Now that you have that big, strong husband of yours to run the ranch, maybe you'll have time for us now and then."

"I would love to." How she had missed the Sweetwater Gulch Ladies' Club meetings. With Michael gone, it seemed she'd never had one spare minute to herself. "Jack is still so injured. I'm not sure if I can leave him this week."

"Already planning on leaving me, huh?" His voice rippled across her like ice water, invigorating enough to make her shiver. "I thought you'd give me at least a week."

He winked and made Susan flutter in appreciation. Lissa took a deep breath, sizing up the man she had married— not bad, not bad at all.

"Mama, Pa likes peppermint too," Chad said, his eager gaze already fastening on the colorful glass jars decorating the counter.

"Aren't we lucky?" She laughed as Susan reached for a small paper sack. Candy crinkled and cascaded into the bag, drawing more delight from Chad.

"I'm gettin' a hammer all my own." Pride lifted the boy up, made him seem so changed, and all for the better.

Whatever Jack Murray was, whatever he wanted, she owed him much more than she could ever repay.

"Give me some of those cinnamon ones, too," he told Susan. "Now, when's this get-together?"

"Thursday afternoon. Every Thursday afternoon." Susan handed him the bag with a grin. "If you're the man I think you are, you'll want your wife to be there. We raise money for many important projects right here in town."

"Susan," Lissa scolded. "Don't mislead the poor man."

"Well, we raised all the funds for the new schoolhouse. And last year we bought the bell."

"My wife will be there," he promised.

The look he gave her made Lissa's toes curl. She could read it in his eyes—how he wanted her to go, simply because she wanted to.

"I'll be just fine, Lissa," he said low, so close that only she could hear the rich timbre of his voice, smell his wood and man scent. "I know these past few months have been hard without Michael. But all that's changed now. I'm here. You go to your meeting. You have fun. It's what I want."

Tears filled her eyes, and gratefulness that this man she hardly knew understood.

She let him take her hand when they left the store, Chad munching on his candy. When Jack helped her up into the wagon, she felt the strength in him, the ease as he nearly lifted her, and her pulse fluttered. She felt all aglow.

"Murray." That lone, cold voice could only belong to one man.

Lissa turned to see Ike Palmer, his sheriff's badge winking in the low sunlight. In a flash she saw the hard set of Ike's eyes, his fists and the wide-legged stance that meant trouble.

Jack faced the lawman with apparent ease. "What can I do for you, Sheriff?"

"I've been meaning to come out to the ranch and talk with you."

"About what?"

"The man you shot and killed."

Jack considered the sheriff's words. He did not miss the double holstered Colt Peacemakers strapped to Palmer's thighs, loaded and ready, or the glint of dislike in the man's steely eyes. "That criminal was on my property, shooting at me and attempting to steal my cattle."

"It didn't take you long to push your way in and take over." A blood vessel stood out in the lawman's forehead.

"That land was legally mine the moment I married Lissa. It's one reason why I came to Montana." Jack wondered what the lawman was up to. "Have I broken the law?"

He heard the shuffling of Lissa's skirts. "Ike, I don't like this. You know those rustlers have targeted my ranch. Why—"

"It's my job," Palmer interrupted, his jaw clenched. "Catching those rustlers are my responsibility. Not yours, and not some man you married for his gunpower."

Jack didn't like the sheriff's insinuation—Lissa was his wife, and she deserved respect—yet his guts told him Ike Palmer was just waiting for an opportunity, just waiting.

Jack refused to give Palmer the fight he was looking for. He held his anger in check and purged it from his voice before he spoke. "I used to wear a badge, same as you, Ike. I'm not looking for trouble."

"Then you will come with me now. We can talk."

"Ike—" Lissa protested.

"It's fine. The sheriff and I will talk. I imagine he wants to know what I can remember of those rustlers, since he's so eager to hunt them down."

"That's right, Murray." A smile twisted along the lawman's face, but it wasn't pleasant. "Let's go."

Jack had no choice. He told Lissa to drive the wagon around to the back of the store, where Susan's husband had promised to load up their newly purchased guns and lumber.

Worry lined her pretty face and made everything he was trying to accomplish fade.

"I won't be long," he promised. "Take Chad home. I'll find my way there."

"Jack."

He turned around.

"Ike wanted to marry me. I never told you. I guess he's mad because I turned him down so many times."

"I can handle him." He took a step. "You really turned him down, huh?"

"I did. For you."

Her smile touched him, soft as rain, as gentle as dreams. So she hadn't married him out of desperation. She had married him out of choice.

All in all, that was good to know, very good indeed. As he strode after the sheriff, his heart felt lighter.

The inside of the jail looked familiar, not this particular building but the barred windows and stone walls and the feel of the office. He saw edges of memories, but nothing more.

A positive sign. He knew he'd been a deputy before. Perhaps it was only a matter of time until he remembered.

"Sit," the sheriff bellowed, rough and hard.

Jack didn't like Ike Palmer's attitude, but he sat down, anyway—best to get this ordeal over with. "What do you want to know, Sheriff?"

Palmer's boots rang with each step. "I want to know about this man you killed."

"I don't know who I killed. I was told no one recognized him."

"Did you shoot first, or did he?"

"I did." Jack formed fists, refusing to be intimidated by the lawman's cold stare. "He was on my land and stealing my cattle."

"It wasn't self-defense."

"Cattle rustling is a hanging offense in these parts."

"So's murder."

Jack's patience snapped. "We both know I'm no murderer. I stopped a crime."

"You killed a man."

"I only meant to unseat him from his horse. I only wanted to stop the rustling, and bring the men to justice. There's no law against that, as far as I know."

A muscle jumped along Ike's clenched jaw. He curled beefy fingers around the back of a wooden chair and pulled it out from beneath his desk with a splintering scrape.

"Now you listen up, Murray. I don't care if you once were a deputy. I'm the law around here. And I do things my way. It isn't your job to bring in those rustlers. It's mine. Got it?"

"Then do your job, Sheriff." Jack bolted out of the chair. Anger licked through him. "There are men stealing from an innocent woman. If you don't put a stop to it, I will."

His threat lingered in the room, echoed in the single, empty cell.

Palmer's eyes hardened. "Then we're in agreement. Do you remember what the men looked like?"

"They were too distant to see well."

"You weren't close enough to see their faces?"

"No. Nothing stands out in my mind. If I remember anything, you will be the first to know. I want those men caught."

"So do I." Unrelenting, the sheriff didn't blink or move. "I am working to catch those rustlers."

Jack felt some of the anger ease from his tight chest. "Let me know what I can do to help."

"The next time you have trouble, you send for me instead of taking after them yourself."

There was no chance of that, though Jack nodded and tipped his hat. Sunshine blinded him when he stepped out into the street. He felt Palmer's gaze, felt the hard, hot fury of the sheriff's jealousy.

"Jack!" Lissa's voice spun him around. There she stood, haloed by the long, lean rays of a golden sun near to setting. Her checked skirts flicked in the breeze, the same one that tossed fine, gold curls across her pretty, heart-shaped face.

"Pa!" Chad dashed across the street, hat brim flapping with each bounding step.

Jack knelt down to greet the boy. "What have you and your mother been up to?"

"Lookin' at the feed store." Chad sighed.

Apparently that place wasn't fun to shop in. "Feed store? I thought buying feed was my job."

Lissa swept closer. "No, it's mine. I thought since I had the wagon already here, I would load up on more grain."

Running the ranch was his job. Jack held back the words because he didn't want to argue. Lissa brushed those curls from her face, and the way she looked made him feel changed and new—as if he was looking upon paradise for the first time and liked the view.

"Is there a good place to eat around here?"

"Maggie's Diner." She lifted one graceful hand and gestured, palm up, toward a neat little blue building.

Chad tugged on Jack's hand. "They got good pie there."

"Good pie. There's nothing more tempting than a good piece of pie." His gaze fell on Lissa, and on the way her eyes sparkled so blue and merry. "Well, almost nothing as tempting."

It was true—Lissa Banks Murray tempted him far more than a plate of sweets ever could.

"Behave yourself," she admonished, but she laughed, too.

He couldn't help but wish away the sharp blows of pain in his skull. He couldn't help wishing he was well enough to show her just how tempting she was.

"Ouch." He jumped beneath her touch.

"It's just an herbal salve." Lissa fingered a blob of the mashed, crisp-smelling yarrow leaves over the entire length of the stitches on his chest.

His hot, hard, very well-made chest.

She swallowed and dipped her finger into the small jar.

"It stings." He gazed up at her from his perch on the kitchen chair, broad shoulders washed by steady lamplight. "Doc didn't say I needed any of that."

"He wouldn't. It's a Crow Indian cure." Lissa snatched up a fresh strip of cloth and pressed it over his wound. Her hand buzzed from contact with his skin. Sensation telegraphed through every part of her body.

Goodness. Lissa took a deep breath and tried to calm her beating heart. She was not looking for love, not even sexual pleasure. *Heavens.* The thought of being pleasured by her masculine, hard-bodied husband left her blushing.

That was no way to think about an injured man. Determined, Lissa wrapped strips of cotton around the breadth of his chest to hold the medicine and bandage tightly in place. "What did Ike want?"

"The sheriff is not a friendly man." Jack breathed in, hiding his pain, but she could feel the tension in his ribs.

"Ike Palmer isn't known for his good humor." Lissa tied the end of the bandage tight. "Did he give you a hard time?"

"Something like that." Jack caught her hand. His fingers, strong columns, heated her skin. "Don't worry. I can handle the likes of him."

As dangerous as any outlaw, Jack rose from the chair with lethal grace and raw power. He snagged his shirt and slipped into it, wincing when he moved his chest, then his arm.

Lissa watched the fabric cover his exposed body from sight, felt regret as he fumbled with the buttons. "I can help," she offered, stepping forward.

"I appreciate it. My arm hurts."

The buttons felt smooth against her fingertips. As she fit button to stitched buttonhole, she lost her concentration. He towered over her, so close she could feel the heat from his body, see the stubble rough on his jaw, so close their breaths mingled.

She remembered the kiss they'd shared, the warm, velvet brand of his mouth, and how her heart had stopped beating. Now it drummed fast and hard, anticipating the dip of his head, the drawing closer of his lips, the closing of the distance between them.

He tasted like sweetened coffee. He felt like a late night dream, all sensation and a whirling, out of control, feeling. She gave up her task and laid her hands flat against the breadth of his chest. Beneath the layers of cotton and sun-browned male skin and steely muscles beat his heart, as fast and furious as her own.

She wasn't ready for this—It was too soon, it was too much—but she closed her eyes and gave in to the dizzying heat of his kiss. It felt so good she wanted him to never stop. She curled her hands in the fabric of his shirt and held on.

His thumb brushed the curve of her chin, sweet and tender, the way a lover's would. She opened her eyes to see him watching her, dark shadows haunting his eyes.

"I was afraid that you might not want me, but after

kissing you I know I was wrong. You are a passionate woman, Lissa Murray."

Lissa Murray. It was the first time anyone had called her that. It felt strange, as if she were a whole new person, someone who could leave the past in the grave, where it belonged. Yet she was afraid, as if letting go of Michael would erase all the happiness they had shared—when her love for him dimmed he would be gone as if he'd never lived.

"You promised me hot chocolate," he whispered in her ear, the brush of his breath meant to tickle her ear and make her shiver deep inside.

It did.

"I'll put more wood on the stove," he offered.

"Your injuries are never going to heal if you keep moving around."

"I don't want you packing wood, Lissa. It's my job now."

That was another thing. Jack's opinion of what his duties were had changed drastically since the letters he'd sent her.

"It can be your job later, as soon as those stitches come out," she argued.

"Forget it. I'm getting the wood, and that's that. The man of the house has spoken," he said roughly, but his blue eyes twinkled, and she wasn't fooled.

"Well, the woman of the house says you had better watch your step, or you'll be sleeping out with the cows."

"That's where you're wrong." Dimples flashed in his cheeks as he headed for the back door. "I'm never sleeping anywhere but at your side for the rest of my life. You can count on it."

He strode out into the darkness, leaving her alone with the cat and the rise of Chad's voice as he played with his toy horses.

Winston hopped onto the table, hoping to find the lid to the cookie crock ajar. Lissa took a while to notice. She shooed the cat back onto the floor, but she couldn't seem to take her gaze from the door, and she couldn't breathe quite the same when Jack ambled back into the room, handily balancing several sticks of cut wood in his muscle-hewn arms.

The memory came to him in dreams.

The burning heat of a late summer Montana sun, the crisp scent of sage, baked earth, and browned bunchgrass. A rock had found its way into his boot, and it bit at the ball of his left foot every time he stepped. He kept low, running on bent knees beneath the cover of scrub brush. The rustling whisper of cottonwood leaves hid the sound of his steps.

Danger. It thinned his blood and sharpened his senses. He heard the low buzz of voices at the water's edge, the almost silent rush of a deep, flowing river, and the twitter of larks swooping low in the grass made heavy by full, dried seeds. He held a rifle in one hand and a Colt Peacemaker in the other.

"Jack." A touch to his shoulder, and he jerked upright, bounding out of the chair.

The sense of danger faded. Lamplight surrounded him, illuminating the front room of his new home. The sofa behind him bore a small, hand-worked pillow and a closed child's storybook.

"You fell asleep reading to Chad. I put him to bed." Lissa reached for the book and hugged it to her chest. Her uncertain gaze met his. "It's only nine o'clock. I think you're not doing as well as you keep pretending."

Jack rubbed his forehead. A deputy from St. Louis—that's what he was. He'd never been in Montana until now. What he'd remembered, that had been a dream, not a memory—not like Lissa.

She laid a gentle hand on his shoulder and steered him toward the hallway. Nighttime made the cabin cozy, the dancing light from the lamps felt like a warm hug.

Home. He'd come home. That was all that mattered—not the past, not the man he had been, but the man he was now, and Lissa, who left fire everywhere she touched him, who made desire burn in his blood.

She was his wife. And he wanted her. How he wanted her.

Chapter Eight

"Look who decided to join us," Blanche greeted from her place at the James's kitchen table. "Is that your apple pie I smell?"

"The one and only." Lissa laughed, careful to keep her pie plate balanced while she accepted hugs from Maggie and Felicity. "I had to bake one for Jack and Chad so I could take this one out of the house."

"How is married life treating you?" Susan asked from her place at the table beside Blanche.

"Tell us *all* about it." Maggie lifted one brow.

"If I had a handsome man like that, I couldn't keep my hands off him," Felicity teased.

"We know." Maggie rolled her eyes, making everyone laugh.

"Being newly wed means being short of sleep," Sophie Johanson added.

"She looks well rested to me," Blanche observed.

Why, they all thought—Lissa blushed. Her friends assumed she and Jack had consummated their marriage.

"Let me take that pie off your hands," Maggie offered. She stole the plate and scurried off to the kitchen counter. Delicious treats sat on pretty plates awaiting consumption.

"I guess we're all here." Felicity pulled out the chair at the head of the table. "Let the Sweetwater Gulch Ladies' Club meeting begin."

Susan Russell produced a new box of playing cards. Maggie circled the table with a teapot and a coffeepot, one in each hand. Cups were filled, sugar and cream stirred, and the desserts distributed, all while the shopkeeper's wife dealt.

"Five card stud, aces wild," she called. As always, at the end of the game, all winnings would be donated to the club's latest cause.

Lissa reached into her reticule and pulled out her bulging coin purse. She emptied shiny coins onto the crisp, lace tablecloth.

"You haven't said one word about your new husband." Sophie peered up from behind her hand of cards.

"Lots of good sex can leave a woman speechless." Blanche counted out her pennies.

"Embarrassment can do the same." Lissa couldn't help laughing. "Really, Jack is an injured man. He needs his rest."

"I bet he likes you nursing him." Maggie winked.

Lissa studied her hand of cards, blushing harder. She remembered the hard planes of his body, so masculine and fascinating, how she felt her own blood heat whenever he touched her, remembered the tingling sparks of his kiss. Physical intimacy—it was something she'd been dreading since she agreed to Jack's handwritten proposal. Yet there could be benefits, too.

"I wouldn't let that man rest too long, if I were you," Susan advised before she made her bet.

Lissa knew darned well what her friend meant, but she took a sip of coffee instead of commenting. "He's been having bad headaches, but he refuses to admit it. He's building Chad a tree house up in the maple out back."

"What a man." Maggie sighed. "Does Chad like him?"

"Chad adores him." Lissa's heart glowed. "Jack has promised him a puppy next."

"I'm glad you found such a wonderful man." Blanche tossed ten cents into the pile. "After all you have been through, you deserve it, Lissa."

She tried to smile. Then the dealer called and the cards were laid down. Maggie won with a squeal, and Felicity took the cards and shuffled.

"How I miss that part of marriage." Elise Pickering tossed three pennies into the center of the table. "My Harry has been gone three long years, and the nights seem longer."

Lissa missed that part of marriage, too. Yes, there were benefits to be had: Comfort. Pleasure. Maybe a new baby.

"Lissa, your bet."

Susan's words brought her back. She studied her cards, trying to decide, but there Jack was—still at the back of her mind, with his sexy, lopsided grin and sparkling gaze.

Well, the hand she'd been dealt wasn't bad, not bad at all. She would make the best of it, both of her new life and her pair of tens. She tossed a nickel onto the growing pile of coins. Her thoughts returned to Jack, to the way her skin heated at his touch, and how her heart drummed when he was near.

She did miss that part of marriage.

"Here comes Mama!" Chad dashed through the house, bare feet pounding on the wood floor. His little fist gripped the spray of wildflowers they had picked together from the meadow.

"Quick. In here." Jack knelt to hold the cup.

Water sloshed as Chad dumped the flowers, stems first, into the offered tin. "She's gonna like these."

"I think so, too. Let's put them right in the middle of the table."

"Oh, Winston." Chad laughed at the smug cat already sitting directly in the center of the table. Winston pulled back one guilty paw and pretended she wasn't trying to knock the lid off the cookie jar.

"Get down, silly kitty."

The feline obliged, eyes eagerly watching the boy's hands. Chad snatched a cookie and dropped to the floor, ready to share.

Well, Jack figured, one cookie couldn't spoil the boy's appetite. He set the cup of flowers right in the table's center and admired his work—not bad. Maybe the forks and knives weren't in the right places, but the plates, the napkins, and the cups sure were.

"I see Winston's been hunting again." Lissa stood on the back porch, surrounded by light, lit from behind by the brilliant green world. "Not every cat is so good at catching cookies."

"We were hungry, Mama." Chad laughed, caught red-handed.

"I couldn't say no," Jack tried to defend himself, but knew from Lissa's glittering eyes that she wasn't angry.

She lifted her skirts with one hand, the other balancing her pie plate, and swept into the house. She brought the sunshine with her. Desire wrapped around his spine, leaving him weak.

"Any of that dessert left?" Some appetites he could satisfy.

"Enough for tonight's dessert." Lissa breezed close to him. "You're lucky Blanche brought her dark chocolate cake, or there wouldn't be one slice left for your sweet tooth."

"Then I owe Blanche a great debt." Jack ached to brush

those curls out of Lissa's eyes. He yearned to just touch her. "How was your meeting?"

"Productive. We're raising funds for a lending library." She laid her slim fingers on his forearm, her silken skin hot against his. Flecks sparkled in her big, luminous eyes.

Every inch of his body responded. "And just how are these funds raised?"

A mysterious smile touched her lips. "We're hosting the annual harvest dance, as always."

She passed by him, and the tiny hairs on his arms stood up. The surface of his skin prickled. He felt like the air right before a thunderstorm—charged and strung tight.

"What have you done?" She looked around. Her reticule thunked to the floor.

He knelt to retrieve the drawstring sack that looked suspiciously lighter than before she left for her meeting. "I thought Chad and I would make supper so you wouldn't have to."

"You even set the table. Look at the flowers."

"We thought you would like those, too." He straightened and laid the reticule on the counter.

"I do." She beamed, her eyes aglow. "You thought of this. You did this, Jack. I can't remember the last time I didn't have to get supper."

"Just trying to satisfy you, ma'am."

"Well, it's working." Her smile pleased him, all sweet curves and luscious softness. "I can't believe you can cook."

"It's an undiscovered talent." The breeze through the windows carried her scent—sunshine and sweetness all wrapped up with spice. "I'd do anything for you. Anything at all. Even peel potatoes."

"My kind of man."

"I hope so." He didn't know where these feelings came from, but he wanted Lissa like no other woman. He didn't need his memory to know this. He only needed his heart.

* * *

Jack's voice rumbled low through the house, blending with a contentment she hadn't known in a long while. Even though it was night and darkness shadowed the corners and the parts of the house not brushed by lamplight, Lissa had never felt so safe.

An owl hooted outside and coyotes called in the distance. She wasn't startled—not even when the night wind drove a low branch from the tall hawthorn bush up against the side of the house.

Lissa set down her embroidery. The wooden hoop clacked against the low table. The low timbre of his voice drew her down the short hallway, to outside Chad's room. With every step closer, she listened as he read about one of Tom Sawyer's exploits. Jack's voice rose and fell with the excitement of the story, and she nearly missed a step, just savoring the sound of him, all substance and heart.

Her throat ached. She tilted her head to peer around the half open door. Jack sat in a chair, the book held open in both hands, his head bent. Low lamplight brushed across his face, burnished his hair, and gleamed off the surface of the pages.

Chad turned on his side, finally asleep.

Jack closed the book and stood. His gaze swept up to hers, and he looked surprised. He hadn't heard her approach. The glitter in his eyes let her know he was glad to see her. "I was just thinking about you."

"Not about Tom Sawyer?" She held out her hand.

He gave her the book. "Tom Sawyer isn't as beautiful as you."

She bowed her head. Golden curls, cascading like sunlight, fell over her shoulder and hid her breasts. Jack thought about what it would be like to brush those curls away. His fingers ached. His whole body ached.

Then she moved away, and his opportunity was gone.

Her skirts whispered, and her shoes gave a light tap against the wood floor as she stepped into their room. She walked in the darkness, drawing him. Starlight silvered the shadows and painted her in hues of gray.

She set the book on the shelf among a half-dozen others. "It means a lot to Chad that you've kept your promises to him."

"It's the least I can do. He's a nice boy. I'm proud to be his stepfather. He's smart as a whip. He learned to hammer nails, straight as you please, in no time. He's building that tree house as much as I am."

"It means a lot to me, too. Not many men would do what you've done. Even reading Chad to sleep every night."

"It's my pleasure."

"You're still an injured man, Jack." Honest concern textured her voice, and he liked it. He liked knowing he mattered to a woman as fine as her.

"I'm on the mend, Lissa. In fact, I'm as fine as ever. And as strong. With strong appetites." He couldn't take his eyes off her, even when all he could see was her silver-limned form, all slender grace and feminine curves. Sharp, physical need speared through him, pumped in his blood, heated his veins. "I want to consummate our marriage."

"Tonight?" she squeaked.

"If you're ready."

She bent to light the lamp. He could not see her face enough to read what emotions resided there, but he knew what he wanted—and hoped she wanted the same.

"I don't know if I will ever be ready, if I can ever have time enough." Gentleness softened her face, shadowed with regret. "If I make love with you—" She stopped, fell silent.

He felt her sorrow ripple through the darkness like shimmers across a deep pond, and he understood. "Then I've replaced Michael completely."

"Yes."

"I didn't come here to replace anyone. All I want is you to look at me and see me—the man who has kept his promises to you, who has made a commitment to you." Truth ached in his throat, raw and honest. "You are everything to me, Lissa. You and Chad are all I have."

His words brushed over her like first light, gentle and stark all at once, changing everything. How could she say no to him? How could she say yes?

He closed the distance between them, laid both hands on either side of her jaw. His big fingers framed her face. She looked up and saw desire color his eyes, intent shape his mouth.

His kiss was hard and exciting. Not tentative, not timid, but as powerful as the man. His lips were commanding, and he seemed to breathe her in until she was without air, without wits, without anything but need—burning, growing need.

She laid her hands flat on the solid wall of his chest. He made her dizzy and hungry and confused. He made her feel so much more. A light heat drifted through her, bright as a rising moon, as enchanting as midnight.

She tilted her head, and he deepened the kiss. Of their own volition, her lips molded to his. She shouldn't want a kiss this much. Yet, as he brushed his big hands down over her jaw and caressed the length of her throat, her pulse stopped. All conscious thought ceased. There was nothing, only the hot, velvety caress of his tongue against hers and the brush of his thumbs at the hollow where her collarbones met.

"I can feel your heartbeat." He spoke with her breath, never breaking their kiss. It felt as if his words were hers. "You want me."

"Yes." It wasn't a lie. She was torn, and yet he was right. She did want. Her pulse snapped light and fast in her veins, beat in her chest with the rhythm of such sweet wanting.

His arms wrapped around her, holding her safe and tight to his chest. She pressed her face into the hollow of his throat, breathless, her lips tingling from the remembered sensation of his kiss. She felt the iron band of his forearms against her back and his steely chest against hers, the solid length of his torso, the muscled strength of thighs.

He was so much man. She tipped her head back. His gaze fastened on hers. He drew in breath, and she knew he wanted her but he wasn't going to push her. The next move was hers, and hers alone. She thought of all he had done for her, all she wanted to give him. He wanted this. She had felt so alone—but not since he'd come into her life, not now, in his presence.

She loosened the delicate button at her throat. The gingham fabric parted. Warm air teased her exposed skin as she freed one button, then another. Jack's hand closed over hers. His fingers spread tingling heat across her sensitive fingertips.

"Let me." How low, those words, how heady, that request.

Lissa took her hands away, lifted her chin to watch his face change. She saw shadowed light caress his cheekbones, saw desire shade his eyes. She felt butterfly tugs at her placket, felt the dress loosen. Fabric slid over her shoulders, catching at the crook of her elbows.

In this heat, she had worn nothing but a chemise. She felt her nipples bud tight against the nearly sheer muslin, saw appreciation quirk in the corner of Jack's mouth—his kissable, beautiful mouth.

He loosened one final button and her dress slid down her hips. Cotton puddled around her ankles, and she shivered—not from cold, for the night was warm. His fingers hooked around the straps of her chemise. Her hand caught his.

"The lamp is on." She blushed.

"I know." His eyes darkened. He wanted to see her, wanted to see everything.

She dipped her chin. "I don't think—"

"Whatever you want." He reached past her to turn down the wick. The sharp scent of kerosene tickled his nose. Shadowed darkness crept back into the room, dominating it.

She was nothing but shade and form. Then, when he touched her, she was flesh and blood woman, silken skin and curves. Desire thudded in his veins. He reached this time and wrapped two fingers around the cotton straps. Fabric slid away, whispering to the floor.

"Jack?"

He wished he could see her. The tremor in her voice told him this wasn't easy for her. "Do you want to change your mind?"

"No." Her hand found his. "I want to do this for you, Jack."

"Not for you?"

He heard her quick intake of breath and sensed she was blushing. "Haven't you missed this?" He ran his finger across her collarbone, felt her shiver.

"Y-yes. I miss the comfort." Her confession whispered across his skin, low and sweet. "My friends have advised me I shouldn't waste any time. After all, I suppose we aren't truly wed until we consummate our marriage."

"Wise friends." He couldn't hold back his grin, especially seeing Lissa's. "Before we make love, I want you to know I'm not doing this for the pleasure. It's my sworn duty as your husband."

"Yes, duty." A smirk lightened her voice. "You are required to give me more children."

"It's a tough job, but I'm ready for the challenge."

She laughed, their breaths mingling. How could she not like this man of strength and humor? "I'm glad you take your work so seriously."

"Very seriously." He gave into the urge to brush those tantalizing curls from her twinkling, shadowed eyes.

He'd come here to replace another man. Looking at Lissa made him want to erase all traces, all memories, all remembrance. He wanted Lissa as his own, all to himself—if not tonight, then in time. In time.

There was not enough light in the room, not enough shadow and shade for him to see her with. His skin prickled with awareness. Except for her muslin drawers, she was naked. Judging by the sharp intake of her breath, she was a little nervous about it.

Hell, he was nervous, too. She was placing her trust in him not to hurt her, not to use her. He would not let her down. He gave a little gasp when he first touched her, felt her body tense slightly at just his fingers on her wrist. He could feel her fast pulse, feel the heat of her.

"Your touch feels nice." Her confession came low, like a caress, soft as the darkness.

"I'm glad you think so." He laid a hand along her jaw, felt the silk of her hair whisper across his knuckles. "I intend to touch you a lot."

She lifted her chin, inviting his touch, inviting his kiss. The world stood still, silenced as his lips descended on hers. She was no longer shy. Her mouth slanted open, ready for the brush of his tongue across the top edge of her bottom teeth. She moaned, a sound of desire low in her throat. Unlike the other times they'd kissed, she opened more to him, inviting him in.

How could he resist? Jack cupped her head with both hands, deepening the kiss, searching out her mouth with his. She tasted like apple, cinnamon and passion, a combination that made his heart thunder, that drove a greater desire through his veins. He found the tip of her tongue with his and sucked gently.

"Undress me," he whispered against her mouth, speaking with her breath.

"I've never—" She laughed, maybe nervous, maybe embarrassed, and leaned her forehead against his throat, just beneath his chin. Her hair tickled his jaw, caught on the stubble of his day's growth. "I've never undressed a man."

"Well, it's time you learned."

That made her laugh again. "Michael and I just—" She twisted half away from him, turning in the direction of the bed, only a few feet away, soft and comfortable and waiting for them.

"I'm not Michael." He caught her chin, drew her gaze to his. Even in the darkness, he could feel the touch of her gaze, felt her shiver.

"I know."

"And I'm not trying to be. I want you to remember that tonight every time I touch you, make love to you. I'm your husband now."

Possessive. He didn't know he could feel this way, towering over her in the darkness with no way to see her, to read the emotion in her eyes, coloring her face. But he *felt* her, felt her heart, her being, without pretense. She was gentle and kind, loving and giving. He liked all that— more than he ever could have guessed when he first decided to marry her, to honor his promise to her.

In answer, he felt the brush of her hand at his throat. Felt the button at his collar release, then one after another until his shirt slipped open with a simple shrug of his shoulders.

Yes, her touch was all the answer he needed. His shirt fell to the floor, and he reached for her, took her hand, and led her the few steps to the bed.

Soft cotton quilt met his fingers as he pulled back the covers. Darkness enfolded them. His pulse thrummed as Lissa settled onto those line-dried sheets, which smelled of sunshine and morning fresh air. He wished he could see her. He wished there was enough starlight to cast faint shadows to see her by.

Then her hand caught his, velvet soft and as hot as fire. He didn't need to see her. He just wanted her touch, wanted to touch her.

"Where are you?" He felt like boiling liquid, ready to explode. She tugged. The strength in her hand pulled him onto the bed.

"I'm on your pillow." Her voice came thin and low, a mix of nervousness and need. "Yours is thicker, because it's new. I think I should have kept it and given you my old one."

"You'll have to fight me for it." He knelt over her. He threaded his fingers through hers.

"No fair. You're holding me down."

"I know."

Her fingers curled against his. He leaned over her, met her kiss, open and wet, full of desire. He nibbled her lips, then her jaw, savoring the flavor of her skin—slightly salty, sweet like angel food cake. He felt the tension in the tight muscles of her neck and caressed that tightness with his tongue.

Relax. He willed the word to her, too breathless to speak. He sensed her body prone beneath his, tensed and waiting, though he still had not touched her. He balanced his weight on hands and knees, giving her time to get used to him. Already he was hot and hard, wanting her so much he hurt, but he had all night. All that mattered was Lissa— only Lissa.

He pressed his mouth and tongue to the hollow at the base of her throat, felt the fast rat-tat-tat of her heart, felt her sharp intake of breath. She was willing. That was all he wanted to know.

He ran his tongue down the length of her breastbone. The soft slopes of her breasts brushed against his whispered jaw. Her fingers slipped away from his. When he caught one peaked nipple with his tongue, her fingers curled around the back of his head, holding him at her breast, asking for more.

She was all hot velvet skin and passion, just as he'd known she would be. He drew her into his mouth, then rolled his tongue around the puckered bud. Another low moan, so soft it was almost a sigh, encouraged him. He sucked softly at first, then harder when he felt pleasure ripple through her.

It wasn't enough. He wanted to touch her, too. He eased his weight down onto her. His erection nudged the silken curve of her stomach. She was all creamy, smooth skin and mysterious curves. And hot, hot need he could feel when he closed one hand over her other breast. As he laved and sucked, caressed and kneaded, she relaxed bit by bit beneath him. Her thighs parted, letting him know she was ready.

She wasn't, though. She couldn't be. Something told him that his cousin Michael hadn't known a whole lot about pleasuring women. Lissa shivered beneath him when he ran both hands across her ribs. He felt smooth skin, rippling muscle. She caught her breath. He heard the smile in her moan, and her thigh brushed his shaft. Red-hot sensation shot down his spine, thundered in his blood, but he wasn't through with her, not by a long shot.

He pressed her thighs apart and knelt between them. His fingers brushed flesh silken and warm, intimate and secret, especially in the dark.

"Jack!" She came off his pillow as if she'd been struck by lightning.

He moved his fingers against her. "You don't like this?"

Her breath caught. "I didn't say that."

His fingers kept caressing, spreading heat and dew. "I could stop."

"No."

He chuckled. She was like the darkness, yet he could

hear the quick rhythm of her breathing, the little sounds of contentment she made in her throat, the heat of her skin. He kept caressing her, discovering more wetness. She opened to his fingers, her hips lifting into his touch. Her fingers wrapped around his forearms, tight and hard. She lay back onto the pillow, moaning softly.

"Jack?" she breathed.

He liked the sound of his name when she said it like that—needy and broken and so dreamy. "Yes?"

"I think—" She couldn't catch her breath.

"You can think while I'm doing this?" His lips grazed hers, hot, enticing. "Then I'm not doing this right."

"Trust me, you are." He was going to make her beg. Fire crackled through her body, arching and jolting until only darkness remained. She couldn't catch her breath. She couldn't do anything but try to resist his touch.

How could she? Pleasure sizzled beneath his fingertips, snapping through her body, twisting her muscles tight. The sensation grew sharper, brighter, then excruciating. "Jack—"

Then he eased over her, all strong steely hardness everywhere his skin touched hers. Darkness framed him, but she could sense his smile. Her lips buzzed right before his mouth descended on hers. She eased back onto the pillows again, thighs clasped around his, breathless and dizzy and wanting—*how* she wanted.

His lips danced with hers, nipping, brushing, moving away. She felt his erection against her inner thigh, sighed when he nudged against her there, where they melted together, nothing but wetness and hardness and sweet, heart-stopping sensation.

"Oh, yes." The words bubbled through her. She clung to him, to the strength in his muscled arms, to the breadth of his back. He entered her slowly, stretching, filling her so that there was only this joining, the beat of her own heart, and him, only him.

He was so much. He withdrew and filled her again. Magical, luxurious sensation rippled through her, left her gasping. Those waves of pleasure built as Jack withdrew again, then filled her completely. Sharp spirals of heat twisted through her. She could not breathe, could not even move, as Jack kept thrusting, kept making that pleasure build.

"Yes." She'd never been this overwhelmed, so at the edge of control. Jack brushed kisses across her face, down her throat, arching his back to catch one peaked nipple with his tongue. Sensation tore through her, so bright and sharp that she gritted her teeth, almost afraid of it.

"Come on, Lissa." His voice shivered across her dampened nipple, breezed across her sensitized skin. He caught her mouth with his and kissed her deeply, all the while pinning her down, moving within her, driving deeper.

So deep. She lifted up to meet him, wrapped her thighs around his hips. Every muscle in her body felt strung taut, ready to break. Her abdomen clenched in a tight ball. This couldn't go on. She couldn't bear it. But his thrusts deepened, quickened, drawing the hottest, sweetest sensation there, where they joined.

She pulsed, her muscles clenching hard around his thickness.

And then it happened. A white-hot jolt of sensation speared through her, a bright, thrilling heaviness that squeezed in every muscle, every bone. Above her, Jack stiffened. She felt his release in the steel of his arms enfolding her, felt it in the tight ripple of his back muscles and in his fast, urgent thrusts. He threw back his head, throbbing inside her, spilling his seed in hot, wet bursts.

Breathless, he kissed her deep and hard, but there was a greater tenderness in his touch, in his kiss, that hadn't been there before.

"You are like no other." His confession rumbled low, vibrating through every part of her.

Tears filled her eyes. She laid a hand against his face, felt the wondrous texture of his day's stubble and the strong cut of his cheek and jaw. Still joined, she felt him thicken inside her, filling her with sweetness and pleasure and a dizziness she'd never known before.

She gave herself over to his kisses. His hips moved, starting up that tight building pleasure all over again. She gave herself up to it, to him.

Jack Murray had kept his vow. He was her husband now, he and no other.

Chapter Nine

She'd left him sleeping in bed, brushed by the first shadows of dawn. He was still healing from his injuries; he needed his sleep. Yet, remembering the night spent together—in his arms, and later, sleeping cuddled against the warm, hard wall of his chest—she hadn't wanted to crawl out of that bed.

The morning's work had called to her, though. She fed her orphaned calves, cleaned their pens, and hauled water.

Now, it was already past sunup, and Chad was out playing in his new tree house. The scents of coffee and of bacon still warm in the oven filled her kitchen. Shadows filtered through the lace curtain covering her kitchen window. The storm that threatened to blow in last night had held off. Dark clouds crowded out the sun, and the wind blew hard and gusty, knocking limbs from the hawthorn bush and the maples against the eaves.

She felt him before she heard him, as if last night's intimacy had brought a new level of awareness. Remembered heat from his touches breezed across her skin, flickered in her veins. There he was, an immovable tower of man and muscle blocking her threshold, one broad shoulder cocked against the door frame.

"Good morning." His smile came lopsided and sexy, as if he were remembering last night, too.

How he'd touched her, what he'd given her, made her shy, but she managed a smile. "How's your headache today?"

"Not as bad as yesterday. Mornings are the worst." He rubbed his brow, the bandage long abandoned. Shocks of thick hair tumbled over his forehead and into his unblinking, far too intimate eyes.

Yes, he was remembering last night. Remembering the way he'd kissed her, touched her, and how she responded. Avoiding his gaze, she swiped her broom beneath the kitchen table. "I kept the coffee warm. I know that helps your headache."

"You're an angel." His voice lured her.

"No, I just know how to cook," she teased, but she could not look up. She kept sweeping, but her skin tingled when he strode past her.

"A cook. An angel. It's the same to me." It was so intimate, the way the words rumbled low in his chest. She remembered being pressed hard against that chest, against him, out of control. "If you have a moment, I want to talk."

"You sound serious."

"I am." He stood, feet braced, looking every bit as dangerous as an outlaw, but uncertainty flickered in his deep blue eyes. "I want your opinion, since this is your land, too."

"You want my opinion?"

He rubbed his brow, pain evident in the wrinkle at his brow. "You've been at this ranching business longer than I have."

"Only because Michael died." She leaned the broom

against the wall, her heart knocking against her ribs. "He never discussed the ranch with me." Jack reached for a hot pad, but she snatched it away from his grip.

"I want to know what you think. I want what happens on this land to be decided by both of us."

Her throat tightened. She reached for the coffeepot, and spilled some. His hand covered hers, reassuring. She saw a steady, caring light in his eyes.

"Is that all right by you?" His voice sounded tight, but his words were gentle.

"I would like that very much." Yes, providence had been with her the day Jack decided to propose marriage. Every day that passed made her more grateful, happier that this man was hers.

He reached for the sugar bowl. "Since we can't count on the sheriff to help us run off these rustlers, I figure we're going to need to hire some men."

"I don't have that budgeted." She watched him stir sugar into his cup—such strong hands, but capable of great tenderness. She thought of last night, of his hands and how they had touched her.

"Can I see the books?"

"Sure." She wished she could just march right up to him and lay her cheek against that broad chest of his, feel the steely comfort of his arms around her. Instead, she moved away. "I keep everything in our bedroom. I'll dig the ledger out from the bottom drawer of my bureau."

Tension ebbed away, softening his broad-legged stance. "Beneath your petticoats?"

"You peeked?"

"I was looking for clean handkerchiefs. Is that your bacon I smell?"

"Keeping warm in the oven."

The way his slow grin spread across his face made her pulse skip two beats. She felt light as the breeze as she hurried from the room. With every step away from him she could hear him, imagine how he moved through the kitchen with the athletic grace of a mountain lion—crisp, efficient, powerful.

She tugged the ledger book from the bottom drawer and caught sight of Jack's clothes folded in the left half, his white drawers touching her everyday petticoats. The sight seemed too intimate—as intimate as last night spent lying naked, spooned on their sides, the weight and heat and presence of his body hard against hers.

He wasn't in the kitchen. She found him on the top step of her sunporch, a few paces away from the spot where they'd exchanged vows. Flowers scented the air. Unfurled rose petals ruffled in the breeze. Yellowbells and bluebells danced, and a hummingbird lingered at the flowering hawthorn bush.

"I caught sight of Hans Johanson along the north property line yesterday." Jack glanced up at her, all business. The breeze tousled his dark blond locks, scattering them across his brow. "He's been having troubles, too. Lost twenty heifers some time between yesterday morning and noon. Some of his best stock."

"Hans has been recovering from a bullet wound one of those rustlers gave him." She gathered her skirts and sat down beside him. "They seem to strike a rancher when he's down."

"That means those rustlers are either spending a lot of time observing the ranchers, or they already know them well." Jack wrapped both hands around the tin coffee cup and sipped deeply. Morning light winked along its surface.

"I thought they were outsiders. I can't imagine men we know as the ones causing such heartache."

"It's a tough world, and all sorts of things are possible." Jack took another sip, facing the wind. "And you have another problem. This is a big place. A thousand acres is a lot of land to keep watch over."

"I don't know how many extra hands we can afford to

hire without compromising our budget. Maybe if we sell extra hay this autumn when the cattle go to market."

Jack took the ledger she offered and flipped through the pages. "We could be worse off."

"True."

"I'm going to take a look at the new calves. Cut out a few to sell. Prices are low this time of year, but we need the cash. I think we should add a half dozen men to the payroll."

"Are you hiring guns or ranch hands?" She twisted to watch the movement of his face.

"Ranch hands. I'm not looking for trouble. And I don't think it will come to that. Besides, Will is handy with a gun. That's good enough for now."

She took a breath, considering. Jack snapped the ledger book shut and set it on the porch behind him. His big fingers dwarfed the tin mug as he drained it. She watched the column of his throat work, saw the vulnerable underside of his jaw. She wanted to kiss him there, to know again the softer side of this man of courage and steel.

"Come with me." He gave a single nod toward the barn, scattering the brazen gold of his hair against his collar. "We need to discuss your calves."

"My calves? You think you're going to sell mine instead of cutting them from the herd?" She kept stride with him across the hard-packed earth. Heated sage and ripe grass scented the air.

"I don't think so. I *know* so. Those orphans are going to be the easiest to sell. They're tame."

"Yes, but I've become attached to them." She followed him into the dimness of the barn. Straw crackled beneath her shoes.

"Attached?" He quirked a skeptical brow.

"Attached." She reached out to rub the first eager calf nose that popped over the pen rail. A long pink tongue darted out and pulled her fingers into its mouth. Chocolate brown eyes gazed up at her.

"I would be more attached to six ranch hands." Jack winked.

"Three calves, no more," she decided.

"Five." He laid one hand on her shoulder, both tender and commanding, as his touch had been last night.

"Four." She turned and saw only him—his mesmerizing eyes, his notched chin, his mouth growing closer that made her heart stop and her breath catch. He kissed her, and she wrapped her arms around his neck, sought the shelter of his broad chest and strong arms.

The kiss had been sweet, just a brush of his lips to hers, but the effect pounded in his heart, drummed in his veins long after—even as he rode the north property line beneath a cloud-filled sky, watching for anything amiss.

This ranch had a lot of problems. He was well enough to start solving them, to start fighting back against the men taking their cattle. Jack swiped his forearm across his brow, considering where to start. There had been no more visits from the rustlers—yet—but his instincts told him it was only a matter of time.

"Pa, I'm getting hungry." Chad wrapped both hands around the saddle horn.

"I suppose it's time to be headin' home." He knuckled back his hat. For as far as he could see rolling green meadows and groves of gigantic timber stretched toward the mountain-framed horizon. The restless heat of the wind puffed against his face.

"Mama was gonna make cinnamon rolls."

"The ones with the icing?"

A solemn nod.

"I'm awfully partial to those rolls." Jack couldn't believe his luck. A ranch like this, a nice boy to call his own, and a passionate woman who could bake. He had it all. The wind rumbled south, bending tall tips of grass and thistle. It felt restless, and called to something in his heart.

The crack of a branch split the air, and the gelding shied. Jack circled the horse around, the call of the wind forgotten, his senses alert.

"Sit here and don't move, Chad. Promise me."

"I promise." Small hands gripped the saddle horn more tightly.

Jack swung down and quickly tethered one rein to the thick rung of the fence. Listening hard, he unsnapped his holster. The walnut-handled Colt felt right in his hand, cold and powerful.

A shadow moved in the copse of pines—a single man riding a silver roan. "Is that you, Johanson?"

"Don't shoot me, Murray," a familiar voice called out, then branches gave way as the rugged man rode out into the heady wind. "Glad to know you're on the mend. I heard you were fixin' to sell a few of Lissa's calves."

"You heard right." Jack holstered his gun.

"The question is, do you have Lissa's permission to sell them? She raises the best breeding stock around."

"And she's proud of it." *And ought to be.* "What will you offer me for four of her hand-raised heifer calves?"

"Come on over to the house and we'll talk. Say this afternoon?"

"I'll be there after dinner." Jack looked over his shoulder to check on his son. The boy was busy kicking the gelding in the sides, pretending to ride. "At the wedding, you mentioned puppies. Still have a few?"

"A few? Hell, I got a whole litter of them. Just eight-weeks-old today, and ready to leave their mama." Hans's gaze traveled to the young boy, who gave an Indian whoop into the wind. "I'll wager Chad would like one."

"We'll pick one out." Jack tipped his hat. He wondered

what his beautiful wife would think about having a puppy in the house.

"I hope you remember who is supposed to clean up after this puppy." Lissa fanned herself with her bonnet, stirring the humid afternoon air only a bit.

"Me!" Chad announced. "I gotta feed him and clean him, and teach him where to do his business."

Jack's amused gaze met hers. "That's right, partner. If you want to have your own horse one day, you have to know how to take care of an animal. And your own dog is a good place to start."

As Chad talked excitedly, Lissa wished she could tell Jack just how much he meant to her. He'd kept yet another promise to her son, another vow to her—that he would love Chad as his own. Her heart squeezed with gratitude, and something more, something greater.

The Johanson homestead came into sight, a tidy log cabin and neat, flower-filled yard. The front door swung open, and Hans stepped out with a ready smile.

It was Jack that Lissa saw. The way he set the brake, swung down from the wagon, greeting Hans with a quick, firm handshake. He moved with strong, masculine grace, with that steel body she had touched last night, felt like no other. When he offered her his hand, palm up, his lopsided grin was only for her.

Heat struck as fast and as electrifying as lightning when she laid her hand on his. Her feet touched the ground, but her body felt changed just from being close to him.

As if he felt it too, he brushed a whisper of a kiss against her cheek. "I'll get a good price for your calves."

His words made her spine shiver. He handed her the covered tin plate, and the scent of cinnamon tainted the air between them. His nearness dazzled her. The strength and breadth of him made her weak.

"Lissa!" Sophie burst out of the cabin, a bundle of wiggling baby in her arms. "Come see how Evan has grown. And are those some of your cinnamon rolls?"

"Enjoy." Lissa left Jack's side, feeling bereft even though she adored Sophie. "Let me see that boy of yours. He's so beautiful."

A round face stared up at her, eyes dark and wise. Sophie beamed, full of pride, and when she spoke her words came low and sincere. "When he was born and we almost lost him, I'll never forget the things you did for me."

"I just washed a bit of laundry and cooked a few meals." Lissa resisted the urge to brush her fingers across the baby's tiny pink knuckles. "It was the least I could do. Look how you helped me last winter."

Sophie's hand came to rest on Lissa's wrist. "Like winter into spring, sadness fades, too. Look at that new husband of yours. And now maybe you can have another baby."

Hope. It was a scary thing. "A baby would be nice."

She thought of last night. Jack's tender, teasing touches, the patient, urgent way he'd joined with her. Her heart skipped, remembering. Even now, his gaze met hers and she recognized a glimmer of wanting in his eyes.

"We're goin' to get the puppy now, Mama." Chad grabbed hold of her skirt. "Pa's gonna help me pick out the best one."

"I'm sure he will."

Jack stole her breath as he strode close, his gaze bold on hers, wise with the passion they'd shared.

"Hurry, Mama!" Chad took off toward the barn, where Hans waited by the open doors. A dog barked, and six little dun colored puppies came running, all awkward feet and floppy ears.

Chad was already kneeling on the ground, where the first puppy jumped up with eager front paws, tongue out. After a few wet kisses, he had fallen in love.

Jack looked up at her, and she read the happiness there,

felt the new binding connection they'd forged last night in the dark.

"Bedtime, partner." Jack caught the puppy just before she dug her little teeth into his boot.

"Puddles is gonna sleep with me." Chad rushed up to wrap his arms around his new companion. The hound washed his face with her tongue.

Chad laughed, and the happiness in the room arrowed straight to Jack's heart. The wind and what lay beyond might have beckoned him today, called to a part of him he couldn't remember, but he was content here. His gaze fastened on Lissa, seated at the kitchen table, bent over the account books, very content.

The puppy snuggled into the covers right alongside Chad. With the lamp turned low, Jack cracked open *The Adventures of Tom Sawyer* and began to read. Chad's small arms wrapped hard around Puddles's middle.

As Chad's eyelids flickered shut—he was exhausted by his exciting day—Jack wondered about his own son, lost to him now, wondered if he had read to the boy and helped him pick out a dog.

Sadness crept through his heart. When he shut the book Chad didn't stir, and neither did the puppy. He turned out the lamp and headed from the room.

Seeing Lissa admiring Sophie Johanson's baby today made him think about his lost past, think about their future. She still sat at the table, with only a single lamp burning low, frowning at the account books. He liked that about her, that she was independent and smart.

He set his hand on her shoulder, felt the warm womanly strength of her.

"Did the puppy settle in all right?" She looked up at him, golden curls tumbling over her shoulders, burnished by the lamplight.

"Tucked tight in Chad's arms."

Her eyes twinkled. "I hope she remembers her house training."

"Probably not. Chad named her Puddles for a reason."

He liked it when she laughed. A brightness washed over her, made her sparkle. "It's awfully late to be working."

"Just worrying over our stolen cattle."

"I thought we were going to worry together." He reached over her shoulder and closed the account book with a snap. "It's too late at night for worry."

"You're right." She sighed, a tired sound, and pushed back the chair.

He turned her toward him. His lips settled over her open mouth and her note of surprise. One hot kiss and she melted against him, all warm woman and need. Her arms twined around his neck, and he caught her fanny with both hands, pulling her firm against him. He was already hard, aching for the intimate feel of her. She pressed boldly against him, her needs unmistakable.

Her kisses were hot and moist, so easy to become lost in. His fingers caught the first button at her throat, hidden beneath a spray of lace. Fabric parted to reveal creamy skin, brushed by light. Last night he had made love to her in the dark, and the thought of seeing her drove fire through his veins.

"What about Chad?" she whispered in his ear.

"He's sound asleep behind a closed door." Jack tugged free more buttons, his eyes never wavering from the soft curves of her cleavage.

"Wait." She pressed a kiss to the base of his throat, then moved away before he could grab her. She leaned over the table and turned down the wick. Flame died, leaving only darkness.

Fabric rustled, then her fingers caught his. She laid his hands on her bare breasts, and his disappointment faded. She felt like heated satin beneath his hands, tasted like spice against his tongue. With blood thundering through his veins, he laid her back on the table. Pressed kisses to her rib cage and stomach. Pulled away her skirts and untied the waistband of her drawers.

When he touched her, she moaned. Need surged through the deepest parts of him. She was hot and wet and swollen, ready for him, as he was ready for her. He unfastened his trousers, leaving them to fall at his ankles. So hard and hot that he ached, Jack splayed both hands against the outer curves of her thighs.

She parted for him, all soft satin and need, all angel and woman and passion. She accepted him inside her with a low, sweet groan, urged him deeper with hands that tugged at his forearms, then pulled frantically at his hips. He drove deeper, teeth gritted against that bright sharp release already beckoning. He felt her resistance, felt the pulsing tightness of those muscles gloving him.

As he set a rhythm, they moved without words, with only mingled breaths and frantic moans and mating kisses of lips and tongues. She came quick and hard, crying and arching, and boldly holding him deeply inside her. She carried him over the edge into oblivion so sweet there was only her and the hot wet pulse of his release.

"It's thundering." Her voice rippled through him.

"That's just my heart," he teased, earning her smile. He kissed that smile, just to taste the soft texture of it, only a shadow in the darkness.

Another boom rattled the windowpanes. "That really is thunder, Jack."

"I know. But if there's a storm out there, then I have to leave you." He brushed the beautiful curve of her face. "I don't want to leave you."

"I don't want you to go." She tilted her hips, and he shivered. Then lightning flashed. Images of her tousled hair tangled around her face, the creamy white rise of her breasts, the curve of her smile appeared and then faded, lingering only in his memory.

A bold peal of thunder shattered the silence.

"I guess I can't ignore that." He thought of the hundreds of cattle he was responsible for, and the shaky fencing that had been ransacked by the rustlers, barely patched. Another flash lit the darkness.

"You have to go." Her voice weighed heavy with regret. He liked hearing that—liked knowing she didn't want him to withdraw, to pull away from this closeness they shared—but he did.

His skin felt cold in the places her body had warmed him. He grabbed her clothes first, handing them to her as she dressed. She moved quickly, all shadowed grace and whispered movements. He pulled on his clothes. Lightning flashed, thunder crackled, calling.

"Take care."

Her words followed him out into the night, into a world driven by wind and storm. His heart ached because despite their physical intimacy they were still so distant; they were lovers without being in love.

Chapter Ten

"There's Pa!" Chad bounced on the wagon seat, his hat brim blowing up in the breeze, all little boy energy and heart. "Ain't he grand?"

"He sure is." Lissa's chest filled with satisfaction. She could not look away from the arresting sight of her husband at work—shirtless, mile-wide shoulders bared to the sun, hammer in hand.

He nailed a split rail into place with two sure, powerful blows of the hammer, then straightened. Sun glistened along the tanned ridges of his back. He rubbed his brow with his forearm, scanning the horizon. When he spotted them, he lifted one strong hand in greeting.

"We brought dinner." Lissa reined in the Clydesdale. The wagon rattled to a stop. Before she could set the brake, Chad flung himself into Jack's ready arms.

"Howdy, partner." Jack's deep voice rumbled with laughter as he swung their son to the ground. Then his gaze swept up to meet hers, and she saw his happiness at seeing her again. "A lovely lady delivering a lovely meal. A man can't ask for anything more."

She handed him the first basket. "Nothing more?"

His blue gaze crackled. "Only one thing."

She blushed, remembering the nights spent in his arms, joined to him, lost in the pleasure he so easily gave her. "Nothing that we can do in front of the ranch hands," she whispered, earning his laughter.

"There's always the bushes." He winked, accepting a second basket.

The four new hands gathered round, offering appreciation for the meal of fried chicken, biscuits, and apple tarts. She poured cups of cool apple cider and ginger water for the men.

When they were settled down to eat, she fixed herself a plate and joined Jack and Chad. They had chosen a spot away from the hired hands and near a clump of sweet-smelling clover.

"Puddles didn't like me leavin'. Not one bit." Chad leaned close to Jack, sitting with his knee cocked just like his new pa. "She cried and cried when she saw me up in the wagon. Didn't she, Mama?"

"She sure did."

Her son looked older, more confident and cocky as he looked up at Jack, imitating his every move. Chad was growing up. He was no longer her baby, but a boy who would have his own dreams one day—thanks to his new pa, thanks to Jack. Lissa's chest ached.

"Lissa." He spoke in warning. His hand shot to the holstered gun at his hip. "Take the boy and climb into the wagon. Quick."

The rustlers? Lissa wasn't used to following orders, but at the sound of alarm low as thunder in Jack's words, she didn't argue. Jack swept Chad into her arms, and stood protectively between her and the sun.

The bunchgrass clutched at her skirts as she turned. She

expected to hear galloping horses and the pop of gunfire. She wished she had more on hand to defend her child with than an empty picnic basket.

Then she saw a brown streak charging toward them. The quicksilver fear faded. Why, there were no dangerous rustlers, no threats at all—only Pete, her bull.

Lissa watched as her husband faced the running animal, tension tightening up his magnificent form. And she realized then that Jack thought the horned bull was attacking.

"Jack, no!" Her words were snatched away by the wind. She swung Chad to the ground as Jack waved his arms over his head, shouting at the animal, trying to divert it from its collision path with her.

Her skirts caught around her ankles as she ran. Desperate, Jack drew the polished gun from its holster. Horror rushed through her as he pulled back the hammer.

"No." She caught his arm, startling him. The gigantic bull ground to a stop before them, front legs braced, kicking up rocks and grass and bits of earth. "He's tame."

"I thought he was charging you and the boy." Jack released a shaky breath. "Most bulls are dangerous."

"Depends on how they're raised." She held out her hand, and Pete nudged it with his big wet nose. His pink tongue shot out and lapped her palm with wide-eyed affection. The gentleness of his touch warmed her, as always. Animals were so easy to care for. Give them kindness and affection, and they returned it. It was that simple.

People, they were different. They became part of a woman's heart, a part of her life.

"I'm sorry. I should have introduced you and Pete earlier."

"Good thing I didn't shoot." A muscle in Jack's jaw jumped. Tension tightened the unyielding line of his shoulders.

"You're angry."

"No," he said, but he sounded angry. "I was afraid for

you and Chad. I'm sworn to protect you, Lissa. I thought you were in danger."

Her heart stopped, leaving her chest feeling empty and hollow. Then his hand closed over hers. She could feel his heat, tangible from a hard morning's work in the fields. She could smell the wood and grass scent of him, see a new scratch from a briar at his chin and the concern fading from his gaze. But more, she felt his need for her, bright as the sun, big as the sky.

"I will always protect you." His words came rushed, breathless, but the solid presence of him felt as unruffled as the greatest of mountains.

She heard for the first time, too, what he meant, what he couldn't say. He was afraid of losing her, too. His past might be a void to him, but the heart, it remembered. It did not forget a loss that great—or want to feel such pain again.

"Howdy, Pete!" Chad charged out of the tall grass, his cowboy hat poking up among seed-heavy tips.

Pete, the big brown bull, lowered his head and stuck out his tongue to swipe the boy's face. Jack tensed, ready to defend the child should the big animal try to harm him.

Lissa laid her hand on Jack's sun-warmed forearm, the texture of male skin and the light dusting of hair wondrous against her fingertips. She took pride in this man of steel and might.

"Mama and me raised Pete from a baby." Chad giggled as the big brown bull nibbled the brim of his cowboy hat. "His mama died, so we gave him milk from a bottle until he got lots bigger. Then he ate grain and hay from my fingers."

Pete jerked up his head. Lissa laughed. "You big baby. Yes, I brought you some grain." She headed toward the wagon's tailgate, Pete following her.

With every step she felt Jack's steady gaze. He came, too, watching the big animal that was taller at the shoulder than the sideboards of the wagon as he twitched his tail at a pesky fly.

Jack didn't trust easily. He kept careful watch, stood silent sentry as she grabbed the tin pail, the bottom heavy with bright yellow corn and dried oats. He stepped closer as she held the pail while Pete lapped up the treat with his big, broad tongue.

Chad dashed up. The gentle bull laid his forehead against the boy's chest and sighed.

"She raises the best breeding bulls this side of Billings," Will said as he shouldered up to the tailgate for another helping of chicken. "There isn't a rancher in this county who isn't clamoring to buy this fellow right here. The rustlers have tried twice, but couldn't drive him from home."

"I train my bulls to come at the sound or sight of a bucket." Lissa set the empty pail and reached to pour Will another cup of cider. "The rustlers don't seem to know that."

"I hope they never do." Jack laid the flat of his palm on the sun-warmed neck of the gigantic bull. Pete turned his head to scent him, then swiped Jack's hand with his tongue. Jack smiled, and her whole heart warmed.

For the first time in a very long while, all was right in her world.

Jack took one last look at his wife. She stood in the open doorway, looking out at the night and listening to the sounds of the storm. Just rain and wind tonight, no threat of lightning yet.

Still, it was a good night for the rustlers to strike—if they dared.

No lamplight shone to illuminate her. Shades of darkness layered her like cloth. Jack found himself moving toward her. She was quickly becoming his center, his northern star.

"The rain feels good." Her voice rang with contentment, with familiarity, although she didn't turn around.

"It's good for the range land." The rain meant less chance of wildfires later in the summer. Jack settled his hand on Lissa's waist. She leaned into his touch, leaned into his kiss, until she was tucked against his chest and moaning beneath the assault of his tongue. "What about the men?"

"McLeod is keeping watch over the cattle until midnight. Arcada is on the other side of the field."

The men guarding this land could be counted on. Jack cupped his hand at the back of Lissa's head and wound his fingers through the silken luxury of her hair. "We are alone for now. For as long as we want."

Rain tapped on the porch roof overhead, dripped off the eaves, drummed against the earth, fell like a curtain of silvery black around them. They were truly alone. Jack caught hold of her collar, released the top button hidden beneath a fluff of lace.

Her kisses burned through his blood, thundered through every part of his body. Her breasts filled his hands, heated silk that felt like nothing he had ever known. She was home and heaven, need and want, wife and lover.

Her fingers plucked at his shirt buttons, smoothed away fabric until there was only air between them. He felt her need, not just for sex but for a man to depend on, a man to trust.

Yet even in her urgent kisses, in her tantalizing fingers curling through his chest hair and then trailing down to wrap around his already erect shaft, there was a holding back—of her heart, of her deepest self.

He wanted that part of her. Wanted her to know he was a man she could trust—now and until the end of time.

"You're ready for me," he whispered in her ear when

his fingers found her wetness, felt the way she arched against his palm.

"Yes." She spoke against his mouth.

"You're always ready for me." His chuckle came low, deep as desire, as dark as the night.

She could not deny it, just as she could not deny her body's reaction to him—swift, hard, melting want. She ached for him deep inside, in those inner muscles clenching tightly at his touch.

He was like dreams that come in the dark of night, all wanting and wishing, impossible to be true. Yet he was flesh and blood beneath her fingers, exciting male scent and taste.

His hands cupped her fanny, lifting her against his hips, and she clasped her thighs around him. His erection surged against the heat at her center, pulsed with his heartbeat against the curve of her belly. His wondrous male hardness was all she could think about, all she could feel, breathless.

Need sparked in her blood, then fed an inferno as Jack pressed her against the unyielding wall of chinked logs, hard against her back, but not as hard as he. She arched against him, wanting that thick pulsing hardness buried deep inside her.

"Please," she whispered.

"You need me?" Low and teasing, his voice rumbled against her chest and within her, as if it were her own.

"Yes." It was always a bad idea to need anyone too much, but when his shaft nudged against her inner thigh she tilted her hips, capturing that part of him within the tightness of her body. There was so much instant sensation there, where they joined, and deeper, bigger, that she had to have more of him, all of him, slow inch by slow inch.

"This must be what you need." His whisper curled along her spine, wrapping her in a cocoon of shivering desire.

"Yes." She ought to be embarrassed, but as his hard

thickness filled her she could only feel a joy and pleasure and caring so great that it threatened to undo her—to blow apart every reserve, end every fear, make her scarred heart new.

Release scorched her like a firestorm, all flaming wind and greedy flame. Bright, blinding heat engulfed her so much that it hurt, it frightened her, it made every part ache and pulse and burn. She felt Jack's release, the pulse of his shaft, the spill of his seed, the groan tearing through his throat, leaving him spent.

A final pulse moved within her, sparking a fast, hard ripple of heat. She hung helpless, draped against his body, held in his arms, weightless and crying out with sharp aching pleasure, with the power of all he threatened to make her feel.

Gradually, the rippling sensation faded. She heard once again the music of the rain, the harmony of the wind, yet she was still in Jack's arms, still under his spell, joined to him.

Instead of letting her down, he only tightened his hold. His face dipped low as he carried her through the house, and she shivered hard at the feel of his mouth at her breast, sucking until the fire of need ignited again. He laid her back on the bed, rising up over her, already hard, setting a rhythm she could not keep.

Already pleasure spiraled through her, bold and dangerous like flames licking high in the sky. Every rippling contraction of her body told her how much she needed him, how she could never let him go.

When he collapsed, spent, leaving her far too sated, she buried her face in his chest and closed her eyes, afraid of what she might feel, what she might say.

When he moved away, withdrawing from within her, leaving her cold and alone, she clenched her hands, fighting against feeling that loss of him. He moved away in the dark, a big presence with gentle hands, covering her up with the sheet.

She didn't stir, and he didn't speak, and she felt the distance between them grow. Tears beat at her eyes as he moved away, leaving her alone when all she wanted was to feel more of that sweet oblivion. Making love with Jack was the only time when it was all right to need him—the one time she did not have to feel alone and afraid.

She heard the back door close, knew he was out there in the rain, waiting for rustlers with his armed men, waiting for the chance to keep more of his promises.

Thunder shattered the peace of dawn. Lissa was startled out of sleep, torn out of dreams. A gentle peach glow warmed the windows, brushed the corners of the room. Then she saw the bed beside her—empty. Memories came of Jack carrying her to bed, laying her down to sleep. He had work to do, he'd told her in that deep, hazy voice, so sexy that it alone, without his touch, could make her shiver. He was out there in the morning.

Another rumbling crackle of thunder sheared the silence. Prickles skidded across her skin, burrowed into her stomach. A distant popping sound confirmed her fears. Gunfire, not thunder, had awakened her. The rustlers. Trouble had returned to her ranch.

Jack! She was out of bed in a flash, pulling on her clothes as she ran for the door. Chad's door was open. No sign of him or his little puppy, and no sound of them, either.

Another string of gunfire sounded closer to the house. Fear clenched hard around her chest. Lissa raced into the kitchen. Her heart stalled when she saw the back door wide open to the sunny world beyond.

Barefoot, she dashed out into the yard. She felt the thunder of cattle before she could see them, a vibrating drum that rocked the earth at her feet.

"Chad!" She ignored the bite of rocks and the stab of fallen twigs. "Chad!"

She saw nothing but green grass and rows of growing corn, empty fields. No little boy's head popped up above the thistles and seed-heavy grasses. "Chad!"

No answer.

Prickles skidded across her skin, burrowed into her stomach. Where was her little boy? The bellow of cattle, sharp and high, spun her around at full speed. She rounded the corner in time to see the first of the frightened cows cresting the hill.

"Mama!" Chad's call came, filled with excitement.

"Chad?" There he was, on the lawn at the edge of the road.

"Look what Puddles did." Laughing, Chad held up the small length of a thin stick. Already Lissa was running as the boy tossed the stick. It flew a few feet, the puppy bounding after it.

Lissa was only aware of the drum of the cattle and the shaking earth as the stampeding animals approached. Dirt spun in the air. The world became a blur of browns and whites, moving cows, and raw, coppery fear.

"Chad!" She screamed his name, running as fast as she could. Rocks bit into the soles of her feet, but the pain hardly registered. One cow overtook her, galloping wildly toward the road and open space, toward where Puddles had retrieved the stick and now was tucked safely in the boy's little arms. But the child, defenseless and small, was not safe from the herd.

"No!" Terror drove her forward. Panicked cattle loped around her, bellowing protest. Like an unstoppable river, the current of wild-eyed animals cut around her. Where was Chad? Where *was* he? Dirt swirled in the air. She couldn't see, couldn't breathe.

"Lissa!" Her name rang above the chaos, strong and

clear, but she would not stop. She would not lose her only child.

His mile-wide shoulders set, Jack appeared out of the dust and dirt and driving animals, tall in the saddle. His horse wove through the milling cattle, headed her way.

"Chad! Get Chad!"

Jack's gaze hardened. Realization passed across the features of his face, turning them to stone. He hesitated only a second, and for the first time in her life she could feel, could hear another's thoughts. He had to make a choice between her and Chad.

Before she could draw in another breath, he was gone, wheeling his mount to the west where she'd pointed. She tore after him, screaming her son's name, but the driving hooves and bellowing cattle created enough din to drown out the world. She couldn't see Jack astride his big bay, couldn't stand knowing her son might be trampled, might be dead.

No! her heart screamed with every step. The herd kept coming, driven by the gunfire from behind. Sharp popping sounds lifted above the drum of the herd and the taste of fear. A cow knocked against her spine, rocking her off her feet.

She hit the ground on her knees, felt the impact of a cow's shoulder against her arm. Pain rocked through her. The blur and drone of motion spilled around her. She tasted dirt and pain. Then a cow, unable to dodge her, jumped over her head.

Lissa ducked and rolled and saw two sets of hooves aiming directly for her. She felt the impact against the curve of her forehead, saw the earth rise up to meet her. She fought hard against the blackness, pure and silent blackness.

* * *

"Lissa!"

He saw her go down in the same instant he spotted Chad, clutching his puppy to his chest, tears running like muddy rivers down his dusty cheeks.

How could he leave her now? Yet the child wasn't safe. She could never live without her son. He knew this without asking, sensed this in the same instinctive way that he felt what she needed in the dark of night when their bodies joined. He knew her—just as he knew he could not live with his choice if he let a child die.

Teeth gritted, he drove the gelding harder, reached down and snared Chad by the waist. He lifted the small boy and tiny dog and swept them high, safe from danger. He settled the child on the saddle in front of him, saw Chad's tears, heard his crying, felt his fear.

"I want my mama," he choked out above the puppy's terrified whines.

Jack spun his gelding around. He saw no sign of Lissa in the herd. Gunplay punctuated the terrified drum of driving cattle, frightening the wild animals into greater panic. She had to be gone, he knew.

Grim, he kicked his tired gelding straight into the fray. Cows, eyes white-rimmed and nostrils flaring, dove around him. One steer after another slammed into the gelding's shoulder, once almost bringing them all to the ground.

"Lissa!" Her name tore from his throat, but he couldn't shout loud enough to be heard. Yards felt like miles. His fear was so big that he could taste it. Cattle thundered over the spot where he'd seen her fall. In a flash he saw the torn earth, the mud where her body should lie. There was nothing.

"Lissa!" He stood up in the stirrups, one hand holding Chad steady, the other trying to keep his gelding from being knocked over by the oncoming cattle.

Then he saw a shiver of blue beyond the shelter of a pine tree, the tall, rugged trunk reaching high but not wide enough to fully protect her from danger. Jack kicked his gelding into a hard gallop, cutting his way to her.

Every step of his horse brought him closer, but he could see her bleeding, see her take another blow from the sharp end of a steer's horn as he raced past.

Jack's breath stopped as he reached out, unable to help her. She didn't go down, though, and then he finally swept her into his arms, onto his lap, holding her alive and whole against his chest, against his heart.

She didn't speak, but he felt her need, felt all he could be to her. He held her and her son tight, felt her tears of relief as if they were his own. Chad was safe. She was alive. It was all that mattered.

"Jack, I—"

"Shh," he interrupted her with a kiss to her temple. They could talk later. He helped her to the ground near the strong split rail fence he'd built, then lifted down Chad and his puppy.

That woman and little boy were his everything. Anger beat hard and lethal in his heart; anger at the men who had dared to put his wife and son in danger.

Jack wheeled the gelding around the charging animals. He saw his profit running away down the road, past fenced barriers to the forest and freedom beyond. He saw the fight up on the hill, where his men had the rustlers trapped. Gunfire filled the air, fast and furious.

"Is Lissa all right?" Will handed him a loaded revolver.

"For now. But not if we don't get these bastards." Jaw clenched, Jack slid to the ground, dodging the bullets whizzing past, thudding into the trees behind them. He kept low, running fast for cover. "You boys did good. You've cut off their only escape."

"What do we do now?"

"Draw 'em out." Jack knew in an instant what he needed to do, felt it in his blood as if he'd done it all his life. He wanted those bastards, dead or alive. He didn't care. They could have killed Lissa or Chad, taken his whole life from him.

"We've got you cornered," Jack shouted to the cowards hidden behind a boulder. "Toss out your weapons."

"Not on your life, Murray."

"Then it will be on yours." This was personal. That scared him. It told him something else. With the better fences and the night watches, only a fool would risk stealing cattle in plain sight, or someone with a different purpose. They had stampeded the cattle past the house. They could have taken the back way, even with the higher fences.

"What do you want?"

"You, Murray," said a deep voice, one Jack didn't recognize. "You killed a friend of ours. And you're next."

Jack spun open the chambers of his Colts. Empty. He thumbed in bullets. He lowered his voice, leaned close to Will.

"We go in after them." Jack took a breath, knew what he had to do. "Will, I want you to circle them from behind."

"And then what?"

"Shoot." He thumbed back both hammers, knowing all too well the fear before battle. "You'll be all right. Just follow my lead."

"You're the boss."

Jack came out shooting. He wasn't scared. He didn't have time to be, with bullets whizzing past him. Anger focused him, made him cold and accurate. He saw nothing but the image of Chad, muddy and crying, of Lissa screaming her son's name.

He smelled the panic in the air, sensed the rustlers' desperation. Every step brought him closer to them, to the men who had nearly killed his family. Jack's Peacemakers spit fire and bullets, and he took down one of the outlaws. Only five more to go. He felt a burning along the outside of his arm, the sting of a bullet. It only iced his determination.

Will's firing dropped one rustler, scared the others out

of hiding. Jack was ready for them. Before they could turn on Will, he fired a volley of shots that caught two more of them, killing all but one of the men. He swung around and dropped him, but not in time. Will's knees hit the ground, blood staining his left side.

"It's not bad, I don't think." The young man looked pale. Strain tightened his face.

"Hold on." Jack checked the dead first, making sure there was no pulse, kicking the revolvers far out of reach. Only then did he check Will's wound.

"You're going to need a doctor." He pressed Will's shirt back over the injury, found a handkerchief and added pressure.

Blood stained his own shirt, but it was nothing, not when compared to the young man's wound. They had to get him to town, and fast.

Jack's gaze swung past the bodies, already wondering how the lazy sheriff would take to the news, then lingered on Lissa's face. Shock slackened her jaw, and he realized for the first time what she must see, realizing for the first time the true heart of the man she married—a man able to kill.

Jack could not remember his past, but he knew this about himself as well as the sight of his own face in the mirror, with a certainty that left no doubt:

He didn't belong here in this haven of peaceful sky and reaching meadows.

Chapter Eleven

"You're a lucky man, Jack Murray." Doc's voice echoed in the small room. "Another inch and you would have lost a kidney."

Jack saw again the image of the stampede, tasted the fear when he'd searched for her in the mud. He knew if he didn't stop the rustlers she would never be safe. "How is Lissa?"

"She's bruised pretty bad, but nothing that can't heal." Doc tied the last edge of the bandage into place. "You're a good man, Jack. She's alive because of you. I'm glad you came to this town, came to her."

Jack reached for his shirt. "Has the sheriff been by?"

Doc shook his head as he moved toward the door. "I sent a message over to the undertaker. He took the bodies, as far as I know."

"Did you recognize any of them?"

"Can't say that I do. I see a lot of people from all over this countryside. I can say with certainty that those men weren't from around here.'' Doc stepped out into the hallway. ''I'll check on Will.''

''Thanks, Doc.'' Jack slipped on his shirt, teeth clenching at the pain in his side and then again in his right arm.

When he'd first rushed to town, he'd been worried over his foreman's bullet wound and Lissa's injuries. Now that the crisis was past, the realization of all that could have gone wrong, all that could have happened, ached through his heart.

What if he would had lost Chad? Or Lissa? Pain as black as his memory wrapped around his heart. He'd done what he'd come here to do, and now they were all safe. He could rebuild the ranch and give Lissa the chance to love him, the way he was beginning to love her. He had a new start, a future, a family that meant more to him than his own life.

Jack headed down the hall, and she was the first thing he saw. Her tangled blond curls, her gentle face, her goodness as soft as morning's light.

He noticed the worry tight around her eyes, and he headed toward her. ''Will's going to be fine.''

''The doctor told me.'' She stepped forward, hand out, then hesitated. Her skirts whirled around her ankles, moving after she had stopped, and he saw the length of the room, felt the distance she wanted between them.

He stopped, not at all sure what he should do. He wanted to wrap her in his arms; he wanted to tuck her close to his heart where she was safe, where she was closest to him.

''Pa!'' Chad dashed across the room Lissa would not cross and wrapped his little arms tight around Jack's knees.

Affection so bright warmed his chest, in the cold dark places a man didn't talk about, didn't want to feel. He knelt down and hugged the boy, his son, and felt the pure power in Chad's tight hug, felt the gentle sweetness of a heart that only knew love, not hatred. Jack knew he would protect this child all the days of his life.

"Chad." Lissa's voice was soft as always, but different, somehow.

The boy stepped away. Jack looked up at her, saw the shadows around her eyes. Lissa took Chad's hand in hers and headed toward the door. "I promised him we would get straight home to Puddles, as soon as the doctor finished treating you. He's worried about his puppy."

"A boy should be concerned for his dog." Jack wanted to touch her, wanted to see for himself the bruises on her body, make sure nothing was broken, to kiss each hurt away. He held back, wary, sensing her uncertainty.

"Puddles and me got all scared by the cows." Chad caught hold of Jack's trousers and hung on hard.

"I got scared too, partner." Jack laid his hand on the boy's head, ruffled his straw blond hair, his heart tight. "How are you, Lissa?"

"I've been better." Her voice was light, but her eyes looked dark. She reached for the door and he caught her hand, watched how his touch shocked her, saw the distrust ripple across her dear face.

"You've been hurt." He saw the smudge of a bruise marking her chin, another across her left cheekbone. He would die before he saw her hurt.

"It's not so bad." She tried to smile, failed.

He laid his hand alongside her cheek, gently cupping the side of her face, wishing he could change what had happened, erase her pain and fear—mostly, her fear. "I need to know what is wrong."

To his surprise, tears filled her eyes, tears so big and silvery he could see the pain in them. "You saved my life."

She said the words with enough reverence to shock him, to make the ache in his chest draw tighter, but the shadows in her eyes remained, darker than ever.

He would do everything, work as hard as he could to be a man she could trust with not just her life, but with her heart. He opened the door, then placed her cool hand in his, leading her out into the street, dreaming of home.

"Murray!" The sheriff's voice was dark and low.

Jack cringed. He had expected trouble. He just didn't want it to happen in front of Lissa and the boy. "Let me get my wife and son in the wagon and headed for home first. Then we'll talk."

"Going to try to run, Murray?" Ike quirked one brow, the curve of his mouth a challenge. He took pleasure in pushing others around, in causing pain.

"I have no reason to run, Palmer, and you know it. I shot only in self-defense. I did what I had to do." Jack guided Lissa away from the red-faced sheriff and the silent town.

Nobody moved as they approached the livery. His chest tightened, and the same cold fire filled his blood as it had in the gunfight. Judging by the sheriff's venom, Jack knew without a doubt that he had a fight ahead.

"It will be all right," he promised Lissa after paying the livery owner to hitch the wagon for her. "It will take Phillips a few minutes to do his job. Please take Chad to the store and get him some candy, anything to help make today a little better."

A gaze as blue as heaven found his. "I think it's better if I speak with Ike. He listens to me. I—"

His kiss silenced her, melted the distance between them, drew her hard against his chest and into his arms.

"I'll come home to you." He stepped away. "On my word."

"Is it true?" Susan Russell met Lissa at the front door of her mercantile, eyes wide, voice low. "Did your husband catch the rustlers?"

"Yes." Lissa saw the relief on her friend's face, felt the

same in her own heart. "Both Jack and Will brought them in."

"Dead, I heard." Susan's hand rested on Lissa's arm. "Good for Jack. We've needed a man like him in these parts. He's saved most of the local ranchers from more serious losses."

Pride washed through her chest, ebbing away some of her fear. Still, the image of Jack on the rise of that hill, charging armed outlaws, shooting them dead, chilled her. She knew Jack had been a deputy, and a deputy protected, and upheld the law, but she had seen him kill with the cold ruthlessness of an outlaw.

"Peppermint, please." Chad tugged on her skirt, his smile trembly but visible. "And a piece for Puddles, too."

Her son was alive today because of Jack Murray, because Jack had shown no fear when he rode straight into a stampede, because Jack had faced armed men and put an end to their lives.

The two sides of him puzzled her—professional killer and tender protector—yet there was no denying what he'd done for her, what he'd come to mean to her.

"And lemon sticks for me," she told Susan. "Oh, and Jack needs more coffee beans."

"On the house. I insist." Susan held up her hand when Lissa tried to protest. "Our livelihood depends upon the ranchers. What he did today helped us, too."

"Pa saved us." Chad sighed, proud of his father and pleased with his paper sack full of peppermint sticks.

Susan turned from measuring out a pound of coffee beans. "The mail came in this morning with a letter for you. Go ahead and help yourself."

"For me?" Who would write her? Lissa had no family. The only mail she had regularly received was Jack's letters. Curious, she circled around the edge of the counter and found the parchment envelope.

"Need anything else?" Susan handed her the candy and coffee.

"Not when you won't let me pay for it." Lissa thanked her friend for her generosity. "See you at next week's meeting?"

"Count on it. Raising funds is very important." Susan's eyes sparkled with mischief. The fact that their ladies' club had been formed for the sole purpose of playing cards was a well-guarded secret, even from their husbands.

The bell above the door tinkled as they left the store. Chad walked ahead slowly, too busy to run as he licked one end of a peppermint stick. Lissa turned the envelope over and studied the writing. Sunlight glinted across the paper and she stopped, turning to stand in her own shadow so she could read the return address.

John Murray. Her heart stopped at the sight of his familiar handwriting. Maybe it was a letter lost in the mail and then found. Maybe—

She tore at the envelope with nervous fingers, the pound of coffee tucked beneath one arm. She tugged out the folded parchment, smoothed it enough so she could read the words written there.

> *Dear Lissa,*
>   *As you must have surmised by now, I chose not to board the train as we agreed. I could not, in the end, take a wife. I am still grieving my beloved Jane. I wish you the best, Lissa, and I am truly sorry.*

Her knees buckled. Emotion sliced through her, knocking the air from her chest. She sat down on the steps to the boardwalk.

"Mama." Chad bounded back to her, his fist still clutching the candy stick. "Want some?"

She read the concern in his big blue eyes—Michael's eyes—and she couldn't breathe. The parchment rattled each time she trembled. She shoved the letter into her skirt pocket, every one of her hopes, of her dreams, dying with each beat of her heart.

She hadn't married John Murray. She'd married a stranger, a man keeping promises not his own.

"Looks like we have trouble, Murray." The sheriff dropped the letter he'd been reading on top of his desk. He stood with a scrape of his chair and a hard, cold glitter in his eyes.

"We had trouble." Jack closed the jailhouse door. "But I stopped it. You'll find the bodies of the men Will and I shot and killed at the undertaker's."

"The men you murdered." Palmer clenched his beefy fists, drew broad his shoulders. "I told you to let me handle it, Murray. But you didn't listen."

"I did what I had to do."

"You took matters into your own hands. Without a badge on your chest, killing those men makes you a murderer."

"How do you figure that, Sheriff?" Jack wasn't fooled. It didn't take a genius to read the malevolence in the lawman's eyes or sense the danger ahead. Something told him he knew a lot about such men—too much. As if he'd been one of them.

"I told you to leave the rustlers to me." Venom stung the sheriff's words.

"You haven't lifted a finger to stop those outlaws. They nearly killed my wife and son today. You can't expect me to stand by idle while I could lose my family."

A muscle jumped along Palmer's jaw. "Is Lissa all right?"

"She will be." Jack strode forward, holding back as much anger as he could, but it rolled through him, unstoppable, a black-red wave of fury that tasted harsh in his mouth. He'd committed no crime. He'd protected his wife, son, and property.

Concern changed the man, resonated in his voice. "What happened to her?"

"She and Chad were caught in the middle of the stampede started by the men I killed." He'd had enough. Jack threw open the door and strode out into the sunlight. "Next time think of that."

"Murray. I'm not through with you yet." The sheriff filled the threshold, a sheet of paper clutched in one hand. "I just got notice of an outlaw loose in this area. Been missing since the same day you rode into town. Or rather, the same day Lissa found you on the road where the old Indian trail leads straight to the territorial prison. Do you think that's a coincidence?"

Anger punched in Jack's guts. "I'm no outlaw. You know it."

"I know that you shot and killed men no one in this county has been able to take down. I don't know one lawman who can shoot like that. Only wanted men have that fine a skill."

"We both know who I am, and why I'm here. Don't think you can scare me away from Lissa. It won't work."

Palmer's mouth was a hard, tight line. "Not yet, Murray. But I can throw you in jail. Don't forget that."

Jack clenched his fists. "Shooting a criminal in self-defense is not murder. We both know it."

"Did you ever regain your memory?" The sheriff strolled down the boardwalk, not blinking, as unrelenting as a Montana blizzard.

"None of your business, Palmer."

"Then there ain't even a small chance you're this criminal who killed a U.S. Marshal in these parts? I'm glad for your sake." Palmer's smile turned bitter. "Because if you were Dillon Plummer, hiding out in my town, then you would be a dead man."

Dillon Plummer. The name burned like a candle in the

dark night of his mind, a faint whisper of memory, yet nothing more.

"I'll be watching you, John Murray," the lawman promised. It was a threat, bitter and undisguised.

Jack walked away, and he was not worried, was not afraid of a small town sheriff.

While Chad napped safely in his bed with his puppy, Lissa did what she had to do. She couldn't feel sorry for herself, or for her situation.

She was the one who'd found Jack unconscious and bleeding on the road. She had been the one who assumed he was Michael's cousin.

Charlie dodged a gopher hole in the meadowland floor as he obeyed the pressure of her knees. He swung left, easy and smooth, cutting the few heifers from the milling herd and driving them back to the fenced pasture.

"Lissa!" The wind carried the distant sound of her name. She looked hard at the dark spot on the road, saw the smudge of a bay horse and rider as they loped closer, still too far away to recognize clearly.

Knots twisted in her stomach. She thought of the letter she'd left on the kitchen table—thought of the husband and father she and Chad stood to lose.

"What are you doing?" he asked when he rode close enough for her to see the good-natured tilt to his mouth as he spoke to her.

"What does it look like?"

"Rounding up cattle is my job around here. Where are the men?"

"I sent them into town to take soup to Will. He's going to be able to walk again." She knew her voice sounded strained, knew she was avoiding his gaze.

"I'm glad to know that." Jack's beautifully shaped hand clasped over her wrist. "Let me take over."

Her chin went up. "I can take care of my own cattle."

"The animals are my job. That's our agreement, right?" He took the whip from her hand, but the look in her eyes, in her cool eyes, stopped him. "You have every right to be angry with me. I didn't keep my word. I didn't stop the rustlers before they put you and Chad in danger."

Her face crumpled. She looked ready to cry. Then her jaw lifted, clenched tight. Tears stood in her eyes, but they did not fall. "You've done more than keep your word, Jack. I don't find fault with you for that."

"Something is wrong." He coiled the whip, watching the snaking leather slide through his gloved hands. He felt her move away before he heard the plod of Charlie's big hooves on the ground, felt the distance as wide and deep as a canyon.

"I shouldn't have killed those men in front of you. I wasn't thinking. I acted on pure emotion."

"You are no mild mannered cowboy." Her gaze met his. Curls which had escaped from her braids whisped around her face, made her look vulnerable, fragile, but he was not deceived.

Lissa was a woman of strength. She could drive cattle, use a whip, and face a stampeding herd to protect her son. "You are not the man I thought you were."

His chest tightened. He thought of Sheriff Palmer's words, remembered the shocked expression on Lissa's face after he'd shot the rustlers. He'd charged the outlaws, known how to draw their fire, how to corner them, how to kill them. He'd reacted without blinking, without fear, without remorse.

What kind of man had he been before he'd lost his memory? Before he sought out Lissa in faraway Montana? Jack didn't know what life he'd left behind in St. Louis, but he suspected he might not have been the best of men.

"I did what I had to do." He lowered his voice, rode his gelding near her so he could lay his hand along her jaw, see the bruises on her face and the pain in her eyes. "I can't swear to the kind of man I've been before I met you, but I will promise you this—I will never show you violence. I will never hurt you."

Tears remained, but still did not fall. He brushed his thumb across her cheekbone, felt the wonder of her silken skin. How could he make things right? He was falling in love with her.

No matter what, he would comfort her, do anything so she knew there was a better side to him. He had a heart, and he would show it to her. Make her know the best he had inside him.

"The cattle can wait." He hung the coiled whip over his saddle horn. "You've been hurt."

"Nothing serious." A smile trembled along her mouth, a tremble he wanted to kiss away until there was only passion and need and her. Only her.

"Let me take care of you."

"You are. You have been." She tipped back her head to gaze up at him, and curled tendrils breezed across her face, teasing him closer. "You saved Chad. You saved my ranch. I owe you more than I can ever repay."

"You have it all wrong. I owe you for everything you've given me." He swept her up in his arms, lifting her from the saddle and onto his thighs.

She melted against him, her silken hair catching on the stubble of his chin. She smelled like sunshine and sweet mountain air. She felt like heaven—warm, willing female in his arms. "Let me show you how much."

Her hands became fists in the fabric of his shirt. "Jack, put me down."

"That's the whole idea." Seeing her in danger today, feeling terror at the reality of losing her, still tore at him. He wanted to hold her close, snug in his arms, and love her until the fear and the shadows in his heart melted away. "Is Chad still taking his nap?"

"Yes, but Jack—"

"And the ranch hands are in town. We're all alone." He pressed a kiss to her temple, breathed in the cinnamon and sunshine fragrance of her hair. Desire beat in his blood, hot and thick, making him hard. Already he wanted her. "I want to make love to you, Lissa."

"We need to talk." She looked so serious. He knew he had to make her forget seeing him kill those men.

"We can talk later. Afterward." He brushed his lips across hers, felt the ready willingness, felt the tension in her jaw. "I'll tether the horses and be right in." He lifted her gently to the ground. "Wait for me."

"Jack, I can't." Her spine straightened. With clenched fists and tight mouth, she looked ready to do battle, not make love.

"Well, then we can have some apple cider and some of your angel food cake." Dessert didn't sound as satisfying, but he didn't care, as long as he was with her. "We can talk. Then we'll see about the lovemaking."

That made her smile. Jack dismounted, snagging Charlie's reins, too, and tethering the horses to the small white fence, well out of reach of Lissa's flowers. Blues and yellows and whites danced in the breezes, reached up to catch the sun, green stems and fragrant petals brushing against Lissa's skirt as she gazed up at him. Shadows haunted her eyes. What had he done that could make her look at him this way?

Jack's heart clenched. "Have I done something wrong?"

"You haven't done anything wrong." She bit her lip, looking very lost. "You're not my husband."

"I know you were still grieving Michael, but I had hoped—"

"No. You don't understand." Her hand caught his wrist, tight as a steel band. "You aren't John Murray."

"What are you talking about?" Ice clenched around his chest. The confrontation with Palmer, the gunfight with the rustlers, the need to round up enough of the herd to salvage their year's profits, all congealed in his throat, choking him.

None of it mattered as much as this woman before him, the tears in her glimmering eyes, so full of pain. His knees buckled, but still he could not believe what she was saying.

"John Murray wrote a letter apologizing for not coming to marry me as he promised to do." Her grip on his wrist tightened, but it was the fear he felt, solid and real.

"You aren't him, Jack. I found you in the road and I just assumed, I just thought, you were him. You've seen how secluded we are. Who else would be using that road? And on the same day? If I'd had any inkling, I wouldn't have married you until you were certain of who you were. And now Chad—"

She released her hold on his arm, covered her mouth with both hands. She sat down on the bottom porch step, all bunched up, looking as if she'd lost her world.

Because if you were Dillon Plummer hiding out in my town, then you would be a dead man. The sheriff's threat rumbled through his memory. A cold shakiness settled in his abdomen. He sat down on the step next to Lissa and tried to make sense of what she'd told him.

"You said John Murray is in St. Louis?"

"According to his letter."

"Then if I'm not John Murray, who am I?"

She paled, but when her hand touched his jaw it was tender. "I know the kind of man you are. I know you are good with my son. I know that you're a fine husband, that you're a man of your word."

"That isn't enough. Our marriage may not be legal." Ramifications thundered through his head, but the emotional blow shook him more. He loved the woman he thought was his wife, wanted nothing more than to be the man she needed. But now—

He didn't know who he was. He didn't know where that left him. And he could not deny the sheriff's threat.

Could he be that outlaw? *Dillon Plummer*—how that name sounded familiar, the way those dreams felt when they'd brought him back pieces of memory. He remembered a sheriff, remembered hunting men in a meadow, the gun heavy and familiar in his hands.

How had he known how to corner those rustlers? How to draw their fire and shoot them dead? He hadn't even considered letting them live, bringing them to the sheriff for justice to be done. He had enacted his own brand of justice, imposed his own law—just as an outlaw might.

Knowing those things didn't make him an outlaw. All it meant was that his memory was gone, just like before.

The growing wind scattered the scent of daisies and roses and asters, and brushed through Lissa's hair the way his hands ached to. He didn't know who he was, but his feelings were still the same.

"You're my wife, Lissa." He laid his hand over hers, felt the luxurious pressure of her fingers against his face. "That will never change."

"How do you know?" She was so close, felt so distant. "We don't know who you are. You could have a life waiting for you somewhere. Your own children. Your real wife."

"I don't."

"How do you know?"

"I know in here." He laid a fist across his chest, over his heart. "I can feel it. There's nobody but you, Lissa. There never has been. And there never will be, if you let me stay."

"Let you?" She needed him so much, in ways she hadn't been aware of until the moment she read John Murray's letter. She hadn't fought hard enough against that need, and it made her feel weak and vulnerable, made her feel foolish for wanting a man who could never be hers. "I don't see how you *can* stay."

"I have nowhere to go. I have no other life but here, with you and Chad."

"But what happens when you remember?"

"It doesn't matter. I won't leave you, Lissa. I won't break my vows to you. I swear it." He kissed her fingertips, wanted to kiss more of her.

How could she keep leaning on him, needing him? Yet his touch stole her fears and all her doubts. For the moment, she knew his kisses and his passion could make everything right.

When his lips brushed hers, sweet and passionate, demanding and possessive, she wanted no other kiss, no other man's touch. His hands caressed the back of her neck, unbuttoned her bodice.

He led her into the house, holding doors and then closing them, stripping her naked at the bedside and then loving her with such tenderness, such raw emotion, that she could not hold back, but gave—touched him until he moaned low in his throat, arched up to meet him when he joined their bodies with one slow thrust, his weight holding her down, his arms holding her up.

Release sheered through her, a twisting downdraft of sensation and sharp pleasure. All she felt was him, the breadth of his shoulders as she clung to them, the heat of his skin all over touching hers, the scent of salt and man and sunshine, and the heart of him, so big and bright, loving her as if they had forever.

As he kissed her forehead, though, his release spent, she could not stop the panic. Who was this man she had married?

"You're still afraid."

"Yes." She would not lie to him. His gaze settled on hers and she read the truth in his eyes, saw the heart of him, shadowed but honest. She saw how he wanted her, the way a man wanted a woman—as lover, friend, soulmate.

How could she let herself want him the same way? He

didn't know his past, or the life he'd left behind. What if the day came when she had to let him go?

She would not love him. She could never love that way again.

Chapter Twelve

Sheriff Ike Palmer watched the sun sink through the bars of the jailhouse window. Jack Murray was trouble, plain and simple. He'd single-handedly thwarted Palmer's plan to force Lissa off her ranch.

Damn. Fury tasted bitter in his mouth. He felt the emptiness of the jailhouse, saw the bustle on the street outside. Men rode down Main, hurrying home to their families, a hard day's work done, eager for the sight of supper on the table.

The door rattled open. Dark and grim, his deputy filled the threshold, more brawn than brains. In a subordinate, those were desirable traits. "What are you going to do about Murray?"

"Whatever I can do." Palmer rubbed his brow. "He killed four of my men. I haven't forgotten Tuckman's murder the day of Lissa's wedding to that man."

"Murray is a good shot."

"Too good for a city deputy." He considered that. Murray didn't act like a man from a city, didn't talk or fight like one. "Ride to Billings and send a telegraph to my nephew in Chesterfield. That's not far from St. Louis. Ask him to do a little digging into Murray's past. Every man has something to hide. I want to know how to bring him to his knees."

"Sure thing, boss." Deakins tipped his hat and trotted down the boardwalk, spurs jangling.

Palmer watched the sun set—and thought of all the ways he'd like to bring Jack Murray down.

At least he knew who he wasn't. Jack's grip tightened on the thick leather reins, and he squinted against the harsh summer sun. The sweet scent of freshly mown hay tickled his nose, lifted on the breeze. Butterflies and dragonflies and finches protested at his intrusion, but still the two great draft horses lunged forward, pulling the heavy mowing machine behind them.

The whir of the blades matched the whirring of his own thoughts. He'd had no dreams in the passing days, still had no glimmer of memory to let him know who he was. His past remained a darkness, full of shadows and unknowns.

He glanced over his shoulder, watching the dirt road as he'd had for the last ten minutes. Dust smudged the sloping hill and all he could see of the approaching wagon—Lissa and Chad, coming with the midday meal. His throat, parched and gritty, ached for the cool, sweet cider she would bring.

The sight of her refreshed him even more: Blond curls shimmering in the sunlight, all slender form and snapping blue skirts. He halted the horses, gave Charlie a pat on the flank to let him know what a good job he'd done. The second gelding tried to grab his hat as Jack turned, his heart filling at the eagerness in Chad's voice.

"Pa!" Chad raced through the tall grasses, only his cowboy hat visible until he burst into the clearing in front of the horses.

Neither animal was startled. The dark gelding stole Chad's hat, while Charlie licked his head. The little boy laughed, then wrapped both arms around Jack's knees.

"Mama said I get to help ya mow. Just like a real rancher." Joy lit Chad's face.

"I could use some help, partner. Mowing hay is tough work."

"I'm tough," the boy said, so much confidence in his grin that it made Jack ache inside.

This little boy depended on him. Jack could still taste the fear in his throat when he'd pulled Chad from the stampeding herd. No matter what his true identity, he would never leave, never dim that bright, shining affection so honest in the boy's eyes.

Being a father and husband was more important than whatever he had left behind, regardless.

"Chad talked me into making chicken sandwiches." She smiled, but her eyes did not shine, did not glow from within when she looked at him.

"He's trouble, that boy." Jack made his voice light as he reached to retrieve the heavy basket from Lissa's firm grip.

"I have it." She moved away, easy as a breeze, gentle and distant and full of apology. "You've been working hard all morning."

"So have you." He swung the hat from his head, wiped his brow with his forearm. "I'll unhitch the horses, then. Looks as if you have everything under control."

She smiled at him as she unfolded a blanket. He knelt to unbuckle the thick leather straps from the traces. He led the horses away, Chad skipping along. He chatted with his son, but his gaze never strayed from Lissa.

How could he look away from her? She drew him like a moth to light. She held him captivated as she spread a red checked blanket in the mown clover, carried the drinking jug from the wagon.

"Hurry up before the bees and ants find us," she called, uncovering the basket.

The wind rippled through her hair, and his fingers ached. How he wanted to touch her again. "Charlie's likely to be more bothersome than bees," Jack teased as the big gelding lifted his head to scent the collection of food Lissa was spreading out on the blanket.

"Tater salad," Chad cheered, dashing away through the tall grass, frightening birds as he ran to his mother.

Charlie tried to follow, and Jack caught him. "Come over here, troublemaker." He tethered the horses in the shade of a cottonwood before joining his family at their meal.

His mouth watered and his stomach growled at the sight of the delicious food, but it was Lissa he looked at most, Lissa who kept his gaze and held it as he sat down beside her. She stiffened a little. He pulled off his gloves to put a bare hand on hers, drawing her gaze.

So much uncertainty was written there. His chest tightened. She had come to care for him over the course of their marriage, but with the arrival of John Murray's letter, she'd withdrawn.

"You don't have to be afraid of me." He didn't know how to lure her back to him, how to recapture the lustrous warmth of her smile. "I'm still the same man I've always been."

"I know." Her fingers found his, twined between them with a surprising strength—almost as if she needed to hold onto to him, to bind her to him for keeps.

"The haying is going well. I've got two of the hands behind me raking over the cutting. Did you find them?"

"And fed them." She unwrapped the sandwiches, much to Chad's joy, and passed the plate to Jack first, then to her son. "Now it's your turn."

"I'm glad. I was about to faint from hunger." He winked, taking a bite. "Feed the breadwinner last."

She laughed, richly and fully, tipping back her head. "We saved a few scraps for you."

"Not good enough for first choice." He took a swig of cider, cool and sweet.

"Nope. You're just not good enough at all." Lissa's teasing voice belied the flash of emotion in her eyes. "Rounding up the cattle, finishing the branding and the fences. And now the first cut of hay. You've been lazy."

"Terrible, isn't it?" He laughed, leaning forward to brush his mouth with hers. She tasted willing and sweet, and it made him remember last night in her arms, made him look forward to the night to come. "As long as this dry weather holds, we'll get a decent cut."

"The storms have been missing us." She picked at her sandwich, then put it down. "Maybe luck is finally on our side."

"We could use it." He studied her hard. "I hope you aren't planning on helping with the haying this afternoon. You're pale. You haven't been getting enough sleep."

"No thanks to you." She felt the heat creep across her face. Jack knew darn well why she was tired. His rumbling laugh only confirmed it.

"I'm glad I'm doing my duty. I wouldn't want you tossing me out on my ear because I wasn't living up to my obligations."

She blushed, glad Chad was chasing yellow-winged butterflies, sandwich in hand. "As long as you keep me pleasured, I guess I'll let you stay."

"As long as I know what's expected of me." His blue eyes twinkled with a sparkling emotion, with affection so honest it made her stomach fall, made her afraid and weak. "It's a tough job making love to you night after night, but I'm man enough to do it."

"I should pick up more strangers on my way to town."

She laughed when he pressed a kiss to her throat, his breath warm against the top of her breasts.

"I'm glad you found me." The teasing had faded from his gaze, from the kissable corners of his mouth. "You've given me a life worth living."

His arms enfolded her, drawing her hard against the plane of his chest. He felt hot from the sun, smelled like cut grass. She wrapped her arms around his neck, afraid to hold too tight, afraid to let go. Her stomach twisted again and she closed her eyes, buried her face in the hollow of his throat.

She didn't want to lose another husband. She didn't want to lose this man of kindness and strength. Fear knotted in her stomach, tight and foreboding, and she feared it was only a matter of time.

"The wind has been hot and mild, and not a cloud in sight until now." Jack strode through the kitchen door, bits of mown grass clinging to his shirt and the brim of his hat. "I have the men raking up everything I've cut in the past few days."

"It can't be dry." Lissa turned from the stove. Water boiled, and fresh strawberries scented the air. "Are you sure it will storm?"

"Positive. It's the way my luck's been running."

Rain would ruin the cut hay. A hailstorm could damage the rest of the grass. Jack glanced over his shoulder at the horizon, where thunderheads gathered, clustered and building. He could smell the rain, feel the coiled tension in the air.

He looked around. "Is today Ira's birthday party?"

"The one and only. Jeremiah came out to fetch Chad about an hour ago. He's spending the night, so we will have some time all to ourselves."

"Hmm. I like the sound of that." Jack kissed her, felt his body respond hard and swift, but there was work to be done, hay to be saved. "It would help if you would bring supper out to the men. I'm going to keep them working until dusk, if we have that long before the storm breaks."

Lissa returned to her jars of cooling preserves. Heat had curled the tendrils around her face into fine, beautiful ringlets. "I'll do better than that. After I finish up here, I'll come outside and help."

He pressed a kiss to her cheek. Her arms circled his neck, and he drew her tight against his body. She smelled like the strawberry jam she was making, tasted like dreams.

"You still look pale. Maybe you should—"

She silenced him with another kiss. "I'm just tired, that's all. Someone keeps me up too late at night making love."

"I guess I could stop." Dimples framed both sides of his mouth.

"Don't even try it." She kissed his smile, tasted it. "Go help your men. I'll be out as soon as I can."

His eyes darkened. His touch felt substantial, boldly affectionate. He lifted his fingers from her chin and stepped away, leaving her alone. She watched him go, all steely dependable man, his tenderness still affecting her as he strode out the door.

Her stomach twisted hard, and she rubbed at her forehead. She felt tired, almost dizzy. Her gaze traveled to the window where lace curtains framed the sight of Jack, heading back out to the fields.

Her heart ached, knowing she already cared for her husband far too much. She had to stop wanting him, stop depending on his quiet, honorable strength. Jack was only theirs to claim as long as he could not remember. That was all.

With one more twist of her stomach, her worries faded to one—she was pregnant.

* * *

Jack gritted his teeth against the burn of exhausted muscles in his back and arms and forked more cut grass into the back of the wagon. A harsh, hot wind hampered his work. The dark clouds gathering overhead told him they were running out of time.

They could survive a hard rain, as far as the crops went. A good rain would turn the rangeland green and give the cattle more fat. A hailstorm could ruin the oats and corn, though, even the grass. Tinder dry from the high winds and hot sun of the past weeks, the golden meadows stretched all the way to the tree line. Lightning this time of year could be dangerous.

Jack threw down his pitchfork. "Lissa. This load's ready."

"Looks like this is as much as we can do." She pointed toward the sky.

"Damn." Jack tugged off his hat. "All right, men. Time to head in. Let's hope some rain falls with that lightning."

A bullwhip of light snapped across angry clouds. Fire streaked from the sky to the earth, the strike miles away. They were safe for now. Jack wasn't taking any chances. The fences were high and sturdy, so the cattle, no matter how they ran, were safe. He just wanted his men and family indoors and away from the approaching storm.

"Aren't you coming in?" Lissa placed her hand on his—leather glove to leather glove, yet he could still feel the heat of her.

"As soon as I send in the second wagon." He lifted a hand toward the other team working the far end of the half-mown field. "You be careful. Let the men unload. I want you safe in the house."

"I'll be fine. Don't worry." She looked exhausted, but beautiful—always beautiful. "You keep out of the way of that lightning."

His heart ached just looking at her. "I'll do my best."

She swept up into the wagon seat, her skirts snapping in the heady wind. With a wave, she gathered the reins and released the brake. The horses pulled, the wheels squeaked, and the two ranch hands jumped onto the back of the wagon and lay down in the bed of soft mown hay.

"Arcada." Jack watched the wagon's progress out of the corner of his eye.

"We're getting ready to head in, boss." With Will still recuperating, the young immigrant had stepped handily into the foreman's shoes, and Jack appreciated his knowledge and hard work. "That dry lightning heads this way, we could be in big trouble."

"I know. All we can do is wait and watch." Jack listened to the approaching thunder, cracking across the silent, waiting land. Sheets of dark rain fell like great gray columns, never touching the earth. Streaks of fire flashed against the twilight sky.

The storm followed them in. Wind tore through the trees, bending the limber tips of pine and fir, sending leaves and branches to the ground. They left the wagons loaded in the barn and rubbed down the horses while Lissa disappeared into the house, soon emerging carrying a steaming coffeepot and a tray of fresh strawberry tarts. The men were content to bunk down and wait. Jack sent Arcada to the neighboring ranch to see if Hans Johanson, still recovering from a bullet wound, needed any help.

"You're a good man." Lissa smiled up at him when he held open the kitchen door. "Hans is still having a hard time getting around."

"Not so good. Just trying to be neighborly." Jack kicked off his boots, dirt-caked from the field, before following her into the kitchen. "A few other ranchers and I are going to cut his fields as soon as we're done with ours."

The house felt empty without Chad and his puppy running to greet him.

She took down a single plate, then grabbed a hot pad to lift a second pot of coffee from the stove.

"You're not eating?" He laid both hands on her slim shoulders.

She shook her head, silken curls tumbling over his knuckles. "I'm not hungry. I may have some coffee, though."

He caught up the glistening curls in one hand, then leaned forward to kiss the back of her neck. She shivered at his touch. "You're pale. I want you to go to bed early tonight."

"Without you?"

"I can always wake you up later." He laughed against the sweet luxury of her skin and hair. He buried his face against her and breathed deeply. She filled him like air, sweet and light, substantial.

She stiffened, and he moved away, turned her around so he could read her face in the half-light—so shadowed, so serious.

"I'm pregnant." She whispered the words.

He could only stare, could just manage to breathe and remain standing. "Pregnant?"

She nodded.

It wasn't surprising, not really, considering all the love-making they'd been doing.

True, he didn't know who the hell he was, but now it didn't matter anymore. Whatever life he'd had was lost to him now. He had a wife and son depending on him, and now a new child. Those were the things that bound a man's heart and determined his road in life, not his past, not whatever he'd left behind.

"Are you unhappy?" She whispered those words, too.

"No. Just thinking." He cupped her jaw with both hands, cradling her dear face. "I guess I did my duty pretty darn well. I was hoping for extended privileges."

"That can be arranged." A smile touched her lips and he kissed her hard, so she would know what she meant to him. Yet he felt it, that holding back of her heart, even while she held him so tightly.

"Watch the storm with me." He wanted her by his side, wanted to watch the wind tangle her hair and warm her skin.

"Gladly."

She didn't light a lamp, so he took both cups in hand and followed her through the darkening room. She tugged open the front door. Outside, night fell with an odd silence. There were no owls hooting, no calls of coyotes on the hunt. Just the clash of thunder rumbling, nearer.

"It's beautiful," she breathed as one bolt of lightning broke apart over and over again.

He needed her so much, his only light in a vast darkness. He pulled her to his chest, and she leaned against him willingly, holding on, her small hands clutching fistfuls of his shirt.

They watched the storm approach in silence, felt the powerful blast of wind and saw branches tumble from tree-tops and strike the ground with snappy fury. They smelled the rain that did not fall as lightning flashed and then thunder crashed overhead.

Lissa tipped her head back, mesmerized by the display of shining, then disappearing, light. The world was so different tonight. She'd said the word she was afraid to believe in, afraid to believe. *Pregnant*.

She'd had her share of problems, had lost babies born too early. As thunder crashed and lightning struck again and again, she hoped this time would be different.

"Jack!" Arcada's voice cut through the darkness. His horse skidded to a stop, kicking up gravel. "On the way back from Johanson's, I saw smoke. We've got a wildfire on our hands."

"Alert the men. Does Johanson know?"

"It was on his land, but the wind's driving it this way. I rode back to tell him just in case the winds shift."

"How big is the fire?"

"Big enough. Jack, are you coming?"

"Yes." His hands caught hers. "I want you to stay with the house. There's probably no real threat, but I have to go make sure."

He released her, but she wasn't the kind of woman to stay, who sat home quietly when her land and her husband could be in danger.

"I'm coming, too. Arcada, saddle up Charlie for me."

"Yes, ma'am." The ranch hand's mount was already kicking up gravel as he galloped toward the barn in the darkness.

"What do you think you're doing?" Jack demanded as she ran to catch up with him.

"Coming with you."

"Not on your life." He spun to face her, standing tall, the receding storm shivering in the sky behind him, limning him with a strange glow. "You just told me you are pregnant. Out in those fields battling a fire is no place for you."

"But I'm more than capable—"

"I know." His voice warmed like a touch, tempted like a kiss. "It's probably nothing. The men and I will have it put out in no time. Stay here so I know you're safe. So I don't have to worry."

"But you may need help. Fires spread so fast in these winds—"

"No." He kissed her, then, and she felt the solid wall of his chest, the steely determination to protect her, as he saw it, from harm.

This was no man she had to help, had to worry about in the dark of night. He could defeat any foe.

"You and this baby are important to me," he whispered in her ear, low and rich and tempting. "You're everything, Lissa. My whole world. Please, do this for me. Stay in the house. I'll be back in time to kiss you to sleep. And more."

She didn't like letting him go, depending on him to fight any more of her battles, but he was already gone, swallowed by the night shadows and the howling wind. Hard drops of rain, just a few, thudded to the ground at her feet, dropped on her head and face.

Just what they needed—a hard rain. Now, if it would just keep falling. . . .

By the time Jack reached the barn, smoke scented the air. Even in the darkness he could see the outline of the fire, glowing low along the ground—widespread, heading their way.

"I want a twenty foot strip cleared up there, along the crest of that ridge. If the fire comes this way, maybe we can keep it from the house and the barn."

"What about the crops and cattle?" Arcada asked.

"We can't save everything. Not unless the wind shifts." Jack fumbled with the harness. Charlie stood nervously scenting the smoke.

"What if it keeps coming?" McLeod asked.

"Then we pray." He sent the youngest hand for lanterns. They would need light to see by if they were going to keep plowing.

The last buckle slipped closed beneath his fingers, and Jack grabbed Charlie by the bit. "Come on, boy." He kept his voice low, soothing the big horse as they approached the burning forest.

The plow skidded along the hard, dry ground, then dug in, turning over rich earth and ripe grass, the dank musty smell thick in the air. He turned over another chunk of earth, then another.

"The rain's stopping." Arcada handed out shovels and axes. "Bad news, boss."

"I know." The fury of the storm remained, tensed in the air like a punch waiting, fist clenched. But it did not strike. Damn the wind. It was blowing hard and southward, directly toward the house. "Tell Lissa to start—"

"She's already at the well." Arcada pointed through the darkness. "Drawing water. We can wet gunnysacks. That will help with the spot fires."

Jack agreed. He kept shoveling. Sweat dripped off him and his muscles screamed from an already long day of hard work, but all he could think of was Lissa. She was depending on him. Even though she didn't say it, finding out he wasn't John Murray had changed things between them. She didn't want to depend on him. He could be anyone—even the outlaw Sheriff Palmer had mentioned.

Clearing the wide strip of land took time. The men worked hard, but the fire, driven into a storm by the wind, advanced like a malevolent army, a front of flame and destruction that glowed orange-red in the night. Jack felt its heat, saw the falling black ash, and pushed Charlie harder.

"Jack!" Lissa's voice. He dropped the reins, already running before he knew what was wrong. The flicker of lantern light brushed low, but enough to see her trying to lift the heavy wooden ladder. "An ember hit the roof."

He saw the flickering flame, a single tongue of light. He hauled the heavy ladder out of Lissa's grip and leaned it against the eaves.

"Here." She pressed a pail handle against his fingers. He heard the water slosh as he raced up the rungs. Embers fell from the sky, shivering like snowflakes in a wind, glowing an eerie shadow of orange.

"The roof's on fire." She followed him up with her own pail.

He knelt before the crackling blaze at the peak, where the first ember had found a niche to grow in, and emptied the water. Smoke tickled his nose, ached in his lungs. He grabbed Lissa's pail and dumped that out, too.

"Wet the roof and keep it wet," he told her. "I have to help the men."

"I'll be all right." Her gaze fastened on his. Even in the darkness he felt it, knew the solid strength of her. She might be afraid, as he was, but she didn't run, she didn't faint or make excuses. She worked as hard as any man. His heart swelled as he watched her. He would do anything for her—anything in his power.

"If this gets out of hand, call me."

She nodded, full of so much gentle strength. He hated leaving her, knew he had to. Smoke already choked the air. The fire, a swirling mass of dancing flame, swept close to the break.

Already, the men were running the line, wetting gunny-sacks in the water trough and slapping out spot fires. Embers whirled in the air. Anything they touched ignited. He joined the men by grabbing up a sack and dousing it in water. Plenty of spot fires burned, and he began beating out one after another.

"The wind's shifting!" He called to the men, the snap and roar of the racing fire drowning his words. The balls of flame rolled just off to the right, along the ground like tumbleweeds, and higher in the treetops, raining down flaming debris.

"It's heading toward the house!" Arcada shouted.

"Lissa!" Already Jack was running. Smoke clogged his throat, gripped his lungs, yet still he ran. The fire leaped ahead of him. He couldn't catch up. He couldn't beat it. "Lissa!"

He couldn't see her in the smoke and the darkness. He

couldn't hear her above the snapping crackle of the flames and the roaring inferno of the wind. "Lissa!"

"Jack!" Her voice rang out, leading him to her. She was still on the roof, beating out embers stubbornly taking hold in the cedar shingles. "The trees are on fire. Look out!"

Chapter Thirteen

He heard the crack of breaking wood, ducked as a limb the thickness of his arm crashed to the roof, where he'd been standing. Sparks and flame shot out, greedily consuming the roof.

"We're losing the house!" she shouted.

There was a bigger problem. Jack saw it at once. A wall of flame now separated him from Lissa, trapping her at the peak of the roof. She just kept beating those flames, tears of anger rough in her breathing.

"Jack! I need more water."

"Lissa." He kicked the burning bough. It broke apart and rolled off the eaves. Someone down below shouted, running to put out the sparks, but he only saw his wife, so determined, surrounded by flames. "Lissa."

"Damned if I'm going to give up." She smothered another growing flame with her wet blanket. "I lost my husband and my babies. I lost that blasted John Murray. I'll be damned if I'm going to lose this house."

She was so fierce. Affection for her ached in his chest.

"Then we fight." He kicked out one spot fire with his foot. "Arcada. Haul up more water."

"Got it, boss." The ranch hand scrambled up the ladder. "McLeod is putting out the fires in the yard. See, the wind is pushing the fire fast."

"If we can keep the roof from burning, it will roll right past us."

"As long as it doesn't burn us, too." Arcada coughed, then handed over the full bucket. He disappeared with the empty one.

Jack looked again at the roof and saw the spot fires. Burning needles fell from the engulfed pine overhead, and his guts twisted. Only a fool would stay on this roof— or a man sworn to earn his wife's affection.

"Jack!" She struck him with her wet blanket. "Your shirt's on fire."

"Watch your hair." He smothered the ember caught in her curls with his fingers.

Flame and heat and storm rolled overhead, jumping from the pines on the front side of the house to the pines and maples at the side. Heat scorched the air. Jack felt the hair on his arms sizzle, and the skin on his face stretch tight. With a roar the ball of fire overhead leaped away, driven by the gusty wind.

"More water." Lissa, face dark and streaked, dunked her blanket into the bottom of the bucket.

"Arcada." Jack tossed the bucket to the ground. Coughing, he choked on smoke. "Over there."

She saw where he pointed in the confusion of smoke and fire. Flame licked at the roof around the stone chimney. "Quick."

Jack beat at the tricky fire until his arm muscles cramped, until only smoke remained. Sweat poured off his face and back. He stood up and looked around. The roof still smoked, but there was no fire.

"We did it." Lissa launched into his arms, his aching, exhausted arms.

Numb, all he could do was hold her, breathe in the dank scent of smoke and ashes. Fires glowed down below where the men were putting out bushes and grass, but they'd done it. They'd saved the house.

"Jack." Arcada called from down below. "The fields."

"Damn." The wildfire had skirted the house—only the flames jumping from treetop to treetop had been a threat—but the wind was driving the wall of greedy flames directly toward the oats and corn.

"Can we save it?" McLeod's shout rose from the darkness below.

"We can try." Jack glanced around the roof.

"I can help—"

"No. This roof was dangerous enough." He saw her jaw tighten, knew he'd made her angry. He touched her cheek, so soft despite the layers of grit and soot. "Keep an eye on the roof. Some of these embers might reignite."

"You be careful." Her fingers wrapped around his wrist. Her touch was a connection that tugged at his heart, that made him remember every night in her arms, every way he'd loved her. "I'd rather lose the crops than you."

"If I have my way, you'll lose neither." He kissed her quickly, sealed his promise to her. He hated leaving, hated that the fire could shift back as the fickle wind gusted again, raining charred, smoking pine needles over her and the roof.

She was capable, his wife. He tried to remember that as he left her, as he raced to help the men beat back the licking wall of flames in the grass, fed by the fire overhead, rolling and jumping between the crowns of the trees.

"You're damn lucky the wind blew this away from the house," Arcada said, welcoming Jack to the line of men at the creek. "With this wind, I don't know if we can stop the fire."

"We can try." Jack grabbed two empty pails and sunk them into the dark creek. He wet the grass and earth, then filled his buckets again. "We have to watch the trees."

"One of Johanson's men is chopping down the pines. It's a gamble, but worth a try."

"If he can fell the trees before the fire comes." The wind gusted again, shooting tongues of flames.

Arcada grabbed a shovel. "If we don't stop it here, it hits more ranches."

"Then we stop it." Lissa's voice, firm with resolve.

Jack's heart jumped out of his chest at the sight of her, slim and delicate, determination strong in her stance. "You shouldn't be here," he reminded her.

"And we can't lose this ranch." In the noise and confusion, she looked as calm as heaven. Soot stained her face and dress, blackened her hair. The eerie light cast from the fire shimmered over her form, limned her in orange and black.

"There's no time to argue about it." Jack felt the embers shiver over them, saw their red gleam as they fell from the sky. "Look, there's the rest of Johanson's men."

"I had word sent. Men from other ranches should be arriving." Arcada sank another bucket into the deep creek.

Jack took heart. They weren't alone. The fire roared larger by the minute, flames reaching higher than a man stood, fed by dry grass.

"We can't let it cross the creek." He sloshed water on the ground. If they didn't succeed, then the fire would spread uncontrolled toward town. "If we get this wet enough, it won't burn."

"We've still got the wind." Arcada, both feet in the current, filled bucket after bucket for the men.

"We can do it." Lissa snatched up a heavy bucket and ran.

Reinforcements arrived. They dug and watered and beat at embers, then at the wall of flames without end. Heat scorched skin and hair, embers set shirts and trousers on fire.

Hell couldn't be any more hot or dangerous. The grass ignited without sparks, simply from the heat. The wind snapped balls of flame into one of Johanson's ranch hands. Jack grabbed the man and dragged him into the creek. "Lissa!"

No answer. He'd lost track of her in the confusion. "Lissa!"

There was only the darkness and fire. The trees moaned from the force of the wind, and a chill snaked down his back. A quick shift in the wind could trap them. Already the fire was licking backward, then shifting forward.

"Get the men out of here. We can't hold it." Jack left Arcada in charge. The burned man moaned, reached out and caught Jack's hand. "Hang in there, Busby. I'll get you some help."

Busby nodded, shivering in the cool creek, his head resting on the muddy bank.

"Lissa!" Smoke and fire blended with the night, choking the air. "Lissa!"

"Over here." Her voice came thin above the explosive crackling fire. "It's blowing back toward the house. If I can just—"

"We need you," he interrupted, reaching out to feel the silken heat of her flesh, know that she wasn't an image or a dream. It was too damn dangerous out here, and he wanted her safe. "We have a hurt man."

"Who is it?" She raced beside him, stumbling along the uneven ground, her hair wet and hanging in strings at her shoulders. Orange light and black shadow shivered across her face, streaked with soot, the concern in her eyes genuine.

His pulse jumped as he admired her, who she was, the kind of woman who fought, who cared.

"Sam Busby." The words scratched in his raw throat.

She dropped to her knees in the mud. Her hand shot out, brushed alongside the man's jaw. "Oh, Sam."

"I've been better, Lissa," the burned man moaned. "Jack, thanks for rescuing me like that."

"Are you burned, too?" Alarm widened her eyes. Concern drew her soft mouth tight.

"Don't worry about me." He couldn't take his mind from the crackling fire consuming their land, threatening all they'd worked for. "I'll get one of the men to carry Sam to the house. You two should be safe there. The wind is blowing southwest for now."

"Arcada!" Lissa stood. "Tell McLeod I need him. Is Sophie staying in town?"

"She was going to leave her baby with Blanche and come help us out," the ranch hand answered, working non-stop, sweat sluicing off his brow.

"Good. I'll need her." She knew little about treating burns, but for Sam she would do her best. "Help is on the way."

"It's already here." Jack pressed a kiss to the crown of her head. Her heart turned over as she gazed up at him. He looked like a hero etched in stone. Light danced off the planes of his face, off the hard, rounded curves of his shoulders.

"McLeod will help you to the house. Just wait for him."

"I will." She was strong, but she wasn't strong enough to carry a two hundred pound man. Lissa brushed her hand over Sam's forehead, speaking low to him.

Jack disappeared in the smoke and grit. The fire was rolling closer. The heat was unbearable. Sweat ran off her skin, wet her corset and petticoats. The wind gusted again, blowing spears of flame and sparks of embers. Fire rained over her, and she squeezed out a few embers in Sam's hair, then a few catching in the fabric of her dress.

Where was McLeod? The crackling roar of the greedy fire filled the night until she couldn't see anyone, anything.

Then there was Jack, checking on her with a look that she could read as easily as if he'd spoken. He cared for her— truly cared.

The knowledge hurt down deep, where she swore nothing would ever hurt her again. Jack was a stranger, his identity unknown. She couldn't let down her guard, had to hold back her heart. He pulled at her with his kindness, his affection, his strength.

No matter what his name, what his past, wasn't he the same man she'd married, who kept his vows, who worked her ranch, who loved her son?

Hot air stung her face and arms. Where was McLeod? "Hold on, Sam."

"I'm trying." The strain in his voice was unmistakable.

He shouldn't stay in the creek much longer. The fire was advancing. She could feel the danger, taste it like the ash and soot in the air. "Jack!" She couldn't just sit here. She couldn't move Sam by herself. "Jack!"

The howling wind answered, bursting along the earth, blowing away the curtain of smoke. Red, hungry flames licked along the ground, skipping over clumps of bunch grass directly toward the creek—directly toward her.

"Jack!" Lissa saw in an instant that she was trapped. Fire fell from the trees overhead, igniting the far side of the bank. Walls of flame leaped high, fed by the building wind. Hot embers and radiating heat licked at her skin, thickened the air. No one could break through the wall of flame.

Sam. She had to figure out how to save Sam. Lissa dropped to her knees. The creek was deep enough, but would it protect them from the oncoming fire? Smoke choked her. She couldn't breathe. She dropped to the ground and took Sam's hand. He was half out of the creek. She had to immerse him completely. She had to—

"Lissa!" Faint but sure she heard Jack's voice, calling to her from the other side of the advancing flames.

"Jack!" She choked out his name, raw and raspy. There was no way he could hear it. Tears from the smoke streamed from her eyes, but from a deeper place inside her, too.

Already the air was burning the fine hair off her forearms. It scorched her as if it were flame itself. She wasn't certain the creek would save her or Sam, even as she stepped into the water. It was hot, reflecting the red-orange walls of flame.

She thought of the life she carried, thought of her son, who had already lost Michael. The flames were too high, too thick. Even if she could run through them, the burns she received would kill her. Besides, how could she leave behind an injured man just to save herself? Sobs tore at her chest. She hurt for Jack, too, for he'd been a man of dreams, a man any woman would be proud to call her own.

"Lissa, you leave me." Sam choked on the words. "You have a chance."

"There is no chance." She looked at the flames, felt the blast of heat. She would be dead if she tried. Without hope, she sank into the creek. The wetness climbed up her skirts and over her along with the certainty that she would die. Flames rolled overhead, gobbling up the cottonwood clutching the creek bank.

"Lissa!" Jack's voice. A black form, shadow against the bright fury of the flames. He reached out, and he was flesh and blood, real and substantial. He caught her hand, then shoved her hard into the creek water. She came up sputtering.

"Quick." He took her hand. His shirt was on fire.

She beat at the small flames licking along the cotton. He was wet, she realized. He was tugging her along the creek bank, his solid body protecting her from the wall of heat and flame snapping overhead, ready to consume them.

She choked and ran, choked and tripped. Jack ran with her through the smaller and less fierce flames along the edge of the creek.

She felt pain and fire like hell itself, and an orange brightness so brilliant that it seemed to reach inside her. Then she was past it, and in someone's solid arms—not her husband 's.

"Jack!" she screamed, but he was already gone. She was on the ground. Men rolled her over to douse the flames in her clothes. Water sluiced over her, and it stung like no pain she'd ever known.

"Jack!" she cried, but knew he was out of her reach, knew he'd gone back to save Sam Busby, knew he might never return.

"Jack?" The blackness faded. Lissa felt pain and heat and softness.

"Shh." It was Blanche's voice, Blanche's touch at her brow. "You need to rest, dear heart."

Lissa opened her eyes and saw her friend's concerned face, saw her own bedroom, heard the thud of rain against the walls and window and roof. "Jack. Where's Jack?"

"Just lie back." Blanche's touch brought pain.

Lissa's head spun. Her leg and arm stung with a pain so sharp and intense that it stole her breath. "He didn't come back, did he?"

"Shhh. Sophie's tending him. He's burned, Lissa. I don't know how severely." Blanche's voice lowered with a sadness so real it tore at Lissa's heart.

The pain from her own burns faded, unable to compete with the horrible rending inside. "I have to see him."

"Sophie gave me strict orders to keep you in bed." A lifetime of friendship shone in Blanche's dark eyes, a sympathy sharp enough to feel. "If my Jeremiah were hurt, nothing could keep me from him. Come, I'll help you.

He's in Chad's room. Sophie thought it best if he could rest alone." *A nice way of saying Jack is seriously hurt.*

Burns could kill a man. Lissa's throat closed, and her leg hurt when she moved it, but it didn't matter. She didn't care.

All she cared about was the man of courage and strength who had risked his life for hers, and for a man he hardly knew.

Lissa stood on unsteady feet, clenched her teeth against the arrowing pain. She stumbled through the room and across the hall. She didn't need to ask to know Chad was safe in town with Blanche's husband. Lissa knew her friend well enough to know the Buchmans would care for Chad like their own.

"Oh, God." Lissa's hand flew to her mouth at the sight of her husband, swathed in white bandages. That was all she could see of him—all but his eyes and tip of his nose were covered.

Her knees shook. Tears blinded her.

"Lissa." Sophie touched on her shoulder. The Crow woman's wise eyes held endless sorrow. "Sam Busby is more severely burned than your husband, so Jack could be worse. His burns aren't deep in most places, so I don't think there will be any scarring, but the burns on his hands and back are serious."

Lissa held back her fear. "Any sign of infection?"

"I've applied a yarrow and goose grease poultice." Sophie poured a glass of water from the basin on the low chest of drawers. "I've covered his burns completely. As I said, some are minor, others are not. And I fear the threat of fever. It could kill him."

Her chest cold, Lissa laid her hand on Jack's bandaged one, a light touch. She hoped it wouldn't hurt him. His fingers stirred, clasping hers, holding on hard and tight, for all he was worth.

* * *

Doc James strode into the kitchen, headed toward the back door. "I have to go check on Luanne Hingle's new baby. If Jack's fever worsens, send for me. Understand?"

She nodded, unable to find the words. She watched the solemn man unhook his tailored canvas coat from the wall peg. Her breath rattled in her chest. She clenched her hands into fists and asked him about what scared her the most. "You said the fever was serious. Sophie said her herbs would take care of it."

Doc's mouth pressed into an unyielding, grim line. "Sophie has done a fine job treating you and your husband. In fact, Sam Busby wouldn't be alive without her care, either. But now we wait and see, that's all we can do. I wish I could give you better news. You have to admire a man like your husband."

She jammed her unbandaged fist into her apron pocket, tasting both sorrow and admiration for the man who stood tall for her, who put her first, even above his own life, who vowed he wouldn't leave her.

"I know this isn't fair, Lissa." Warmth softened Doc's lined face. "You don't deserve to lose another husband."

She watched the doctor leave, hope draining from her chest with every breath. Jack was strong, but she'd helped Sophie change the bandages and felt the heat of his body and the fever burning his brow.

Her throat closed, and she sank into the closest chair, where Jack always sat, at the round oak table. She could lose him as easily as she'd lost Michael. How could she tell Chad they might bury another pa?

"Mama?" Booted feet slapped on the floor, startling the cat from her perch beneath the table.

"Chad." She opened wide her arms, welcomed his little body tight against hers. "I'm so happy to see you. Did you have fun staying in town?"

"Ira and me played ball." Chad's eyes shone. "But I missed my pa."

Big blue eyes, full of love for Jack, met hers, and Lissa's stomach fell. How could she tell Chad the truth? How could she lie to him? "You know your new pa got hurt fighting that fire."

"We saw the big flames. The rain done put it out, though." Chad leaned against her side, his arms winding around her waist in an awkward hug. "I wish it didn't burn up my tree house. How am I gonna fight outlaws now?"

It hurt to smile. She brushed flyaway bangs from his brow, treasuring this little boy while he was still small enough to want affection from his mother. "I bet when your pa's all better he'll build you another. Look up at the ceiling. It burned clear through over by the chimney."

"Pa can fix that, too." That voice was so full of pride, as bright as any noontime sun. "I can help. Pa showed me how to hammer."

Lissa managed a wobbly smile. "We'll see. Now go wash your hands. It's nearly dinnertime."

Chad dashed off, chattering of the things he saw in town and wanted to tell his pa all about.

Holding back her fears, she grabbed the bowl of broth, stirred in the dried, crushed lovage to reduce fever, and headed toward Chad's room. Jack lay quietly, breathing raggedly. His presence was hardly perceptible in the still, summer-hot room.

"Jack." She laid careful fingers against his face. This afternoon, they had removed some of the bandages. Reddened skin, not blistering, still intact, felt hot beneath her knuckles.

His eyelids fluttered open. "Lissa."

The way he said her name melted her heart, made her forget old resolves and fears, made her see only his broad-shouldered form cutting through the wall of flame, iron-strong and undefeated. He'd rescued her, shielded her from being burned with his own body.

How could she not love this man? How could she ever keep her heart safe from him?

"How's Sam?"

"Doc says he's going to be fine, thanks to you." She filled the spoon, then held it to his lips. "He's not the only one who is alive because of you."

His eyes filled, a wondrous shimmer of emotion that left no doubt. He loved her. This man with no name, with no past, he loved her in a way no one ever had.

He closed his mouth at the sight of a second full spoon. "I don't want anything hot."

"You have to eat this, for us. It will make you well."

"I already am. You're safe. Chad's safe. That's all I care about."

She brushed a kiss to Jack's brow, unable to stop herself from falling even harder for this man of unflinching courage, this man made of the stuff of dreams.

Chapter Fourteen

"Sheriff, the fire's out," Deakins announced as he kicked open the jailhouse door. "At least, according to Hans Johanson. The town's out of danger."

"About time." Rain sluiced down the barred window and dripped steadily through a crack by the stovepipe. "I heard it started on Lissa's land. Seems to me that husband of hers could have started it."

"Folks say it was a lightning strike. There's no doubt. Too many of the ranch hands saw it."

"Did any mail come on the stage today?"

"Yes, sir." Deakins slapped a small pile of envelopes on the polished desktop. "Heard Murray was burnt pretty bad."

"That so? A pity." The quicker the man was out of his way, the better. "Maybe the bastard will die from his burns and save me the trouble."

Deakins didn't answer.

Well, not everyone had as much gumption as he did. Palmer didn't mind doing the dirty work a lot of people balked at. He sorted through the envelopes, caught sight of a familiar hand—his nephew in Chesterfield. This was the news he'd been waiting for.

Palmer tore open the flap, pulled out the single sheet of paper. At first he thought it was bad news, that there was no dirt his nephew could find on the invincible John Murray. When Palmer skimmed the words penned there, he knew he'd hit pay dirt.

Deputy John Murray was alive and well in St. Louis, living in his apartment above the tailor shop, alone, still grieving for his wife and son, according to those who knew him.

That meant the man who was masquerading as Michael's cousin, as Lissa's groom, was a man with a secret and a past. Palmer laughed, triumph tasting as satisfying as fine whiskey.

His instincts had been right all along. It would take only a little more digging to bring almighty Murray down.

"Deakins, as soon as Lissa's husband is up and around, let me know. I need to pay him a little visit."

"Pa?" Chad's voice spun her around in the chair.

Lissa saw the little boy, eyes wide, worry crinkling his brow. She held out her hand. "Come on in. He's sleeping. I told you he was hurt pretty hard fighting that wildfire."

Chad nodded, stepped forward in silence, mouth open. "Pa's gonna wake up, ain't he?"

"We sure hope so, cowboy." Her heart twisted as he leaned against her side, his need and fear as endless as a midnight sky. Lissa lifted her son onto her lap.

"My first pa never woke up." Chad sighed, and his sorrow touched her, made tears sting her eyes.

"I know. We hope that doesn't happen to this pa."

"I'm prayin'." Chad bowed his head.

"What's that you have in your hand?"

"The book. Pa read it, and I felt better."

"Maybe we should read the story to him?"

Chad cuddled in her arms. In the stillness of the afternoon, with rain tapping at the windows, she began reading aloud from *The Adventures of Tom Sawyer*.

Jack.

The name echoed in his head, distorted by a dream. *"Jack, you're going to miss this life."*

Sunlight burned his eyes. He sat straight in the saddle, rifle resting over the saddle horn, riding next to a man dressed in a plain blue shirt and dark trousers, a black hat tipped low over his brow and shading his rough-cut face from the sun.

"Nah. I'm restless. Need a change." His own voice, his own feelings and memories, just out of reach. "I've been in Montana a long time. Done all I can here. I'd like to get some land, make a fresh start in life."

Darkness pounded in his skull. A memory came, so close he could almost touch it. Then it vanished, lost in fog and night.

Lissa's voice, low and soft. He couldn't open his eyes. Pain engulfed him. Fire licked across his skin, over his back, in his throat. Darkness claimed him, no matter how hard he fought.

"How's he doing?" Sophie stepped into the room, her voice low, concerned.

"He's still burning up." She wrang the washcloth out over the basin, the splash of water loud in the room, but not as loud as Jack's labored breathing.

"He's hot, all right." Sophie laid her hand on Jack's brow. "I'll draw more water, steep more tea."

"Thanks, Sophie." Lissa's gratitude knotted in her throat. She hadn't been alone since the fire. Will had returned to help Arcada run the ranch, repair the roof and fences that had been burned. Blanche had come with enough cooked meals to see her through most of a week, then she'd washed the soot from the house and done load after load of laundry.

"Jack, can you hear me?" Lissa smoothed the hair from his brow, let the dark, blond locks fall between her fingers. "Jack?"

He murmured, lost in fever, but he knew her voice. She dared to hope, dared to believe he would awaken, that he wouldn't leave them. She bathed him, kept him cool, spoon-fed him the steeped tea Sophie swore by.

Toward dawn, he felt cooler. He breathed easier. He looked less pale, and she felt he was less lost to her.

As first light broke through the curtains, swathing the room in a peach glow, she held Jack's hand and didn't let go. She refused to let go of the man she could not let herself love, yet could not help loving.

Jack woke up, already sitting, breathing hard. The maze of dreams he'd had over the last week confused him, ached in his head. Disoriented, he blinked, trying to see in the inky blackness.

"Jack." Her voice was liquid moonlight, bringing substance to the night. She moved, and he saw her shadow. She drew nearer and made him feel more alive. "Let me touch your brow."

"I'm better." The words rasped from his damaged throat. The doctor said his voice would return, but it would take time, like the burns on his back.

"Yes. You feel cooler. But you still aren't out of danger." She sat on the bed beside him. The feather mattress dipped beneath her weight, the ropes squeaked a bit. Her hand brushed the side of his jaw, silken skin against his day's growth. "Another bad dream?"

"Not bad." Just disorienting—the days and nights spent in bed, half-feverish, racked with pain, had been impossible to count. "I want up. I want to sit on the porch."

"No." She brushed a kiss to his brow, velvet heat and tender comfort. "You take a chill now, and that fever could return with a vengeance."

"I'm tougher than that." Troubling images remained in his mind—of the Montana plains, the rugged mountains of the Rockies, the pine and fir he knew by scent. He had no doubt the dreams were memories, disjointed pieces of himself. "I need to get up, Lissa."

"You're an injured man. You need to stay in this bed and rest."

He laid his hand on hers, felt the satin wonder of her skin, and the burns on his fingers protested the touch. He did not let her go. "Come with me. You've sheltered me from trouble enough. I'm better."

"I'm not going to let you take any more risks. I've come close to losing you twice now."

"Please."

"No," she said, but she smiled.

He eased up off his side. Pain screamed across patches of his back where the skin and muscle felt tight. He sat all the way up, put his bare feet on the ground.

"Change your mind?" she asked with another smile in her voice.

"No. Just catching my breath." Truth was, pain sliced through his flesh and muscle like a dull-edged knife. He'd spent too many days in that bed—he didn't even know how many—fighting the pain and the fever. "I'm going to stand up any minute now."

"You are so stubborn." Her voice was warm and fragile, as if she were too afraid to hope he was improving. "I could push you back into bed if I wanted to."

"Have mercy. I'm a weak man."

That made her laugh, a brightness in the night that could warm any darkness. "Let me get the lamp so you don't trip."

"I'd appreciate it." He could see the faint shadow of

her movement, all elegance and grace, heard the *clink* of the crystal chimney, then the scrape of the match. Flame leaped to life, brushing Lissa's face. She lit the wick and doused the match. She had no idea that every time she breathed it affected him—her every move, her every smile, her every word. "I don't suppose you have any sweets in the kitchen."

"I think there's a piece or two of angel food cake I could let you have, with the proper reward."

"Reward?" He stood, tried to keep steady on his bandaged feet. "Lady, if you're trying to get me to kiss you, you've picked the right bribe."

"I thought so." Her lightness shivered over him like a flame on a wick.

He caught her hand in his bandaged one. Her skin was red in spots, but still soft. He kissed her knuckles, remembered the bright hot fear when he thought she was dead, consumed by that towering wall of fire. Any amount of pain now was worth her life, worth having her here to look at, to hold, to touch.

"You took care of me." He remembered her voice, the caress of her hand at his brow, the solid comfort of her fingers twined around his.

"Somebody had to do it," she teased, but there in her eyes he could see her true meaning, see the glistening spark of affection she had never once confessed.

His chest squeezed, and he was grateful—very grateful indeed.

The kitchen was dark, the front room curtains drawn tight against the starlight. While Lissa lit a lamp at the table, he crossed the room and pulled back the ruffled fabric. The sky above was dark with clouds, but a few patches of stars broke through.

"You haven't mentioned the baby." His footfalls echoed in the stillness as Lissa looked up from the drawer, knife gripped in one hand.

Lamplight sparkled along the steel blade, illuminated the blue of her eyes. Her mouth opened and in that moment before she spoke, he feared he already knew. The foul smoke, the upset, the burns she had to have suffered that night even though he did his best to protect her from the fire, they all must have taken a toll on her body. She must have lost the baby.

She put the knife down. Her movements filled the room, her nightgown shimmering in the darkness as she drew near.

"No, Jack." She laid her hand along his jaw, her touch more than tender. "The doctor wants to examine me one more time to be sure, but everything seems fine. At least, so far."

He heard the thinness of her voice, but his own emotion, so strong and sharp that it filled him up, gave him hope. "A baby." It seemed impossible, and yet good, so very good. "We're going to have a baby."

Lissa's smile radiated across her face, but her eyes were dark. "There's something else I should tell you, before you get too excited."

Again, that wobbly voice. The happiness dimmed, and he brushed those tangled curls from her eyes. "Tell me."

Her throat worked. Tears glimmered on her cheeks. "The last two times I was pregnant, I didn't carry the babies long enough. I'm afraid it could happen again."

He'd seen the graves on the small knoll facing the setting sun and the mountains, and he hurt for her. "That doesn't mean it will happen this time."

"It could." Her fear, her failure, lowered her voice. "The first one lived only a day. He was so very tiny, too small to breathe well on his own. And the second little boy lived two whole months, even though he was born almost as early, but when the diphtheria passed through he was too small to fight it. I lost him a day before I lost Michael."

He folded his arms around her, held her tight against

his chest, against his heart. Her sorrow felt like his own, and nothing had hurt so much before. Nothing.

"I don't want to fail you, Jack. I—"

"Shh." He kissed her mouth so she would not say such words, silenced the fears he could not bear. He tasted her tears and her hopes, her passions and sorrow. He held her so tightly that he could not tell where she began and he ended. The night wrapped around them like a cloak, and in the darkness they were not alone, and it felt as if they would never be alone again.

"Looks like we lost most of the crop." Jack stood with his back to the sun, hands on his hips, as solid as the mountains at the horizon, as strong as the land.

Lissa squinted against the low, bright rays to study the devastation. "All the oats, half the corn."

"Damn." Time had passed before Jack was strong enough to be up and about, and even then his major burns, still bandaged beneath his shirt, drew the color from his face and made his eyes pinch with pain. He walked stiffly, but without complaint. "Damn."

"At least we still have the hay. The fire missed half our fields. The cattle are all safe."

"I'm grateful for that." He knuckled back his hat, but he didn't sound grateful. "I should have stopped the fire. Look at all it did."

The scarred land, the blackened skeletons of trees and bushes looked like an ugly wound on the peaceful land. "You did what you could, Jack, and more. It's all the ranch hands and the neighbors have talked about for weeks."

He shrugged, said nothing, but his disappointment in himself, his defeat at the situation, lined his face, weighed down his shoulders. "We're lucky that cattle prices are up."

"We could mortgage the land."

"Not unless we have to." He sighed, a release of frustration. "We'll see what the rest of the summer brings."

"Good things." At least she hoped so. They'd had their share of hard luck. The sound of laughter drew her gaze. There, in the yard by the house, was Chad playing chase with his puppy, the growing dog awkward on her too-big feet. The barking and laughter blended together into a happy noise, a sound that made Lissa's chest warm.

Good things. How she wanted them for her son and for the baby she carried, for this husband of hers with no name.

Horse hooves crunching in the gravel broke apart the moment of closeness. Lissa stepped out of Jack's arms to see a figure in black, hat slung slow, riding closer.

" 'Morning, Lissa."

"Sheriff." She saw the grim line of his mouth, and her stomach fell. "What brings you out our way?"

"It's your *husband* I want to talk to." Ike Palmer, tall and lean, dropped his knotted reins. He placed both beefy hands on the handles of his holstered revolvers. "Got a minute, *Murray*?"

Jack didn't miss the distaste in the sheriff's voice. "I've got time, Palmer. What do you want?"

"Answers." A cynical grin shaped the word.

Warning prickled along the back of his neck, tightened into a cold ball in his gut. "Answers to what?"

"Your true identity." That grin widened, grew menacing. "You see, I had a friend of mine check up on Deputy John Murray. Seems Michael's cousin is alive and well, and still at his job in St. Louis."

Trouble. Jack tasted it, smelled it. "I don't see that it's any of your business."

"Well, considering my friendship with Lissa, I thought she might want to know she didn't marry the right man." Palmer's fingers caressed the polished walnut handles of his revolvers. "Lissa, you know I care for you. If you want me to throw this varmint off your land, it will be my pleasure."

Lissa paled. Jack saw the tension tight in her jaw. The wind whipped at her pink gingham dress. Then she lifted her chin, all fire, all fight. "I already know Jack isn't John Murray. We've known for some time, Ike."

"Damn you." The sheriff's mouth twisted as he drew one revolver, cocked the hammer. He swung off his horse, all boastful power and confidence. "I knew I didn't like you, Jack, or whatever your name is. Now I know why. You've been taking advantage of her, maybe threatening her."

"That's not true." Jack saw the lawman's intent. "I'm no danger to Lissa."

"Did you threaten to hurt her? Or her son?" Palmer jammed the nose of the revolver against Jack's temple.

Pain shot through his head. "No, I—"

"Ike!" Lissa's voice rang high and clear, vibrating with fury. "Stop it. Right now."

Jack saw her hand curl around the sheriff's upper arm. "Ike!" Lissa fumed. "Put down the gun—"

"Palmer." Jack kept his voice low, but threatening. "Put the gun down. I'm not armed."

The sheriff didn't relent. His gaze traveled to Lissa, who was shouting at him to lower his revolver. "Did he hurt you, Lissa? Did he?"

"No." She kicked Palmer in the shin. "Let him go right now."

"Ow. That hurt." The sheriff's attention slipped a notch.

Jack grabbed Palmer's wrist, twisted the gun from his temple in one quick movement. Before the sheriff could protest, he was on his knees in the dirt and Jack was holding the cocked revolver.

"Don't even try drawing your other gun." He towered over the sheriff, then released the hammer. "I'm not your enemy, and you know it. I didn't force Lissa into marrying me, or staying married to me."

"It's true, Ike." Lissa held out her hand.

She wanted the gun. Jack considered it, knew it was pointless to threaten a sheriff. He laid the revolver on her palm. Anger snapped like blue sparks in her eyes. Her jaw was clenched tight as she threw the revolver into the dust at Palmer's knees. "You know how I feel about threats and firearms on my land."

Palmer stood, swiping the dust from his knees. "Lissa, I only meant to protect you."

"Don't lie to me." Her voice tremored with fury. "When you threaten my husband you threaten me, Ike. I can't believe you would do this. I thought you were my friend."

"I was Michael's friend." Palmer reached down to retrieve the revolver.

Jack heard what the lawman did not say. He might have been Michael's friend, but he had coveted his friend's wife—and wanted her still.

"A friend wouldn't storm in here and try to kill my husband. What if I hadn't known the truth about Jack? You didn't think about me, or how the truth could have hurt me. You only cared about waving your gun around. You know that's one of the reasons I could never marry you. You have a violent side."

"What about him?" Palmer holstered his gun. "He could be the outlaw missing in these parts."

"I'm no outlaw." Jack stepped forward, fists tight, spine set. "You can count on that."

"On what? Your word? From a man hiding behind a woman's skirt?" The sheriff's face soured. "A United States Marshal is missing, presumed dead, killed by a man on the loose in these parts. Now, for all I know you could be that man."

"Or not." Jack's heart jumped. His palms felt clammy,

but he kept his hands fisted, his resolve firm. He would not let Palmer see his fear.

"I've sent away to Billings for the outlaw's description. As I see it, it's fifty-fifty odds that you're an outlaw." Palmer caught his gelding by the bit.

"Then it's fifty-fifty that I'm not." Jack met the sheriff's gaze, didn't blink, didn't back down.

"Don't be leaving town, or I'll hunt you down myself." Palmer swung up in the saddle, but his gaze never wavered—black, cold, hateful. "I don't take kindly to a murdering, thieving outlaw hiding out in my jurisdiction. Remember that, *Jack.*"

"I'm no outlaw, and I don't run."

"How do you know? Or did your memory come back?" Palmer laughed, as he reined his horse around. "Lissa, I won't arrest this joker yet, because I know you need someone to run your ranch until roundup. But if he's the man I think he is, then I'm coming back with my deputies and enough gunpower to take him in. There will be nothing you can do or say that will stop me."

Rocks and earth churned beneath the gelding's hooves as the sheriff galloped out of sight. Jack watched the lawman go.

"I'll speak with him." Lissa's jaw was still tight, her spine straight as a post. Anger rang in her words, sparked in her eyes. "He can't start throwing accusations around like that. What if people start to believe him? You're no outlaw. You—"

"Lissa." He knew he was gruff, knew he should lower his voice, but he couldn't.

She gazed up at him with startled eyes, too wide, too hurt. "No. I don't believe it."

"What if it's true?"

A family of larks settled down on nearby thistles, bobbing and squawking. Baby birds flapped their wings for their mother's attention. Jack felt nothing save for a great coldness settling in his chest.

"It can't be true." Lissa's chin never wavered. "I know who you are, the kind of man you are. You're honorable and courageous. You're Chad's new father, and the father of the baby I'm carrying. You're my husband, not an outlaw. Palmer is just jealous, he's just posturing—"

"No," he interrupted with a voice that was harsh and steely. "It makes sense. The horse I had, it wasn't mine. The saddle wasn't my saddle. I still had money in my billfold. I figured someone had tried to rob me, figured maybe they'd failed, that maybe the wildcat had come along and interrupted."

"You're the most gentle man I've ever known." Sunlight danced in her hair, in curls as gold as heaven. She looked like an avenging angel, all steel velvet and grace, determined to protect him, to believe in him.

His heart broke into a million pieces. "I'm also the most deadly. You can't deny it."

"No." She tucked her lower lip between her teeth. "I know you, Jack. You're not a bad man, not at heart."

"We don't know what I was before I came here." He swept off his hat, raked his hand through his hair. "I could be an escaped felon. Look how I handle a gun. I can shoot at a group of men and kill almost every one of them, even when they're shooting back at me."

"I saw." Her throat tightened. Emotion knotted there, and she could barely breathe.

"I'm deadly accurate with a gun. I can outshoot men who steal for a living, men no other law-abiding citizen in these parts could bring down." Wind tousled his dark blond curls over his forehead, leaving half-wild, rakish locks hiding his eyes. With his hard voice and steely strength, he looked every bit a criminal, a man living on the wrong side of the law.

"You're still my husband." She meant those words, even

if they frightened her. "The sheriff still has to prove you're that missing outlaw. He has to prove it, not just accuse."

"All it will do is buy me some time." His eyes darkened with what could only be sorrow.

"You might be someone else, Jack."

"No. I've had some dreams. Nothing that made sense, until now." Iron-strong, he stood with his back to the sun. Golden light limned him like an archangel, but his face was dark—so very dark. "I know I've lived in Montana a long time. I know however I made my living, I did it carrying a gun."

"Maybe—"

"No, Lissa." He stepped away, into the wind, scattering the birds from their perches on the thistles. "I know the outlaw's name. I recognized it."

"But Ike never said—"

"He talked to me earlier, in town. Let's just hope to God I'm not Dillon Plummer, that I don't match his description. He's a murderer, Lissa. And that man, he could be me."

Her heart broke with every step he took away from her. A wall as high as the sky separated them now. She could feel it even if she could not see it. She knew what kind of man she'd married—the best of men, one honorable enough to tempt even her wary heart. And yet how could she lean on him now? Need him? Love him? Jack said there was a possibility he was an outlaw. Tears blurred her vision, but she did not look away, did not stop watching him—not until he was nothing but a blur in the golden fields, and then nothing, nothing at all.

Chapter Fifteen

"Mama, Puddles doesn't know how to share."

Lissa looked up from creaming sugar and butter to see Chad sitting on the floor, one cookie in hand, the other hand empty. Puddles sat on his lap. Winston sat daintily next to her boy, her belly hiding her toes.

Puddles leaped up and grabbed the last cookie from Chad's fingers, and the child laughed. "See? Winston and me otta get some too."

"I see." Laughing, too, Lissa set down her mixing bowl and stole two more gingersnap cookies from the crock.

Scenting the treat, Puddles leaped up, her mouth still lined with cookie crumbs, eyes bright and happy.

"Smells good in here." Jack's smiling voice spun her around. He stood shirtless in the threshold, framed by the mid-morning light, bronzed skin glistening.

"Pa!" Chad jumped to his feet, racing across the room to wrap his arms around Jack's knees. "We've been eatin' cookies."

"Got any for me?"

"Yep!" Chad raced back to the table, the puppy bouncing at his heels. The lid to the crock clinked.

Jack's gaze brushed hers, warm but not intimate. "Thought I'd stop by and bring the men some cider. It's getting hot out in those fields."

"I got caught up in preparing for the ladies' club meeting this afternoon. It's my turn to host." Lissa glanced at the clock. "I should have thought of you and the men working under that sun."

"Don't worry about it. I like taking a break to see my family." He thanked Chad for the handful of cookies.

The sight of the big man and small boy—standing in the sunshine nibbling gingersnaps while the puppy jumped up, trying to join in—made Lissa's heart ache.

She gave Winston a final pat and knelt to pull up the cellar door. Cool air met her. She grabbed a jug of unopened cider.

Two big hands reached down out of the light. "Let me. That's pretty heavy."

"I can manage." She looked up, saw his handsome face, his smile that did not reach his eyes.

"I know. But let me do it. Make me feel manly."

She wasn't fooled. She handed him the heavy jug and started up the short ladder. At the top, Jack took her arm, helping her up. She didn't need the help, but he had been busy doing small tasks for her, things she could handle and always had—because she was pregnant, she knew. It was nice that he worried over her.

With the sheriff's visit everything had changed. She didn't want to lean too much on Jack. Didn't want to depend on him, need him. If his fears were true and he was the missing outlaw, then he couldn't stay no matter what his promises were, no matter his honor.

It was there, in the way he held himself just a step away, in the cool sadness of his eyes even if he smiled, in the lack of his touch. He knew it, too. His time with them could end. All he had accomplished here, everything he'd become, wouldn't matter one whit against the wrongs of his past.

Sheriff Ike Palmer wished to hell he could have arrested Jack—rather, Dillon Plummer—on the spot. Plummer was the cousin of a notorious criminal, and notorious in his own right. Arresting him would be a boon to his career.

Palmer wanted to be more than a small town sheriff. He had bigger aspirations, dreams he couldn't reach while sitting behind a desk piled with papers. He needed money, real money, and the chance to prove himself. In this land of the free, home of the brave, any fool could be voted governor. He didn't see why in blazes he couldn't be there one day.

A fine home, money, a beautiful wife. Most of all, power. That was what he really craved—being able to destroy a man, any man, with the snap of his fingers.

The jailhouse door crashed open. Deakins scrambled inside, out of the bitter heat. "No mail from the capital."

"Damn that sheriff's office." Were they a bunch of morons?

"Maybe next week, Sheriff."

"Next week isn't good enough. I want that bastard out of the way now." He should have hired better guns, ones who could have brought down that outlaw when they had the chance instead of getting themselves killed by him.

Palmer made a decision. He hated to spend money, but this time he had no choice, unless the sheriff's office decided to answer their mail. "Get ahold of Clayborne. Tell him I'm going to need some more men. The best he's got."

*   *   *

"Lissa, I can't believe the devastation." Felicity James stepped down from her buggy while her sister, still perched on the seat, set the brake. "We're just lucky that wildfire didn't reach town. We owe a lot of thanks to your husband and the men who did what they could to stop it."

"The rain stopped it," Maggie added as she climbed down, balancing a crystal cake plate. "But the men sure took the vigor out of it, or we would all be in terrible straits."

"We managed to save the house, so I don't feel like I have cause to complain." Lissa accepted a hug each from the James sisters, then thanked Arcada, who hurried from the barn to take their horse and buggy. "Come in. I have some lemonade and ice tea."

"Look. There's Blanche."

A wagon kicked up a dust cloud, but the woman behind the reins was a welcome sight. "You're looking much better, Lissa. The burns have healed."

She held up one bandaged hand. "Just have this one left to go. Sophie's balm worked wonders. And so did your loving care."

"I do what I can for my friends." Warmth from nearly two decades of caring shone in Blanche's eyes. "Here, take this plate of tarts from me. I'm going to spill the entire thing if I try to get down without tripping on my skirt."

"Where's your buggy?" Lissa reached up to take the covered plate, balancing it quickly when the tarts started to slide. "Did Jeremiah take the children somewhere?"

"Jeremiah is itching to head up to Billings before school starts and he'll need the wagon for that. All those books he gets to buying wouldn't fit inside that buggy, not with all our little ones." Laughing, Blanche dropped to the ground, kicking up dust and offering a hug. "Wait. We can't start without everyone else."

"There's Sophie." Felicity pointed.

A woman on horseback, skirts flying, crossed the burned out fields, loping toward the house.

"It's hot in this sun." Lissa swiped her brow. Her morning sickness always came in the afternoons and stayed. This pregnancy was no different. She took a step toward the house. "Go inside and help yourselves to refreshments. I'll stay to greet Sophie."

"No. We'll just stay right here." Maggie offered a mysterious smile.

"I heard someone has a big secret," Felicity teased. "Probably as a result of all those sleepless nights in the company of her new husband."

"Yes," Blanche chimed in. "Certain pleasurable activities can result in certain conditions."

"All right, who told?" Blushing, Lissa took a step back. Their shade trees had been burned somewhat by the fire, and Will had the men chop them down. Now there was no shade.

Blanche's eyes twinkled. "All right, it was me. I can't keep a secret that big. Besides, I thought everyone should know. We can celebrate, especially after all that's happened." She gestured with one upturned palm toward the scarred land and fields, the missing trees, the scorched yard and garden.

"We're all so happy for you, Lissa." Felicity beamed. "Tell us when the baby's due."

"January. It seems so far away." Worry knotted in her stomach, but excitement bubbled there, too. She was almost afraid to hope that this time the baby would live, that she would carry to term.

Maggie took her hand and squeezed. "It will be here before you know it. And that handsome husband of yours, he must be happy with the news. What with him losing his own son back in St. Louis."

Lissa's throat closed. No one knew of Jack's secret, that he wasn't truly John Murray. Apparently the sheriff was keeping that piece of information to himself. For now. "Jack is very happy."

"We'll keep our fingers crossed for a son." Blanche laid her arm across Lissa's shoulder. "Not that little girls aren't nice, because that would be wonderful, too. But a son, seeing as how both you and Jack have lost sons, it would be a nice gift to get one back."

"Yes." Tears filled her eyes. Friendship, true friendship, was a rare thing. She cherished these women like her own family. They all knew her fears, and in their quiet congratulations she knew they understood. "Hello, Sophie."

The Indian woman slid off her bareback pony. "Baby Evan is teething, and I just couldn't get him down for his nap for Hans. Hans is a good father, he just doesn't know what to do with a teething baby."

"Who does?" Blanche teased, earning laughter from everyone.

"Elise. Susan." A second wagon rolled up, the tanner's wife and the merchant's wife side by side. They weren't in their own buggies, either.

"Let's just show her now," Blanche suggested.

"Yes, let's." Sophie handed Arcada the reins to her painted pony and adjusted the leather sack slung over her shoulder. "The plants won't do well drying out in this heat."

Lissa swiped her brow. "What's going on?"

"Surprise." Susan leaned over the back of the wagon and lifted a canvas. "We heard from Will when he came to buy supplies for the ranch that your gardens were damaged—"

"So we all took plants from our own gardens for you to start a new one," Blanche finished.

"I brought herbs and native plants." Sophie unwrapped her sack, revealing yew and yarrow and strong-scented sage and wild licorice.

"Susan and I brought flowers and roses from our yards." Elise brushed her fingers over the soft petals of red and pink roses, over dogwood and lily, their sweet fragrance filling the hot summer air.

"And the James sisters and I brought vegetables. Everything you can think of. Beans and beets, and cooking herbs."

"And the men and I will plant them for you," Arcada added, returning to unhitch the wagons. "You ladies go ahead inside. Lissa, you just call if you need anything."

"Thank you." The words felt so small when compared to her friends' generosity. She saw Jack at the barn watching, his gloved hands wrapped around the handle of an ax. He'd been working hard, and sweat darkened his hair, sparkled on his shirtless shoulders and chest.

It hurt, not being alone. And for once in a very long time, she was grateful.

Jack tried to peek in the window, but Winston sat on the sill, blocking his view. The wind breezed back the curtain, and the screen obscured what he could see of the room on either side of the cat. The women's voices, breaking into laughter, rose and fell. He was too far away to make out what they were saying.

"I wonder what women do when they're all alone." McLeod grunted as he lifted a heavy shovel full of dirt.

"They talk about men." Will unwrapped a wet cloth from around a tomato plant and fit it into the ground, careful not to damage the roots.

"Nah, they talk about babies." Arcada knelt to water the potato plants he'd just transplanted from the back of Blanche's wagon. "Women like babies."

"And religion," the youngest hand, Jesse Winters, piped in. He looked up from his digging. "My mother and sisters always prayed a lot."

"Probably because they had you in the house," McLeod teased, and the men laughed.

Jack pulled his hat brim low against the sun. He didn't know what the women were doing, but he was certain he'd heard the shuffling of a deck of cards.

His gaze shifted to the acre-size garden. Most of the sweet corn and root vegetables had survived the heat from the fire, but the beans and peas, the patch of tomatoes, and the carrots had taken a beating. Much of her hard work had been ruined.

He was touched by the kindness of Lissa's friends. They cared for her. She'd grown up in this town, and her relationships with others were lifelong. He'd heard from Hans how Lissa had helped after Sophie's baby was born, and Sophie fell ill, how the other women had pitched in, just as the men had to cut Hans's hay fields.

How would they feel once they knew he was an outlaw? Dillon Plummer. How that name sparked glimmers of memories in the blank part of his mind. The dreams he'd had flashed back to him—stalking men in a field, standing in a jail, hunting others—as a criminal, as a man who killed?

He didn't want to shame Lissa that way. Worse, he hated waiting, hated wondering what the sheriff was going to do next, what information he'd gathered.

"All done, boss. Except for the roses." Arcada straightened, holding an empty bucket in each hand. "McLeod said he'd plant the rose bushes."

"Then let's get started on the fence. I have a feeling the deer will be by tonight if we don't." Jack dug another fence posthole, sweat dripping off his back. The harder he worked, the less he had to think, but he couldn't help it.

The women's laughter rose again. Whatever plans they were making for the harvest dance must be amusing them.

Good. He wanted to see the shadows gone from Lissa's

eyes, the worry from her face—the worry he'd put there, the fears he'd planted.

He believed he was who the sheriff thought he was. Nothing else made sense. Hating the trouble he knew would come, and all because of him, Jack turned his back to the house and the women's laughter, and forced the shovel deep into the ground.

Lissa pushed open the screen door, the coming night alive with the drone of insects, the hoot of an owl, the first distant calls of the coyotes. Twilight cloaked the land with a purple-gray haze, the shadows deepening over hill and forest.

She saw him in the garden, heard the rhythmic scrape of a saw, smelled the fresh, sharp scent of sawed wood. Head bent, saw gripped tightly in one hand while he held a piece of wood with the other, Jack worked in silence as the night enfolded him. Darkness stole him from her sight.

"It's too dark to work," she said.

He dropped the saw with a clatter, then swore. "I didn't hear you there."

"You were pretty absorbed in your work." She stepped out onto the porch, hugging herself.

"I want this gate to latch right. I'm an inch or two off." He returned to his work, his breath labored as he sawed the thick length of the board. She could see only the brush of his movements against the darkness.

"I can light a lantern for you," she offered.

"If I need one, I'll do it." His voice was light and friendly, but his words stopped her.

He wasn't mean, he wasn't harsh. Lissa knew he was still the same man, strong and hardworking, keeping what promises he could, but since Sheriff Palmer's visit, Jack had withdrawn. So had she. While neither had said it, they both knew their relationship, the happy future they were working for, was forever changed.

"I left your supper in the oven. It's still warm."

"I'll be in after I'm done here. It may take a while." He shrugged. "I know that you were sick a lot today. You must be tired. Don't wait up for me."

Midsummer had passed, but the nights were still late in coming. Winston rubbed against her ankles, hopping up from her cool spot beneath the porch and ambled into the house.

"What if I want to wait up for you?"

Her question lingered in the warm breezes. She heard Jack put down his saw, heard wood *thunk* to the ground. Saw the shadows of his movement, felt his approach.

"I'm going to be in very late." His words rang low, and he knelt on the ground. She heard the sounds of wood rubbing against wood, and the jingle of a hinge. "Besides, I don't want you getting tired, not in your condition. You need your sleep."

"I'll miss you." She wanted to find a way to erase Palmer's words and Jack's fears, to make it all right again. To bring him back to her arms.

"It's harvest time. We don't know what's going to happen, Lissa. I want to get as much of this work done as I can. For you. In case I have to leave." The bang of a hammer shattered the stillness. Three pounds, and he stopped, then pounded twice more. "There. Now it fits."

She heard the whisper of a hinge, heard the click of the metal latch as the new gate shut tight. Most of all she felt his sorrow. The first star of the night peeked low over the horizon, and her hopes felt like that star, only a speck in the darkening sky.

"The fence is beautiful."

"I aim to please." He knelt to gather his tools. She heard the *clunk* and *clink* of wood and metal coming together.

"I carved the posts and cut a heart into the garden gate. I'm glad you like it."

"I do." She laid her hand over the smooth knob of the posts. "I can't believe you stopped your work to do this."

He stopped, sighed. "All the trouble your friends went to, bringing you new flowers. I would hate to have those deer hanging out there in the grove eat up all your new rose bushes before morning."

Thinking of her, that was all he seemed to do, and of her son—for she had heard from Chad of how Jack had promised to rebuild the tree house this weekend. He was such a proud man, so determined to do the right thing.

Discovering he could be a killer and an escaped criminal had hit him hard. "Will you talk to me now?"

"I wasn't aware that I ever stopped." Jack opened the gate, then closed it. The fence separated them.

"I think we should discuss what happened. About the sheriff's threat."

His silence was his answer. He took a step away, then another. "I don't see there's anything to talk about. As long as there are doubts, I'm not good enough to be your husband. You're a fine woman, and if it's true then I'm nothing but a criminal, and I don't belong here. End of story."

"How can you think that? You've been a hero to me. You saved my ranch and my son. You even saved me."

"I killed men for you, nothing heroic in that." *A hero?* He wanted more than anything to be wrong, but in his heart, a darkness answered.

How he ached, hearing both the hurt in her voice and the affection. She cared for him, truly, just as he'd wanted so long ago.

He walked away from her, afraid to reach out. Was he an outlaw? If so, he wasn't good enough for a woman so fine, as beautiful as dawn, didn't deserve her, would bring shame to her.

He heard her behind him in the dark, fumbling with the latch. It was new and stiff and made a crisp *clink* when she finally opened it.

His chest tightened. He didn't want to talk about what was to come. "Lissa, please. Let me work."

"But—"

He caught the gate before it snapped shut, held it open for her. Her sunshine-sweet scent tickled his nose, filled his being.

He wanted nothing more than to take her to bed, strip away her clothes and kiss every part of her, to love her as he had throughout their marriage. But did he have that right?

Not until he knew for certain who he was, and what promises he could make to her.

"Come on. I'll put you to bed."

"It's early." Her protest shivered through him, and when he took her hand the heat of her, the gentleness of her, touched him all the way to his soul.

Tonight, he would lead her to their room, help her with her clothes and into her nightgown. He would tuck her in safely with a kiss good night. Then he would walk away. He had work to do, this woman to honor.

He would honor her best by respecting her, by giving her nothing more to regret.

Chapter Sixteen

"I'm heading out with the hands to cut the cattle." Jack sat down on the edge of the bed to pull on his trousers. "We have to decide which to keep for breeding and which to sell. Did you want to come?"

Lissa squinted against the low morning rays slanting into the room. He stood up from the chair, his steely frame casting a long shadow into the room.

Her heart stopped just looking at him. "Blanche is coming this morning. We're making preserves."

"Did you need me to watch Chad?"

"No. Blanche is bringing her children. They will play together in the yard. Her oldest can keep an eye on the younger ones."

"Just let me know if you need anything. Will shouldn't ride all day with his leg still mending, so he should be in the fields or the barn. Just send him to fetch me."

"I will." How she wished she could touch him, wrap her arms around his strength, breathe him in like air, but he'd avoided her touch. He wasn't cold, just cautious.

She heard his footsteps retreat, and reached for her blue gingham work dress. Soft calico whispered against her fingers as she tugged the dress on. In the heat, she wore only drawers and a camisole. The cotton caressed her skin as it slid down her body, her hips, her legs.

"Jack, do you want me to bring breakfast out to you and the men?" She began buttoning her dress.

"We'd appreciate it." His voice came muffled through the thick walls of the log home. "It's going to be another long day. I can send Will in to get the food. Would that be easier?"

Her fingers stilled. There, at her waist, was a gap in the fabric. The buttons didn't meet. She looked up and caught her reflection in the mirror. The white muslin of her chemise showed against the edges of blue checked placket.

"Lissa?" He hesitated outside the room.

She could only stare at her stomach, at the dress that had fit her just yesterday.

"Lissa?" His hands cupped her shoulders, gentle as always. "Is something wrong?"

"Not wrong." Her throat closed. She could not talk, could not breathe.

"Your dress doesn't fit." Jack's words were soft against her ear.

"No, it doesn't." She found her voice. She had lost babies. Now she laid her hand on her stomach, hoping this time would be different.

"The baby?" His hand covered hers, and she could lean against him, feel the steely hardness of his chest, the strong protection of his arms.

"This is just the beginning. Before too long I'm going to be too big to button my shoes." How she wanted this child.

"You're going to need new clothes." His voice against her ear sounded so good, so happy.

"I already have them. I just need to dig them out of the attic."

"I'll do it. I don't want you climbing any ladders, not unless there's a roof fire." He squeezed her, his hug warm and tender, sustaining. "And no heavy lifting. Agreed?"

"Sure. I'll just stand around while you do my bidding." *Really.* "This is a farm, Jack. I can still do my normal work."

"No climbing. No heavy lifting." He released her, but his heart, his affection didn't end when he stepped away, or when he headed toward the door. "What do I look for up there?"

"A trunk. It's the blue one."

His smile flashed and it almost, almost, felt right, without strain, just as it used to be between them.

Pregnant. He'd been worried about that ever since the sheriff paid him a visit and levied his threat just to insert a wedge in their marriage.

It had worked. Jack considered the baby. Although in his heart he feared Palmer was right, that he was the missing killer, Jack had to find a little hope. For Chad, for Lissa, and most of all for her baby.

"These cows here are the springer heifers Lissa bottle-raised two years ago." Will gestured with one gloved hand into the unforgiving rays of the sun. "These are usually the best breeding stock. They're tame, gentle, and easy to handle. Plus, they come when they see a bucket. Easy to take care of come winter."

"Looks like they come without a bucket." Jack laughed as the curious cows lifted their big heads, watching the men with thoughtful eyes. One sniffed the air, then hurried over.

"That's Clover. She's a handful. There's nothing worse than a pet cow, you know. They don't herd well."

"Or behave well." Jack laughed when the big brown cow came up and nosed Will's saddlebag.

"Hey, that corn in there is for my horse." Will waved his hand at the cow, who wouldn't budge.

Encouraged by Clover's boldness, the others followed, maybe fifty of them, all curious tongues outstretched, trying to figure out where the grain was hidden.

"I guess we leave these. We'll never get them to the railroad in Billings."

"Right, boss. Not unless we took wagons of corn for them to follow. Feedin' them all that way would put a ranch out of business."

The cows became obstinate over the lack of grain and refused to move aside for the horses.

"Like I said, they make great breeding cows. Easy to handle if there's a calving problem." Will shook his head. "Outta my way, Clover. I'm not giving you any grain."

A movement caught Jack's eye. A brown blur down low in the field, running adjacent to the big, split rail fence. He blinked, and there Pete was, dashing toward them in this pasture instead of the other.

"Do we have a fence down?"

"Didn't last night when McLeod rode it. Every inch of it, just like you wanted."

"Then we have a problem. That bull shouldn't be in with these heifers." Jack had made sure the fence was too high to jump, strong enough to deter a stampeding herd. "Come on."

The gentle cows would not scatter at the wave of his hat, so he had to weave around them. Pete, dashing full speed, skidded to a stop in greeting just before he collided with Jack's gelding.

"Will, got that grain?"

"It's for my horse," the young man insisted. Then he laughed. "Some days, a man just can't win."

"I know the feeling." His gaze traveled to the fence line,

then back to Pete, who was licking the toe of Jack's boot. "Come with us, Pete. Will has a treat for you."

"He prefers a bucket." Will untied the small burlap bag from his saddle pack and held it high.

Pete's nostrils flared and his big pink tongue shot out.

"Follow us, Pete." Jack led the way down the fence line and shook his head when the gentle cows followed, too, hoping for some of the corn.

There it was, a hole in the fence. Piles of shavings and the clean cut of the wood left no doubt.

Rustlers.

"Mama, I can't find Winston." Chad poked his head in at the kitchen door, his hair rumpled with bits of grass from his morning of playing.

"Maybe Winston doesn't want to be around so many loud children," she teased, turning from the stove.

"If I were her, I'd run from all those ruffians out there," Blanche added from the basin, where steaming water curled into the already hot air. "Look at those wild things. Whose children are they, anyway?"

Lissa laughed. "Apples don't fall far from the tree."

"I think they've had too much summer. I'll be glad when school starts." Blanche gingerly lifted a steaming hot jar and dried it with care. "Jeremiah is already planning his lessons. Is Jack going to be taking the cattle up to Billings before or after the dance?"

"Before, I think." He hadn't spoken much of anything. He was working so hard in the fields. Already stacks of hay dotted the south side of the barn, which sported a fresh coat of whitewash and a repaired roof, just as Jack promised long ago. "Cattle prices are up. With the tough winter we had last year, many animals died."

"That will be good news for the ranchers. And maybe for our fund-raiser." Blanche glanced up at the clock. "It's time, Lissa. Let me grab the hot pads, and we'll get these preserves off the heat."

Lissa held the pan while Blanche skimmed off the foam with a long handled spoon. Then together they filled the sparkling clean jars. The scent of sugar-sweetened berries lifted with the steam, and the purple-blue jam brightened the wooden counter.

"Whew, is it hot in here." Blanche whisked the emptied kettle from Lissa's grip. "A red-hot stove in the middle of August is never a good idea."

"I can smuggle up some of the lemonade I mixed this morning. It's in the cellar."

"Do it. The children don't need to know we sneaked a few glasses. There has to be some reward for slaving away to make the winter's preserves."

Laughing, Lissa pulled the ring handle in the floor and stepped down into the dark cellar. She grabbed the covered pitcher, cooled and sweet-smelling. She handed it up to Blanche, whose hands were dripping with washwater.

"I noticed your stomach is showing." Blanche grabbed two cups from the cabinet.

"Just barely." Lissa curled her fingers around the pitcher's metal handle.

"Excited?"

"And scared." She didn't mention that today, even though she tried to not think of it, was the day her last baby was born. "But that's normal."

"That makes two of us. I didn't want to say anything at our last club meeting, because of your announcement, but—"

Lissa studied her dear friend's smiling face. "You're pregnant, too?"

Blanche nodded. "I wasn't sure last month, but I am this one. I suppose your morning sickness has passed already?"

"I'm still a little queasy in the afternoons."

"Then we can be sick together. And fat."

"And happy." Lissa filled both glasses. "This lemonade tastes like heaven. I took a sip this morning, before you came."

"Hmm. It does. I think we should set out the meal, I—"

A door swung open, and Lissa heard Jack's low laughter, rich and merry as he stepped into the kitchen with Chad at his knee, saw the big rugged man with his riding boots, his shirt half-buttoned, his hat gripped in one hand. He listened patiently to Chad's account of the morning. When he looked up, his gaze arrowed to hers, and he smiled, truly smiled. But she saw the shadows in his eyes—trouble.

"I'm going to town," he said, "do you need anything?"

Chad spoke up. "Candy."

Jack laughed, but all Lissa could manage was a wobbly smile. She recognized the tense set of his wide shoulders, the clenched angle of his jaw. Something was wrong.

He caught her hand, his touch reassuring. She felt the calluses on his fingers, the strength of him. He pressed a kiss to her cheek. "I have some business to take care of. I can't say when I'll be back."

"I'll walk you to the barn." Her stomach tightened. Something had stirred Jack's anger.

"It's best if we talk later. Stay and have a good time with your friend. And don't worry. Promise?"

His blue eyes sparkled with warmth, with caring. There was a time when he would have held her tightly to his chest, as close as possible, instead of standing with the room between them.

She nodded, and he was gone. The power of his stride carried him quickly from her sight. Her chest tightened. She ached in a way that made her feel empty and lonely without him, even if she didn't want to.

She never wanted to care for any man that much, so that his loss, his absence, left her less of a person, with less of a heart.

* * *

Jack pushed open the jailhouse door, prepared to meet trouble head-on. Anger drove him and he waited in the threshold, met the sheriff's gaze.

Palmer sat behind his desk, surprise widening his eyes. That quickly faded. "Didn't think you were man enough to darken my door."

"Did you think I was a coward? That I'd spend my time hiding from the law?"

A muscle jumped along the sheriff's temple. "Truth is, I never figured you for a coward. Or a fool. You know I'm itchin' to lock you up."

"Got to have charges that will stick." Jack slammed the door behind him. They were alone, just the way he wanted it. "How about bothering some real criminals? Lissa has some more rustlers."

"I thought you killed them." The sheriff stood. The set of the man's mouth, the lack of surprise in his eyes, told Jack something.

"I did. But now there's a few more. Not more than two or three, judging from the tracks. They took a few of the springer heifers, some of our better stock."

"Lissa's pet heifers?"

"No. So far, the rustlers haven't been able to drive them off." Jack thought about that. Lissa's gentle cows would bring a good price, not for beef, but for breeding. Ranchers would pay good cash for such stock and not ask any questions. "I imagine it's just a matter of time. I know your opinion of me, Palmer, but we both don't want to see Lissa lose everything."

"No." The sheriff's mouth was hard, but the flicker in his eye, the lift of his voice, spoke otherwise. "Planning on going somewhere?"

"I guess it depends on you." Jack looked his enemy straight in the eye, saw the cold hard heart of the man, felt the same power in his own. "I'm not afraid, either way. And as far as the rustlers go, if you don't catch them, I will."

"You can count on me." The sheriff smiled, and Jack wasn't fooled.

He wasn't fooled at all.

"The rustlers are back," Jack said as he pushed open the screen door, the hinge squeaking. "And we're on our own. The sheriff isn't going to help."

Lissa looked up from tightening the lids on those jars cool enough to close. "Did we lose much stock?"

"A dozen or so heifers."

"The very valuable animals." She tried not to meet his gaze, tried not to feel the distance between them. "Did Johanson have some losses, too?"

"No. Just us. So far." Jack hung his hat on the peg. "Where's Chad?"

"He went home with Blanche. Puddles went, too."

"That's why the house feels so empty. Do I smell huckleberries?"

"Blanche and I made preserves today. Her family is going to go picking this evening. I wanted to go, too, but I wasn't sure when you would be back."

"I see." He unbuckled his holster. "So it's just you and me for the night."

"Looks that way." Her chest squeezed. She feared what he did not say, feared he didn't want to be alone with her. "I want to get enough berries to dry so I can bake with them this winter. I was going to ride up into the hills and do a little picking."

"Up in the hills?" He gazed out the window, troubled. "I don't want you to go alone."

"I guess I could ask one of the men. I've always been safe. I'm not going far."

"There are clouds on the horizon. It smells like rain. We could have another thunderstorm."

"I know how to avoid lightning. And wildfires." Really, it was better that she stand on her own two feet, even though she was weary of it, even if she just wanted a strong shoulder to lean on now and then. She'd learned the hard way depending on someone wasn't always for the best.

"I left your supper wrapped up in the cellar. Some left-over chicken and potato salad. And there's a glass or two of lemonade left in the pitcher."

He caught hold of her arm, his grip gentle but as binding as steel. "Let me go with you. I can eat later."

She wanted to be with him, but was it a good idea? He'd been pushing away from her, keeping himself distant. She had been doing the same.

"I insist." Jack reached for his gun and his hat. "Come on. I'm pretty good at berrying. I used to pick huckleberries all the time when I was a boy."

A coldness arrowed through her heart. "Are you remembering?"

A look of surprise crossed his face, a face made handsome by the warmth of his eyes and the gentle brush of his very masculine, very sexy smile. "I guess I did. Hmm. Maybe I'd better eat a bunch of those huckleberries and see what else I can remember."

She laughed, the flicker of humor in his gaze so welcome. This was the Jack she knew, the one she cherished. At the same time, she feared what he would remember— and how it would tear them apart.

The wind felt cool and the sky cloudy when they reached the line of trees. Tall pines and firs crested the low hills, and Jack scented the breeze as he dismounted. Rain.

He caught hold of Charlie's bit, and the big horse waited

patiently as Lissa swung down, ruffling skirts and all. Charlie nudged him, looking for a treat.

"Here." Lissa withdrew a new carrot from her skirt pocket. She held her hand, palm up, while Charlie lifted the treat daintily with his lips. The wind whipped her skirts around her legs, hugging her form. Jack could not force his gaze from the length of her legs, from the curve of her hips, or the small roundness of her stomach.

Not sure what he should feel, what he should think, Jack grabbed down the metal pails from his saddle horn and tethered his gelding to a low tree. He reached for Charlie's reins, the big horse still crunching on his carrot, and did the same.

"Look. It's a wonderful crop this year." She breathed the words. She lured him when he should turn away and force distance between them. "I'll start right here. My bucket, please."

She held out her hands, elegant, stained purple-blue from her preserve making. Those hands, he knew how they felt laid flat against his chest, knew how soft they were, how gentle. His blood thickened as he remembered all the ways she'd touched him, how he wanted her to touch him again, and shouldn't.

He handed her the bucket, unable to speak. She smiled, and he could not look away, even when she turned and knelt down before a low, flat-leafed bush, then began plucking ripe, blueberries from supple stems. The berries plunked into the bottom of the bucket. He stood there, simply watching her, craving her like air and sunshine and late night passion.

Just pick the berries, he told himself. He'd made a promise, one she knew nothing about. He would do right by her. He wanted to make sure she never regretted their time together.

He left her picking berries and knelt down before a bush several yards away. He could hear her if she called out, but he could not see her. It was better that way. If he couldn't look at her, then it didn't hurt so much not being able to need her.

"I'm eating almost as much as I'm picking." Her voice tempted him. "How about you?"

"Looks like I'm guilty, too." He looked up, his picking forgotten, to see her approaching with a brimming bucket. "Did you want to head home?"

"I'd like to get more." She knelt near him, smelling of forest and spice and sweet, wild berries. "But it's starting to rain."

"A little rain never hurt anyone." He stood, held out his hand. The leaves and branches overhead shielded them, but he could hear the occasional thud of a raindrop.

"I'm going to empty my bucket so I can pick more berries."

He should let her go. The pail wasn't heavy. She would come to no harm doing it by herself. When she walked from his sight, though, he felt bereft, so he climbed to his feet, his bucket nearly full, too, and joined her. He took the canvas sack from behind his saddle and held it so she could empty one pail, then the other.

"I have a good gallon, don't you think?" She looked up, her eyes as blue as those berries, as rich and sweet.

"A good gallon." He could only repeat her words. Heaven help him, she affected him like no other.

"Did you remember anything more?"

"No. No image. Just an impression. Sunlight. Laughter. A brother, maybe." The memory was impossible to capture. "My remembering, does it frighten you?"

"A little." She set down the empty pail, then reached to take the sack from him. "My family used to pick huckleberries every year. We were poor, but happy. My mother used to be the best cook. She made huckleberry juice and preserves, tarts and pies and cakes, pancakes and syrup, and dried berries for winter. We needed a lot of gallons for that. Mama would pack both a dinner and supper, and we spent all day in the woods.''

"Where is your family now? Do they live far from here?" Jack followed her into the clearing, where rain fell in slow, hesitant drops.

"They're dead. When I was ten, we all got sick with scarlet fever." She bowed her head, her sadness as gray as the rain. "Only my older brother and I lived. And he was killed in a mine accident a few years later."

"I didn't know."

"I don't talk about it much."

She was alone. No wonder she had no one to help her with the ranch, no one to depend on, to reach out to. She'd been alone for so long, growing up without anyone to lean on. He'd been trying to keep his distance—to do her justice by keeping his promises and by not taking anything she would regret giving him later—but she looked so lost, remembering her sorrows. He laid his hand against her cheek, felt the silken heat of her skin and the cool rain mixing with quiet tears.

She'd told him several times she didn't want to lose another husband. It hadn't occurred to him, it never occurred to him, how much she still cared, how much she needed him.

His lips found hers, and she opened for him, molding her body against his. She felt like summer heat and autumn storm. She was passion and need in his arms. He held her tight, and she clung to him. And then somehow they were on the ground, in a bed of soft grass surrounded by fern and berry bushes, guarded by silent pines.

Jack tore his mouth from hers, out of breath, uncertain if she wanted him, but the way her eyes flashed affection changed something deep inside him, some long ago belief, some wall he'd always kept around his heart. Whatever it was, he felt vulnerable and unprepared for the way she cared about him, cared for him.

"Don't stop." Her hand curled around the back of his neck and pulled his face to hers. Her lips caressed and teased and nibbled. When he reached for the button at her throat, she kissed him harder, erasing all doubt.

He tried to resist her, control his need for her, yet it burned brighter than ever, endless and everlasting. Jack fumbled with the last of her buttons, saw the calico fabric give way to soft muslin beneath. He undressed her, and she undressed him.

Rain tumbled from the sky—ever harder, skin temperature—drenching them as they lay together, naked and wanting. She was so beautiful that it stole his breath and all of his heart. Her soft breasts, generously pink-tipped, filled his hands, fuller than before. Her stomach curved a little, drawing his attention, too. When he laid his hand there, and then his kisses, she grew still. Their gazes met. All he could not say knotted in his throat, burned in his chest.

She was carrying his child, and the wonder of it, the power of it, washed away the past and gave hope to the future. As if Lissa knew his thoughts, she pulled him over her and his shaft brushed her inner thigh.

He wanted to enter her slowly, but she reached for him, pulled him down into her with one fast movement. Everything he felt, everything he was, was her—sweet love and body heat and rippling pleasure. He held her tight, already fighting the lure of release. But he was too frantic and she was too ready, and when she came, her muscles gloving him tight, he did, too—in one long agony of pleasure that left him so in love with his wife that it hurt.

He held her tenderly, kissing her face, her lips, her throat. The rain fell, making them new.

Chapter Seventeen

Lissa looked into Jack's eyes, the nighttime all dark around them. She knew he wanted something. She didn't know if she could give it to him. A heart was a fragile thing, and already she'd lost too much of hers, buried with those she had loved. He kissed her, and now wanted more than a kiss, wanted deep, intimate affection, a love she was afraid to give again.

"Cattle prices could go higher, but I doubt it. I want to take the herd in now. We'll make a decent profit with the current high prices. What do you think?"

She looked at her husband, seated at the table, tossing a few ripe huckleberries into his mouth. How handsome he looked, with his hair rumpled and wind-tossed, his shirt stretched tight over those rock-hard shoulders. "Will and I can take care of the ranch while you're gone."

"The rustlers may be a little trouble, but I figure they won't be able to herd all those pet cows of yours, the ones I'm keeping for breeding, so maybe we won't have too many problems." His grin flashed in the low lamplight.

She broke a smile, knowing he was teasing her. "I'll miss you."

"I'll miss you, too. I may be gone longer than a month. Depends on how fast we can move the herd in this heat, and on how long it takes in Billings."

"I know." Michael had always waited until the weather was cooler to move the cattle, but she knew as well as Jack did that the prices would be lower the longer they waited. "You're leaving now to get out of having to help me put up the garden."

"You caught me red-handed." The chair scraped, he stood, and he strode toward her in the half darkness, those sexy dimples framing his lopsided, kissable smile. "I'm just trying to get out of all the work."

"Yep. It's just a leisurely ride up to Billings. Not work at all."

"Exactly." He folded his arms around her, and she settled against the firm warmth of his chest. He smelled like ripe berries and grass and rain, especially rain. "Take me to bed. Have your way with me. It's your last chance for pleasure for a long while."

"Oh, you never know when I might find myself another husband lying in the road."

"You'd better not." His laugh rumbled through her, touching every part of her, as rich as late night dreams.

"Pa, you can't leave." Chad had a death hold on Jack's knees, and he couldn't take a single step. "You gotta stay. Me and Puddles need you pretty bad."

"I need you, too, partner." Jack laid his hands on the boy's back and hugged him as tight as he could. Love bubbled in his chest. "You know I have to go sell the cows. They can't make it all the way to Billings all by themselves."

"I know." There was so much sorrow in that sigh. "But can't Will do it?"

"No. Remember how Will got shot? He can't ride all day for a while yet. That means I have to go."

"But you were gonna help me teach Puddles. She still don't sit so good."

"Your mama can help you." Jack knelt down.

"But I want *you.*" Chad's arms were wrapped tightly around his neck.

"There's another reason I have to go to Billings." Jack kissed the boy's brow. "Remember I told you that once you learned to take good care of your puppy, you would be ready for your own horse?"

"Oh, boy. Is it true, Pa? Do I really get my own horse?"

"I'm going to pick one out for you, just like I promised."

"Thank you!" Chad's hug turned bruising, then he hopped away. "You'd better hurry, Pa. I need that horse pretty bad."

When Jack turned to Lissa, he was laughing, and so was she, but strain crinkled the areas around her eyes. The wind brushed her soft face, danced through her golden hair, played with the loose, blue-flowered dress not quite concealing her stomach.

He didn't want to leave her. He couldn't bear to ride away, but he was doing it for her—selling her cattle, insuring there would be money in the bank to pay her debts and the hired help and see her safely through the winter— just in case he wasn't there.

He had to prove Palmer wrong, too. He had to try to find out who he wasn't.

"Be safe, Jack." She laid both hands on either side of his jaw, her blue eyes clear and luminous, showing the strength and colors of her heart. "You come back to us."

"I promise it," he vowed, and he would.

Blanche's backyard afforded little privacy, but he kissed her, anyway, tasting her lips, breathing in the summer scent of her hair, remembering the feel of her. It wasn't enough, but it had to see him through the nights ahead, sleeping on the ground without her in his arms.

He rode away, glancing back only twice. She waved once, and then stood still and silent, her skirts ruffled by the wind, watching him leave.

"Tell me you didn't climb a ladder to pick these peaches," Blanche said the moment she stepped through the threshold. "Sophie, tell me you didn't let her."

"I didn't let her." Sophie patted her little son on the back, then put him down on the floor. "Hans and I are going to come over and pick the fruit in the orchard for her. Will is too busy with the second cut of hay, and he's helping Hans with the work. It's the least we can do in return."

"You don't need to do anything." Lissa reached down a third glass to fill with cool cider. "But I do appreciate the help."

"You're really starting to show." Blanche cringed as children's shouts echoed outside the house. "Four more days until school starts. I'm counting."

"I don't know how I'll ever let this one leave my skirts." Sophie sighed, her gaze affectionately fastened on her son, who immediately rolled himself over on the floor.

"Believe me, you'll be glad to get rid of him in five years." Blanche yanked on her sunbonnet strings, the bow stubborn. "I'm cranky today. Morning sickness."

Lissa handed her a glass of cider. "Maybe this will help."

"Thanks." Blanche sipped. "Jack has been gone a while. Have you heard from him?"

"No. I don't expect to. He's taken all but the yearlings and the breeding stock."

"Selling off the herd?"

Lissa reached for a paring knife. "We've had more trouble with rustlers. Jack wanted to sell the cows before they were stolen.''

Sophie quietly reached for one of the knives on the counter. Lissa saw the way her two friends exchanged looks.

"What?''

"It's just a rumor. Something Jeremiah heard the other night when he stopped by the general store.'' Blanche lifted the bucket of fragrant peaches from the floor. "You know how rumors are.''

"Hans heard it, too. It's about Jack.''

"It's that sheriff, that's what it is.'' Blanche set the bucket on the counter. "He told Susan Russell's husband to let him know if anything was missing out of his store. This was after Jack and your hired man Arcada came in for supplies, just before they left town.''

"Did Ike accuse Jack of stealing something?'' A cold foreboding spilled through her. "Jack's gone. He can't defend himself from those kind of rumors.''

"Then Ike told the Russells that Jack was only posing as Michael's cousin, that John Murray never showed up at all.'' Blanche waved her hand dismissively. "Now, I don't believe that for a moment. Anyone can see what fine a man you married.''

"And look how he's helped out, with Hans still recovering from that bullet in his back,'' Sophie added. "A liar and a thief wouldn't do something like that.''

In her heart, Lissa knew Sophie was right. "Jack isn't Michael's cousin. He isn't John Murray.''

Blanche paled. "Do you mean the sheriff is right?''

Lissa saw Jack's credibility and his reputation disintegrate, like old leaves in a strong wind. "Jack is a good man. The truth is, he's never regained his memory from the accident. We don't know who he is.''

Shocked silence filled the room. Sophie peeked around the kitchen wall to check on her son, who was struggling so hard to try to crawl.

"Does that mean the rumor is true?" Blanche whispered the words as if she, like Lissa, was too afraid to voice them aloud. "Is Jack the missing outlaw? The one who's killed up to twenty innocent people, they say, and has done everything from robbing banks to rustling cattle?"

"Jack isn't that outlaw." Lissa felt it with a certainty. "He's the most honorable man I know."

"Others don't feel that way." Sophie's words were kind. "Hans won't say a word against Jack, not after how he's helped us, but some people are having hard times on their spreads. They're looking for someone to blame."

"Some think Jack's been behind the cattle rustling in these parts. It's nearly bankrupted some ranchers. It's a serious thing." Blanche hung her head. "I don't believe the rumors," she added.

"But you know how rumors can get."

"I know." Lissa's hand shook as she grabbed a peach from the brimming bucket. She sliced it in half, then pitted it. Anger scorched her chest, made her breathing rough.

"Maybe the rumors will die down by the time Jack returns." Sophie sounded hopeful.

"Maybe." In her heart, Lissa knew differently. She could feel it like a dark, cold wind.

As Lissa clutched the strings of her reticule tightly in both hands she knew she was angry enough to snap the strings in two. Light shivered in the sky as afternoon turned to evening. A cool breeze whispered in the trees and kicked up small dust devils in the street.

She didn't even knock, just pushed open the jailhouse door. Anger rang in her step, in the strength of her arms as she pushed the door too hard and it slammed against the wood wall.

"Hell, Lissa. You scared the crap out of me." Ike Palmer

swiped one hand through his dark locks, the other hand firmly gripping a loaded Peacemaker.

"You haven't seen anything yet." She yanked the door shut, withering the protesting deputy with a single stare. The lean-limbed man bowed his head and mumbled about checking something outside.

"There's one thing I find greatly unattractive," the sheriff began in that smooth voice of his. "And that's a woman with a temper."

"I've known you most of my life, but I'm only now beginning to see the real Ike Palmer." Distaste for the man soured her mouth.

"You haven't the faintest idea." He looked smug.

Anger flared. "You started those rumors. You told everyone Jack is an outlaw. You know he isn't—"

"I don't know that."

"Don't interrupt me." She slammed her fist on the edge of his desk, rattling the gun and the box of cigars lying there. "How can you hurt a good man?"

"A good man? He's a killer. He's—"

"But you, you're the sheriff. You were too lazy to get off your duff and hunt down those dangerous men."

"I tried—"

"Don't lie to me." She heard her voice rise, knew she was the most angry she'd ever been. "Don't you ever call me friend, stop me on the street, or think that for one instant I would want you for my husband if Jack weren't around."

"But Lissa, I never—"

"I know you did. I don't want you spreading any more rumors about Jack."

"What are you gonna do to stop me? Yell a little louder?"

His insult felt like a slap, this from someone who had always been her friend. "You've gone too far this time, Ike. I'll never forgive you for this."

"You'll thank me in time. He's a criminal, and I'm going

to prove it. The mail is due on the stage today. If I get what I'm looking for, I'm going to hunt him down. I told him not to leave town."

"He went to sell the cattle, and you know it."

"I just hope he brings back your money, and so do a lot of people in this town, people who are hurting because of the outlaws. Who's to say Jack isn't behind all their trouble?" Ike sounded sympathetic, but she wasn't fooled.

Ike's spurs jangled in the silence, echoing in the empty jail cell. He pulled open the door. "I'll look for you at the harvest dance. You'll save me a waltz?"

"Never."

"Well, we'll see what happens between now and then. A woman in your condition and without a proper husband just might have to change her mind."

What she wanted to do was give the sheriff a good kick in the shin. Lissa stepped out onto the street, her anger so hard and tight she didn't know what to do. The day had been long; she'd been helping Blanche put up gallons of plums since dawn. Now she was tired, so very tired.

Jack should be home in a few days.

Lissa jumped out of bed. She couldn't remember the dream that woke her, but the pop of gunfire echoed in the night air. A cool breeze fluttered through the curtains and she pulled them back, gazing out at the darkness.

She saw silvered shadows and a thousand shades of black. Will had brought the breeding cows close to the barn, where they would be more easily defended by one man, but the animals were quiet, bedded down on the ground for the night. Only Pete the bull seemed disturbed, restlessly roaming the length of the solid fencing.

The gunfire continued, but it wasn't over her animals. Lissa grabbed her housecoat and slipped her bare feet into her shoes. She checked on Chad—sound asleep with his puppy—and hurried outside.

She saw a flicker of light in the barn, and then a man emerged, orange flames lighting his face. "Will. Do you know what's going on?"

"Sounds like it's coming from Johanson's place. I'm going to head over there and see if Hans needs any help. Here's the rifle. Bolt yourself in the house. Don't come out, even if there's trouble."

"But I can—"

"The cows aren't worth your life. Besides, I need to know you're in the house in case I decide to shoot any prowlers. Agreed?"

"Agreed." Lissa took the repeating rifle Will handed her. "I'll wait up until you come home. Be safe, Will."

"I'll do my best." The young man dashed off, caught his horse, and galloped off into the night.

The darkness felt ominous, the shadows deeper than before. The crispness of the night air made it clear. Summer was over, autumn was here. Shivering, Lissa headed for the house and bolted herself in.

"The rustlers got away with nearly the entire herd." Sophie's quiet statement echoed through the staircase of the empty schoolhouse.

"The entire herd?" Lissa nearly dropped the pie plate she carried. "Will only told me your losses were bad."

"Bad isn't the word for it." Sophie stepped up onto the landing and led the way into the upper story, her moccasins quiet, but her sorrow rang clear. "With Hans injured by those first rustlers, and now all but a few cows gone, we have nothing to sell—only the hay the neighbors helped him cut."

"You won't have to move, will you?"

Sophie set the crystal cake plate on the cloth-covered table. "Probably. When is Jack expected home?"

"Any time." In truth, six weeks had gone by since he'd left—six weeks without a letter, without a word, without anything.

"Hans wanted to offer him our land first. I don't know if it's worth much with the mortgage on it, but it's better to sell if we can than go bankrupt."

"Oh, Sophie." Lissa set down the pie in order to give her friend a hug. Tears knotted in her throat, and she didn't know what to say. "I wish there was something I could do to help."

"Me, too. But what's done is done." Sophie stepped away, the light of friendship bright in her eyes. "Tonight is a time to put sorrows aside. To dance and celebrate, and raise a lot of money for a lending library."

Lissa tried to smile, but could not help feeling sad for her friend, for good people who didn't deserve such hardship.

"The same thing happened to Maude Hubbard's family." Felicity James strolled in carrying two covered platters, bowed backward by the weight of them.

Lissa jumped to help.

"Nonsense, these big platters will poke you in your tummy." Felicity's eyes sparkled. "You can clear a spot on the table for me."

"How about right here?" Lissa pushed pies and cakes aside to make way for the infamous James sisters' delicious fudge.

"What happened to the Hubbards?" Sophie stepped forward and took one huge platter from Felicity before she accidentally dumped them both on the floor.

"Rustlers struck two days ago. I just heard about it myself. Took their entire herd, except Maude's pet milk cows that were too stubborn to be chased around by a bunch of rustlers." Fudge safely on the table, Felicity led the way toward the staircase. "That's the third family in as many weeks."

"What's Ike doing about it?" Lissa held the banister tightly, careful of the steep steps.

"He's supposed to be hiring more deputies, although I don't know what good that will do unless he actually goes after the outlaws." Felicity shook her head. "Maybe we should elect your husband as sheriff, Lissa. At least he knows how to handle rustlers. How are you doing in this heat?"

"Fine." She brushed the curls out of her face and stepped outside into the cooler breeze. Though the sunshine was hot, autumn was here. "I think we have just the cider to take up."

"Felicity and I will do it. You shouldn't be carrying those heavy jugs." Sophie reached for a crate in the back of her wagon.

"Then I'll start decorating the tables." Lissa climbed into her own wagon and found the box of candles. She scooted the carton to the edge of the tailgate with her foot, then hopped down to the ground.

"Where's your man?" A shadow fell across the lawn at her feet.

She whirled around, startled. "Mr. Hubbard. I'm not sure when Jack will return. He took the cattle to the sale—"

"Did he skip town?" A vein throbbed along the side of his throat.

"No, of course not. He's coming home." His fury radiated like heat from a stove. "Is there something wrong?"

"Damn right, there is. I knew your pa, but I can't keep quiet anymore. It ain't right, you hiding an outlaw in this town. We're peaceable people. Now look at what's happened."

Her throat went dry. "I heard about your misfortune. We've had our share of trouble from the rustlers, too."

"Funny how your man was out of town when all this happened. Who's to say he ain't behind all this, stealing from hardworkin' folk? The sheriff says he's a cattle thief."

"The sheriff is wrong." Lissa held out one hand to stop him.

Milt Hubbard slammed his fist against the bed of her wagon, shaking the vehicle, rattling the cider jugs. "This is your fault. Don't think I don't know what your husband's been up to."

Lissa saw his naked violence, smelled the alcohol on his breath. She took a step back.

Hubbard followed her, shaking his fist, his face growing redder with each word. "Go ahead and run. But you tell that man of yours, wherever he's hiding out, that he ain't gonna get away with it."

Lissa's back hit the broad trunk of a pine. She couldn't retreat any farther. "Jack didn't steal the cattle, Milt."

"No one else around here would do it." That fist slashed the air.

Lissa thought of her baby, saw the unreasonable anger gleam in the drunk man's eyes. She reached up and slapped him, the sound reverberating in the schoolyard. "Don't you threaten me, you big bully."

"Yes, how dare you!" Felicity ran up behind him and swatted him with her reticule, a heavy object that made a terrible cracking sound when it collided with his skull.

"It's her fault. You heard what that man of hers is. Probably ain't even a legal marriage." Hubbard rubbed his head. "He ran off with your money, didn't he? Sold your cattle and kept the cash. Just like a thievin'—"

Anger tore through her. "You don't even know Jack. He would never—"

"Shame on you, harassing a pregnant woman." Blanche barged up and smacked the man with the brim of her hat. "And you smell like a vat of whiskey."

Lissa was startled when Sophie touched her hand.

"Come with me," the quiet woman whispered. Then she led her away from the scene. Lissa could hear Blanche warning Milt Hubbard that she was still in the clutches of morning sickness, and that made her terribly cranky. That would have been funny if Lissa hadn't been crying so hard. Anger warred with a terrible hurt that started deep inside her chest and radiated through her entire being.

"Milt is drunk," Sophie whispered. "Jack would never do those terrible things."

Rumors were powerful. Lissa took a deep breath, hoping Chad never had to hear what other men were saying about his beloved pa.

Fiddle music drew Jack down the street. The lighted schoolhouse shone a block away. The night was cool as autumn tightened its grip on the land. The ground crunched beneath his feet.

He saw her from the doorway, through the mesh of the crowd and the whirl of dancers. She wore a blue dress, the exact shade of her eyes, the color of heaven. Her hair was tied up in a fancy knot, with her soft, ringlet curls framing her angel face.

The long hard miles of riding, the cold nights, the hardship of the trail, all faded, became nothing at the sight of her.

"Pa!" The excited note of Chad's voice rose above the merry music and drone of voices from the crowd. The boy, just a little bit taller and wearing a black coat and trousers raced toward him, arms flung wide.

"Hello, partner." Jack knelt to take the child in his arms, and his chest ached at the sweetness of Chad's hug. "I think you grew a whole foot while I was away."

"I've been waitin' forever."

Jack brushed at the boy's bangs, in his eyes again. "I'm

sorry I took so long getting back to you. But I had to take my time so I could find the right horse for my son.''

"You did get me a horse. Oh, boy!" Awe flickered in those big, dark eyes. "Just like you said."

"Just like I said." Jack stood, took the boy's hand. "I have her tucked into the best stall in the barn back home, just waiting for you."

"Can we see her right now?"

"Let's ask your mother." Jack laughed, glad to be home, glad to see that he meant something, *was* something, and not just a man without a name, without a past. He was Chad's father. Lissa's husband. If that's all he ever knew about himself, it was more than most men could dream of.

"Hey. Murray."

Jack felt a blow to his back, and he spun around, releasing Chad's hand, feet braced. He didn't fall. The shove wasn't enough to knock him to the ground. He faced Milt Hubbard, red-faced and drunk.

"I wanna talk with you, Murray. Or is it Plummer?"

"Chad, go find your mother." Jack felt the low, tight clamp of his spine, knew he was looking at trouble.

"Well, answer me." Hubbard shoved Jack hard.

He braced his feet, caught the man by the wrist and held him prisoner. "Wait until the boy is out of the way."

"Why would a man like you care about a little boy, or about anyone?"

Jack released his grip. The rancher broke away and rubbed his wrist, the band of bruising already visible. "I care a lot. What's gotten into you, Hubbard? Last time I saw you it was at my wedding party. You were more than happy to eat the meal Lissa and her friends prepared. You weren't complaining then."

"That was before I knew you was a liar and a thief."

The music stopped mid-note. Faces turned toward them.

Tense silence settled about the room, thick and cold as fog.

"I'm no liar. And I'm not a thief." Jack saw a few men muscle close to Hubbard, saw the equally dangerous anger in their eyes, in their stance.

He saw the guns holstered, felt the weight of his own. "This is a room full of people. Of women and children. Let's take this outside."

"We wanna know what you done with our cattle."

"Yeah, did you sell my cows with the rest of your herd?"

"Yeah, Jack." It was Palmer's voice this time. "Tell them what you did with the cattle."

"Tell us." Now there were five men closing in on him.

"I didn't take anyone's cattle. Sheriff, help me calm down these men. You don't want any trouble in the schoolhouse. People could get hurt."

"You mean *you* could." Hubbard threw a punch.

Jack sidestepped, unharmed. "I'm not Dillon Plummer. I have evidence. I—"

"My boys ain't gonna have nothing to eat this winter because of you." Hubbard threw another punch, then a second.

Jack dodged both of them.

"The rustling has started up again, just about the time you were supposed to have left town." Jim Anders stepped forward, fists clenched. "I lost my entire herd. Everything. Even the milk cow. How am I gonna pay my mortgage? I got children needing food and a roof over their heads. And you stole from them. Get a rope, boys."

"I got a rope," the sheriff offered.

"No!" Lissa's voice, sharp and high. "Mr. Anders, you're drunk. You're all drunk. Don't you dare—"

"Havin' a woman defend you, huh, Plummer?" Bob Riley jeered. "Hiding behind her skirts while you steal from us. Now lettin' her beg for your life."

"Calm down, now." Jack held up both hands, trying to

figure out how best to stop the men. He had guns, but violence was no solution. These were ranchers, not outlaws. "Anders, put down that rope and listen to me."

"Grab his hands!" Anders shouted.

"Let's take him outside," another added.

"Yeah, the maple in the yard will be a good place to hang him." Hubbard balled his right hand into a fist.

"No!" Lissa saw the punch, saw Jack dodge the blow. As powerful as he was, he was only one man.

He stood tall and calm, his shoulders braced, trying to get the drunken men to listen to him. He dodged another blow, but Anders hit him from behind. Jack dropped to his knees, and the men descended on him.

"Mama!" Chad's anguish tore through her. He hid his face in her skirts, crying for all he was worth. She could not leave her son. She could not save her husband.

"Sophie will take him." Blanche fought through the crowd and lifted Chad by the forearms. He fought her, but he settled against Sophie, crying inconsolably, his heart breaking.

"Palmer, stop those men right now." Blanche, still cranky from her bad bout of all day morning sickness, took after the sheriff. "This here is a civilized gathering—"

Blanche's scolding became background noise as Lissa pushed her way through the crowd. Her round shape made it hard to squeeze through the wall of people frozen by the sight of violence.

"Jack." She gasped. Men surrounded him, had lifted him up between them and were carrying him out the door. "Jack!"

The men ignored her, tumbling out into the cool night. What would make them stop? She snatched a broom that leaned in the corner of the foyer.

"That's enough, boys." Palmer shouldered past her. "Put him down. This is a civilized town. We don't stand for vigilante justice."

"He deserves to hang." Hubbard grabbed the noose from Anders.

"He will, trust me."

Lissa watched in horror as Ike Palmer approached the group. Jack hit the ground; she heard the air rush out of his lungs. He lay on the cold, hard dirt, gasping for breath. She pushed past Milt Hubbard and dropped to her knees. "Jack."

"Lissa, I don't want you in the middle of this."

"I'm fine. But you're not." She laid her hand against his jaw, felt whiskery stubble, the heat of his skin, and the wetness of blood.

"Out of the way, Lissa." Palmer took her by the shoulder. "I don't want to push a pregnant woman, but I will if that's what it takes for me to bring in my prisoner."

"Prisoner?"

"Your husband is under arrest."

Chapter Eighteen

The cell was cool with the night's frost. Jack's head pounded, his lip bled, and his ribs ached something fierce, but he wasn't seriously hurt. It wasn't himself he worried about. It was Lissa. He had hated the horror on her face, hated knowing she had to live with consequences she hadn't created.

Midnight passed; he could tell by the circling motion of the stars. The harvest dance had broken up an hour before. He'd heard the creak and rattle of buggies and wagons rolling past on the road outside. The small, barred window didn't allow him to see much, but he could hear the murmur of voices as families walked to their homes in town, and the faint, tinny piano music at the saloon across the street.

How was Lissa doing? It was all he could think about. The image lingered in his mind of her sitting at one of the candlelit tables, the light glittering in her golden hair, the softness of her face as she leaned to speak with one of the James sisters.

Her pregnancy had advanced while he was gone. He'd known it would, of course. The roundness of her stomach was unmistakable now. She looked serene sitting there, happy, and the instant he'd stepped through the door, he'd taken that serenity from her.

Bitterness twisted his stomach, soured his mouth. After finding the best price for their cattle, he'd spent an extra week trying to figure out who he was, or wasn't. The local sheriff wasn't too helpful. Sure, he tried, but he was young and new at the job. The former sheriff had died of a fever, leaving the office unfilled for a few months.

So, Jack and Arcada had leafed through the wanted posters and the leaflets about wanted men, and tried to find a match. Nothing. At least he could say with confidence he wasn't an outlaw.

He'd ridden home with such great plans. His conscience clear, he envisioned building up the ranch, maybe buying more land, adding an addition to the house with a play-room for Chad, a hobby room for Lissa, and a nursery for the baby. He even thought about breeding some horses, to diversify a little. Most of all, when the workday was done, he envisioned coming home to bask in the light of Lissa's smile.

How he'd missed her. How he'd ached for her, hurt without her to complete him. When the ranch had rolled into view, it was dark—no lights warming the windows, chasing away the night. Then he remembered her plans for the dance, and headed to town—headed straight into trouble.

Until he could prove the sheriff wrong and hunt down the true rustlers, his wife and son would not be safe.

"Now I got you right where I want you."

Jack's head ached at the sheriff's triumphant voice. "I

didn't throw the first punch, Palmer. You saw what happened. Half the town saw what happened."

"Assault is only the charge I'm using to keep you here." Palmer's spurs clinked against the stone floor as he paced in front of the barred cell door. "This morning I'm getting the mayor to authorize sending a messenger. That damn sheriff's office isn't answering my letter. I bet they'll listen when they find out who I have cooling his heels in my jail."

Jack's head pounded at the brightness of the new morning's light. "I'm not Dillon Plummer."

"Bull." Palmer kicked the bars. The door rattled.

Jack's head screamed with pain. He hadn't taken that hard a punch last night, but it had been directly over his old injury.

A door squeaked open. "Palmer?" Lissa called, her voice tense and tight.

He remembered how she'd fought through the crowd to reach him. He remembered being afraid someone would push her or knock her to the ground. She might be strong, but she was fragile, too, and she was carrying their child.

"Don't get your hopes up. I'm not letting her see you." Palmer turned away. A door closed, and he couldn't hear anything more, but at least the piercing, bright sunshine had faded.

In the dim corner cell, Jack rubbed his forehead. He knew Lissa would get him out. He'd made sure Arcada had the evidence they searched so hard for during their stay in Billings.

"You thought I was angry before," she warned Ike the minute he stepped into the jailhouse. "It's nothing compared to what I'm feeling now."

"Why did you bring him?" Palmer gestured toward the man behind her.

"Arcada insisted on coming. And I'm glad. I don't trust myself alone with you."

"You can't control yourself around me, is that it?"

"I would never want you, Ike. Surely even a man as thickheaded as you can figure that out by now." She would never forget the sight of Jack being dragged away, cuffed and ostracized, nor the solid strength that held him up, unbowed and proud even in the dark, even against the angry mob.

Jack was no outlaw. If she'd ever had her doubts, they were silenced now. He could have outshot all of those men if he'd chosen to, or at the very least outfought them, but he wasn't a violent man. He was made of much finer stuff. He sought peace, not conflict, solutions, not problems.

"I'm not going to let your *husband* go because you insult me." He raked one beefy hand through his dark hair. "What is it that you want, Lissa?"

"I'll go to Billings myself if I have to. That's the closest sheriff, besides you. I'm going to ask for their help."

"To put away your husband, you mean?" He laughed.

"No, to prove his innocence. I intend to ask the mayor to make sure you hold off with your brand of justice until I return."

"You?" Palmer shook his head. "Right. You're going to prove your husband isn't an outlaw. Good luck. I—"

Arcada stepped forward. "I have the proof."

Lissa lost her breath. She gazed up at him, speechless. The ranch hand pulled a folded piece of paper out of his shirt pocket and handed it to her. The double holsters he wore caught the light, the gleam of the loaded pistols a statement to the sheriff—a statement no one could miss.

"What the hell is that?" Palmer demanded. He reached to snatch the sheet out of her hands, but she dodged him.

"Leave her be, Sheriff." Arcada's voice. "You don't want to cross me."

Lissa's fingers shook as she unfolded the page—a wanted notice. She saw a drawing of a dark-eyed man, unkempt and wild-eyed. Studying the caption beneath the portrait she read, "Dillon Plummer. Five-foot-ten, brown eyes, missing front teeth." She lifted her gaze, then handed the paper to Palmer.

He glanced at the sketch. The arrogant triumph on his face dimmed a notch. "Why should I trust you? You're on Jack's payroll. You could have faked this—"

"I didn't. The real Dillon Plummer was arrested a month ago in Colorado for various crimes, including the murder of a United States Marshal in Montana Territory." Arcada laid both hands on his hips, inches from his gleaming revolvers. "You can ride up to Billings and check with the sheriff if you doubt my word."

Lissa felt numb. Her knees wobbled. She laid her hand on her stomach and settled into the closest chair. "You could have told me."

"Palmer was the one who needed to hear it," Arcada said simply. "You already knew Jack was innocent."

She had. It just would have been nice to know Jack could be easily freed. "Release him, Ike."

He turned his back to her, one hand rubbing his chin back and forth. She could hear him breathe, hear Arcada take a step closer.

"There's still the matter of the missing cattle. Entire herds. I can't overlook that."

"You know he was in Billings. If you need proof, you can see the bank receipt. It takes time to sell cattle and to prove your own innocence." Lissa shifted in the chair.

"He assaulted Hubbard."

"Hubbard assaulted him."

The sheriff faced her, his mouth a hard, fine line, unforgiving, unrelenting. "I've changed my mind about marrying you, Lissa. It would be too much trouble teaching you your place."

He lifted the ring of keys from the wall peg with a sharp angry jingle, then strode away, spurs clicking.

She held her anger in check, her hands fists, wondering how she could have considered his proposal at all, so long ago now. She'd been blinded by grief, had just lost Michael. She'd known Palmer all her life, and had never seen the blackness of his heart or the way he liked to harm others.

Bootsteps, slow and powerful, drew her gaze. Jack strode through the threshold, shoulders straight, upright and strong. His gaze met hers instantly, and her heart soared. It was a rich, light, dizzying sensation, more powerful than anything she'd ever known.

He took her hand, and her entire body tingled. "You're a beautiful sight."

His goodness and his respect, love, and honor for her shone in his eyes, rang in his voice. He was truly a man she could believe in—now, and for the rest of her life.

"You're hurt." Her stomach twisted at the sight of the bruise over his eye and the swollen cut to his lip.

"It's nothing." He dismissed his injury with a shrug. "All I could think of was you. After what happened last night, what you had to endure."

"Me?" Her heart had ached for him all night. "You were the one locked up in a cold cell. I bet you didn't have a blanket. You were hurt. I didn't know if I could get you released this morning."

"I'm not the one who grew up here, who knew everyone at the dance last night. Those are your friends, and I embarrassed you—"

"Don't say that. Don't ever say that." She didn't care if they were on the boardwalk in the middle of the town. She wrapped her arms around him, felt the steady strength in his shoulders, and buried her face against his chest. Tears pricked behind her eyes, and she tried hard to fight them.

His arms folded around her, and he just held her for a long time. The street noise and the sounds of the town vanished. All there was, all there would ever be, was Jack.

"I don't want to bring shame to you." His voice rang so deep and low.

"You can't do that." She stepped away, but wouldn't let go of him. "I've lived with you for more than half a year, I've slept with you, made love with you. I've seen the way you stand up to injustice, and the way you refuse to use violence on unarmed men. No matter what happens, I believe in you. I know the kind of man you are deep inside, where it counts."

His throat tightened. Her words made him hurt. Jack knew people were watching them, or he would have taken her in his arms again, held her close, as if he'd never let her go. He didn't need memories to know he'd never loved anyone the way he loved Lissa. Right now. Forever.

"Compliment a man like that, and you're likely to make him hungry." He wanted to make her smile, needed to see the gentle light that warmed her eyes when she laughed. "He might want some huckleberry pancakes, sausage, eggs. A pot of his wife's fresh coffee."

"Didn't eat well while you were away?"

"Nothing was right while I was away." He caught her hands in his. "You look as if you've been eating."

His gaze traveled to her belly, and she laughed. "I look as if I ate a melon."

"You've been surely doing something." Wickedness twinkled in his blue eyes. "I'm hungry for that, too."

His hand settled across the curve of her abdomen. Her heart skipped at the tenderness of his touch. She looked up at the humor fading from his eyes. A different emotion shone there—a reverence, an affection so great it made her hurt inside, deep inside, where dreams and fairy-tale wishes lived.

"He's not kicking right now." She laid her hand on Jack's, felt the wondrous male texture of his skin.

"You can feel him?"

"He's a late night kicker. Right when I'm half asleep he starts up." Over Jack's shoulder Lissa saw a few ranchers lining up on the boardwalk across the street, watching them.

Jack glanced over his shoulder, held their gaze, then turned back. "We'd best be going. I don't know how welcome I am."

"You belong here. With me." She laid her hand in his, smiled when his fingers wrapped around her elbow to help her up into the wagon. She settled her skirts on the seat and was proud when he climbed up into the wagon beside her and took the reins in his capable hands.

He was her husband and she loved him. She knew the man he was. She didn't care what anyone thought.

He released the brake and touched the reins against Charlie's backside. The Clydesdale handily pulled them down the quiet morning street, made quieter by the sight of Jack, freed from jail.

Lissa caught sight of Susan Russell in the front door of her shop. She waved, and Lissa's chest tightened. She waved back, grateful for Susan's show of friendship.

"Things are likely to get worse before they get better." Jack sounded grave as he headed the wagon out of town, down the sloping road toward home. "I don't know why the ranchers are blaming me for their losses, but I have a suspicion who planted the idea in their heads."

"Palmer?"

A muscle in Jack's jaw jumped. "He's the law around here. He can make life difficult for me, and for you."

"I don't care. I believe in you." Just looking at him, just sitting beside him, filled her with a sweet pride. She laid her hand on his forearm, felt the heat of his sun-browned skin, the texture of downy hair and steely muscle. "I missed you."

His gaze met hers, sparkling with an affection that touched her deep inside. Then mischief flickered, and he pulled the wagon to a stop.

"What are you doing?"

"Going to say a proper hello to my wife." He set the brake, took her hand in his, and helped her down to the ground. "I can't wait."

She laughed. "We're only a mile from home."

"That's one mile too long for this man." Jack patted Charlie's neck, and the big horse stomped his front hoof, uncertain that it was a wise idea to just stop along the road. "As I see it, there's trees and a little privacy, and that's really all we need. Come here."

Her shoes crunched over fallen leaves. She laughed as he tugged her into his arms, against the grandeur of him. How good he smelled, how wondrous he felt. His mouth found hers and she opened to him, already enchanted by the heated caress of his kiss, of lips and tongue and passion.

"Over this way." His kiss ended, and he led her through low bushes and beneath a yellow and orange maple. Graceful limbs stretched overhead, dappling the sun and shade.

"This should be just fine." He drew her against him, fiddled with the bow at her chin. Her ribbons came loose and he dropped her best sunbonnet on the ground. "I want to make love to my wife."

"We're close to home," she reminded him as he popped open several buttons on her dress. "Close to our own bed."

"I've always wanted to make love on a bed of leaves." He slid the fabric down her arms, and the garment puddled over the curve of her stomach. "Besides, once we get home Chad will come running, the ranch hands are there, there's business to be done. No, if we go straight home there will be a long wait before we can be alone."

He lifted the dress and the chemise over her belly, and the garments slid to the ground. His mouth curved into that sexy, lopsided grin she loved so much, but the laughter faded and could not dim the shine of love that gleamed in his eyes. "You look beautiful."

She blushed. "Soon I'll look like a watermelon."

"You are beautiful to me." His hand curved beneath her jaw, tipping her chin upward. His gaze met hers and there could be no doubt, not a single solitary doubt, that he meant those words, felt them from the bottom of his heart.

Tears burned in her throat and behind her eyes. This time when he kissed her it tasted like magic. Every touch set her on fire, changed something deep inside her. He laid her down on the warmth of his shirt spread over a bed of leaves. He took his time touching her, caressing her breasts and her inner thighs. His words tingled against her mouth when he broke their kisses long enough to speak, to tell her how much he'd missed her, to admire the changes in her body.

How could a woman keep her heart from such a man? Lissa had tried, had vowed to herself when she buried Michael she would never hurt like that again, never hand over her love and a part of herself, knowing how vulnerable it made her. She had lost far too many people, buried them and mourned them. She had agreed to marry John Murray for the convenience, for comfort, and more children.

This man she had found on the road and brought home, he wasn't convenient. He was myth and reality, legend and truth, a man as grand as the mountains, and when he kissed every curve of her pregnant stomach, he was a man who owned her heart—completely, without reserve or doubts, without any conditions at all.

When he entered her, joining their bodies in a rush of

heat and need and wanting, it was with more than just passion. It was with love, pure, true and unbreakable.

"Pa!" Chad ran out of the house, the puppy barking at his heels. "You came!"

"I hope you saved some breakfast for me." Jack set the brake and hopped to the ground. He caught both of Lissa's hands. It was good to be home, so very good. He helped her to the ground, unable to look away from her, from this woman to whom he owed so much.

"I ate all the pancakes, me and Puddles." Chad's arms were flung out and then wrapped tight around Jack's knees. "Maybe Mama could make you some more. Me and Puddles could eat more sausages."

"Oh, you could?" Lissa laughed, tipping her head back just enough to scatter those luxurious gold curls. "I suppose I could be talked into cooking up lots of sausages."

"I would like that." Jack straightened, stood in the light of her smile. "After I eat, I'll take Chad to meet his new horse. Would you like that?"

"Oh, boy!" Chad raced toward the front steps. "Hurry up, Mama. You need to cook real fast."

Laughter filled him up. Jack took Lissa's hand in his, felt the snap of want and the memory of every time he'd loved her. Her fingers twined with his, holding him tightly, and they walked to the house together. Yep, it was good to be home.

"Why did you let Murray go?" Deakins strode into the jailhouse with an envelope in hand. "We finally got the goods on him. Look. It's from Billings."

"Why in the hell did they wait so damned long?" Palmer kicked the chair, sent it flying across the room. It slammed into the log wall with a crash that echoed through the empty jail and straight through his heart.

"That sheriff from Billings is probably just busy. That's why he took so long." Deakins dropped the letter on the desk. "Want me to ride out to the ranch and bring him in?"

"No, damn it. There's no way in hell Jack could be Dillon Plummer." He clenched his fists. He wanted to hit something. Instead, he grabbed up the envelope and tore open the flap. He knew what he would find, but he just had to see it—just in case that high and mighty Jack whatever-his-name-was and his hired man weren't telling the truth. It wasn't a big hope.

He unfolded the sheets of paper. There were two. The handwritten scrawl from a rather talkative lawman who told of Plummer's capture, just like Arcada said. But there was more—mention of a missing marshal who Plummer admitted to killing. The body had never been found.

A chill snaked down the back of Palmer's neck. He knew before he looked at the second page he would see words describing a lawman whose characteristics were the same as Jack's. Jack Emerson—thirty-two years old. Born December tenth, federal marshal, twice-decorated, six-foot-two, dark blond hair, blue eyes.

That chill snaking down his neck wrapped around his spine and paralyzed him. He'd thrown a United States Marshal in jail and was framing him for cattle theft, a hanging offense.

"Somethin' wrong, Sheriff?" Deakins inched closer.

"Nothing is wrong." He folded up the sheets of paper and shoved them into his shirt pocket. He would burn the information as soon as he could get away from his deputy.

Whole herds brought in thousands of dollars at a time. Rustling was good business. Soon the fine citizens of Sweetwater Gulch would soon be witnessing a lynching.

* * *

"Are you done yet, Pa?"

"Look at my plate. Is it empty?"

"No. But you could have gotten real full. Did you?"

Lissa loved seeing her son so happy. He shone like a midday sun in Jack's presence, all bright joy and adoration for the man he imitated at every chance. Jack set down his fork and cocked his head, his smile lopsided on his face.

Chad did the same.

"Let's share that last sausage, and then we'll head out to the barn. Is that a deal?"

"Deal."

Puddles barked, Winston eyed the open jar of maple syrup, and Lissa poured Jack a second cup of coffee.

"He can take it with him to the barn," she explained when Chad looked ready to protest.

Jack dipped the last link of sausage into the syrup, cut it in two. "What did you do with the sugar?"

"I was making apple butter yesterday." She snatched the sugar crock from the counter. "If I'd known you were coming, I would have baked a pie."

"Hmm. You could always bake this afternoon." Jack took the crock from her grip and grabbed a spoon.

"Hurry, Pa," Chad pleaded, holding open the door. "Please?"

"Getting your first horse is a mighty important event." Jack' s voice rang deep and low, but his eyes twinkled and he gave her a wink. "Would you like to accompany us to the barn?"

"It would be my honor." She took the arm he offered and stepped out into the cool morning, her heart and her life brimming full.

Chapter Nineteen

Hard frost crunched beneath Jack's boots as he headed for the barn. Late autumn scented the foggy air. White coated the green of the grass and iced the shallow puddles in the yard. A few stubborn leaves clung to overhead branches, rattling in the wind.

Winter wasn't far off.

A low growl, deep and threatening, drew his attention. Cows huddled together, milling against the split rail fence. He heard the growl again, a wildcat's cry, and then the lower, threatening rumble of the bull.

"Will!" Jack couldn't face a wildcat unarmed. He threw open the barn doors and ran for the tack room. No answer. Will had promised to ride the fence line all night. He was probably sound asleep in his little cabin uphill from the barn.

Jack grabbed the repeating rifle from above the door-frame and a handful of bullets from the shelf. All was calm in the barn, the horses and milk cow watching him with surprised gazes.

The wildcat's cry split the air. There wasn't much time. Jack raced out into the morning, skidded on ice and hopped over the fence. He fired a shot into the air, but the wildcat didn't startle. Jack kept running toward Pete, who stood facing the cat, all four feet braced for a fight, head down.

There was no choice. A mountain lion and livestock didn't mix. Neither did children. He heard the cabin door open and Chad's voice ring in the cold air.

"Mama, I'm goin' to feed my horse, like Pa says!"

Lissa's answer was lost across the distance.

"Lissa! Keep the boy in the house!"

The wildcat leaped just as he squeezed off a shot. Pete charged. Jack fired again, but the nimble cougar was already a blur in the fields. Probably hedging its bets, it would return when the pickings were easier.

Jack checked to make sure Chad was nowhere in sight. Knowing the boy was safe, he gave chase. Pete was already charging after the fleeing cat. Jack ran, then stopped when he was certain the cat was no immediate threat to his family or his herd.

Lissa opened the back door when she saw him coming. The wind battered her dress, plastering it tight against her body. The grace of her struck him, as always.

"What is it?" There was fear in her voice.

"Not the rustlers." Jack set the rifle on the pegs high on the wall of the porch, out of a small child's reach, and swept into the warm kitchen. "A mountain lion is bothering the stock. Must be sick or hurt to be hunting this low this time of year. There's still a lot of good hunting for the cats up in those mountains."

"Did he get any of my cows?" Lissa closed the door behind him.

"He wanted to, but that bull of yours was putting up a good fight. Good thing I went out to do the barn work when I did." A fire crackled in the fireplace, warming both rooms, and the cookstove puffed smoke every time the wind gusted. The heat felt good. He grabbed the coffeepot from the stove so Lissa wouldn't have to. She looked tired, and was moving slowly. He worried about her. "I'm going to need to pack a meal. Some of that beef jerky would do us just fine. I don't want you to do any extra cooking."

"I baked just yesterday. I have fresh biscuits and bread." She pushed the sugar jar in his direction.

How beautiful she was. Since he'd been back, everything had changed. Everything was better, felt right, felt whole.

Chad tugged on Jack's trouser leg. "The big cat didn't get my Comet, did she?"

"No, son. Your mare is tucked safe and sound in the barn. The mountain lions can't get in there." He sipped the steaming coffee. "I'm going to take either Will or Arcada with me. We're going to hunt down the cat, so we don't have to worry about someone when he plays outside."

Lines tightened around her eyes. "Good. I can get a bedroll together for you right now."

"No, I can do it. I just need one more cup if I'm going to head out. I'll ask one of the hands to do the barn work this morning. I don't want you out there cleaning pens and milking the cow."

"I'm perfectly capable, but it's nice to be pampered." She brushed a kiss across his cheek. He turned and caught her mouth, tasting her heat, her passion. As always, his body responded. Need and desire mixed in his blood. "Let me go gather up a meal for you and Will."

"I'll be home for supper." He knelt down to explain to Chad that their work with his new mare would be postponed for a day. As he spoke, he glanced over the boy's head to watch her move around the kitchen.

He loved her. How he loved her.

* * *

"Pa said a man has to treat his horse right." Chad tossed one of Jack's rolled up socks the length of the cabin. Puddles took off, obediently hunting it down. "And that goes for his dog, too. Pa said one day Puddles can bring back a geese we hunted. But first I gotta teach her to bring things back."

Tiny snowflakes fluttered outside in the twilight, weightless, swirling but not quite falling. The air smelled like winter, and the house felt cozy with the fire in the hearth.

Lissa gave the dough one last sweep with her rolling pin, then began carefully cutting it into pieces.

"When's Pa gonna be back?"

"I expect him any time now." Lissa pinched the dough in place over the two pie plates.

"I wanna show him how good Puddles retrieves." Chad dropped to his knees to praise the half-grown puppy that came loping across the wood floor, floppy paws sliding. The boy's shoulders were braced just like Jack's often were, the half-smile on his face an exact replica.

Love and a rare happiness joined in Lissa's heart. The baby moved, then gave her a good kick in the ribs. She laid her hand there, listening to the fire crackle at the hearth, smelling the chicken potpies ready to bake in the oven, a treat for Jack when he came in from the cold.

Puddles stopped retrieving and lifted her nose. A noise echoed somewhere outside the house. The dog barked and raced to the door.

"Pa!" Chad dashed to the window.

Lissa took one look at the dog barking protectively, and she knew whoever was outside their door couldn't be Jack. She lifted the curtain over her kitchen counter and saw a rider dismount at her front steps. The sun was near to

setting, and shadows cloaked the man's face. She knew it
wasn't Hans Johanson by the look of the horse.

"Chad. Please take Puddles into your bedroom."

"Yes, Mama." Chad, shoulders sagging because his
beloved pa wasn't home yet, obediently called Puddles to
him. The young puppy wasn't sure, but at a second command ran to her little boy's side.

A knock on the door rattled it, and fear leaped into
Lissa's heart. Had something happened to Jack? She threw
open the door, tried to stay calm. Tried to remember how
Jack had already faced another mountain lion and won,
so long ago now. He was a strong, intelligent man, and a
good hunter.

"Bill Lambert." She saw the rancher's rifle and the hard
look on his face. "What's—"

"Where's that husband of yours?" he interrupted, his
voice brittle and tense. "Where is he?"

"He isn't home yet. I can tell him that you called."

"That ain't good enough." The rancher's hand shot
out, throwing wide the door. Lissa jumped back, startled,
then she saw the men with him—maybe six, maybe ten.
Snow caught in the lamplight, shivered on the hat brims
and shoulders of the angry mob. "I ain't gonna ask again.
Where is he?"

"T-tracking a mountain lion."

"Sure he is!" A voice jeered in the back. "He's out
stealing another herd right now."

"Quiet!" Lambert lumbered in the door. He towered
over her, his face set and his hand tensed around the stock
of his rifle. "We're gonna wait until that bastard shows."

"If he knows what's good for him, he'll take off for
Canada at a dead run," another called.

"He didn't stand and fight at the harvest dance. He's a
damned coward."

"Out of my house." Anger popped through her. She

grabbed her broom from the corner and held it tight. "Get out. Don't you dare insult my husband, you big oaf."

"Lissa." Lambert took her by the arm and tried to push her away.

She smacked his knuckles with her broom handle. "Don't you manhandle me." Her pregnancy made her awkward, but she gave Lambert another smack on the back of his hand. "I want you off my property, Bill. How dare you push me around? You know how I lost my last two babies."

Some of the rage slipped from Lambert's face. His shoulders sank a little. "I didn't mean to hurt you, Lissa. I just lost my whole herd, breeding stock and all—everything my wife and sons have worked for."

"And that's my fault?"

"Well, no." His grip on the rifle slackened. "It's just that we got reason to think your man is responsible. Palmer arrested him for being that outlaw."

"Palmer also released him when Jack proved he wasn't."

"You don't know who he is." Reggie Gannon stepped forward. "I tell you one thing. No one can vouch for that man of yours. He's not around every time a herd goes missing."

"But he brought in the other rustlers."

"Don't mean he wasn't one of them." Lambert shook his head. "We're waitin' for him whether you like it or not, Lissa."

"Not in my house. And not on my porch. All of you. Out." Lissa swung her broom, so angry that tears blurred her eyes. "You wait in the dark, in the snow. Get off the porch."

"Lissa." Lambert grabbed the broom, stopping it before she could do harm. "We'll wait where we want."

"No you won't." Jack's voice, as deep and as powerful as the encroaching darkness, sliced through the drone of the arguing men. "Lambert, let go of my wife."

Lissa heard the click of a revolver's hammer, saw the crowd of men part. Jack's boots knelled on the wooden porch as he stepped into the pool of lamplight. He strode toward her with the strength of a hero, with the unyielding courage of legend, as dangerous as any outlaw.

"You heard what I said," Jack ground out. "Let go of my wife."

Lambert released his hold on her broom. "We've been waiting for you, Jack. We've got business to discuss."

"Looked to me like you were manhandling a pregnant woman." Jack released the hammer of his gleaming Peacemaker, then holstered the gun. He stood proud and unafraid, his voice hard and clear. "Never threaten my wife again. Do you understand?"

"Where have you been, that's what—"

"Do you understand?" Those words were as lethal as a bullet.

Lissa's heart soared. Even though he was outnumbered, there he was, protecting her, standing up for her in a way no one ever had.

Lambert ducked his head. "I hear you. But I want my cattle back. Where did you take them?"

"I never touched your herd, Lambert." Jack caught her hand. "Are you all right?"

"Shaky, but I'm fine." She wanted to thank him, to tell him all he was to her, but the tension in the air, the hard, angry faces of the ranchers and ranch hands, kept her silent.

"Go inside. I'll be right with you."

"I won't leave." She knew the men crowding onto her porch, had known them all since grade school. "I said you were hunting a mountain lion, but they wouldn't believe me."

"It's a likely story, Jack. And a mighty big coincidence." Lambert's hold never loosened on his rifle. "I want my animals back."

"Where's the cattle?" Gannon demanded.

"If he don't talk, maybe we ought to take everything from him and his family, and see how he likes it!" Vic Bell shouted.

"Hell, might as well hang him now."

"I've got a rope."

Jack tensed in the shadows, his strength and power unmistakable. "This is America, boys, where a man is innocent until proven guilty."

"Where were you today? I bet it proves you guilty," Lambert challenged.

"I said I was tracking a wildcat that had been threatening my herd. I can prove it." Jack gave Lambert a shove. "Out of my way."

Lambert, a smaller man, stepped aside. The crowd parted as Jack strode toward his horse standing in the shadows. "Lissa. Bring me some light."

She grabbed the tin lamp by the door and carried it past the men who had threatened her, who threatened her still. Her knees shook, her blood felt shivery in her veins, but she held her chin steady. She would not falter as she neared the steps.

Jack reached out. His fingers brushed hers as he took the light. His face was set in stone, and his gaze was steady and certain. "Thank you."

Her belief in this man would never end. He turned the wick, and a flame of light danced over the skiff of snow crusting the earth and illuminated the back of his gelding, where a mountain lion's body lay tied behind the saddle, limp and lifeless.

"I was out hunting a wildcat." Jack faced the men. "I have a carcass to prove it. And if that isn't enough, Will was with me. You all know Will. He's no liar."

The foreman stepped into the shadowed light, his revolver raised and ready. "I say Jack's telling the truth. I was with him the entire day. And any man who accuses Jack of stealing cattle is accusing me of the same."

"I want to believe you, Will." Lambert strode forward, his step as harsh as his voice. "I lost everything today. I'm going to find the man responsible, I swear it. I can only hope you ain't involved."

"Go home, boys." Jack held the lamp, but his free hand curled over the handle of his revolver.

The men, understanding what Jack didn't say, filed off the porch and into the night. He waited until the last man had mounted up and galloped away before he nodded to Will.

Will lowered his rifle. "I don't like what I saw tonight."

"Neither do I." Jack's anger tasted bitter in his mouth, but he swallowed it, anyway. Acting out of anger never did anyone a bit of good. "Lissa, how are you?"

"Scared." She stepped into his arms, fragile and trembling. The mob tonight had threatened her. She had every right to her fear. "Chad is in his room. I need to go to him."

"I'll be right in." He released her, even though he wanted to hold her tight and to protect her for all he was worth.

She took the light, leaving only darkness in her wake.

"I have something for you."

Lissa looked up at Jack's voice. The length of her unbound hair shimmered down her back, and she held the brush in mid-stroke. Her heart thumped. The air in her chest escaped. He stood framed in the threshold, iron-hewn and darkly handsome, but it was the object held in his hands that made her stomach drop, that made her throat ache.

"I bought this when I was in Billings. This is for the

baby." His footsteps tapped on the floor. He set the cradle down at the foot of the bed.

The baby. She could not lift her gaze from the sight of the carved spool sides, snug and safe. She thought of the trunk in the attic, pushed back into the corner where a part of her heart had been buried. Her tears and grief and emptiness were packed between the folds of the tiny baby gowns and hats and socks stored there. Amid the quilt and blankets were a hundred lost hopes.

She set down the brush, laid her hand over the breadth of her stomach. Life kicked there, just beneath her palm.

Jack raked a hand through his hair, looking lost at her lack of response. "When I was up in the attic before I took the cattle to market, I saw the crib tucked beneath the eaves. I thought maybe this would work real nice, until the baby was bigger. I can bring it down for you. Maybe dust it off and give it a new coat of oil."

"The cradle is beautiful, Jack." She somehow found her voice, somehow faced the hole in her heart. "I don't want you to bring down the crib. Not just yet."

"But I thought—"

Where he had hoped to please her, she could see he now thought he'd failed. She trailed her fingertips over the finely carved sides, over the spindles of wood perfectly made. "I would like nothing more than to lay our child here. But I want to see him safely born first."

"I see." His arms folded her tight to his chest. She heard the dependable beat of his heart beneath her ear, felt his steady comfort. His kiss brushed her brow, so tender and loving that tears burned her eyes.

Loving hurt. It hurt to open up her heart again, but protecting her heart and keeping her distance could never be worth missing a single opportunity to love this man— to feel his magnificent presence, to hold him tight in her arms.

"This baby is going to be fine, Lissa." His voice vibrated through her, becoming part of her. "You have to believe."

"I guess I have no other choice." She closed her eyes when their lips met.

Love opened up a woman's heart, claimed a space, made her vulnerable. The chance to truly love Jack, to truly love him, though, made her brave.

"Jack."

A man's voice, hard and angry, distorted by dream. A shaft of light penetrated the darkness, flickering across the nighttime room. He saw the knob of a four-poster bed, felt the quick bite of fear at his chest, heard the fast, shaky breathing of someone else—a little boy, littler than he was.

"Jack. Joey. Show your faces, boys. Come out, or hell if I won't make it harder on you." That voice brought more fear, loud enough to echo, to draw a gasp from the little boy.

Joey. A brother. Jack wrapped his arm around the child protectively. He knew Father was lying. He always lied about hitting. That's how they'd lost Mama, even though Jack had tried to protect her.

He'd stood right between Mama and Father, but when the blow hit, it had broken Jack's arm. And Mama, well, she'd never woken up. They buried her two days later.

Jack had cried at the funeral, even though he was eight years old, for the grief at losing his mother beat at him. The guilt of not being strong enough to protect her hurt him more than any of Father's blows ever could.

Now he had to protect Joey. From this day on, Father would never break Joey's arm. Jack would make sure of it.

"Hide, Joey." Jack pushed the boy beneath the bed and tugged the hem of the quilt all the way to the floor. Then he stood to face his father's wrath. "I was the one who spilled the last of the milk, Father."

Footsteps crashed through the silence. The lantern tossed swing-

ing light through the room, then straight into his eyes. Jack didn't wince when he heard the clink of a buckle or the hiss as Father jerked off his belt.

"Come here, boy. You need to pay for what you done. Maybe if I beat you enough, then you'll learn. You'll learn—"

Jack bolted awake, heart slamming against his ribs. The dream didn't evaporate, but stayed in his mind, lingered like fog on a cold morning. He wanted to believe it was a nightmare, spurned by the ugliness of the angry mob on his doorstep, but he knew better. Deep in his guts he knew he'd remembered a piece of his childhood, one best left forgotten.

No—best remembered. At least he knew he had a brother. Jack thought about that, and tried to push the images of violence from his mind. Then he realized he was alone. The pillow beside him was empty, the sheets tucked neatly into place to hold in the warmth.

Jack tossed back the covers. The air was nippy, but not cold. He padded on stocking feet around the bed and into the hallway. Chad's door was shut tight, so all was well. The boy hadn't become sick in the night and needed Lissa.

She was all right, wasn't she? He worried about her, about the pregnancy, but the contented silence of the house wrapped around him like fog. A faint glow beckoned him toward the front room. The cabin looked different in shadows, but the sweetness, the coziness, felt the same.

She sat at the table, a lamp lit before her, the wick turned low. Light sparkled in her long hair like stardust. With elbows propped on the table, she sat still as the night, her face buried in her hands.

"Couldn't sleep?" he asked.

She jumped. Her hands flew from her face. "You startled me."

"Next time I'll make more noise." He waited for the tension to ease from the tight line of her jaw and shoulders.

"Want me to stir up the coals? You look as if you need some tea."

"I just need you." Her gaze met his, her big, luminous eyes drawing him closer, drawing him in. "I didn't want to wake you, so I came out here. I'm still angry over what those men—men who were good friends to Michael and me, men I went to school with—accused you of—"

"That was desperation talking. And hopelessness." He settled down across the table from her, leaning into the pool of light that surrounded her like a halo. "Lambert and some of the other men lost everything they have worked for."

"That gave them no right to do what they did tonight. Scaring Chad. Upsetting me. Nearly attacking you."

"They are entitled to their anger. They just need to direct it at the men causing the trouble, not at me." He took her hands in his, felt the tremble of fear and anger. "I will put an end to this. You can count on it. When I find the men responsible, all of this heartache will stop."

"You shouldn't have to do Palmer's job just to prove yourself." Absolute faith rang in her voice, clear as church bells, certain as dawn. "You never need to prove yourself to me."

What had he done to earn that? He'd married her, done right by her, that was all. "I guess the right woman found me in the road last spring. Think where I would be if old spinster Mills came across me."

"She's a terrible cook. You're very lucky I picked you up and claimed you." Lissa laughed, leaning into his arms, the night shining in her eyes.

"Damn lucky," he agreed, then led her back to the warmth and comfort of their bed.

Chapter Twenty

Lissa heard the laughter, muffled by the log walls and thick chinking. She caught herself smiling. Jack must be back from town.

"Here's my head count of the springer heifers." Will handed her the account book. "I have them in the southwest pasture. Twenty of them were your orphans from last year. I figure they should start calving early spring."

"Thanks for moving them closer to the barn." Lissa pulled out a chair at the kitchen table and sank down into it, grateful to get some weight off her aching feet. "What about last year's calves?"

"The hands and I herded them into the small pasture directly behind the barn. That mountain cat is dead, but that doesn't mean there aren't others." Will's youthful face looked more serious with his responsibilities. "We'll have a small herd of steers. That has me worried, because prices go sky high come spring."

"We'll buy in late winter, when some ranchers are running low on feed and want to sell extra animals." Once again she heard the high call of laughter outside, where snow laced the ground in a thick cover and dripped off trees beneath the midday's sun.

"Jack wanted me to keep you current on all this," Will explained. "Sounds as if he's back from the bank."

"I hope he got the mortgage." Lissa pulled herself out of the chair and headed toward the window. Sunshine sparkled on the glass. Outside, a broad-shouldered man ran around the yard with a little boy, flinging snowballs. "Looks like we just bought the Johanson's land."

"Yep. It's good for the Johanson's. They won't be going bankrupt from their losses." Will closed the tally book and straightened. "And it's real good of you to let them stay in their home for the winter. I'm proud to work for people like you and Jack."

"Will, I'm glad to have friends like the Johansons. And you. You've stuck by me, no matter what. I can't tell you what that has meant."

"Jack let me know that with the big bonus he paid me from the cattle drive." Will ducked his chin, hiding emotion. "Well, I best be getting back to the barn."

Her heart twisted. "Thanks, Will."

The foreman strode out into the cool day. Lissa set the teakettle on the stove to heat and grabbed her cloak. She pushed open the door. Wind gusted. Cold air stung her face, and made her breath rise in great clouds. How she loved winter.

"We own another five hundred acres," Jack announced, then dodged a snowball.

"Gonna get you, Pa!" Chad vowed, scooping another handful of snow into his mittened hands.

"I don't know about that," Jack teased. "I'm fast."

"Me, too." Chad tossed the clump of snow.

Jack didn't try very hard to elude it. The snowball slapped against his chest. "You got me. I can't believe it."

"See? I'm good." Chad laughed when Jack came after

him and then tackled the boy. They rolled together in the snow, Jack gently tickling him. Laughter rang merry and loud. Then Jack was on the bottom and Chad was sitting on his chest.

"I give up. You win!" the big man declared, much to the boy's delight. Jack's eyes twinkled when he looked her way. "There's your mama just standing there. She's a pretty big target, don't you think?"

"Don't you dare." Lissa was laughing. "I just came out to see if the sale went through. Sophie is my dear friend. I want to make sure everything went well."

Both Jack and Chad stood. Both reached down to pack snow into their mittens.

"It went well." Jack's lopsided grin gave away his intentions. "Hans has the money he needs to see them through the winter and into spring. Sophie is happy, because she doesn't have to worry about moving with a baby in these temperatures. We have more land. It's a great situation."

Lissa took a step back. "I see that. I'm so glad the banker trusted you to take over their mortgage. You are a pretty shady character."

"The shadiest." Jack stalked closer, despite Chad's giggling. "I'm also a sure shot with a snowball."

"No!" Laughing so hard made it tough to run.

The soft snow splatted against her shoulder. She turned around. "You're going to pay for that. I was going to make you both hot chocolate with whipped cream, but I've changed my mind."

"Not fair," Jack protested, catching up to her, sweeping her safely into his arms. He kissed her hard, a wonderful passionate kiss that made her blood heat, that filled her with pure happiness. "Give us the chocolate or I'll dump you into the snow."

"Never," she squealed, choking on laughter as Jack tipped her downward, the cold ground ever closer.

"Change your mind?"

"Yes!" He swept her back to her feet, but he didn't let go of her. His touch was claiming, and left no doubt that he loved her as she loved him.

"We get whipped cream, too?" Chad asked.

"Whipped cream, too," she promised, almost too happy to speak. They headed toward the back door, stomping snow off their boots and sweeping snow off their coats.

It was good to be a family. So very good.

"Where are you taking those tarts?" Jack's protest filled the front room.

Lissa tucked the last pastry on the platter and covered it. "These are for my ladies' club meeting. We are discussing the bid for purchasing a building. By the new year we should have a location for the lending library."

"And you need to eat strawberry tarts for that?" He rose from the chair and set aside the book he'd been reading.

"Sugar helps keep the mind clear when making decisions." She tugged the plate out of his reach. "I left plenty for you and Chad in the pantry."

"I'm glad to know you didn't forget me and your only son." His eyes sparkled. "Want me to drive you to town? It's snowing pretty hard."

"Charlie is safe as a kitten. I can handle him myself." Lissa reached for her coat. "But you could harness the sleigh for me."

"Sure. Let me do the heavy work." He winked, then stole a kiss, leaving her lips tingling.

"I have to make you earn those strawberry tarts."

"I thought I earned something last night."

"What happened last night? I don't seem to remember." She let him open the door for her, then stepped out onto the porch.

"Is my lovemaking that forgettable?" His voice rumbled

against her ear, driving hot sparks of desire through her veins.

"Oh, right. I remember now." She started down the steps. "My memory is a little foggy."

He chuckled harder. "I guess I will have to refresh your memory. Say, tonight. After Chad is asleep. Meet me in our bed."

"Now, that's a promise I can keep." Her heart felt full, so very full. Snow fell, making the world new and fresh, making their problems feel small and far away.

Will led his mare into the barn to unsaddle her out of the wind and snow. "The rustlers hit again. Ranchers can't afford to lose entire herds. They're angry."

"And desperate." Jack wondered just how long it would be before other accusations came his way, questions about a past he no longer had, a life he did not remember— and up until now, hadn't wanted to.

"Who was it this time?" He bent to retrieve a harness.

"The McBains." Will swept off his hat and shook the snow from the brim. "They're my cousins."

"Lost everything?"

"The rustlers cleaned them out last night while they slept. They didn't hear a thing."

Jack saw the herd huddled together in the field against the cold north wind and snow. Their ranch hadn't been hit lately. It made him look guilty, for a man who was stealing cattle would not steal his own herd.

"Do your cousins think I did it?" Jack hung the harness on its peg, his gaze never leaving Will's.

Will's expression wavered. "Ian isn't going to come riding up to your front door with a gun in hand, if that's what you're asking."

"That's not what I'm asking."

"My cousin thinks there's a reasonable chance you're

guilty, but then he knows me enough to know the last thing I would do is work for a rustler.''

Jack considered that. "He's willing to listen to reason?"

"Maybe."

"Would he let me take a look at his fields?"

"We can ask." Will stood tall. "I'll ride out with you. He's just on the other side of town."

If he could find the real rustlers, he could wipe away all suspicion—for once and for all.

Palmer nearly slid off his horse at the sight of the man riding tall and silent beside Will Callahan. Jack Emerson looked like U.S. Marshal material, no doubt about it. Tough, proud, intelligent, not a single glimmer of fear as he faced the townspeople who suspected him of devastating crimes.

They suspected him because Deakins had been spending time in the saloons, planting the idea. It was all according to plan. Tonight his men would hit another ranch, one neighboring Lissa's. Even though the price of beef was low, it wasn't too hard to drive the herds north. Pay off enough people, and anything was possible—especially for profit.

His bank account was getting fatter. He didn't need Lissa's land. He didn't want her, anyway. He had enough cash to leave Sweetwater Gulch, to move on and move up.

"Where's he heading?" Palmer lowered his voice as he dismounted, so only Deakins could hear him.

The deputy tethered his horse, but his gaze never left the sight of the two men parading right through the center of town. "Look at those revolvers strapped to their belts. And rifles, holstered."

Palmer didn't miss the gun-power. His spine quaked a little when Jack Emerson and Will Callahan rode close.

Jack didn't blink, but met his gaze steadily—a challenge, no, a dare. That damned marshal was taunting him.

Emerson rode on past, straight through town, his hired man at his side. Wagons and riders moved aside for the men, letting them pass.

"Mount up," he bit out. "I want to know where those men are going. Maybe I can use it to prove his terrible guilt. Rustling is a hanging offense in this county."

Poor Jack Emerson. By tomorrow, he was going to find himself swinging from the knotted end of a rope.

"I appreciate you letting me take a look at what happened." Jack could see the worry on McBains' face, knew the man was facing near ruin. "You say the rustlers came sometime after midnight?"

"I heard a mountain lion, or I thought I did, so I mounted up and rode out about ten last night." Ian was a young man, friendly and pleasant, and as he rubbed his jaw, muscles flexed in his arm. He was a strong man, too. "I spent a long while riding the meadows, making sure the cattle were safe."

"Nothing unusual?"

"Not even any cat tracks, so I rode in. I walked through my front door just as the clock was ticking off midnight. I heard the cat again, so I climbed out of bed around four. When I rode out, I found my herd gone."

Jack saw the tracks of shod horses, clear, crisp tracks frozen into the snow, maybe ten men this time, more than the last bunch, but one thing was the same. Jack crouched low to study the imprints of steeled horseshoes. "Isn't this Phillips's work? He's left-handed, and our horse's shoes look just like this."

"Then it is someone from town." Will knelt down to look at the distinctive prints, too. "Yep, sure does look familiar. What do you think, Jack?"

"The horses were shod or purchased from the town livery. I'm going to head out and check with Phillips." Jack straightened, gazing up at the sky. Snow clouds hung low along the northern rim of mountains, dark and ominous.

Ian McBains looked, too. "You had better head home before the storm hits."

Jack looked again at the tracks. Sheriff Ike Palmer came to mind. He was the only man in town who had nothing to lose, and he had been damn angry when Jack had put a stop to the first round of rustling.

Now all Jack had to do was to find proof of the sheriff's guilt. He would start with the livery owner. He'd learn who had recently bought or shod a lot of horses.

"I'm going to stop by my mother's house," said Will. Wind blew hard against them, smelling of snow. "She is heartbroken at Ian's losses. He sold his beef cattle almost as early as you did, so it was his breeding stock that he lost."

"You stay on with your family if you need to, Will." Jack eyed the sky. "This storm isn't anything to be riding in. If you're needed at home, maybe it's best to stay."

"We'll see what happens." Will tipped his hat and headed his horse east, down the street off Main, where picket fences lined the road.

Jack dismounted in front of the livery, tethering the gelding with a single knot. The horse nosed his hand, and Jack patted the animal. "We'll be home where it's warm in a bit, fellow."

He looked up and saw Deakins ride into sight. It wasn't hard to figure out why Palmer's deputy had been on the road out of town. Not hard at all.

Instinct twisted hard in his guts, and Jack knew he was right. He knew before he stepped foot inside the livery that the sheriff was guilty.

* * *

He had the answers he needed. Now he had to figure out the best course of action. The wind grabbed at his hat brim, sliced through his wool coat, howled through the trees. He was the only one on the road from town; even the birds had found shelter.

He heard the click of a hammer, the only warning before the bullet knocked off his hat, dropped him from his saddle. He hit the ground hard. Breath whooshed from his chest. Something warm ran down his face—blood. Something cold wet his back—snow.

He grabbed for his holster, anyway, had both revolvers in hand and firing, even though he couldn't focus. He saw a blur of dark movement against the white ground and squeezed off two bullets, saw the form tumble forward, saw another, and shot.

"Hold it right there." *The sheriff's voice.* Cold, biting steel pressed against Jack's temple. The gun was cocked and ready. "Give me one reason, any reason, to pull this trigger."

The fight was over. Jack looked up at a man capable of hurting those he'd known his entire life, a man who had a name and friends, a past and memories. All that, though, weighed little against the blackness of Sheriff Ike Palmer's heart.

Lissa pushed open the mercantile's front door, her platter empty, laughter in her heart. Blanche was talking about Jeremiah's dusty office and how she hoped to go through the room to donate books to the new lending library. The boardwalk at her feet was slick with new snow. She looked down, careful of her step.

Blanche clucked her tongue. "Look at that."

Far down the street she saw horses and riders, all but obscured by distance and the thickly falling snow.

"Looks like Ike has himself a prisoner." Blanche shook her head, stopping before Russell's General Store. "It's about time he actually got some work done. I swear Jack ought to run against him next election. He'd win for sure on looks alone—"

Blanche's voice faded. All the sounds on the street faded except the quiet plop plop of the snow and the clomp of horse hooves on ice. She saw a bay with three white socks that looked just like Jack's gelding. And—

Lissa's knees wobbled. Her feet shifted, threatening to slip out from under her. She grabbed the post outside Susan's store with both hands. Somehow the air had thickened, and she couldn't draw it into her chest.

Those were Jack's boots on the feet of the man slung over the back of the bay gelding, tied to the saddle like a dead man.

"No!" Horror moved her forward. Her feet slid on ice. She righted herself, her bulk awkward, and ran out into the street. Snow slapped against her face, clung to her eyelashes, hampered her skirts.

"Jack!" She caught hold of his ankle, then grabbed the gelding's bit. The animal slowed, but could not stop.

The man holding the reins turned around in his saddle. "Lissa. Get back on the boardwalk."

She grabbed hold of the reins and yanked hard. They tumbled out of Palmer's grip. She soothed the agitated gelding with her voice and a pat to his neck as she circled around him. Jack lay head down, face down over his saddle. The dark gold of his hair hiding his face was stained with blood.

"Lissa, stop it." She vaguely heard Palmer's voice, the din of bystanders, the whisper of snow.

Was he dead? She could not believe the worst. Couldn't bear to. Jack. Tears filled her eyes and made her movements jerky as she reached out and laid a hand on his shoulder.

No, he was breathing. Relief washed over her as cold as the snow, stronger than her fear that he was dead. Her hand shook as she smoothed back the tangled locks from his face, saw the bloody wound from his hairline to the crown of his skull.

"Lissa." Big hands cupped her shoulders.

"Get away, Palmer." She pushed him hard. "You did this to him."

"He didn't give us a choice. He's the rustler, Lissa. I hate to be the one to tell you—"

"Stop this." She pushed him again, hard in the shoulder.

"Damn it, Lissa. I know this isn't easy—" His feet slid on the ice, and he struggled for balance.

"Jack?" She said his name, hoping he would hear, would stir. "Jack?"

More footsteps, then arms trying to tug her away, but she fought them. Blood dripped into the snow. She was determined to lead the gelding away from the group of milling deputies. Jack needed help. He needed a doctor, he—

"I'm right here." Doc James broke through the crowd. "Give me the reins, Lissa."

It was hard to let go, to let the leather slide through her fingers.

"I'll take good care of him," the doctor promised.

"Hey, you can't take my prisoner." Palmer stopped the doctor, one hand resting on his gun. "We'll take him to the jailhouse. You can treat him there."

"Ike, no. There's no heat in the cell." Lissa grabbed at him.

He pushed her away, so hard she slid on the ice. Doc James grabbed her arm, held her up. Fury licked through her veins when she looked up at the sheriff, his expression smug and triumphant.

"I don't know what's happened. Something has changed you, and it isn't for the better." Her words lifted in the snow-filled air, carried by the harsh winter wind. Bystanders along the street fell silent again.

"Do you want to know what happened?" He jerked the gelding's reins, bringing the horse and his unconscious passenger closer. "I lost my wife."

"I lost my husband." Her gaze traveled briefly to Jack, bleeding—heavens, but he was bleeding. "And this one needs medical help."

"No one cared about my Stella." Ike's voice was lowered, grew cold as steel. Where there should have been emotion, his words were cold, final. "She labored in that bed trying to give birth to my son, and Sophie Johanson was too good to come help—"

"She was bedridden with a troubled pregnancy—"

"She didn't care. And good old Doc here was running all over the countryside, tending the rich governor's son over in Swift Creek. There was no one to help her. What good were you people, then? Friends stayed silent, family could do nothing."

"I came as fast as I could," the doctor argued, grabbing back the reins and leading the gelding toward the jailhouse. "It's not my fault there isn't another doctor in this town. I've been saying it for years, but folks around here would rather spend their tax money on more deputies. I don't know what good that's done, you sitting around with your men while criminals run free."

"I got a criminal, Doc. You can't complain."

Bitterness, that's what it was—hard and cold, lacking heart. Palmer had suffered a loss no worse than her own, and she knew the pain, knew the hopelessness.

"I gave you a chance, Lissa, but look at you." He spit out the words, so low only she could hear. "You bedded down with that bastard. Who would want you now?"

Lissa staggered, shocked. The jailhouse loomed in front

of them, a gray shadow of stone and timber in the falling snow. How close had she come to being just like Palmer? How close had she been to closing up her heart, replacing love with nothing at all?

Loss was a part of life. She knew that all too well. But so was love, so was laughter, and so was caring about family, friends, and neighbors. Just like the seasons, life kept turning, from birth through death, and no one could stop it. No one could snatch back lost moments, or breathe life into a loved one gone and buried. The strength was in the letting go, in finding the courage to go on and love again.

Lissa watched the man who had done neither, who had let his heart remain as cold and dead as winter where nothing could grow. Look how ugly he'd become, his only pleasure inflicting pain on others.

"He took a bullet to the head." Doc's voice rumbled low, speaking only to her. "This is very serious, Lissa. I wish I could give you hope."

Hope. Lissa considered the word, felt it resonate in her heart. "We've come this far. We will just have to believe."

"Jack." Father's voice, this time not slurred by drink. "You boys hop up into the wagon. We're taking this load in."

"Yes, Father." Jack took his little brother's hand and helped push him over the tailgate. Laughing, Joey jumped up and into the pile of sweet dried hay, as fresh smelling as a Montana morning.

"Get up!" Father ordered the oxen, and the wagon squeaked to a start.

Jack caught hold of the tailgate and pulled himself up the rough, scarred wood and into the bed of soft hay, falling back beside his brother.

"I wanna be just like Father when I grow up," Joey said on a sigh, basking in the heat of the summer sun, shining with the kind of hope only the innocent had.

"Not me." Sure, Jack loved the animals and the wide-reaching

openness of the Montana plains, but wanted something more. He was going to be a sheriff, and make sure no little boy's mother died the way his had.

Ike Palmer blocked the threshold with his considerable bulk. "You're not going in there, Lissa."

"Yes, I am." She saw red when she looked at him, this man who took pride in shooting down her husband. "Jack is innocent until proven otherwise. And he is innocent, I guarantee that. You shot a good man, the man I love."

"He's a cattle rustler. It's high time you faced the truth."

"I know the truth." Anger twisted inside her, hard around her stomach.

"The truth is he's a cattle rustler from Wyoming. I have the wanted poster and a name to match. Blackjack Thomas. Look." Palmer pulled the poster from his shirt pocket and unfolded it several times, the paper shaking.

She took it from him and studied the rather general picture. Blackjack Thomas was a man under six foot, with dark blond, shoulder length hair, a handlebar mustache that he shaved now and then, blue eyes, and a cleft in his chin. Lissa looked at the picture and saw a stranger. She knew her Jack's face well enough to fill her dreams.

"You can't fool me, Ike." Lissa shoved the poster back at him, slamming her fist against his chest. Paper crinkled, echoing in the cell.

Lissa heard a groan. Jack! "Let me by." She planted her feet and shoved, but Ike's hands banded her wrists, imprisoning her.

"Since when did you lose respect for a pregnant woman?" Doc said, his voice low with censure. "I need an extra set of hands. Let her by."

The sheriff met the doctor's gaze. Lissa felt the lawman's cold hate, and shivered. Without a word, Ike shifted, just enough to let her through.

"He's conscious," Doc told her, "but I don't want Palmer to know yet. Jack is drifting in and out. He isn't making sense."

"Maybe this isn't as bad as last time, when I found him on the road. He was unconscious for a long while, and he still woke up. He didn't have his memory, but—"

"No, Lissa." Doc took her hand. "This time is different. I've seen it before. He's drifting away."

"He'll come back to me." Certainty rang through her, holding her up, as strong as hope. "I'll sit with him. I want to be with Jack."

She pulled her hand away, heading straight toward the open cell door. A lantern licked a thready light across the man lying still on the cot. Frost clung to the stone walls and crackled beneath her shoes. Her breath fogged in a great cloud as she fell to her knees.

"Jack." He looked dead, he really did, so ashen that he was gray, so motionless that she couldn't even see his breath. Only the faint traces of clouds lifting in the air marked that he lived at all.

He mumbled, turned toward her. His eyes opened, but he didn't focus on her. He looked through her, never blinking, so very far away.

"Joe." He rasped the name, then closed his eyes.

He was lost to her, lost in memories forgotten for so long.

"Lissa." Doc's hand was on her shoulder. "It's too cold for you here."

"I'm wearing my coat." Her chin came up.

"It's freezing in here."

"I can't leave him." Her back hurt, and she was cold to the bone.

"What about the baby?" Doc's voice came gently.

She knew he was right. She'd been worried about that,

yet every time she thought of leaving Jack defenseless and unconscious, she couldn't do it. He was her husband, and how she loved him.

"Lissa." Doc's gloved hands covered her own. "It's nearly midnight. It's important to think of your own health. You're carrying something mighty important."

"I know." Tears stung her eyes. "I've been thinking of nothing else."

"Good. Blanche said she's keeping the stove hot, and has a bed ready for you. Go to her house. Eat a good meal. Sleep the night through."

"How can I leave him?" Despite the blankets, Jack shivered so. "He might not wake up."

"I will stay by his side." Doc helped her to her feet. "I know it's a hard decision to make, but you must take care of your baby. It doesn't mean that you are abandoning Jack."

"It feels that way." How could she sleep, worrying so?

"You'll be warm and rested. That's what you need," the doctor assured her. "Besides, there's nothing more we can do but wait."

It was like leaving her heart behind. "You'll send for me if he starts slipping away?"

"I will."

Her back ached, low and hard. It was not good for the baby—Jack's baby—that she was here in the bitter cold. The deputy keeping watch in the corner barely glanced at her as she let herself out into the street, into the full force of the blizzard.

The snow swirled around her, blocking out the world, even the ground at her feet. Tiny pellets of ice slammed into her, drove deep into her wool clothes. She could not see anything but darkness, could not hear anything but the howling power of the wind.

She found her way by feeling along the storefronts, then along the length of the picket fences, to the shadow of

Blanche's home. She stepped up onto the sheltered porch and out of the driving snow. A lamp burned in the window, in the kitchen where Blanche was waiting.

She hoped Jack would find the way out of his storm, too.

Chapter Twenty-One

"I didn't mean it."

Jack looked up from the floor, saw the big man standing in the shadows, his head down. A blizzard beat at the north side of the house, the scouring sound of ice against the thin walls, the howl of the angry wind. Snow blew in through the cracks. A single lamp burned on the table, the wick low, barely illuminating the room.

"I didn't mean it at all." Father wept, his grief as powerful as the storm outside, as dark as the night. He grabbed a whiskey bottle from the top shelf and cracked the seal. "Now she's gone."

They had buried Mama that morning with snow falling on the casket, with only a few mourners gathered. Grandma, refusing to look at them, cried how she'd known her daughter's marriage to an Emerson would come to no good. Violence was in the blood. Like father, like son. A person couldn't expect more from a man whose own father put two wives in the grave.

"She made me do it." Father sniffled, sucking down alcohol, trying to forget. Hopelessness cloaked the room, muffled the world

outside until there was only Father's grief, only his endless sorrow.
"She just got me so damn mad."

Jack felt the bitter bite of winter at his toes and fingers. He
wanted to go to bed with his brother, cuddle into the cold sheets
and shiver until sleep claimed him. He tried to sneak away, but
Father called after him.

"Don't think you can escape it. Judge me all you want, but
you will be like me one day, boy. You mark my words. There are
some things in life a man can't escape."

Jack ran from the room, fighting tears. The bedroom was freez-
ing. He stripped down to his long johns and snuggled into bed,
his little brother already breathing slow and even, fast asleep. Jack
shivered, aching for warmth, for a lit hearth where a fire always
crackled merrily, for the scents of cinnamon and sunshine and
an apple pie baking in the oven . . . .

"Jack." A woman's voice. Rich as music, drawing open
his eyes.

"Hello there, sleepyhead." Lissa's smile was like coming
home, like the deep abiding warmth and safety of no place
else on earth. "I've been waiting for you to wake up."

How tired she looked—as beautiful as an angel, but dark
shadows smudged the smooth skin beneath her eyes and
drew in her cheekbones. His heart caught. "This jail cell.
It's freezing. And Lissa, you are carrying our child."

"I am watching over my husband, the man I love." Her
touch felt like paradise.

He leaned into it, cherished it.

"Let's see how you're doing, Jack." Doc drew a stool
close, the clatter of wood against stone echoing in the
chamber. "I frankly didn't think I would be talking to you
again."

"I remember what happened. I remember a bullet being
fired from the bushes up ahead. Palmer and his men
ambushed me like a bunch of cowards."

"I can't believe I ever called that man a friend." Lissa's

voice tightened. She sounded angry, yet he knew she was hurt, too.

"People change, that's all. Sometimes things change people." Jack winced against the pain in his head and the sharper hurt when Doc looked beneath the bandage. "How long was I out?"

"Less than twenty-four hours."

Lissa left the room, a swish of skirts and elegance, taking his heart with her. Jack saw the concern on Doc's face.

"You are the luckiest man I know." Doc leaned back and tugged on thick wool mittens. "How's your head?"

"Hurting like son of a gun." Jack tried to sit up. Nausea dropped him back onto the pillow. "Palmer's arrested me for the cattle rustling."

"He claims that his evidence is irrefutable," Doc said, though he looked skeptical.

"Irrefutable, huh?" Jack breathed in and out, trying to think through the black, suffocating pain. Palmer was just trying to shift the blame, trying to frame Jack for crimes he couldn't have committed.

He knew who he was. Well, maybe not entirely, but he had memories, a family, a past, a childhood, and a name.

"Here's some hot tea. This will help warm you up a bit." Lissa smiled, and made his heart stop.

She loved him. It shone in her eyes like the brightest sun, like moonbeams and stardust and dreams. He would give anything to be the man she needed. Jack accepted her tea, accepted the heated brush of her kiss. She was heavy with his child; the fabric of her skirt stretched over the generous curve of her belly when she settled down on the stool at his side.

He thought of all he had promised her, of the commitment he made to her. He'd had no right, no business marrying her in the first place. He could see that now, and wished he had made different choices.

He could never claim a wife and child of his own. He

was his father's son, a man who killed, a man who didn't blink in the face of violence. That was the one truth he could no longer escape.

"I'm going to get you out of here." Lissa's determination was as big as a Montana sunset, all fiery color and light. "Jeremiah's friend is a lawyer, and—"

"No." Jack gave her back the cup of tea and sat up. His skull pounded and dizziness swam through his head, but he gritted his teeth. He could be determined, too. "Send a telegram to the district judge."

"But he's talking about hanging you." She choked back tears.

"I deserve a trial. It's the only way I'm going to prove my innocence—and I *am* innocent." Jack covered her hand with his. Her hands were like ice even in the middle of the day. "Do it, for me. Only a higher authority can make Palmer come to heel."

"But—"

"Just do it." His words were harsher than he meant, but there could be no argument.

Hurt glittered in her eyes. "Jack, I—"

"Do it." He softened his voice, but held back all the gentle feelings she made burn to life in his chest.

Sheriff Palmer was a dangerous man. He preyed on his friends and neighbors, and he intended to kill an innocent man to cover his own crimes.

Lissa was not safe near such a man. She was not safe here with him, her own husband. Jack turned to the doctor. "Take Lissa out of here. And don't let her back in."

"It is too cold for her, and with the problems she's had before, I agree." Doc stood, took the empty teacup from Lissa's fingers.

"No. Jack needs me. I'm fine, really—"

"I don't want you here." It was only the truth. Looking at her tore him apart, so he turned away. "Get her out of here, Doc. And make sure she gets in contact with the judge, like I asked."

"Will do." Concern crossed Doc's brow, but he didn't ask, didn't judge. He took Lissa by the elbow. "Come, let's get you some rest."

"No. I can't believe—"

"Believe it." Jack felt his chest tighten, his heart harden. "And sign the telegram from me—Jack Emerson."

"Why can't I see Pa?" Chad asked as soon as Lissa cleared the table.

"Because your pa is in jail."

"With Ike?"

"Because of Ike." Lissa bent to fill the basin from the stove.

"But I wanna see him."

"We can't." She straightened, set the enamel basin on the counter.

"But he's my Pa! I gotta tell him about how well I'm ridin' Comet."

"I know you miss him, Chad." Lissa's heart ached with the loneliness, with the injustice of it. "We just have to be patient."

Will pushed open the back door and ambled in, his snow-covered coat dripping on the floor. He shrugged it off and hung it on the peg by the threshold. "I'm going to town, Lissa. Did you want to come?"

"Yes." She reached for a bar of soap. "Can you wait for me, or are you in a hurry?"

"I'll be pleased to wait." Will glanced at the stove. "As long as you provide me with a cup of coffee and a couple of your sweet rolls."

"You have a deal." Lissa grabbed a knife and began shaving lye into the washwater.

"Folks are saying he's guilty." Will waited until Chad had fled the room, excited about a trip into town on the sleigh. "Folks say Palmer has the proof he needs."

"I've heard what folks say." She slid the cups into the water, then the flatware. "Do you believe it?"

"Of Jack? No." Enamel clanked on iron. Will set down the coffeepot and padded over to the table. "I think Palmer has the wrong man, and he's being stubborn about admitting it."

"He wanted me to send a telegram for him. I had to have Jeremiah ride all the way up to Sweet Creek Flats to send the wire."

"Do you think it will help him?"

"He thought so." She scrubbed the knives, then the spoons. "Ike wouldn't let me see him yesterday."

"I could try to persuade Palmer to change his mind."

Lissa glanced over her shoulder. "I like the sound of that."

Hammering echoed in the cell and reverberated through his head. Despite the cracking pain, Jack climbed up on the cot to look out the tiny window. He could see the street, coated thick with snow, smell the scent of wood smoke in the air.

If he stood on his toes he could see the bright color of raw lumber leaning against the awning post of the jail, and the feet of the men as they worked—building the scaffold.

"When's the hangin' gonna be, Sheriff?" a man asked. He sounded like Anders, a man who had lost his herd and held a grudge against Jack.

"As soon as we get this thing up." Palmer sounded cocky, proud of himself—too damn proud.

Jack listened to the hammering and doubted the judge could intervene in time.

* * *

"What are they buildin', Mama?"

Lissa opened her mouth but could not force an answer around the knot in her windpipe. Her gaze arrowed to the scaffolding.

"Will, stop the sleigh."

The floor was already built. Sawdust and mud littered the base of it, the bright wooden surface already slick with falling snow.

"Mama, what are they buildin' that for?"

The sleigh skidded to a halt. She climbed out, careful not to slip. "Chad, I want you to stay with Will. Will, could you take Chad over to Blanche's, please? Tell her what is happening."

"Sure thing." Grim-faced, Will snapped the reins against Charlie's behind. The horse and sleigh pulled away, Chad's question high in the air.

"Mama, what's it for?"

She knew. Cattle rustling was a hanging offense. Sheriff Palmer was wasting no time.

"Ike." She caught him by the arm, forcing him to turn around.

"Why, Lissa. I didn't think you would have the courage to show your face in town today."

"Why wouldn't I?" She wanted to wipe the smugness off his face. "Jack is innocent."

"I have proof. Anders says he saw a bay horse with socks and a blaze, just like Jack's, ridden by one of the men who stole his herd."

"He saw Jack clearly?"

Ike's eyes glittered. "He saw a man fitting Jack's description. That's good enough from a distance."

"It's not proof, and you know it." Lissa felt cold with anger. "Give him a trial, or let him go."

"Not on my life." Palmer flipped the hammer from one

hand to the other. "No one can say I'm not doing my job.
I've stopped the man who has been stealing from our
friends and neighbors."

"Don't you dare hang him." Lissa grabbed hold of Ike's
collar and held him hard.

"Don't dare me." He had to struggle to break her hold,
and when he did he held her wrist hard enough to bruise
it. "I can have your beloved husband swinging by his neck
by supper, if I've a mind to."

"Don't you—"

"Let me take you down a peg, Miss High and Mighty."
Ike wrenched her wrist, dragging her after him.

Lissa stumbled on chunks of ice and snow, struggling
to keep on her feet. Her added bulk made it harder. She
slid to a breathless stop behind him in the jail office. He
grabbed a burlap sack and upended it. An old hand gun
bearing the ranch's brand etched into its wooden grip
clattered to a rest on Ike's desktop.

"You took that from Jack when you arrested him." She
wasn't fooled.

"No. Ian McBains and Deputy Deakins found it. I hear
he wanted to give Jack a chance to prove his innocence
first, since your husband is Will's boss, but Jack couldn't
do it."

"No." Lissa recognized the old Colt as one of the extra
guns they kept in the tack room in case of an emergency.
The last time she'd seen the gun was just after Jack brought
in the mountain lion. "Anyone could have grabbed the
gun and dropped it in McBains's field."

"Anyone with a bay gelding matching your husband's
description. Old Lady McIntosh, who was up tending her
ill husband late at night, swears she saw Jack ride past her
cottage on North Fork Road driving a herd of cattle."

"By himself?"

"With his accomplices." Palmer's grin glittered with triumph. "This comes as warning to your ranch hands. If I find any more evidence, they may be the next to hang."

Fury threatened to overtake her. She fought for breath, feeling the tension tight in her shoulders, clutched around her spine. Pain sliced through her stomach. She was only upset, that was all. She breathed deep, trying to relax. "I'm going to prove you wrong, Ike. I don't know how, but I'm going to—"

"Palmer!" Jack's voice interrupted, ringing in the corners of his cell. "Get Lissa out of here."

"You're in a fine position to be giving orders."

"I don't want her here."

"I want to see him." Lissa turned her back on the sheriff's evidence.

Palmer grabbed her by the arm. "You're leaving. And if you're lucky, you'll be a widow before nightfall."

"Jack?" she called as Palmer escorted her to the door. She tried to fight him, as strong as she was, but the baby she carried was priceless. She did not want to risk falling. "Jack? Answer me."

Nothing. Not a word of love. Not a request for help. Nothing.

"See? He's guilty." Palmer chuckled as the snow struck her face, as the bitter wind burned her exposed skin.

"Jack." His name still tumbled from her lips, ached in her heart.

The only answer was the ring of the hammers in the still morning air.

Jack heard her tears, felt the weight of what he'd done as Palmer slammed shut the jail door and he was alone.

His memories might be patchy, but he knew enough to know why he had never married, never wanted a wife and family, never wanted to face his past. Lissa was safer away from Sheriff Palmer, and away from the man his father swore he would grow up to be.

Jack just needed rest, that's what Lissa told herself as Blanche tucked her into bed in the family's spare room. Jack had hit his head. He wasn't himself. Tomorrow he would be glad to see her, would welcome her with that lopsided grin she loved so well, had kissed so often.

A tiny voice inside her, the one that often spoke truth, reminded her there was another problem, one not even the strength of her love could soothe away. Jack had remembered, she was sure, and he was going to leave her.

"Sleep well," Blanche's voice caressed the sincere wish like the lamplight in the room. She turned down the wick, the flame died, and only the dark grayness of a stormy afternoon remained.

Lissa felt fatigue weigh down her body like lead. She closed her eyes, drifting off into a world of darkness and no dreams.

A sharp pain tore her awake, followed by another. A tight clamping around her stomach brought tears to her eyes, panic to her heart. *It can't be.*

"Blanche!" She stood, hand on her stomach. Her water broke, running down her legs onto the polished floor, and she felt the ebb of her last hopes. It was too early. Much too early.

The door flung open. Lamplight from the hallway tumbled into the room, brushing over Blanche, wearing an apron, a paring knife in hand. "Lissa? Lissa, what's wrong?"

Another pain clamped tightly, and she groaned, unable to hold it back.

"Oh, Lord." Blanche slipped the knife into her apron pocket and grabbed Lissa's arm. "We have to get you back to bed. Jeremiah! Run and get Doc. Then ride out to the Johanson's ranch and fetch Sophie. Hurry!''

Jack. Lissa thought of him locked away in that cell, ice white on the bars. "Tell Jack."

"Jeremiah will." Blanche's touch was comforting, solid, stable in a world overtaken by pain.

"I can't lose this baby." Lissa gritted her teeth, determined this time would be different. "Please, don't let me lose Jack's baby."

It was too early, though. Much too early.

Chapter Twenty-Two

"I want you to drink as much of this as you can." Sophie knelt beside the bed, one of Blanche's china cups in hand. Steam lifted from the cup, curling invitingly.

Lissa managed to shake her head. "I can't."

"It's pineapple weed tea." Sophie held the cup to Lissa's lips. "You must drink. It will build up your blood for childbirth. It will give you strength."

Another contraction gripped her. Pain built in her back, tightened like a vise around her stomach. Sweat gathered on her brow, dampened her body. She gasped for breath. "I still have seven weeks to go."

Sophie nodded. "Drink."

Lissa did, sipping the tart tea, letting it slide down her throat. "Michael Junior was born this early. He wasn't strong enough to breathe on his own."

"Drink more." Sophie tipped the cup.

Soothing tea sluiced over her lips, into her mouth. She tried to swallow, and swallowed tears instead. She'd known all along this could happen. How could she bear to lose Jack's child?

The contraction released her, and she leaned back into the pillows. Exhaustion enveloped her.

"Rest as much as you can." Sophie set down the cup, took her hand.

Lissa heard Sophie turn to whisper to Blanche, but the words were lost to her as another wave of pain washed over her.

"Here's some more tea." Sophie padded quietly into the midnight dark room.

"No more tea." Lissa gritted her teeth. "Besides, it tastes terrible."

"It will help with the pain." Sophie sat down beside her. "You look pretty tired."

"I'm ready for this to be over." The contraction ended. Lissa leaned back into the pillows. "Something is wrong with the baby."

"Doc and I are doing all we can."

Another clamp of pain gripped her. Lissa lost her breath, sat up into her friend's arms, gritted her teeth. Sweat sluiced down her face. "I can't go on like this."

"It won't be much longer now. Here, drink up."

The contraction released, only to wash over her again. She couldn't breathe. She couldn't bear it.

"Sophie." Doc looked up from the foot of the bed. "Get down here. We have a problem."

Lissa felt dizzy with pain, felt the weight of exhaustion. Sharp, hard contractions left her helpless. What was the problem? What was the doctor saying to Sophie?

She felt the wetness, felt the tearing pain. She was bleeding. She didn't even have to ask. What did it mean? What about the baby? Was he going to die? The thought of losing Jack's baby rent her in two, left her weak, left her crying.

Sophie took her hand. "We need you to push, Lissa."

"I don't think I can."

"You have to." Sympathy burned in those dark eyes. "The cord is around the baby's neck, and I can't loosen it."

Lissa pushed. Pain ripped through her, unnatural and like nothing she'd known before. She felt her own blood pool beneath her, felt her heart dying a bit.

Sophie took her hand and held on tight. She didn't have to question her friend to know the truth, to know what both Sophie and the doctor feared.

The baby might already be dead.

Jack heard the clang of the outer door, then the drum of footsteps. Glass *chinked,* then light licked along the floor, coming closer. He wondered if Palmer had given up his promise to hang him in the morning, and wanted to do it now, in the dark of night, when no one could stop him.

The sheriff stepped into sight, the swinging lantern flickering orange flames. Jack's chest tightened. It looked as if he'd run out of time.

"Jack." Jeremiah Buchman's voice rose in the darkness. There in the shadows the tall man emerged, behind Palmer. "Lissa's in labor."

"Labor?" Alarm buzzed down his spine. Fear settled into a cold ball in his guts. "It's too early. She's—"

"Having a hard time." Jeremiah stepped into the light, his long face grim. "Sophie and Doc are both with her. There is a problem. Lissa is losing a lot of blood."

"Will she be all right?"

"There's no telling. She's losing strength fast." Jeremiah bowed his chin. "Open the door, Palmer."

Palmer's face was bowed, too. His voice, when he spoke, was strained. "You understand this is just for the night."

"I understand." Jeremiah shrugged. "Sometimes being mayor pays off. And being friends of a mayor does, too."

"I don't like it," Palmer growled low, over the sound of keys clanging in the lock. "My deputy and I are staying close. You try to run, and we'll do whatever it takes to stop you."

"You get to be with Lissa, Jack." Jeremiah tugged open the barred door. "She's asking for you."

"I could lose her." The knowledge left him cold, numb, and unable to move. His anger and his worries died with the thought of Lissa's suffering. "Is she home?"

"She's at our house." Jeremiah stepped aside. "Come with me. Palmer, this is decent of you."

The big sheriff said nothing. His head remained bowed, and his tipped hat brim covered his shadowed face. He said nothing as Jack walked away, out into the world with fears as dark as the night.

"She's been in labor since early afternoon." Jeremiah spoke over the crunch of their footsteps in the frozen snow, despite the bitterness of the winter air. "Blanche is worried we will lose her."

Jack's heart felt as brittle as the ice at their feet. The Buchmans' house shone in the darkness, every room lit, a cozy sight on such a frigid night.

"I hope we're in time." Jeremiah's hand paused on the doorknob. "I just want you to be prepared, Jack. The news may not be good."

"I'm prepared." He felt pain so deep it froze him, dark as the night, bitter as the wind. They stepped into a silent house, so silent that a clock's tick could be heard two rooms away. Fire snapped and crackled in the hearth and wood popped in the belly of the kitchen stove, but that was all.

Jack knew without asking, was afraid to ask. Just like that, a man could lose everything—everything that mattered to him. He thought of John Murray, the man he'd inadvertently replaced, who had lost a wife and child. Thought of Ike Palmer, who had lost a wife and baby. Thought of Lissa, who had buried a husband and two sons. How did they go on living? Jack didn't know if he could take another breath.

"Jack." Low and solemn, Sophie's voice whispered in the upper shadows of the stairwell.

His heart broke—one piece at a time, a slow, horrible rending that left him unable to move. He heard the soft squeak of a board on the stair, heard the faintest brush of her moccasins against wood.

"Do you want to meet your son?" She stepped into view, cradling a tiny bundle in both arms.

"Lissa?" He choked. Tears stung his eyes.

"She's resting." Sophie laid the baby in his arms—so light, it could have been nothing but the blanket. "He's small, but that's to be expected. He's a strong baby. I think he just might make it. I'm giving Lissa plenty of rush skeletonweed and baneberry tea. It will bring strength to them both."

"Thank you, Sophie." Overcome, he was afraid to move, afraid to break the magic, afraid to believe that Lissa was truly fine.

"Take a look at your son. He's a handsome boy." Sophie lifted the corner of the blanket, revealing a tightly scrunched face, round and sleepy.

Lissa's nose. His chin. He stared in amazement at the baby, their son. Tears wedged in his throat, filled his eyes at a love so strong it overwhelmed him, so enormous there was no end.

"He's had quite a hard time of things so far, with just coming into the world. He's tired like his mother, but he is perfect." Like song, Sophie's voice tugged at his heart, made it safe to believe again. "Come upstairs and see your wife."

"Are you sure she's fine?"

"As sure as I can be." Sophie smiled, leading the way up the stairs and into the second story. "She's sleeping, too, which is good. She needs to heal and gather her strength. Being a new mother isn't easy."

A door creaked open. A single lamp had been turned low, brushing the bed, caressing the sweet face of his wife. She looked so peaceful, but he saw at once how pale she was, how exhaustion bruised her skin.

A fire crackled in the hearth, keeping the room warm. Jack sat down in the chair by the bed, hating to disturb the woman who had given him the greatest of gifts, the finest life he'd ever known.

Lissa stirred. Her eyes flickered open, and her smile shimmered with joy. "Jeremiah said he was going to try to get you out of jail."

"He forced Palmer into letting me go. Of course, there are two armed men stationed at both doors, but I'm not going anywhere."

"You'd better not." She lifted up on one elbow, her hair of gold framing her face, glinting in the low light. "What do you think of your son?"

"I think he's mighty fine." Pride made his voice thick. "You did good, Lissa."

"I'm so glad he's able to breathe." Her voice sounded thick with tears, too, and weak, so very weak. "He didn't make a sound right away after he was born. But then he let out a tiny little cry. He's going to be fine."

"I know he is." Jack leaned forward, brushed her brow with a kiss. How tired she looked, how beautiful. His heart might be breaking, but he didn't want it to show—not now, not during their last time together. "Palmer's going to haul me back to jail soon, but I want you to know something."

"What?"

"Living with you and having the privilege of loving you has been the sweetest thing I have ever known."

Tears sparkled in her eyes, but the love for him, the love they had together, shone through. "You have made me a stronger person, Jack, just from knowing you. And you've given me another son."

She brushed her hand along the side of the baby's face, his eyes scrunched tight against the light. "What are we going to name someone so precious?"

"Joseph." His throat filled. "Joey. I would like to name him Joey."

Palmer sat in the dark room. An opened bottle of whiskey scented the air, growing warmer from the fire in the stove. Flames crackled and popped, and an occasional wind gust rattled the door and released a puff of smoke. Otherwise, the night was quiet.

Three more hours until dawn, when he had decided to hang Jack Emerson. Palmer thought of that, remembered the look of grief on Jack Emerson's face when he thought he could lose Lissa to childbirth. Memories he didn't want washed over him, hard and sharp, more painful than any wound. Stella had died in his arms, crying in agony. Doc hadn't been at *her* side. Sophie hadn't been crushing *her* herbs. The mayor hadn't been arguing on *his* behalf.

Hanging Emerson was right. It solved a dozen problems, and it gave Palmer a new chance. Maybe that was what he needed—a new town, a more satisfying job, money to buy whatever he needed. Money would protect him. It could have convinced Doc to stay in town in case Stella needed him. It could have bought a finer home, a better life for the son who never lived.

Bitterness filled the empty chambers of his heart, the dark emptiness of his soul. He'd heard Lissa lived. Of course she had. She might not be rich, but she had the biggest spread in the county. She had assets, and that had guaranteed a doctor at her side.

Palmer took another drink, hating the man he'd become. He'd lost his hope, his heart, and his humanity. Now all he wanted was the oblivion a good bottle of whiskey could give him—and revenge. How he wanted revenge.

He would hang Jack Emerson two hours early, before his wife, the great mayor Jeremiah Buchman, or any other Good Samaritan could stop him. It would be just the dawn, a few of his friends, and Jack Emerson hanging from a noose.

Lissa laid Joey down to rest in the cradle Blanche had brought down from her attic, dusted, and cleaned. The baby was very tiny, but he carried Jack's blood in his veins. He was strong. He would live. She knew it in her heart.

"Chad wants to see his new brother." Blanche stood in the threshold, growing round with her pregnancy, a little blond boy at her side. "Can he come in?"

"Chad." Lissa held out her arms and her son dashed across the room. He tumbled against her.

"You didn't tuck me in last night. Mr. Buchman said you couldn't come because of the baby."

"Tonight I will read to you. That's a promise." Lissa brushed the locks from his forehead and kissed his brow. "Come meet Joey."

Solemn, Chad's hand slid into hers. He peered over the top of the cradle, his face seriously studying the baby asleep beneath the blankets. "That's my brother?"

"That's him." Lissa took hold of Joey's tiny clenched fist. "You're a big brother, now. That's something special."

"I know." Chad nodded, his shoulders set, his spine straight, his posture just like Jack's. "Joey, I'll let you play with my dog when we get home. And when you're bigger, I'm gonna teach you to ride."

Lissa's throat filled. The first light of dawn beckoned at the windows, peach and gold, the colors of a new day.

Their baby was safely born. Now she would find a way to save Jack, just the way he had always saved her. It was only six o'clock. She had two hours—two hours to ask Jeremiah and the ranch hands to help her with a plan.

Jack saw the light change from gray to peach, felt the morning come with the reverence of nature—birds sang, a rooster crowed, a wind whispered along the frozen ground, all announcing the new day.

He hadn't slept since leaving Lissa's side. He sat in the darkness. His life before knowing her was patchy, but what he remembered was bleak—a small house, lonely and silent. His days always ended in that house, in the quiet, so lonely he hurt.

She had given him everything he'd ever dreamed of, ever wished for: The beauty of a woman's love, the honor of being a father, a rare happiness found in precious moments—really just normal moments made up from the sight of Lissa's smile over the supper table, or reading his son asleep, or picking berries in the rain. Those moments made up the pieces of a man's life, made it whole.

"Ready to hang?" Palmer strode into sight, his stride cocky, his grin triumphant. Why didn't that surprise Jack?

"You know I have a right to a trial."

"Too bad life is unfair." Palmer slid the key in the lock. "Of course, you'll be dead before anyone will know."

The door swung free. "And lucky me. I have the honor of placing the noose around your neck."

"How are you going to silence the livery owner? How are you going to keep Will quiet? Those men know the truth."

Palmer shrugged. "Threats have worked with the stable man. And accidents happen all the time on a ranch. Will should remember that."

The morning sun stung his eyes as Jack stepped out into

the street. The scaffold smelled of new lumber and rose up against the east horizon, silhouetted by peach and gold.

There was no one out so early in the morning. Only Anders, Hubbard, Lambert, and a few of the men who had threatened him now strolled out of businesses and saloons. Palmer tugged him up onto the floor of the scaffold.

He thought of Lissa, thought of all he had wanted to do for the boys. Hunting and fishing, and sending them to college—these were the dreams he'd nurtured. Now, he would not have a hand in his sons' lives, or their futures.

Palmer drew down the noose. "I want you to see we spared no expense in building this scaffold. We wanted to do a good job, one we could be proud of."

Jack said nothing. He would not spend the last moments of his life arguing with a murderer. Palmer pulled the hemp over Jack's head. The rope was rough and scratched his face, bit into his neck.

"Tight enough, Emerson?"

Hearing that name spoken startled him. A memory, vague and shadowed, flickered through his mind. *Emerson, Emerson. Marshal Jack Emerson.* He was a Federal Marshal out of Helena. He'd been taking Dillon Plummer to trial.

Looking into the glittering darkness of Ike Palmer's eyes, Jack saw the truth. The sheriff knew Jack's true identity, and had for some time.

"Say good-bye, Marshal." He whispered the words.

Deakins hit the lever. The floor dropped out from beneath Jack's boots. The noose snapped tight around his neck.

Chapter
Twenty-Three

Jack caught hold of the rope above his head, fighting even though he knew it was useless. Down below, Deakins laughed. Anders spit a stream of tobacco that hit Jack square in the chest.

"You're taking a long time to die." Palmer gave him another hard push, sending him swinging. The rope pulled harder at his throat.

Then he heard the clink of shod hooves on ice. A shot rang out, the rope gave, and Jack tumbled. He hit the wood flat on his back. Pain and shock bolted through him. Blood covered his hands from where the noose had rubbed his skin away. He tugged off the rope and drew in fresh morning air.

A shadow covered him, tall as the sky, invincible.

"What are you lawmen doing hanging my brother?"

Jack saw the glint of the marshal's badge, saw the blond curls and broad shoulders, the blue eyes so like his own. It all rushed back—the memories lost, the past buried, the dreams that came in pieces in the night now whole.

"Look out!" He saw Palmer draw, tried to jump up.

A shot rang out. Surprise twisted Palmer's face as the gun fell from his injured hand. Blood dripped down his arm, stained his sleeve.

"Don't even think of firing on a Federal Marshal, boys." Joe Emerson wheeled his horse around, keeping his eye on all the men. "Up against the wall, all of you. Or I start shooting."

"But this here's a cattle rustler," Hubbard belted out.

"There's not a chance in hell of that." Joe fired his gun, cracking ice an inch from Hubbard's boot. "Move."

The rancher stumbled up against the jailhouse wall. Jack still struggled for air as his brother dismounted. "The judge couldn't believe the telegram. Told me to ride down and fetch you. I pushed hard all the way. Looks like I came in time."

"Your timing and your aim couldn't be better." Jack hugged his brother, felt good to know Joe was safe, not lost, as he'd feared from his dreams. "Palmer and Deakins are the rustlers. I say we escort them to the territorial prison to await a fair trial."

"Sounds reasonable to me." Joe tossed him a set of handcuffs. "What about the others?"

"They may be drunk, but that's their only offense." Jack took pleasure in relieving Palmer of his other gun and the knife in his boot. He cuffed the man and tossed him into his own jail, beside his whimpering deputy.

Joe helped himself to the coffee simmering on the jailhouse stove. "I still can't believe my eyes every time I look at you. I thought you were dead. Plummer confessed to shooting you in the head."

"I woke up and I didn't know where I was." Jack grabbed two cups from a nearby shelf and held them while his brother poured.

"We had men looking for you. We didn't think you were this far south, judging from Plummer's crime spree." Joe grabbed the sugar and measured out four heaping tea-spoons. Then he offered the jar to Jack.

"There are some things I have to do first, before we leave." He thought of Lissa, wondered what kind of future they could have now.

"I'll stay here and keep an eye on our prisoners. They are lucky I'm in a good mood." Joe grinned, and a broth-er's love shone there, as strong as the affection in his own heart.

Joe hadn't grown up to be like Father. He'd grown up to be a marshal, too, a protector of others.

Cradling his cup of coffee, Jack stepped out into the street.

The plate holding her breakfast muffin slid from her fingers at the sight of the man in the door. "Jack!"

"Pa!" Chad raced the length of the room and wrapped both arms around Jack's knees.

Lissa stood, shaking. "We were just talking over how to stop the hanging."

"Help already came." Jack's gaze arrowed to hers.

Want and hope and love telegraphed through her entire body, warmed the cold hurting places in her heart. "Are you free?"

"Free and clear." He opened his arms, and she fell against him, breathed in the solidness of him, of muscled chest and invincible shoulders. "Palmer is cooling his heels in jail. I need to take him to a judge for trial."

"He was the rustler?"

Jack nodded. How bleak he looked, how dull the shad-ows in his eyes.

She knew. He wasn't just taking Palmer to justice. He was leaving. "You remembered everything."

He nodded.

Her knees wobbled a little. She'd known that one day

he would have to face his former life. He would have to go back, see what he was missing, make a choice. How wonderful to have him alive, though, to know that he was safe and happy rather than buried in a plot on the hill, forever silenced.

"Come. Let's have one last meal together before you go."

He nodded, and she knew his regrets were as great and painful as hers.

Jack didn't want to go, didn't want to leave the light of Lissa's smile or the warm comfort of her presence. He didn't want to lift Chad from his knee or walk away from his baby son, so helpless and fragile. Time was passing, though, the hands on the face of the clock ever moving.

"Will you be coming back to us?" Sad knowledge was in her eyes. She already knew the truth.

Jack took a breath, felt all eyes on the room studying him, measuring him. "I made a vow to you. I swore I would never leave you."

"You made that vow as John Murray, a man come to marry me. But you aren't John Murray, Jack. You can't fulfill another man's promises. Only your own."

She saw his jaw tense, heard the emotion in his voice. "I don't want to leave. I have to."

"You have your own life to return to. I know that." She did. Jack Emerson was the man she loved more than the need to breathe, but she knew what she had to do. She tried to have the courage to do it, and do it well. "Let me pack you food for the trip."

"We'll stop in Sweetwater Flats for dinner." Jack bowed his head. "I plan to send money to help out." His gaze traveled to his baby son, tummy full, asleep in Lissa's arms, then to Chad.

"You made me enough money this year by saving my

herd, and again by selling my cattle when the prices were the highest. You don't owe me anything.''

"You're wrong. I owe you everything.'' Jack hugged Chad, who started to cry. He held him tight, then gave him over when Blanche came to take the boy from the room.

"The town has an opening for a sheriff.'' Jeremiah shook Jack's hand. "Maybe you should think of us if you are looking to change jobs.''

"I won't forget your offer.'' Touched, Jack felt honored to know some of the people he had met in this town— the Buchmans, the Johansons, the Russells. They had never judged him or doubted his integrity. He would always be grateful.

Lissa walked him to the door, her chin set, tears silvering her eyes. They did not fall even when she kissed him. She tasted of huckleberries and coffee, of passion, late nights, and sweet dreams.

"Thank you for all you've given me.'' He stepped away, his fingers lingering against hers. He didn't want to let go, but he would do what was best. If it meant leaving them to protect him, then he would do that, too.

"At least write. Let me know how you are doing.'' Lissa tipped her head back, her gaze full of longing. "I will miss you.''

"Not as much as I will miss you.'' He swallowed, his throat aching. "You don't know me, the kind of man I am, what I come from. If there were any other way—''

"I know the man you are, Jack Emerson.'' Her fingertips brushed his mouth, soft and gentle. "You are the most amazing and gentle man I have ever known. I truly wish you had been John Murray—because then I would never have to let you go.''

"I'm sorry. I wish—''

"Me, too.'' She stepped away, the love in her heart for

him rare and unmistakable. "You go. I am going to be just fine."

She memorized his face one last time. Life was a cycle of seasons, of change and loss and birth and life. The one thing she had learned was that she couldn't hold too tightly to the people she loved. It was the way of things. She had to let him go. She loved him that much.

"Whatever you do, Jack Emerson, don't ever forget us."

"There's no chance of that, my sweet angel." He kissed her one last time, then simply walked away.

"You put away a murderer and a rustler." Joe's voice drifted back on the frigid wind as they headed toward Helena. "That ought to feel good."

"Damn good. Palmer hurt Lissa intentionally. He hired men to steal her cattle so she would marry him, and he could sell her land."

"Prime Montana range land is very valuable."

What was valuable about Lissa's ranch were the people on it, the memories born there: Chad's delighted squeal as he sat astride his mare, walking her around the yard. The love in Lissa's eyes when he caught her looking at him. The beauty and magic she made of his life, and the way she'd shown him his heart.

"What's ahead for you, brother?" Joe slowed his gelding.

"I want to see my house."

"I packed up your belongings and sold it." Joe laughed. "We thought you were dead. Had a real nice memorial service, though. Annabelle Marten baked up those puffed chocolate pastries. They were so good I proposed to her."

"Over a dessert?"

"A man can't be choosy. They are the best desserts in the county." Joe laughed, shaking his head. "Losing you made me realize I was alone. You can't always let the past affect you, brother. Sometimes you have to take the bull by the horns, wrestle it, and win.''

"You? Married?" That was a laugh. "What is Annabelle Marten going to think when she gets a good whiff of your feet after you take off your riding boots?"

"She's going to love me despite my flaws." Joe seemed certain of it. "Besides, she's already acquainted with my riding boots."

"You devil."

"A man's willpower gets weak around a woman who knows how to make pastry." Joe shrugged. "We're almost home. It feels mighty good."

Home? No. Home was a hundred miles behind him. Where his children waited, where his heart remained, and where his wife slept alone thinking of him.

She missed him most in the mornings—his cheerful humor over breakfast, the dent he made in her sugar supply every time he sweetened his coffee, the way he spent cold, snowy evenings spending extra time with them where it was warm by the fire.

Now she had plenty of sugar and an empty place at the table.

Will had moved on, taken his bonus from the cattle sale and his savings, and gone into partnership with his cousin. After losing everything, the McBains had needed a partner with cash. She'd heard from Susan that Will was happy running his own place and working alongside his cousin.

Arcada had taken over running the ranch with quiet competence. He had also taken Chad under his wing, and was helping the boy improve his riding skills.

Joey was thriving. He was still small for his age, but healthy. He slept most of the night, liked to watch Puddles play with her ball. He had Jack's smile, lopsided and adorable.

She missed him at night, and her days were not as happy. She had not lost her heart, though, as she had when Michael died. No, now she was wiser. Loving only made a person's heart stronger. No matter what, love was the one thing that could never die.

It was snowing as Jack made his way through the church cemetery. His insides felt as cold as the frozen snow at his feet. He'd come back, seen the life he left—one of service and duty and loneliness. He still had his old job if he wanted it, but he hadn't taken it.

There it was—John Emerson's grave. Jack stared at the simple headstone. The day he'd buried his father, he'd vowed never to drink and never to marry. The cycle of violence in his family would die with John Emerson—but it already had.

Jack had feared he was his father at heart, down deep where nightmares lived. He'd lived with a woman for nearly a year, though, suffered through difficulties and injustices and hardship. Never once had he felt that horrible rage that used to overtake his father.

And what about Joe? Joe was getting married. If his little brother could face the past and win, then so could he.

No, Jack already had won. He remembered the man he'd been with Lissa, how there had been no memories and no Father's curse—just happiness and tenderness and a deep, abiding love.

He was his own man, memories or not. How he lived his life, how he treated others, how he loved his wife— why, it was all his choice.

Chapter Twenty-Four

"Mama! Come see my snowman!"

"Close the door. You're letting in the cold air." Laughing, Lissa laid Joey in his cradle. Puddles lay down nearby, keeping watch over her baby. Her son was fed, changed, bathed, and asleep. She left him to rest, then grabbed her coat from the peg.

Cold air rushed to meet her. Snow crunched at her feet. Chad came running, wrapped in dark blue wool, his mittens caked with snow. "See how big he is!"

"I see. You did a great job."

"I gotta get a carrot for his nose." Chad rubbed his brow.

"Let me go in and get you one." Lissa turned toward the house, where the windows were lit by warmth, and smoke curled from the chimney.

"Look!" Chad's voice cut through the still afternoon. "It's Pa!"

"Jack?" Could it be true? She whirled in the snow, squinting against the low rays of the sun where a dark silhouette, tall and broad-shouldered, rode into view. "Jack!"

He drew his gelding to a stop and dismounted. Chad was in his arms, holding him tight, chattering about snowmen and baby brothers and how well he could ride.

Jack held Chad close, listened patiently and answered, so enamored by the boy it shone in his eyes, rang low in his voice.

Chad ran off to the barn to fetch Arcada, as Jack asked. They were alone. Her knees wobbled when the big, iron-hewn man turned to her and held out both hands.

Their fingers met. His gaze brushed hers, intimate as a touch. So much shaded his eyes, remained unspoken between them.

"Did you come to see your sons?"

"Not just my sons." He had dreamed of her touch at night, ached for her smile to light his day. All he loved was her, was connected to her, was from her.

"I just took a pie out of the oven." Lissa stepped back, tilted her head and met his gaze. "Come in, have a bite, see Joey. He's grown."

"I'd love nothing more." Jack followed her up the steps and into the house. Apple pie cooled on the counter, Puddles jumped up to bark a welcome, and a baby's startled cry filled the cozy room.

"Look at him. Isn't he something?" She lifted the baby from his cradle, all gentle elegance. "Well, when he isn't crying at the top of his lungs."

Jack laughed, his chest tight. "The crying isn't so bad. As long as a person is deaf."

"Unfortunately, I'm not." She stepped close, cradling his son, held out one hand. The touch of her, the feel of her, was like a brand to his soul.

"You're here to stay?"

He heard both the hope and the uncertainty in her

voice. How could he tell her how she filled him up, made him better, made him whole? "If you will have me."

"Any day of the week." She was magic and stardust and heart. She was his dawn and his dusk, his day and his night.

"Let me marry you the right way this time. Let me give you my name and my own promises." Jack held out his arms and she stepped against him. She felt perfect beneath his chin, next to his heart.

"And I will give you mine." She kissed his throat, his chin, his mouth.

She tasted like forever, like angel food cake and coffee. "I love you, Jack Emerson."

"I love you. Now and forever."

Her eyes filled, and he saw the depth of her affection for him, but it was nothing compared to the power of emotion that lived in his heart—and always would.

BOOK YOUR PLACE ON OUR WEBSITE AND MAKE THE READING CONNECTION!

We've created a customized website just for our very special readers, where you can get the inside scoop on everything that's going on with Zebra, Pinnacle and Kensington books.

When you come online, you'll have the exciting opportunity to:

- View covers of upcoming books
- Read sample chapters
- Learn about our future publishing schedule (listed by publication month *and author*)
- Find out when your favorite authors will be visiting a city near you
- Search for and order backlist books from our online catalog
- Check out author bios and background information
- Send e-mail to your favorite authors
- Meet the Kensington staff online
- Join us in weekly chats with authors, readers and other guests
- Get writing guidelines
- AND MUCH MORE!

**Visit our website at
http://www.zebrabooks.com**